ARMADA:
THE FIRE

ARMADA: THE FIRE

Book One
The Armada Saga

Robert Oliver

PROSPECT PACIFIC PUBLISHING

ISBN: 979-8-9944434-1-5 (paperback)
ISBN: 979-8-9944434-0-8 (hardcover)
ISBN: 979-8-9944434-2-2 (ebook)

Library of Congress Control Number: 2026902757

This is a work of historical fiction. While major events, dates, political actions, and public figures of sixteenth-century Europe are grounded in the historical record, many private conversations, motivations, relationships, and certain sequences of events have been fictionalized for narrative purposes. Some timelines have been compressed, and minor historical figures combined, in order to preserve narrative momentum and clarity. The names of non-historical persons or events are the product of the author's imagination or are used fictitiously. Any resemblance of such non-historical persons or events to actual ones is purely coincidental.

This novel forms part of a multi-volume historical narrative. While each volume stands independently, character arcs, political developments, and historical consequences continue across the series. Dates and events are consistent across volumes, with dramatization applied only where the historical record is silent or ambiguous.

Cover design and art by Robert Oliver.

First edition: February 2026

Prospect Pacific Publishing
www.prospectpacific.com

To the Lord Jesus Christ, and to the memory of the late Dr. Gertrude LaDean Golladay, my English 101 and 102 professor at the University of Texas at Arlington, who taught me how to put a paragraph together.

"No man commands the storm.
I am the storm!"

– Queen Elizabeth I

Chapter 1
The Burden of Empire

12 September 1553

The bells of the Cathedral of St Michael and St Gudula toll for Vespers as the late afternoon sun slants low across Brussels, the heart of the Duchy of Brabant. From the high hill of Coudenberg, the city unfurls below like a tapestry of tiled rooftops and twisting streets, the air thick with the mingled scents of smoke and autumn damp. Stirring faintly in the wind, the Habsburg banners hang over the gates of Coudenberg Palace, their crimson and black silk whispering of empire.

Inside the palace, tapestries depicting the victories of Burgundy and Spain line the corridors of polished stone and timber, their muted colours dulled by candlelight. At the centre of a private council chamber, Holy Roman Emperor Charles V—King of Spain, Archduke of Austria, Duke of Burgundy, sovereign of the Seventeen Provinces of the Netherlands, King of Naples and Sicily, and ruler of territories in the New World—sits in a carved walnut chair before a broad table strewn with maps and instruments. His shoulders stoop beneath the weight of years and empire. His pale face is drawn, the strong Habsburg jaw pressing his lower lip into a near-permanent frown.

Corpulence burdens him; gout gnaws at his joints. He shifts carefully, as though each movement must be negotiated in advance. His knees burn. His once fiery hair has faded to a soft chestnut threaded with grey. The cost of campaigns—mud, cold, sleepless nights—has etched itself into his bones. His physicians have urged him from rich meats to boiled river fish and thin pottage, but tonight even that gentler fare lies untouched.

Don Ruy Gómez de Silva stands close at Charles' right, one hand discreetly poised near the Emperor's elbow. A cup of pale Rhenish wine rests on the table within easy reach, watered at the doctors' insistence. Silva watches without staring, a man long practised in reading weakness without acknowledging it.

At length, Charles lifts his head.

"Send for Philip," he says. His voice is low, gravelly with fatigue. "It is time."

Silva bows and signals softly to the waiting page at the door. The boy slips away at once.

Charles exhales, his shoulders sagging. For days he has rehearsed the words he must speak—crowns to be passed, duties that cannot be refused. Naples and Sicily will soon lie in Philip's keeping, the southern gates of Christendom his to defend. And beyond them, England: a realm divided by faith, a spark that could either ignite Europe or be bound by alliance.

Mary Tudor rises unbidden in his thoughts—solemn as a child beside her mother, Catherine of Aragon. Now she is queen, hardened by exile, fear, and unyielding belief. Her throne is precarious. England needs strength. Spain needs England.

With a muted grunt, Charles plants both hands on the chair's armrests and leans forward. His breath rasps. His swollen knees tremble as he forces himself upright inch by inch. Silva steps in at once, slipping an arm beneath Charles' forearm, bearing part of the Emperor's weight without ceremony.

Charles reaches for his polished rosewood cane and steadies himself. He sways, then lifts a hand slightly—an unmistakable signal. Silva holds but does not tighten his grip. Charles remains on his feet, leaning on the cane.

A Habsburg emperor does not ask for help. Even when the battle is against his own body.

Moments later, footsteps sound beyond the door. Philip Habsburg enters. Silva straightens at Charles' side.

Philip is twenty-six, slight of stature—fair hair cropped close. A neat moustache and beard frame a controlled mouth. He wears dark princely attire that mirrors his reserved nature, his narrow build held rigid by posture rather than ease. He bows.

Inside, resentment stirs. His father's gaze weighs on him as it always has—measuring, unrelenting. His throat tightens.

Several instruments lie scattered across the council table: astrolabes, compasses, a small globe of the known world.

Philip steps closer and reaches for an astrolabe. The cool brass turns beneath his fingers as he traces its markings, as though certainty might be found among the stars. For a heartbeat, he imagines how many worlds his father commands—and how small he himself feels by comparison.

He sets the astrolabe down more sharply than he intended; it seems to mock him. His hand moves instead to a small compass. He lifts it, watching the needle quiver as he turns it slowly. How easily it spins. How rarely it settles. It feels like a mirror of his own directionless future.

Charles braces both hands atop the cane's carved head and leans forward slightly, the effort visible in the tight line of his mouth. He does not sit. Sitting means rising again. Pain never leaves him, but the weight of empire steadies his voice. His gaze is fixed on his son.

"I have spoken many tongues in my life, Philip," he says. "Spanish to God. French to men. Italian to women. Latin to scholars and priests. And German to my horse—so the grooms swear."

A faint, fleeting smile touches his mouth. Charles shifts, pain tightening his jaw, his breath shortening.

"But to you, my son, I speak as a father—to pass on what remains of my strength, my wisdom, and my burdens."

Philip inclines his head, but inside he bristles. *Always the burdens. Never the freedom.* His fingers tighten unconsciously around the compass.

Charles' hands, once firm and decisive, tremble slightly as his grip tightens on the cane, the weight of his future abdication settling like a heavy cloak upon his shoulders.

"So much of this empire," he continues, "has been bought with blood and prayer. And now it must pass to younger hands."

He shifts his weight, grimacing. Silva steps closer, sliding a hand beneath Charles' arm as the Emperor turns towards a side table where a velvet cushion bears the crowns. Charles moves slowly, leaning heavily on cane and courtier alike. Each step draws a wince.

Reaching the side table, Charles leans both forearms against its edge, resting his weight there. After a long breath, he lifts one hand and crosses himself.

"Soon I place two crowns in your keeping—Naples and Sicily, the gates of the Mediterranean. By my word you are named their king. Remember, Philip: these are not ornaments. They are shields."

Philip sets the compass on the table, fingertips resting on the brass for a beat—then he lets it go. His blue eyes narrow. "Father, Spain already presses hard upon me. Two more crowns—must the load never lessen?"

Charles straightens slightly, anger lending him strength. He leans hard on the cane, pain flaring bright across his face.

Still standing, he snaps: "Do you think I bore them lightly? I stood before the Turk at Vienna, the heretic Martin Luther at Worms, and the French at every border. Every crown is a chain—but it is also duty."

The effort costs him. Silva guides him carefully back towards the chair. Charles lowers himself into it with a hiss of pain, knees aflame.

Philip's jaw stiffens. He has heard these tales a hundred times. *Your chains, Father, not mine.* From the council table, he picks up the compass again.

An impatient flick of Charles' fingers sends Silva to lift the cushion of crowns from the side table. He sets the cushion on the council table. Philip leans in towards the crowns. His left hand hovers—then closes around the nearer crown. He tests its weight and sets it down, then does the same with the second, aligning them on the cushion. He keeps the compass in his right hand. The crowns were lighter than he expected, yet heavier than anything he has ever held.

"And there is more," Charles says. "I hope it will please you more than the rest." His chest heaves, every word forced through pain. Philip's stomach tightens.

Charles continues: "You understand well that our lands stretch across continents, our influence weaving through the courts of Europe. But remember this, my son, strength does not lie solely in conquest. It lies in unity—in alliances forged not just in blood, but in marriage and faith."

Philip feels a cold coil tighten in his stomach. He knows what is coming. His voice is taut.

The compass remains in his hand when he asks, "Marriage, Father?"

"You will wed Mary Tudor, Queen of England."

Philip freezes. Mary—older, a stranger, ruling a land that already curses his name. His hand tightens on the compass until his knuckles pale.

"Father, you speak of alliances, of unity. But Mary? She is over a decade my senior—but that is the least of my concerns. England fears me as a foreigner and will never yield me a true king's authority. Do you ask me to bind myself to her for the sake of politics alone?"

Charles' voice hardens.

"Do you suppose I married your mother for love?" He coughs, harsh and wet. Silva steadies him at once. "We Habsburgs marry for survival. England must not fall to France, nor to heresy. With Mary, England becomes our shield. Do you shrink from your duty?"

Philip's gaze drops. His chest tightens. A hostile country, a woman not of his choosing, a people who will spit when they hear his name. Words erupt from him before he can restrain them.

"Father, you ask me to walk into a hostile country. In my place, would you choose to take on such a burden?"

Charles' face softens briefly. He has rejected a betrothal to Mary Tudor before—when she was a child—and remembers it now.

"Marriage is a weapon, a chain, a bond. With Mary, England becomes our ally—a bulwark against Protestantism and the French king. Together, Spain and England will shield the faith."

Philip lowers his gaze. *Always faith. Always the empire. Never me.*

Charles coughs raw.

"We Habsburgs marry not for love but for the survival of kingdoms. Do you think I cared for comfort when I wed your mother from Portugal? Or when I bore this emperor's crown for the first time at your age? No, Philip—we are not mere men. We are custodians of empire." He gestures to the map spread across the table. "Of this."

A faint smile creases his lips, though his dark-brown eyes betray exhaustion. The words strike Philip like hammer blows. His fists clench at his sides. *Custodians. Never men.*

Eyes closed, he masters the wave of pain before speaking, softer but still edged with command.

"Philip...I was younger than you when I wore my first crown. I did not ask for this burden. It was God who placed me here, as He has placed you. Know that we do not choose our paths. We just obediently walk them."

Philip's voice breaks through, barely restrained. "And if I fail?" The fear he hides slips out.

Charles grips his cane like a sceptre. His body trembles, but the memory of crowns steadies his words.

"Then you rise again. A king does not have the luxury of failure. We stumble, yes—we bleed, we suffer—but we do not fall. You will face challenges. Enemies will curse your name. But you will endure, my son, because to endure is to reign. And the moment you doubt that truth, you have already lost. Learn that lesson well."

Philip closes his eyes, fighting the knot in his chest. *Endure. Always endure. Even if no one loves you.*

Charles' expression softens—just for a moment—a rare paternal flicker. Philip exhales, the anger ebbing, leaving only exhaustion.

"You are allowed to doubt, Philip. A wise ruler often doubts. But action must always follow resolve. You will be King of Spain in time. And with Naples, Sicily, and perhaps England, you will wield power enough to shape Europe's destiny. And history will judge you not by your doubts, but by what you achieve despite them."

Philip nods once. "You...honour me, Father." His voice is calm, but his hand trembles at his side.

Charles raises his trembling hand towards the crowns. "My son, take them. I have carried them long enough. Take today's wisdom, too. Rule with strength, rule with faith, and rule with the knowledge that you are never alone, for the empire stands with you."

Philip inclines his head, composed but conflicted. He sighs.

"Very well, Father. I will serve as you have taught. I will do as you ask. But not without my reservations."

"Remember that your greatest strength is patience—and your greatest enemy is complacency."

A heavy silence lingers. Philip glances back at the compass where he left it. He picks it up again, turning it slowly between his fingers. The needle quivers, never quite still. For a moment, he imagines the English court glaring at him, a stranger and foreigner. The thought twists in his gut. He sets the compass on the table and turns the case a fraction, watching the needle swing, quiver, and settle.

"You always knew where north was, Father," he says quietly. "I am still trying to find it. I will not fail you."

Philip goes to one knee, hand to chest, head bowed.

"At your command, Your Majesty."

Charles lays a weary hand on his son's shoulder.

"You have my leave to withdraw."

Philip rises, bows, and approaches the door.

Charles remains seated, staring towards the window.

"One thing more, my son," Charles says, without turning.

Philip stops and turns. "Yes, Father?"

"In England, let them think you slow. They fear resolve, but they mistake patience for weakness. Be wise. Be watchful."

"Yes, Father. At your command." He bows again and exits.

Outside, the bells continue to toll. The empire does not pause for pain.

***

Philip enters the adjoining chamber. The panelled door closes behind him with a muted thud, muffling the weight of his father's presence. Silva waits in the antechamber, watchful as ever. For a moment Philip stands motionless, his breath shallow and unsteady, the tension of the exchange clinging to him like the heavy velvet of his doublet.

Silva follows quietly, his footsteps soft against the stone floor. He waits, knowing better than to speak too soon.

Philip moves to the tall window, pushing it open just enough for the cool dusk air to wash over him. Outside, the faint sound of church bells drifts across Brussels, echoing like distant warnings.

"He does not see me, Don Ruy," mutters Philip. "Not as a man. Only as a vessel. A tool forged to carry the weight of his empire, to marry for his treaties, to bleed for his ambitions."

He turns sharply. The dim light catches his fair hair and a rare flash of emotion.

"Two crowns he set before me, as if one would not be heavy enough. And now—" His tone hardens, almost biting. "Mary Tudor. A queen unknown to me—her years exceeding mine—set before me as though she were no more than another pawn in the game of state."

"She is Queen of England, Your Highness," says Silva softly, stepping closer. "You are her equal, as your father has declared you. Why would you not want a marriage that binds one of the strongest realms of Christendom to Spain? Why would you not want a holy alliance—one that could stand against France and crush the Protestant heresy before it devours half of Europe?"

Philip gives a short, humourless laugh.

"Holy, you say? What is 'holy' about using a crown to buy loyalty, about turning marriage into another weapon of politics? England will despise me. And Mary..." His words falter. "God bless her, but I believe at her age she is desperate for an heir, desperate enough to take a stranger as her husband. What am I to her, Don Ruy? A saviour—or a breeder?"

Silva's dark eyes are calm and patient.

"You are a Habsburg, my lord. And a Habsburg does not choose his fate. He accepts it."

Philip spins towards him, anger flashing in his eyes.

"Accept it? Accept being a counter in my father's game? Moved here, married there, sacrificed for his empire?"

The silence between them sharpens. Philip's chest rises and falls as he tries to calm his breath. His anger softens into something heavier, something that presses on him from all sides.

He sinks into a high-backed chair and lets his hands cover his face.

"I have never been free, Don Ruy," he says quietly, the words barely audible. "Not for a single day. My father speaks of God's will, but what of mine?"

Silva places one knee on the ground, his voice a calm tether against the tempest of Philip's thoughts.

"Your father is right. England is the key. If Mary loses her crown and the French take it, the whole balance tips—and the heretics will only grow bolder. This alliance could decide the fate of Christendom, Highness."

Philip lowers his hands, staring at the floor, lost in thought.

"Then I am to be the shield again," he says bitterly. "Always the shield."

"You are the son of an emperor," Silva replies. "A curse and a crown in one."

Philip stands suddenly, walking to the window once more. The last light of the setting sun traces the edges of his figure, throwing his face into shadow. He watches the city below, the smoke of hearth fires curling into the evening sky.

For a long moment, he is silent, his hands gripping the windowsill.

Finally, he speaks firmly and coldly.

"Then let it be done. I will wear all these crowns. Reluctantly, I will take Mary Tudor's hand. But I will not be consumed by this ruthless game of kingdoms."

He turns from the window, standing straighter. His eyes are sharper now, and his expression is resolved.

"Have Renard carry our assent to the terms—and press for the safest articles," he tells Silva. "And Don Ruy, should I marry this queen, I want you to come to England with me. The more men of Spain at my side, the better."

"Yes, Your Highness, with pleasure."

Philip glances up. "I will find my north, Don Ruy."

9 October 1553

At Hampton Court Palace, upriver from London, the warm glow of candelabras washes the council chamber, light flickering across intricate tapestries. Queen Mary Tudor, in deep crimson embroidered with gold, sits at the head of a long oak table. Her black jewelled hood frames a face tempered by struggle and authority. The hearth crackles. Around her the murmurs of the Privy Council fade as they wait for the ambassador's address.

Monsieur Simon Renard, the Emperor's envoy, steps forward and bows.

"Your Majesty, I bring greetings and a proposal from His Imperial Majesty, Charles V, Holy Roman Emperor, Archduke of Austria, and King of Spain."

Mary's gaze holds him. Her voice is calm, firm.

"Proposal, Your Excellency? Pray, what matter does the Emperor place before us?"

Renard straightens. "His Majesty admires Your Majesty's piety and defence of the Holy Catholic Church. In these turbulent times, he believes England must take her rightful place at the heart of Christendom, united with Spain to shield the Church from heresy."

Mary's fingertips brush the carved arms of her chair. "England must remain a beacon of the true faith. But what does the Emperor propose to achieve this unity?"

"To that end," Renard says, "His Imperial Majesty offers a union most noble. His son, Philip—Prince of Asturias and Duke of Milan—extends his hand in marriage to Your Majesty."

Her eyes widen. The chamber stills. Advisers glance between queen and envoy. Mary shows nothing, but her grip tightens on the chair. A servant moves softly among the councillors, refilling goblets with sack wine or ale; Mary waves the servant away. She will not have her resolve mistaken for warmth born of wine.

After a pause, her voice cuts clean. "A bold proposal, Your Excellency. Prince Philip's lineage and piety are not in question. But you know how such a union will be viewed here. My people will call it domination, not alliance. England's sovereignty must not be touched."

Renard bows his head. "His Imperial Majesty understands these concerns."

"Indeed, he should."

"This alliance would preserve England's laws and independence," he continues. "Together, England and Spain can stand as a wall against the tide of heresy."

Mary leans forward. "And the Prince himself—what does he bring beyond title and faith?"

A faint smile touches his mouth. "He is strong, steady, the kind of man who will be a constant, dutiful husband. He has ruled wisely, with a fair hand. Disciplined, yes—and his loyalty to the Church is absolute. In him, you see the best of his bloodline."

Mary sits back, contemplative. "This is no small matter. A marriage such as this is not merely for myself, but for my realm. I shall weigh it with the gravity it deserves."

Renard bows. "For Your Majesty's consideration." He gestures. An aide draws back a cloth to reveal a likeness of the Prince by Titian, recently delivered by imperial courier from Brussels.

Mary rises and walks to the painting. A small smile touches her mouth, and she lowers her eyes a moment, only to lift them again with quiet, almost unguarded light. She presses a finger to her lip.

"Your Majesty's wisdom will surely secure England's future," Renard says. "His Imperial Majesty awaits your response with hope and respect."

She returns to her throne and stands before it, signalling the end.

"You shall have my answer in due time, Ambassador. For now, this matter remains within these walls. I will consult with my council."

Renard withdraws with another bow. Voices rise at once as the councillors begin to argue the proposal's weight.

Seventy-year-old Bishop Stephen Gardiner, the Lord Chancellor, rises first, one hand on the table, the other smoothing the seal-string of a folded brief.

"Majesty, the match promises strength," he says, voice careful, "but England is a skittish horse. London men mutter at 'Spaniards in our streets.' If we ride too hard, she throws us."

William Paget is already half out of his chair, calm where Gardiner is weighty. He inclines his head to Mary, not to Gardiner.

"Your Majesty, I say the horse wants a firm hand and a clear road. A Spanish alliance checks France, brings us allies for the true faith, and—by God's providence—an heir. Without an heir, we purchase only reprieve."

William Paulet, Marquess of Winchester, fingers the beads on his rosary once and lets them fall. He lays his white staff of authority along the table's edge, and as he speaks of coin, one finger idly traces a nick in the painted wood.

"The Exchequer wheezes," he says bluntly. "Debts of the late king, a coinage in need of honesty. Spain brings dowry and credit. With Spanish silver, we mend the realm's purse."

Sir William Petre, ever the drafter, clears his throat.

"With Your Majesty's leave: a treaty can guard our gates. Let it be written—Philip shall style himself 'King' during Your Majesty's life, yet he shall appoint no foreigner to office, command no fort, carry no jewel or child out of England without Your Majesty's consent. Our laws stand. Our courts stand. Our ships and garrisons remain under English captains. These are but first heads of agreement, madam. If Your Majesty approves, we will set them into articles for fuller debate when Parliament meets."

Henry FitzAlan, the Earl of Arundel and Lord Steward, turns his signet against his thumb and speaks silk over steel. When the talk turns sharp, he lets it turn once—slowly—before stilling it.

"Spoken wisely, Sir William. And let it also say: should God deny issue, this realm returns wholly to itself—no Castilian claim, no Imperial encroachment. So the people hear 'marriage,' not 'merger.'"

Across the table, William Herbert, Earl of Pembroke, paces a step, then stills. His knuckles brush the hilt at his side before he folds his hands.

"France will not sit idle," he warns. "Guise stirs already. If we clasp Spain, we cross the French. Expect raids in the Channel, mischief in Scotland."

Sir John Bourne, Principal Secretary, dips his quill and does not look up.

"Then we prepare writs for musters," he says, dry as parchment, "and brief the Wardens on the marches. France rattles her blade whether we wed or no. Be assured of that."

Sir Robert Rochester, Comptroller of the Household, bows from behind Mary's chair. He shifts his white staff upright by his boot, palm flattening on the knob as if to pin the room to order.

"Madam, the commons love you for restoring the Mass. Tie our altar back to Rome with a Spanish knot, and the faithful will hold fast."

Sir Edward Waldegrave murmurs assent, but his eyes flick anxiously towards Gardiner.

Gardiner lifts a palm for quiet.

"Majesty, I do not say 'no'—I say 'slowly.' We must carry the realm with us. Proclaim first that England's liberties remain. Let Parliament see the treaty before the people see the pageant. If we look to Spain and forget our own, Kent and Devon will remember us with pikes."

Paget's smile shows the slightest edge. He spreads his hands, easy, practised.

"Or we lead, and the country follows. Majesty, delay feeds rumour. Set terms now, send word to Brussels tomorrow, and announce when the ink is ready. Confidence is a policy."

Pembroke tilts his head, eyes half-lidded.

"And what of the Londoners, Master Paget? Apprentices do not read treaties. They read faces, and theirs sour at the talk of Spaniards." He glances towards Mary—then away too quickly. "Your Majesty knows I will draw a sword for you. I ask only that you not set us to cut our own streets to pieces."

Mary lifts a hand. The argument stalls. "You tell me the same truth from different doors," she says. "France watches. England grumbles. The Treasury coughs. The faith needs friends. I am not blind to any of it."

She turns to Petre. "Draft the terms you named. Add Arundel's clause on our full freedom if God denies heirs. Make it plainer than a market tally: no foreign appointments, no garrisons yielded, no child or jewel taken out without my sign and seal."

"To be laid before Parliament, madam?" Petre asks.

"Before Parliament and the people," Mary says. "I will not have it whispered that I sell England for a husband."

Gardiner bows, grave. "I will preach the safeguard as I preach the sacrament, Majesty. But—" He hesitates, then says it. "Kent's restless. Wyatt's friends mutter. London, too. Give me leave to speak with the mayor and aldermen, to cool the city before the heat takes."

"You have it," Mary answers. "And you, Lord Pembroke—quiet your captains. I want readiness, not bravado."

Pembroke inclines his head, jaw tight. "As Your Majesty commands."

Paulet raises his ledger a fraction. "And the money, madam?"

"Find it without selling my vow," Mary says. "We will have no new riot over Spanish subsidies."

Paget steps in, smooth as ever. "If Your Majesty speaks first to the City—Guildhall, perhaps—assure them their charters stand and their benches remain English, they will lend at gentler rates."

Mary holds his gaze. "You will stand beside me when I speak, Lord Paget—and you will own that counsel before the City, not only before your queen."

Paget's smile tightens; he bows. "Willingly, madam."

She draws a breath, then looks from face to face—the men who have carried her to the throne and will quarrel over every mile of the road ahead. "Then hear me plain. I will marry for England, not against her. I will take Philip's hand, but I will not yield my crown, my courts, or my conscience. Any man who says otherwise shall answer to me."

A murmur ripples and dies.

Mary rests her palm on the arm of her chair. Her ring clicks once against the carved oak. "Set your hands to it. Sir William, bring me the draft by tomorrow's Vespers. My Lord Chancellor, prepare the city. My lords, keep order in your shires. We move—carefully, but we move."

The council bows as one. Beyond the chamber, the wind presses at the casements, and somewhere in the palace a bell begins to toll for evening prayers. Mary turns once more to the Titian likeness, studies the steady young face, and lets no one see the flicker of fear behind her resolve.

***

A single candle lights Mary's private apartment. The furnishings press in with the stillness. Beside the letter, a small cup of hippocras—spiced wine sweetened with sugar and a shaving of cinnamon—has cooled untouched. Her physicians recommend it for her sleep, but sleep comes no easier for a queen than for a penitent. On her desk lies a letter bearing the Emperor's seal, delivered that same day. Behind her, the Titian likeness of Philip stares. She runs a finger along the parchment's edge, then looks back at the painting.

"A Spanish prince...a Catholic alliance." Her voice is low, tired. "But at what cost to me—and to my people?"

She turns the chair to face the portrait, rubs her temple, and closes her hand around her crucifix. Far bells toll—solemn reminders of the faith that has carried her through years of hardship.

"Would they despise me for this? Or see it as strength—unity?" she murmurs, and crosses herself. "Grant me wisdom, O Lord."

She looks again to the letter: promise and peril in the same hand. Her gaze steadies on the candle flame. Her thumb circles one bead of the rosary, once, twice, then stops. Resolve takes hold.

26 October 1553

A grey, chilly morning in London. Fog clings to streets. The bustle is muffled. Within Whitehall, the air is close with expectation. Weeks of rumour and argument have hardened the court. Today the Queen must speak with those closest to her.

The Presence Chamber fills with councillors and leading courtiers, eager, wary. For Mary, the marriage means faith, peace—and an end to loneliness. For England, it is an alignment some will bless, others curse. She feels their eyes as she mounts the dais. William Paget, Baron Paget de Beaudesert, stands behind her with the sealed scroll.

"Your Majesty," Paget intones, steady, official. "The document is prepared."

She nods, lips set, and draws breath. She holds her crucifix. The words will unsettle, but they are necessary.

"My lords, my faithful councillors," she begins. The room holds its breath. "We bring tidings of a union forged not only for my heart, but for the greater good of this kingdom. We enter into marriage, to the glory of Almighty God and the benefit of this realm, with His Royal Highness Prince Philip of Spain."

Silence seems to expand, as if time itself lingered on the edge of what must come.

"We know some will grieve," she continues, voice hardening. "Some would disrupt the peace this union seeks to secure. Let none in this realm offer slight or scorn to the Prince's people. Such offence shall be met with our full displeasure and punished accordingly. The first offender shall be laid fast in the Tower at our pleasure."

She fixes her eyes on the lords near the dais. "This is not a light matter."

A quiet tension hangs in the air. Faces tighten. She does not care. Authority stands where she stands.

"We do not seek mere compliance," Mary says. "We demand loyalty—to your queen, to your country, and to God. We stand at a turning. We adjure you to choose peace."

She steps back. Murmurs break like surf. The message is clear. Paget reads the proclamation aloud, each word sealing the course she is set. The nobles will bend—or break.

As she turns to leave, a chill runs down her spine. The decree will not silence England's fear or the Protestant ferment. Words are one thing. The people are another.

Chapter 2
Chains of Paper

8 February 1554

Valladolid burns gold in the last light. The palace stays dim. In his chamber, Philip crosses the floor, boots hard on stone. A small brazier glows in the corner, and on a sideboard the remains of supper—Castilian beef stew, a plate of quince paste, and cakes baked with olive oil—stand cooling. Philip paces until hunger goes quiet. A messenger's report rings in his head like an iron bell.

"They would bind me like a prisoner?" he mutters. *King of England in name only—subject to Mary's council and forbidden to act? And if the Queen dies, no claim at all?*

Don Fernando Álvarez de Toledo, the Duke of Alba, stands by the window, arms folded.

"The terms are harsh, Your Highness. Mary's council will not let England fall under Spain's sway."

"Harsh?" Philip turns, eyes blazing. "They are humiliating. A figurehead paraded through a foreign court while her council rules. They fear Spain more than they trust Queen Mary."

Alba chooses his words. "The English are proud. Her position is fragile. The winter rebellion hardened them against any hint of foreign rule."

Philip turns away. He hears his father's calculus: the Empire needs this marriage. *A pawn. On my father's board. England the prize.*

A knock. Don Pedro Dávila, Marquis de las Navas, enters and bows. Attendants bring a velvet-lined chest and set it down.

"Your Highness, the gifts for the Queen and her ladies are ready—the diamonds, emeralds, pearls. The great table diamond alone is worth fifty thousand ducats."

"Jewels," Philip says bitterly. "Am I to buy favour with trinkets while her council chains me?"

Dávila hesitates. Alba answers. "Diplomacy, Highness. If you must marry, do so on your terms. Let the world see the splendour you bring."

A grim smile, but the mask does not hold. "A gallant suitor," Philip says. "Very well. If this must proceed, let it proceed with magnificence. Let them see Spain's wealth, the Habsburg name. Let them tremble at what they defy."

He opens the chest. Light flares from the stones. He lifts the table diamond, mounted as a rose. It presses cool and heavy in his palm.

"Such," he says, "is the cost of a crown I may not bear."

He returns the stone to its velvet bed. Silence settles. The jewels glitter indifferently.

"To the Queen," he orders. "Make it grand—as grand as the insult. And know this: their paper binds my hands, not my will."

As the chest departs, Philip sinks into a chair by the fire, fingers gripping the chair's arms. A goblet of dark Castilian wine waits beside him; he grips the wood instead and lets the wine go cold.

"The Emperor believes this marriage will bind the realms," Alba says, softer.

"Perhaps," Philip replies. "But I will not be a token forever. If they think parchment and councils can pen me, they misjudge Spain—and me."

The sun slips. Shadows rise. Firelight carves his face into angles of pride, resentment, and unbending will.

4 May 1554

Madrid's Alcázar gardens breathe a new season. Weeks pass, and the turmoil of court gives way—at least in appearance—to the soft tread of spring. Orange blossoms scent the air. The court hums beyond. Philip walks with his son, eight-year-old Carlos, the boy's blond hair tousled, his small stick flashing like a sword.

Philip schools his expression as they walk. The iron stays behind his teeth.

"See these gardens?" Philip's voice is uncharacteristically soft. "Each path tended like a realm."

"The Empire, Father?"

"Yes. Spain, the Indies, lands across Europe—gardens of a kind. One day you may tend them."

"And England too?"

"Perhaps. The Netherlands are ours by heritage, yet complicated—proud, fierce. They require wisdom as much as force."

"And England? Would I be king there?"

"England is a possibility with challenges. Queen Mary rules now. She works to restore the true faith. If England binds to us, it will be by alliance, not conquest."

"Alliances? Like a marriage?"

"Precisely. I will marry Queen Mary to strengthen our ties. You too may one day forge bonds for the realm."

"I would be strong," Carlos says. "Make everyone obey."

"Strength matters," Philip says, resting a hand on his shoulder. "But loyalty is won, not seized. A wise king listens, chooses for his people, not only for his crown."

"Will I be a good king?"

"You have a king's blood," Philip says, kneeling to meet his eyes. "But goodness is made. Learn. Be just. Keep the faith. Then you will honour the name you bear."

"I will be a great king some day," Carlos declares.

Philip rises with a wistful smile. "We shall see. For now—be a boy."

They walk on.

12 July 1554

La Coruña's harbour blazes in crisp morning light. Scores of ships bristle at their moorings. On the quays, stevedores roll casks of dried peas and salted cod towards the waiting holds. They stack sacks of hard biscuit and barrels of wine and vinegar for the voyage. The smell of tar and fresh-cut timber wrestles with the sharper tang of brine and shipboard rations. The *Espíritu Santo*, a great galleon under Habsburg colours, the Burgundian cross vivid against a white field, rides at the centre, her lion figurehead gripping a cross.

On the docks, Prince Philip, clad in a finely embroidered black velvet doublet and Spanish hose, his sable-lined cloak over his shoulders, surveys the preparations with stoic determination. A silk canopy, borne aloft on poles by attendants, shields him from the glare of the rising sun—a mark of dignity as much as of comfort. The Duke of Alba stands beside him with a tally of ships and stores. Nearby, young Carlos counts the ships. He is kept close by his governess and by Philip's guards.

"Over one hundred ships, Don Fernando. Enough to remind England of Spain's power—but not to cast the shadow of conquest."

Ruy Gómez de Silva nods, faintly smiling. "England will be impressed, Your Highness."

"And the men?" Philip asks. "Do they understand?"

"They are prepared and loyal. Europe watches."

Trumpets peal as carriages roll in with the last of his suite. Nobles flash with jewels. Priests bear relics, their prayers threading the din.

A young naval officer named Diego Flores de Valdés approaches the Prince and bows.

"Favourable winds, Your Highness. We could sail within the hour."

"It pleases me," Philip says. "Inform the captain."

He turns to his son. "Hold our kingdom together—as princes must pretend to do—while I am gone." The governess curtsies and leads Carlos away.

As Philip boards the *Espíritu Santo*, drums roll across the harbour.

"Weigh anchor! Loose the sails!" the captain bellows.

Sailors swarm the rigging, their shadows sliding over the deck. Canvas bellies out like great white wings, snapping in the wind, while cannons along the gunwales wink in the sun. The sea answers in its own steady heartbeat against the hull.

On the cliffs and the pebbled shore, crowds press close. Caps lift; hands cross themselves. Gulls wheel overhead with harsh cries.

At the prow, the Prince stands alone, hands clasped behind him, a dark figure against the brightening water. Spray drifts in the air, touching his cloak with salt. He does not wave.

The fleet inhales. Ropes groan, sails snap, masts creak in chorus. Hulls press forward, cutting white wakes that unfurl like banners across the sea. The sound of a multitude of men at work rises—drums of boots on decks, the rasp of pulleys, the bark of orders, the answering shouts.

On shore, crowds roar. Farmers, wives, children, priests—faces lifted, arms flung high. The shouts swell, crest, and then break apart as distance swallows them. From the decks, sailors answer with ragged cheers of their own, voices mingling with trumpet calls and the thunder of cannon salutes.

But the sea is patient.

Mile by mile, the land dwindles. The cheering thins, overtaken by the steady hiss of waves at the bow, the slow and endless beat of the ocean's drum. The Prince remains fixed at the prow, eyes on the line where water meets sky.

And behind him, the fleet surges into the Atlantic, each ship a prayer cast upon uncertain waters.

16 July 1554

A steady south wind carries the *Espíritu Santo*. Timber speaks in creaks and sighs. On the quarterdeck, Philip leans on the rail. Ruy Gómez de Silva stands beside him. Sea and sky stretch like judgement.

Philip breaks the silence. "I have never seen England. Strange land, strange people. And soon—a stranger for a wife."

"Yet a wife who shares your faith, Highness. No small thing," Silva answers. "What do you look forward to?"

Philip's mouth quirks. "You talk like a man who has worn a ring, Don Ruy. I have, once. I do look forward to a wife again...but just as much to what it might steady: my father's empire, braced against France."

"Yet you are apprehensive."

"Of course—England is not Spain. They do not trust us. Every word, every gesture will be measured. They will say, 'Philip is ambitious. Philip seeks to dominate.' I will have to move carefully. They must see me as an ally, not a master. Winning their hearts will be hard—perhaps impossible."

Silva gives a quiet smile. "You do not gild your words, Your Highness."

Philip also chuckles under his breath. "And for Mary herself? Her years have not been kind, so I hear. I suspect there will be no great love between us. It would be nice if there were. But if she shares my commitment to duty, we may yet succeed as partners—as companions in purpose. That much is clear."

Philip stares at the horizon again.

Silva reads the tension. Two fingers rest on Philip's sleeve, then lift—a promise of steadiness without presuming. "Walk with the steel and grace that have carried you so far. This queen may have had little room for love. She is born to rule, as are you. Together, you may build what neither could alone."

The sails snap. Wind speaks in the rigging. The words hang. The food smells from the galley drift up faintly to the quarterdeck, where the Prince stands apart, appetite dulled by thoughts heavier than any ration.

After a time Philip nods. "You are right, Don Ruy."

"And England will learn it," Silva says.

They stand in companionable silence. The horizon glimmers with the promise of England—and its trial.

20 July 1554

Southampton's harbour brims with pageant and purpose. Trumpets blare from the quay, drums rattle in answer, and the townsfolk surge forward in a sea of caps and kerchiefs. The air is alive with salt, tar, and trampled rushes. Children dart between soldiers' legs. Merchants shout above the din. Pie-sellers and bakers jostle for space at the edge of the crowd, hawking hot pasties and coarse oaten loaves spread with honey to those who can reach the trays between soldiers' elbows.

Out on the tide, the *Espíritu Santo* glides in like a floating citadel, her gilded prow gleaming in the pale sun, banners snapping in the stiffening breeze. The creak of rigging and the snap of canvas roll across the water, answered by the roar of welcome from shore.

"Furl sails! Heave to!" the captain of the *Espíritu Santo* bellows from the quarterdeck, his voice cutting through the clamour like a blade.

Couriers ride to London, and church bells along the coast ring to herald the Prince's approach. Bishop Gardiner and the Council have set the route and rites.

On the quay, a delegation of English nobles waits, velvets and jewels bright under the sun. Above, English and Spanish banners fly on this welcome day. On shore, bells and cheers collide. Philip stands at the prow, face composed, thoughts divided between resolve and dread.

The Duke of Alba approaches Philip. With measured confidence, he addresses the Prince.

"Your Highness, the fleet lies at anchor. All is prepared. England awaits."

"So it begins, Don Fernando. So it begins, my friend. England and Spain—bound by the Church and bound by this marriage. Let us hope the ties hold as firmly as our resolve."

From the quay, musicians play lively galliards.

"They seem welcoming enough," Alba offers. "The court has prepared well."

"Welcoming—and suspicious," Philip answers. "They will seek fault."

Silva steps forward. "It is not their approval you seek, Highness, but their queen's. Win her heart and England follows."

"You speak as if hearts were easily won," Philip says, softening. "Mary's heart may be the Church's—as is mine. I am apprehensive. The people, Don Ruy, are another matter."

"True, but you have navigated far more treacherous waters than these."

Philip chuckles a little and adjusts his cloak as the wind tugs at it. "Words and acts—they will weigh them all."

"Make fast! Lower the gangplank!" the captain roars. Lines are thrown. The gangplank thuds into place. The first of the suite descends.

Philip appears at the top. "The sea was steady, Don Ruy. England—God help me—will not be. I am ready."

"Ready and resolute, Highness," Silva says, hand on his shoulder. "This land may question you. History will not."

Philip straightens and descends, boots ringing on wood.

The crowd swells—cheers and bells. When his boots touch English soil, the air hums with possibility and dread. His face stays still. The weight shows in the set of his jaw.

Henry FitzAlan, Earl of Arundel, comes forward to the very edge of the quay, his heavy robe of ermine lifting in the salt breeze, the fur flashing pale as frost against the dark water. He bows deeply, the jewelled chain at his breast catching the low sun. Behind him the courtiers arrange themselves in a loose half-circle, their expressions a study in restraint—measured curiosity, guarded calculation, a few smiles already rehearsed.

"Your Highness," Arundel declares, his voice carrying over timber and tide, "in the name of Her Majesty and the people of England, I bid you welcome to our shore. You do us great honour."

Philip inclines his head in return. "My lord, I thank you. I am honoured to set foot upon English soil, and to be received in such friendship, at the threshold of what is to come between our realms."

A herald in the royal tabard steps forward, the cloth heavy with the arms of England and edged in gold thread dulled by sea air. At Arundel's signal, a pursuivant gives a short, formal trumpet call—no fanfare, just enough to mark the moment. The herald advances bearing a velvet cushion: upon it the badge of the Order of the Garter, encircled with *Honi soit qui mal y pense*, and beside it the collar of roses and knots.

Arundel bows first to Philip, then to the insignia itself. Setting aside his white staff, he lifts the cushion and fastens the badge with practiced hands, deliberate and unhurried. The ferrule of the staff taps once against the planking as he resumes it, a single, final sound.

"By the Queen's command," FitzAlan says, "this token is bestowed here, in welcome, the fuller rites and solemn investiture to follow at court."

The collar is displayed, not yet laid upon Philip's shoulders. Spanish courtiers murmur softly at the courtesy—honour granted, ceremony reserved—while the tide laps at the quay, witness to a promise made in public and deferred with care.

"Convey my gratitude to Her Majesty," Philip says. "I look forward to meeting her and fulfilling the vow that joins our realms."

Applause rises. Banners of England and Spain lift in the breeze.

Silva leans close. "A fine start, Highness."

"She will see the same steadiness," Philip says. "This is the first step."

The procession forms. A few cheer. Others whisper of the foreign prince who will marry their queen. Philip walks with measured authority, deeper into the land that will test him.

***

Afternoon sun kisses the Church of the Holy Rood. Bells toll solemnly as Prince Philip of Spain, flanked by members of his entourage, enters for a Mass of thanksgiving for his safe passage. Everything has been timed to the quarter-hour; prayers, receptions, and removals stitched together without pause. Inside, the air is cool and heavy with incense. Spanish courtiers, imposing in their black velvet and gold-threaded garments, kneel beside English dignitaries in a rare blending of two worlds.

Kneeling, Philip crosses himself. "Lord, thank you for safe passage. Strengthen my resolve. Bless this union."

A priest murmurs in Latin and sprinkles holy water. Sunlight dazzles as they step out of the church. Sea air fills the lungs. An usher offers a silver cup of sack in thanks for his safe arrival; Philip touches it to his lips out of courtesy more than thirst.

A gentleman in fine English dress approaches, bowing with the courtly precision of one long used to ceremony.

"Your Highness," he says, "I am Anthony Browne, Viscount Montagu. Her Majesty appointed me your Master of the Horse. I am honoured to serve you."

Philip inclines his head, measured, princely. "I am pleased to make your acquaintance, my lord. Her Majesty's arrangements are...thorough."

Montagu smiles faintly. "The Queen and Council have prepared all. England is eager to receive you—and careful in her preparations."

Eager—and cautious. "Thank you, my lord."

The treaty terms have rung in his ears since England first sent them. None of this is new, yet hearing them recited by the Queen's own man tastes no sweeter.

He asks, with a crease sharpening at his brow: "Tell me, my lord—what place is set for me in this realm?"

Montagu hesitates. His eyes flick once towards Ambassador Simon Renard, standing near the Spanish suite, as if searching for permission. When he speaks, his tone is courteous but steady.

"Your Highness shall be accorded all honour due a prince of Spain and consort to our sovereign."

Philip's voice remains even. "As her consort. Not her equal, is that correct?"

Montagu carefully produces a folded parchment—one of the marriage articles already rehearsed in Brussels. He smooths its edge between two fingers, draws out the folded article, and opens it just enough to confirm the line.

"The terms are plain enough," he says. "Your Highness is honoured as consort—but the governance of England remains in English hands."

He glances down once, then adds quietly, "You may not appoint to English offices without the Queen's express assent." He hesitates, then finishes carefully. "And should Her Majesty predecease you without issue, Your Highness shall claim no governance of the realm, nor guardianship of any successor being under age."

He folds the article shut again with deliberate neatness. "Precedents, Your Highness. England guards her own authority closely."

Philip nods once, the motion small but tectonic. The sting is familiar. He has braced for it since the treaty drafts crossed his desk. Still, the formality of its recitation in English air draws the old iron taste to his tongue. He feels the heat rise—but keeps the flame banked.

He beckons Renard with a slight tilt of his head. "Excellency, I will have clarity in every particular. Speak with the Council and set down the limits plainly. No shadowed phrasing."

Renard bows shallowly, a courtier's smile held tight. "At once, Your Highness."

He turns and vanishes into the waiting knot of English ushers.

Among the Spanish suite, whispers stir like cloth in a draught. A Castilian nobleman leans close enough for only Philip to hear.

"Highness, it appears they mean you to walk a pace behind the Queen in all things. Strange terms for a marriage that joins two realms."

"Strange, yes," Philip replies, voice cooling to tempered steel. "But not unexpected. England yields little to strangers—even when those strangers come as husband."

"It casts a shadow," the nobleman murmurs. "Many will take it for insult, Your Highness."

Philip's gaze shifts to the pale horizon. "Let them take it as they please. I do not come for vanity. I come for alliance. If I walk a step behind, England will yet feel my strength beside her."

Montagu, sensing the tension like a hound scenting weather, clears his throat softly. He then forces a diplomatic smile.

"Your Highness, Her Majesty awaits you at Winchester. If it please you, we shall begin the procession."

"It pleases me," Philip says at last. "Let us proceed."

***

Since early evening, the streets of London have been buzzing with anticipation. The city, ever restless, seems to hold its breath as town criers march through the cobbled lanes, their voices rising above the din of daily life. Bells toll from church towers, their peals mingling with the clatter of cartwheels and the murmur of gathering crowds.

A crier wearing a tall, wide-brimmed felt hat and clad in a crimson coat embroidered with the royal emblem stands atop a wooden platform in Cheapside, a parchment scroll unfurled in his hands. Shopkeepers and apprentices crane their necks.

"Hear ye, hear ye! By order of Her Majesty Queen Mary, it is proclaimed that His Highness, Prince Philip of Spain, has arrived safely at Southampton. By God's grace, he prepares to unite with our sovereign in holy matrimony in Winchester, for the peace and prosperity of this realm and the preservation of the true faith!"

The crowd erupts into murmurs, some whispering their hopes for stability, others voicing wary scepticism of the Spanish prince.

"So 'tis true then, is't? The Spanish cur's made landfall?" a fishmonger says to his neighbour who shrugs.

"Aye, so what's it portend for us poor souls, eh? More cursed taxin'? Another war to feed with our sons?"

A vendor cuts in, loud.

"Hold your clack, you two! An' it please Her Grace and put the Church to rights, that's good coin by me."

The crier lifts his hand. "By order of the Lord Mayor, bonfires shall be lit tonight in every parish in celebration of His Highness's arrival. Constables will be posted at every crossing. Let us all make merry."

The proclamation draws scattered cheers. Children ring handbells until the sound spills into the lanes, while older faces watch and measure the cheer.

Meanwhile, in the Guildhall, the Lord Mayor of London issues final instructions to his attendants.

The Lord Mayor, seated at a grand table, gestures for his clerk to step forward with a stack of parchment.

"Ensure every parish has the wood it needs for the bonfires. And remind the constables to keep the peace—celebrations of this sort can quickly turn unruly," he orders.

The clerk bows and responds. "At once, my lord. Shall we also dispatch musicians to the main squares, as was done for the Queen's coronation?"

"A fine suggestion! Music will lift people's spirits. Let them see this is a time for unity."

***

At Winchester, far from the bustling streets of London, the Queen's Council convenes in the Great Hall of Winchester Castle, where preparations for the royal wedding are well underway. Messengers had already been dispatched to summon England's greatest lords and ladies to the city. Carriages roll into the castle courtyard one by one, bearing richly dressed aristocrats, their banners fluttering in the warm summer breeze.

Bishop Stephen Gardiner, Bishop of Winchester and Lord Chancellor, stands tall and formidable amid a small knot of advisers, his robes sweeping the stone floor of the vast, echoing hall. Firelight chisels his hawk-like face. His dark eyes spare no one.

"Her Majesty wishes the ceremony to reflect the grandeur of this union," he says. "Every noble family is to be present—no exceptions."

"My lord," an adviser begins, "there is unease about the Spaniards—talk of foreign hands—"

"Then we answer in splendour and order," Gardiner replies. "This is a marriage of equals, in the world's hearing, for the glory of God and the strength of England. Remind them of their duty—to the Queen and the faith."

***

Later that evening, in London, the city transforms into a patchwork of flickering light. Bonfires blaze in every parish, their warm glow reflecting off the faces of revellers. Children dance around the flames while vendors sell spiced wine and roasted chestnuts. Musicians play lively tunes, and the air buzzes with excitement and speculation about the Prince who would soon wed their queen.

21 July 1554

Winchester's streets hum with reverence and celebration. Summer sun warms stone fronts. The air smells of flowers, candles, and strewn herbs. Tudor roses ripple on flags. From the lanes beyond the procession, the smell of roasting meat and new bread drifts in from taverns and cookshops making ready for the lords and gentry flooding the city.

Hooves echo on cobbles as the Queen's carriage appears. Queen Mary descends in crimson velvet trimmed with ermine. A gold-embroidered veil falls from her hair. Her crown glints. At the carpeted approach to the cathedral, Mayor William Lawrens and his wife await.

The Mayor bows. His wife curtsies and advances with a great hammered-gold goblet that glows as if lit from within.

"Your Majesty," the Mayor says, steady and reverent, "in the name of the City of Winchester and her people, we present this remembrance of loyalty and devotion. May it bring blessings to your union and prosperity to the realm."

"Thank you, Mayor Lawrens, and the good people of Winchester," Mary replies warmly. "You do honour to us, and you do honour to this ancient city, and to England."

The crowd cheers, "Huzzah!" while Mary inclines her head to the Mayor's wife and ladies.

"Your Majesty," the Mayoress says, curtsying low, "the women of Winchester pray for your health and happiness, and for God's blessing upon your marriage."

Mary smiles and inclines her head in answer.

"I thank you," she says simply. "God hear your prayers."

As Mary moves on, the crowd parts cleanly before her, voices rising once more in loyal noise. Behind her, Winchester breathes out, already carrying the moment into memory.

***

Inside the cathedral, candles and coloured light from the windows flood stone and air. Mary walks up the aisle. Rich gowns rustle. The organ sounds the solemn *Gloria in excelsis Deo*. Incense hangs sweet and heavy.

She kneels and crosses herself. Bishop Gardiner steps forward.

"Almighty God, bless your servant Mary, and the union she enters. Make it a strength to your Church and a light to this kingdom."

Mary's lips move. *Lord, guide me. Make me steadfast in this path. Let not my enemies prevail. If it be Your will, bind this realm to righteousness—and to Philip, whom You have set before me.*

The organ's last notes fade into the high vaults and leave only breath and candle-pop. Mary keeps her head bowed a moment longer, fingers tight around her beads, as if she could hold God to the words she has just prayed. When she rises, she does so with care—queen first, bride second—and the long aisle waits for her like a road that does not permit turning back.

***

Evening. Wolvesey Castle—Bishop's palace—softens beneath banners and garlands. The Queen's ladies escort her to her chamber. Within, silks rustle, gifts are arranged, plans murmur.

A knock. A servant enters and bows.

"Your Majesty, His Excellency Ruy Gómez de Silva and Señor Juan Rodríguez de Feria have arrived. They bear a further gift from Prince Philip."

"Admit them."

Two Spaniards enter—dark cloaks, grave courtesy. They bow. Silva presents a velvet-lined box.

"Your Majesty," he says warmly, "His Highness sends this token—a sign of his devotion and joyful anticipation."

He opens the lid. Diamonds and emeralds blaze. Green fire dances along the walls.

Mary smiles—real, unguarded. She reaches, fingertips grazing light. "His Highness is gracious—and generous. His earlier gifts delighted my ladies and me. Tell him they wear his gifts with gratitude." She pauses, voice lowering. "Tell him I look forward to our meeting—with the goodwill of a wife who seeks not only alliance, but harmony."

They bow and withdraw. She touches her crucifix then takes a jewelled pendant. It burns like a captured flame in her hands. She turns it slowly. Duty mingles with apprehension—and a quiet hope.

Lady Jane Dormer steps near, eyes bright.

"Another gift, Your Majesty. He means to win every heart in England—beginning with yours."

"He is wise to know women's hearts matter as much as men's in these things," Mary answers, wry warmth in her tone. She touches the pendant to her breast.

"This is not mere wealth. It feels as if he sends part of himself."

Jane lowers her voice. "Not all hearts here are easily won, madam. Some whisper that Spain will grip us by the throat. But if he is as generous in spirit as in jewels, he will silence them."

"He will have my loyalty—and, God willing, my affection," Mary says after a moment. "I am not blind to the nature of our union, nor am I so hardened I cannot hope." Steel enters her voice. "If England doubts him, let them not doubt me. I am their queen. My crown shines by its own light."

Outside, Winchester celebrates. Inside, Mary, alone with the fading light, weighs the jewel—a tangible promise from the foreign prince who will stand beside her as king consort.

22 July 1554

Wolvesey's halls ring with hammer and saw. Fresh timber scents the air. Iron hisses beneath the hammer. Damp stone breathes cool. Light spears through high windows and dances in dust.

Master Laurence Bradshawe, Surveyor of Royal Works—tall, thin, exact—stands like a conductor with a surveying rod and silver-tipped stick. He watches carpenters raise a doorway beneath the Great Hall's vault.

"The new door must align with the stone," he says, tapping an uneven lintel. "No gaps. No rough cuts. This is not a barn."

"Yes, Master Bradshawe," the carpenter answers, wiping sweat. He smells of sawdust and the cheap ale and onion cheese the men broke their fast on at dawn. "The frame will be fitted by nightfall, the hinges by morning prayers, God willing. It will be as befits Her Majesty."

Bradshawe strides to a run of panelling. "Trim to match—walnut, not oak. The grain must run true. The Queen deserves perfection."

He tests the near-finished door—dark wood polished, ironwork in Tudor scrolls. A gloved finger runs the edge. He crouches to check the threshold and rises with the faintest smile.

"This will do," he murmurs. "Wolvesey shall be worthy of a queen."

***

Inside the cathedral, beeswax and sawdust lace the air. Master John Norris, the Queen's Usher, stands on the dais, framing and gesturing as a gilded canopy lifts into place. Bolts of tapestry lean against stone.

"Higher!" Norris calls. "The canopy must crown the dais. The throne must command."

He turns to the hangings. "The Tudor rose faces the aisle. The Habsburg eagle flanks it. This is not decoration. It is language."

"At once, Master Norris," the weaver says.

Bradshawe arrives, dust on his boots and satisfaction in his eyes.

"The alterations at Wolvesey are nearly done," he says. "Her Majesty's audience chamber is ready."

"Excellent," Norris grins. "The cathedral takes shape. The merchants have been difficult over costs."

"They always are," Bradshawe says. "When it is done, they will boast they helped make history."

"The dais will be ready tomorrow," Norris says. "It will carry the weight of an empire."

Bradshawe claps his shoulder. "You have done well, Master Norris. Her Majesty will be pleased—and Prince Philip as well, if he has an eye for detail."

***

By evening, the nave has transformed. The gilded dais catches the last stained light. Tapestries marry the Tudor rose and Habsburg eagle. At Wolvesey, Bradshawe tests the new door's smooth swing and the dais's polish. Pride rises in him: they are not merely building. They are setting a stage for history.

Chapter 3
The Queen's Marriage

23 July 1554

Rain falls in a soft, steady drift. Prince Philip of Spain approaches the ancient city of Winchester. The white stallion, in a gilded saddle, gleams even under the grey sky, a bright figure against the damp fields.

Four attendants walk beside him with the folded silk canopy and poles. Philip wears a dark-blue cloak and a wide-brimmed black leather hat. His face is calm, alert, the weariness of travel held in check by habit and authority.

At the Hospital of St Cross, the sound of hooves sloshing through mud mixes with the muted chatter of his entourage. Grooms hurry out. Philip dismounts. The attendants unfurl the canopy and lift it over him. He passes beneath it on foot towards the gate.

Ruy Gómez de Silva steps forward and adjusts the angle of the canopy to shield Philip from the rain.

"Your Highness, the city awaits," Silva says with a faint smile. "A fresh mount is ready."

Philip glances towards the distant gates. "Good. Let us not keep them waiting."

He hands off the white stallion to a groom. Another groom leads up a sturdy bay. He rides on towards Winchester. Townsfolk line the narrow streets in the drizzle. A few brave voices cheer him. Others watch with guarded curiosity as the Spanish prince passes. From open doorways, the smell of morning pottage and fresh bread drifts out—barley and leeks stewed to a thick mash, coarse loaves split to take butter—comforts for townsfolk who welcome him with their eyes more than with their voices.

The Great West Front of Winchester Cathedral looms, its stone streaked dark with rain. Bells toll in slow, solemn time. Philip dismounts at the Great West Door, flanked by his courtiers and English escorts.

He enters, walks to the high altar, and bows his head. Bishop Stephen Gardiner begins the welcome rite by stepping forward and lifting his hands.

"Almighty God, we beseech You to bless this intended union. May it bring strength and unity to Your Church, and peace to these realms."

***

After the brief welcome service, Philip returns to the Dean's House, then crosses through the garden to a reserved lodging at Wolvesey Castle. He feels a tightness in his chest at the thought of meeting his future bride today. *I hope she will not recoil from me. Perhaps I shall find in her a partner in rule, not only a crown to be worn.*

The rain fades to a fine mist. Philip changes into a white kid-leather doublet, heavy with gold embroidery, and a French-grey satin surcoat. He crosses the gardens of Wolvesey Castle, his boots gritty on wet gravel. He enters the stair-tower and climbs a spiral stair to a private chamber where Queen Mary waits.

The chamber is still. Curtains stir in the damp air drifting through the open windows. Mary stands by a table with gilded candlesticks and a small globe. She wears deep purple brocade. Her attendants step aside as Philip enters.

She rises at once, her face alight.

"Ladies—withdraw to the outer chamber. Remain within call."

The women withdraw in a flutter of silk. Candlelight catches the silver on Philip's surcoat as he approaches. Their eyes meet without formality for the first time alone. For a breath, the weight of state slips away.

"Your...Your Highness...my lord—welcome to England," Mary says, her voice shaking with joy. "My heart is gladdened beyond words to see you. I have prayed for this moment every day."

She extends her hand. Philip removes his hat and, after the briefest hesitation, kisses her fingers—cool skin, a tremor she conquers in a breath.

"Your Majesty, the honour is mine. Your kindness crosses the sea long before I do. The road was long, indeed. To stand before you now is worth every mile. With Spain and England joined, we may do more together than either alone, not merely as crowns allied, but as purpose shared."

"Under the circumstances," she says, "let us set ceremony aside. To you, I am simply Mary."

"And I am simply Philip."

Her smile softens. She gestures to the table where two silver goblets of sack await, the pale Spanish wine catching the candlelight.

She sits opposite and lifts her goblet. "You are much more handsome in person. Titian did not do you justice."

He smooths the edge of his glove with a thumbnail. When he looks up, the smile holds: the eyes do not.

"Thank you, Mary. Your countenance pleases me."

She blushes and recovers with a small laugh. "And you are not as tall as I imagined. I feared I might have to crane my neck to meet your eye."

He grins. "Then I am glad to spare you the strain. If you wish me taller, I will stand on a stool." He lets the line land. Her laugh comes quick and real.

"Or I could wear my crown a little higher," she says, tilting her head and opening her eyes wider.

The humour lingers, but her eyes soften as she studies him more closely. "Your presence does not want for height, my lord. You carry yourself as if you were a head taller than any man."

"You strike neatly, madam. I shall remember it."

He eases back. The edge in his gaze warms. "I confess I have half dreaded this moment."

"Dreaded?" she asks, curious rather than offended.

"Not the meeting," he says quickly, a hand lifted in mock alarm. "The pageantry. The expectation. I feel more like a player waiting for his line."

"You? An actor?" she says, amused. "I thought princes were bred for such performances."

"I have been taught how to walk, how to stand, even how to smile," he says. "One might suppose I frown without end."

Her laugh, bright and unguarded, breaks the tension. "Had I curtsied to you as a lady would, I might have toppled into the rushes. A fine match we are. A prince weary of pomp and a queen with clumsy steps."

The humour lingers. The burden lifts a little.

"At least we agree on this," he says. "We both survived the preparations. A victory of its kind."

"I must warn you," Mary replies. "I am not always so accommodating. I have a temper."

"A temper?" he says lightly. "That may keep things interesting. Perhaps I will start an argument just to see it."

"Careful, sir," she says, eyes bright. "A princess who yields a point may yet gain the game. Spain sends me a prince—and finds I am no novice."

He offers his hand. "Shall we face it together?"

She takes it with a mix of confidence and shyness. "Yes. Together. England is not for the faint of heart."

"Nor Spain," he says. "We will manage."

He looks at her a moment longer. "You know, Mary, in some ways you are more Spanish than I am. Your blood runs hot with Castile and Aragon. I know that fierceness."

"Do you truly think so?"

"I do. It comforts me. In you I find not only a queen and wife, but kin."

They smile, the weight of rank eased by candour.

"I think we can restore the Church to her proper glory," Mary says. "That rests heavy on my heart."

"On mine as well."

"We can mend what is broken and bring stability," she says. "The people will see the strength of our union."

Philip folds his hands. "Indeed, that is my hope. A united Christendom is strength. France watches, and others. They must learn that England and Spain stand as one."

"They will," Mary says, leaning forward. "Our faith and purpose will show them this alliance is more than policy. 'Tis Providence."

Philip glances at her fingers, tight in her lap. He reaches and takes her right hand.

"Mary, your kingdom is proud. Your people may need time to accept me as a foreign prince. I will tread carefully, honour their customs, and prove my loyalty."

"Philip," she says, tasting the name, "my people will see in time. You are what I prayed for. A partner. A protector. A king willing to guide England to greatness."

"And you, Mary, are the heart of it."

Relief softens her face. She lifts her goblet. "Philip, my dear—our union is a blessing for England, for Spain, and for the faith."

He raises his goblet. "To our future, Mary."

"Say my name again, Philip."

"Mary. It is a sweet name."

They drink. Promise and complexity weigh the air. For Mary, this feels like fulfillment. For Philip it is a measured step in a broader design.

They speak for half an hour about hopes for their realms. Philip is restrained yet warm, a man who weighs words. Mary's relief shows in every smile. Candlelight flickers as quiet accord grows. Outside, the rain finally gives over. The gardens shine under a thin moon through rags of cloud.

They descend together into the damp sweetness of the water meadows by the River Itchen. They walk side by side. Attendants keep a respectful distance.

24 July 1554

On Tuesday morning, Master Richard Tisdale, Mary's tailor, arrives at the Dean's House with an array of cloaks for Philip. He lays out silks and velvets, rich with embroidery.

Tisdale bows. "Your Highness, Her Majesty sends these for your consideration, that you may be attired as befits the sacred day."

Philip examines the pieces and nods. He chooses a dark-purple cloak, richly worked, that complements his measured style.

Tisdale signals to his assistants, who lift the chosen cloak with care and set it across Philip's shoulders. The weight settles—heavier than it looks.

"It will sit well upon you, sir," Tisdale says, adjusting the fall at the collar. "The Queen has an eye for such matters."

Philip studies himself in the polished metal mirror. The purple is sober, imperial without ostentation. English enough to reassure, Spanish enough to remind.

"Tell Her Majesty I am grateful," he says. "And that I will not dishonour her with excess."

Tisdale bows again, but hesitates. "If I may, Your Highness—there are those in the city who would have preferred brighter colours. More triumph."

Philip's mouth tightens, almost a smile. "Triumph belongs to armies," he answers. "Not to husbands."

The tailor inclines his head, wisely silent now. The assistants gather the rejected garments, folding them away like abandoned arguments.

When they have gone, Philip remains standing. Outside the window, Winchester stirs—footsteps on stone, a cart rattling, a distant bell already being tested for the morrow. England is awake, and watching.

He draws the cloak closer around him.

Tomorrow, he will kneel before an English altar, swear English vows, and be proclaimed husband to a queen who rules in her own right. He will smile, and bow, and speak the words required of him.

But tonight, he feels the seam between what is given and what is taken—and knows how easily it can split.

Philip turns from the mirror and extinguishes the candle.

The room falls dark, and the day before his marriage passes into memory.

***

That evening, the Great Hall of Wolvesey Castle glows with candlelight. Rich tapestries hang high. Pre-wedding rites begin.

Philip enters in a black coat worked with silver and white hose, the dark-purple cloak he chose earlier falling from his shoulders. The metal catches the light. The white hose emphasises his frame.

Mary sits in purple velvet, her gentlewomen bright in silk and brocade. She rises.

"Phil—Your Highness," she says warmly. "You honour us. You wear your chosen cloak beautifully."

Philip bows. "I am dressed to meet the grandeur of the occasion. Thank you for Your Majesty's generosity."

They speak in low tones for a time. Formality thins. Familiarity grows. The clink of goblets and a murmur of voices fill the hall as the last details fall into place. Servants drift between the tables with trenchers of roast capon and venison in claret, bowls of pease pottage and baskets of new bread; later, platters of custard tarts and marchpane crowns will close the meal for those who can still eat for excitement.

***

At the same hour in Paris, in a dim room above a tanner's shop on a narrow lane, Master Thomas Stafford bends over a rough table. The air smells of damp and cured leather. A chipped jug of thin red wine and a heel of coarse rye bread sit on the table between them, barely touched. No man has come for comfort. Three English dissenters sit with him: Master Edward Deane, a stern yeoman with broad shoulders; Master Henry Cobhale, a wiry merchant; and Sir Peter Carew, Devon-born, court-bred, and twice burned by Mary's favour.

"On the morrow they wed her to a Spaniard," Stafford says, voice low and sharp. "And with it they yoke England to Rome."

Deane slams a palm down, jolting the jug and sending a smear of wine across the rough wood. "A papist prince to rule us, and foreign at that? Treachery."

The boards creak under Cobhale's boots as he paces. "Mark me. Once this Philip plants himself, he will send our gold and grain to Madrid. We will be beggared."

"And worse," Stafford says, eyes narrowing. "They will silence our faith. Mary speaks fair of order and mercy. I do not believe it. She will close our churches and pulpits. She would burn us if she could."

Carew shivers. "Next they'll bring the Inquisition to England," he says.

Stafford's fingers lock on the edge of the table until his knuckles pale. "The crowds in Winchester would cheer a queen who sells their freedom. Do they not see?"

Deane strikes the table again. Carew flinches.

"They will see when Spanish soldiers march their streets and claim their houses," declares Deane.

"We cannot wait," Stafford says. His voice hardens. "If this union takes root, we will pull at weeds for generations. England was free under our Josiah, King Edward. It might have been free under Queen Jane Grey. Under Elizabeth it would be free. It can be free again."

Carew looks up, doubt creasing his brow. "How? The queen crushed Wyatt's rising."

"Wyatt was too bold," Stafford says, and a grim smile cuts across his face. "There are other ways to fell a ruler. Not open rebellion. Not yet. We fan grievances—in Parliament, among merchants, even at court."

"And when the time comes?" Deane asks.

"We strike," Stafford says. "For England. For the Protestant cause. For Elizabeth."

Cobhale snorts. "And for revenge."

"For justice," Stafford snaps. "And for freedom."

"And if we fail?" Carew asks.

"Then we die as Englishmen," Stafford whispers fiercely, "not as slaves to Rome."

They nod, grim and set.

25 July 1554

The seven great bells of Winchester Cathedral peal over the city. Crowds press for a glimpse. The cloud cover thins to a pale light as St James's Day, or the Feast of Santiago in Spain, dawns with its familiar gravity and pomp, though here it falls upon an English morning.

Inside, incense sweetens the air. Whispers ripple and still. Sunlight pours through stained glass. The clock strikes eleven. The wedding Mass begins. The organ sounds. Heads turn to the West Door.

Prince Philip enters the long nave. His black boots are soft on stone. Gold thread in his garments catches the light. The collar of the Order of the Garter—newly bestowed—hangs at his shoulders. A gold crucifix rests on his breast. A jewelled English ceremonial sword rides at his waist on velvet.

As befits a king-consort, English noblemen bear a canopy of estate above him as he advances, then draw it aside at the choir steps. At the altar, Bishop Gardiner waits with missal in hand, priests and servers arrayed. Philip slows before the steps, composed. Spanish nobles follow, their dress a show of Spain's weight.

Edward Stanley, Earl of Derby, goes before in crimson lined with ermine, the Sword of State borne aloft. Ruy Gómez de Silva and Don Juan de Figueroa take their places near the rail. The litany flows on.

Half past the hour, Queen Mary enters from a side door. She wears rich purple velvet trimmed in ermine and set with pearls. Her train runs yards behind, carried by her ladies. A crown gleams on her head, hard with diamonds, rubies, and pearls. Jewels weigh her neckline and sleeves. Eyes follow her.

Care has marked her face, yet hope lights it today. She is both monarch and bride.

Mary and Philip meet at the choir steps. They bow to one another. A few words pass, too soft for others to catch.

Bishop Gardiner, in opulent vestments, taps the crozier's ferrule once on stone—a quiet gavel. He looks at the people. He lifts his hand. *"In nomine Patris, et Filii, et Spiritus Sancti."*

He proclaims the banns and asks in English if any know cause to forbid the joining. Silence holds.

Figueroa advances with a document from the Emperor. Gardiner raises it high.

"By decree of His Imperial Majesty Charles the Fifth," he proclaims, "Prince Philip is sovereign King of Naples, King of Sicily, and Duke of Milan, with the privileges of a monarch."

The words carry clean across the nave. The point is plain: Spain itself will not have him treated as a mere consort but as a king in his own right. Mary has ensured they all hear it.

The Earl of Derby bows and places the Queen's hand into Philip's. Gardiner turns first to Mary, tapping the ferrule.

"Mary, wilt thou have this man, Philip—King of Naples, King of Sicily, Duke of Milan, Prince of Spain—to be thy wedded husband, to live together after God's ordinance in the holy estate of matrimony? Wilt thou love him, comfort him, honour and keep him, in sickness and in health, and, forsaking all others, keep thee only unto him so long as ye both shall live?"

"I will," Mary says. Though soft, her voice holds.

Gardiner turns to Philip. Philip meets his gaze.

"Philip, wilt thou have this woman, Mary—Queen of England, Ireland, and France—to be thy wedded wife?"

"I will," Philip answers. His baritone carries to the farthest arch.

Gardiner joins their right hands for the handfasting.

Philip speaks first. "I, Philip, take thee, Mary, to be my wedded wife, to have and to hold from this day forward, for better, for worse, for richer, for poorer, in sickness and in health, to love and to cherish, till death us depart; and thereto I plight thee my troth."

Mary replies in turn, steady now. "I, Mary, take thee, Philip, to be my wedded husband, to have and to hold from this day forward, for better, for worse, for richer, for poorer, in sickness and in health, to love and to cherish, till death us depart; and thereto I give thee my troth."

Gardiner blesses the ring. A deacon brings a single plain gold band upon a small dish.

Philip takes Mary's left hand. As he slides the ring home, he says, firm and clear, "With this ring I thee wed, and with my body I thee honour, and with all my worldly goods I thee endow."

Gardiner lays his crozier lightly over their joined hands. "Those whom God hath joined together let no man put asunder."

They kneel at a *prie-dieu* before the high altar. The Mass proceeds. At the close, Gardiner presents a joint chalice, sign of both spiritual and political bond. The organ swells. The royal chapel choir breaks into "*Te Deum laudamus.*" Polyphony climbs into the vault.

They rise. Mary looks at Philip, bright in her eyes. He bows and offers his arm. England and Spain bind themselves in the sight of heaven and earth.

The Garter King of Arms, Gilbert Dethick, steps forward and proclaims their titles—first in Latin, then in French, then in English. His voice rings. Murmurs answer.

"By the grace of God, Philip and Mary are hereby proclaimed King and Queen of England, France, Naples, Jerusalem, and Ireland, Defenders of the Faith, Princes of Spain, Naples, and Sicily, Archdukes of Austria, Dukes of Milan, Burgundy, and Brabant, Counts of Flanders and Tyrol."

The cathedral bells peal again. The crowd within and the crowds without cheer. Mary's eyes glisten. Philip's smile is measured, yet real.

The Mass ends. The congregation rises in a rustle like wind in grain. Trumpets flare. The couple walks down the nave through a wave of acclamation.

"God save Queen Mary and her King!"

"Long live their Majesties!"

Gold embroidery flares in coloured light. Noblemen and gentlewomen stream behind. Mary's ladies in purple velvet bear themselves with solemn grace. Spanish courtiers move with reserved pride.

Mary leans close and whispers for Philip alone. "This is the happiest day of my life."

"Indeed, Mary," he answers softly. "A happy day for the Tudors and the Habsburgs."

They step into the brightness beyond the great door. For a breath, the world stops. Power gathers around their joined hands. Mary beams and laughs, thinking only of joy and the promise of what may be.

The bells answer them, rolling across stone and water, carrying the sound of union far beyond the city walls. What has been joined in joy this morning will soon be tested by crowns, councils, and the hard weather of power.

***

The late-afternoon wedding banquet begins at Wolvesey Castle. High vaults carry music. Musicians on a dais strike up "La Mourisque" from Tielman Susato's *Danserye*. Their rhythm threads through talk and the light ring of silver on plate.

Under a canopy of gold and crimson, King Philip and Queen Mary sit on a dais. Philip's smile lingers. He lets his gaze take the measure of the hall—who looks away, who holds his eye, weighing glances, tallying allies and doubters. Mary's joy sparkles, but he feels the weight of a crown not yet his.

Dignitaries crowd the place—Scotland, Ireland, Spain, the German states, Hungary, Italy, Flanders, Poland. Lords and gentlemen take a long table to the right. The Privy Council, bishops, envoys of Emperor Charles, papal emissaries, observers from France. And even a well-dressed Indio in a Spanish nobleman's train draws quiet glances. On the left, ladies speak in low tones, their silks whispering.

The musicians shift to a Spanish pavan. A few brave souls take the floor. Their measured steps match the stately air.

At a lower table, a nobleman tears at a capon with little grace. He flicks a bone over his shoulder. It strikes a young servant. The boy staggers, recovers, gathers the scraps with a murmured apology, and slips away.

Across the hall, an English lord at the high table watches Philip with cool disdain. He wets his lips, touches two fingers to his collar, and lets the smile arrive a heartbeat late. He then smirks and lifts his cup, drawing out the sip. Philip notes it. *This wearies me.* His gaze meets the man's. The noble colours red and looks away.

Tension sours and clears, like weather. Servants pass with platters of venison haunch in claret, roast capons under winter herbs, deep bowls of beef pottage and stewed peas, baskets of fresh manchet bread and trenchers laden with fruit tarts. Spiced wine and warm loaves scent the air. Heat and splendour thicken the room.

"Madam, I feel a chill," Philip says, voice low. "I am not convinced your subjects—"

"Our subjects, Your Most Catholic Majesty," Mary says.

"Our subjects," he echoes. "However, I am not convinced they will accept me as their king."

"My love, you are king by the grace of God. They must accept you as their lawful sovereign. To deny it openly is sedition."

"A king in name only," Philip says. "If I am King of England, where is my authority—my seal, my council seat, my right to appoint?"

"In good time, my dear," Mary replies. "I will press the Privy Council and Parliament to amend the marriage treaty. I will speak with my Lord Chancellor Gardiner."

"Does your word as queen weigh nothing? Can you not command it?"

"Parliament has been standing before my time," Mary says. "My father, King Henry, respected it. I owe duty to my ancestors and to English custom."

"This England is strange to me," Philip says. "I will never win its heart."

Mary takes his right hand and sets it to her breast. "You have England's heart," she says. "Right here."

She kisses his cheek. Philip glances around the hall. "Where is the French ambassador? Not that I care about the French."

He scans the room again.

"And where is Princess Elizabeth?"

Mary's face hardens. She knew well enough why Elizabeth was not present. The smile dies. She sets the goblet too hard. Wine leaps and runs. Her fingers find the crucifix and clench until the chain tightens.

"FIE—bastard whore's daughter usurper!" she cries.

Silence falls. She breathes. She forces herself to stand. Her words cut sharp across the hall. Philip keeps his face still, answering with the careful smile of a man who knows too well how quickly affection could sour into suspicion.

"Musicians, play on. Dancers, dance," she says, voice rough. "This is the happiest day of my life. The happiest day..."

Her eyes fill with tears. She sits. The room remembers itself. Sound climbs back. She looks at Philip in apology and manages a small smile. He answers with his own. She raises her gold cup to the hall.

***

Nine o'clock. Candlelight casts the crucifix's shadow like a watchful guard. Mary and Philip, in nightdress, sit at a small table. Philip rubs at his temple. The day had been long—a tide of ceremonies, endless courtesy. He had given smiles, vows, assurances all day. Now, in the hush of candlelight, his weariness sharpens into impatience. The temporary royal chamber is quiet but for the soft scrape of Philip's knife.

Mary holds a goblet of sack. Her hands tremble. On the wall, Titian's portrait of Philip seems to watch with polished calm.

"The painting will go in our bedchamber at Hampton Court," Mary says. Her voice shakes as she tries for steadiness.

"As you wish, Mary," Philip says without looking long.

She leans forward. "I love you, Philip." She grasps his hand. "Today would have been perfect if you had not spoken of that bastard heretic daughter of the Boleyn witch! That king's whore, that great whore, that she-devil who bewitched my father to put away my mother and to betray the true faith!"

She crosses herself, hand unsteady. Philip crosses himself as well, almost by reflex.

"She even turned my father against me," Mary says, louder now. "He declared me the bastard. I was the unhappiest woman in Christendom. Mistress Anne Boleyn did not deserve the sword. No, my lord. No. She was a witch who deserved the stake!"

Philip sets his knife carefully. He straightens and fixes her with a cool look.

"Madam, pray do not judge your sister too harshly," he says. His tone is calm. Impatience edges it.

Her knuckles pale around the stem of the goblet. The crucifix chain bites lightly into her palm. Mary slams the goblet. Wine pools on polished wood.

"That little whore," she says. "Spawn of a whore!"

Philip leans back and drums his fingers once on the arm. "She did not choose her birth, and England will not forget that, madam. Would you fault the Almighty for that? See her as an ally, not an enemy. From what I hear, Princess—"

"Lady Elizabeth," Mary snaps. "I am too generous to call her even that."

"Your sister is loyal to you," Philip says, breath slipping out through his teeth. "She has not been proved a traitor. She has the love of your—our subjects."

Mary stands so fast the chair skids. She paces. "Yes. The love of her devil's brood of Protestants who would throw me from my throne, crown her, and make a heretic kingdom." Her voice breaks. Her fists knot. "For your sake, for mine, for our children—for my Catholic realm—I must keep her watched. I do not trust her. She wants my crown. Do not let her bewitch you, Philip."

A thin smile touches Philip's mouth. He sits straighter. "Bewitch me?" he says, almost amused. "Do you take me for a fool? I am a Habsburg prince. My duty is to the Church and to England's rightful queen. And I remind you, Mary—your throne stands more secure because I sit beside you."

Mary's shoulders sag. Her face grows pale. She drops to her knees before him.

"Philip," she says, voice shaking with raw hope, "give me a child. Give me a son. Then we keep my father's bastard off the throne. Until God says otherwise, England belongs to the Catholic Habsburgs and the Catholic Tudors."

Philip lifts his cup and turns the wine with a lazy wrist. He studies her with cool detachment.

"Madam, I am a son of the Mother Church," he says. "I desire with all my heart to see England in the true faith. Your sister is not our enemy. Will you summon her to court?"

"Nay," Mary cries. The word tears from her. She sinks back into the chair and clutches the edge as if to steady the room. Tears break and run.

Philip rises slowly and smooths his gown. Candlelight crawls along the folds. "I fear your anger blinds you," he says. "Your love for me, at least, is steadfast. That is enough for tonight."

He turns towards the bed. His shadow stretches long across the floor. Mary sits fixed, the goblet tight in her hand. Tears track down her cheeks. The face in Titian's portrait seems to hold the room with a cool and private satisfaction, removed from pain, untouched by tears.

Philip pauses at the table beside the bed. His fingers brush the folded papers laid there earlier, half-seen beneath the candle's guttering light. He does not open them. He knows what they contain.

One line, written with careful courtesy, returns to him unbidden—*with the Queen's counsel*.

He leaves the papers where they lie and draws the coverlet back.

The words do not follow him into sleep.

Chapter 4
Yet a Keen Sour Follows

31 July 1554

Night deepens over Woodstock Manor, Oxfordshire, with thunder. Rain lashes the leaded panes. Wind howls along the gatehouse like a restless spirit. Lightning flares and the rain-slick court flashes cold and white.

In her dim chamber, Princess Elizabeth Tudor, twenty, stands by the narrow window. She wears a plain gown of dark velvet. A single candle gutters on the table and sends a tremble of light across her ginger hair. A cup of small ale cools beside the candle.

She holds a small locket, a precious keepsake that bears tiny likenesses of herself and Anne Boleyn. She opens it. Enamel faces glow for a heartbeat. Her fingertips trace her mother's features and her expression softens.

"Mother," she whispers. "They took you. Now they would bind me with the same chains of suspicion."

She looks for a long moment, hazel eyes set with sorrow and defiance. She snaps the locket shut. She touches the cold glass with her fingertips and watches her reflection blur in the rain.

She tilts the locket. The enamel catches the flame. She lifts the diamond ring she wears to the pane and scratches. Each stroke gives a thin squeal in the hush. Her hand moves with purpose, the stone biting the glass like a graver. Lightning throws her words into view.

"*Much suspected by me, nothing proved can be.*"

Below it, she scratches her own signature: "*Quoth Elizabeth, prisoner.*"

She holds her breath over the last word. Her lips bend into a bitter smile that refuses to die.

Thunder rolls closer. Stone shudders. She steps back. The lines gleam faintly in the candlelight, a vow cut into glass.

She turns into the room. Shadows run over her face and steel her features. The storm outside answers the tumult within. It promises an end. It promises light after the dark.

For now she is a prisoner. If she is not killed first, she knows she is meant for more—much more.

1 August 1554

Morning clears the air and leaves the flagstones dark with rain. From the manor kitchens, the smell of barley pottage and frying salt pork drifts out into the yard, breakfast for guards and grooms if not for their royal charge. Outside the gatehouse, Elizabeth dances a galliard, quick and springing. Her slippers barely sound. She hums a lively tune as the sun catches loose strands of hair. Her hem turns in bright arcs against grim walls.

Mistress Katherine "Kat" Ashley, Elizabeth's lifelong governess and confidante, lately returned to her lady after hard questioning in London, watches with a shawl ready. Amusement and concern share her face. Mistress Anne Denny of Elizabeth's household clasps her hands and cuts wary glances towards Sir Henry Bedingfield, custodian and gaoler of Elizabeth, dour in his post with arms crossed.

Elizabeth glances at Bedingfield as she turns.

"Master Gaoler, my dear sister forgot my wedding invitation. Was I an oversight?"

Bedingfield shifts but keeps his gaze steady.

Elizabeth adds, "And what kind of man is my new brother-in-law?"

Bedingfield replies, "He is quiet and mannerly, Your Highness. Carries himself as a prince. Loyal to the Mother Church. He chooses slowly in all things. He tries to fit in, yet he is like a fish out of the sea. The people do not warm to him."

Elizabeth laughs and moves through another figure.

"Poor Master Gaoler. You sound almost tender towards my sister's new husband."

She spins and looks at Kat. "What say you, Kat? Will this Spanish fish live in our cold English water?"

Kat steps in and sets the shawl on Elizabeth's shoulders. "Your Highness, keep such thoughts close. Storms pass. Loose words linger."

Elizabeth's smile tilts.

"Storms clear the air, Kat. I do not fear them."

Mistress Denny gathers her courage.

"Your Highness, they say King Philip offends easily. He keeps his state very close, revealing little beyond what duty requires."

Elizabeth tilts her head. "Then for England's sake he must learn to swallow pride. Our weather and our temper do not bend."

Master Thomas Parry, keeper of Elizabeth's accounts, newly restored to some favour after the Council's examinations, strides up and doffs his hat.

"Good morrow, Your Highness. Mistress Ashley. Mistress Denny. Master Gaoler."

Bedingfield's mouth thins at that name. His fingers tap the keys at his belt—one quick click. He gives a short nod and replies, "Master Parry."

Elizabeth curtsies in play.

"Good morrow, Thomas. How fares your cousin Blanche Parry?"

"She fares well, Your Highness."

Parry looks at Bedingfield. "And how fares the Spanish King? Has he grown used to English ways yet?"

Bedingfield keeps his tone flat. "The King learns his role, as we all must."

Parry smiles.

"The English prefer an Englishman to sit on the English throne. They fear he will pull us into war with France and bleed our coffers. They say he sulks for lack of an English crown. Offended to be only a consort."

Elizabeth stops. The play falls from her face.

"Offended, you say. Let him take comfort in the Queen. My standing with her is delicate ground. One wrong step and the whole floor shifts beneath me."

Kat lays a hand on Elizabeth's arm. "Do not dwell there, Your Highness."

Elizabeth's voice lowers.

"Every day, Kat. From the Tower to this wretched place, I think of my mother. Of Lady Jane Grey. Of those who stood too near the throne and lost their heads. Every day."

Mistress Denny whispers. "Surely Queen Mary would not—"

Elizabeth cuts her off. "Oh, would she not? If I must die, let it be swift. Let me fly by the sword as my mother did. I will not cower."

Bedingfield steps forward. "Your Highness, many see you as a threat to the Church. Yet under my charge no harm will come to you."

Kat says, "Yes. Never fear, Your Highness."

Elizabeth's smile turns sardonic.

"In England no one is safe. Least of all a Protestant Tudor princess."

Elizabeth turns back to the dance, her steps light, her thoughts anything but, hidden beneath the rhythm.

17 April 1555

Sun pours into the Queen's Bedchamber at Hampton Court Palace. Queen Mary looks in a mirror on the wall. She steps back to get a fuller view of her torso. She laughs at her reflection and rests a hand on her swollen belly. Philip stands near with a small smile.

"My lord, have Lady Elizabeth summoned to court."

Philip does not answer at once. He watches Mary's hand settle over her belly—possessive, resolute—and reads the decision already made. A clerk is signalled; the order is carried outward at once, before doubt can find breath.

28 April 1555

The Presence Chamber at Hampton Court glows with amber light through tall casements. It is easy for talk, yet heavy with gold and tapestries. Philip stands close to his wife, a goblet of watered Rhenish in his hand.

Elizabeth enters in deep green velvet threaded with gold. She curtsies low before Mary, then rises and takes both her hands and kisses them lightly.

"Your Majesty. I have longed to see your face these many months. It seemed years. I am ever your most loving servant."

Mary leans forward. Suspicion edges her glance. Her fingers tighten for a breath.

"His Majesty believes as much, but do not lie to me, madam. I am not so convinced."

Elizabeth turns to Philip. His face is neutral. His eyes flicker with curiosity. She curtsies lower, rising with measured deference.

"Your Majesty."

Philip extends his hand, and she touches it lightly to her lips. He bids her rise with formal courtesy—no more, no less—yet Mary notes every bit of it. Her smile holds, but something sharp flashes behind it—jealousy wearing the mask of doctrine.

"Lady Elizabeth," she says, cutting the moment. "It does my heart good to see you in such...good health."

Elizabeth steps back. "Thank you, Your Majesty."

Mary's mouth tilts into triumph.

"Madam, I bring good news. God willing, before the year turns, I will give birth to your first nephew, the next King of England. Long may he reign."

Mary lays a hand across her belly, eyes bright with pride.

"You are to remain here and assist my ladies. Your lodging is ready."

Elizabeth inclines her head. "I am honoured to serve you and my future sovereign."

Mary's smile falters. Suspicion creeps back.

"Yes, your most Catholic sovereign. Unlike you, my son will be raised in the true faith of Saint Peter. What I began in blotting out heresy, my son will finish. Am I clear, madam?"

Elizabeth's hands tighten on her skirts, yet her face does not change.

"Yes, Your Majesty."

Mary's voice sharpens and rises to mock her sister.

"'Yes, Your Majesty.' Your hypocrisy stands out like coal in snow. You pretend to honour the Mass and the Blessed Sacrament. You are the spawn of a witch. I am under no illusion."

Elizabeth keeps her tone even.

"Is there not one Christ, Jesus, and one faith? The rest—are we not tangled in men's quarrels?"

"Quarrels?"

The word hangs. The room seems to hold its breath.

Philip steps in.

"Madam, for the child's sake and for your health, be calm. For my sake also."

Mary yields a little and sinks back.

"Yes, my lord."

Philip turns to Elizabeth.

"Sister-in-law, count me a devoted brother, an advocate, and a friend."

Mary sneers.

Elizabeth answers with grace.

"My cup runs over, Your Majesty."

Philip goes to the table, pours a light cordial from a silver ewer into a goblet, and hands it to Elizabeth.

"Come. Taste this spiced lemon cordial our steward favours."

Elizabeth takes it and sips.

"'Tis sweet. I love sweetness. Yet a keen sour follows."

Philip smiles and claps his hands once.

"The balance is its charm, madam."

Mary's hands clench in her lap. The air tightens.

23 August 1555

The chamber feels sepulchral. Heavy curtains shut out the summer. A single candle burns low. Mary sits motionless with a Catholic prayer book open at "Prayer for a Woman with Child." Tears blot the page. A pewter cup of warm milk-posset cools on the stool by her chair, the nutmeg skin unbroken.

Behind her stand Philip, Elizabeth, and Dr John Caius, Mary's physician. Silence bears the news.

Caius speaks softly.

"Your Majesty, there are times when the body gives signs that do not end in birth. Desire is fierce. Nature can deceive."

Mary's shoulders stiffen. Another tear falls on the page.

Elizabeth folds and unfolds her arms. She looks from Mary to Philip.

"Your Majesty, nature is cruel. Do not take it for a measure of your worth."

Mary turns a fraction and fixes Elizabeth with a look that holds both bitterness and kinship.

"You do not understand, madam. My own body has failed me. I prayed for a son—for England's sake. And now there is only waiting. Nothing. What is a queen without an heir? What am I, if not a disappointment—a woman who has fallen short?"

Philip steps close, voice steady.

"Listen to your sister, Mary. Your worth is more than children. You are the heart of your people. You have restored the old faith. Be proud of that. That is your legacy."

Mary searches his eyes.

"Is that all I am to them? Will they remember my faith and my fight, or only what I could not give?"

Elizabeth moves nearer.

"History remembers you for not yielding. A true Tudor queen."

Caius clears his throat. "Rest and quiet will ease the strain."

Mary closes the book with trembling hands and clutches it to her breast.

"Madam, leave me."

Philip steadies Elizabeth and guides her out. Caius follows to the corridor, closing the door softly behind them.

Philip speaks low. "Mary breaks under her own hopes. Her faith consumes her."

Elizabeth keeps her face still. "She is a Tudor. Tudors do not break. We crack under weight."

Philip turns to Caius.

"Excuse us, Doctor. I will speak with the Princess."

"Of course, Your Majesty."

Philip and Elizabeth withdraw to a smaller privy room. She inclines her head. A Spanish guard closes the door at Philip's nod, leaving them alone with the hush of the corridor and the faint hiss of rain at the casement.

"Your Majesty?"

"Call me Philip. With your permission, I would like to call you Elizabeth. I will sail soon for the Low Countries."

"Sail? You would leave when she needs you most? I know love was never in your marriage contract. Loyalty was. You are bound to Mary."

Philip's control frays. *I do not need this. Not now.*

"Everything is wrong. Am I king in name only? Do I wear a crown? No. Your people will not have me. There is no heir. My father's realms require me. I must tend to them."

Elizabeth steps in, eyes fierce.

"And what of England? What of the Queen? She can barely rise. She needs a husband, not an empty room. Do your duty."

Philip sighs.

"I am a husband, and a consort without power. Your sister—"

"She loves you," Elizabeth snaps. "You swore to stand by her. Yet you run."

Philip's look hardens.

"She knows the empire claims me. I do not flee. I stand in the role carved for me."

Elizabeth's voice goes cold.

"That is your excuse. Is this how you wish to be remembered? The prince who left his wife in her darkest hour?"

The cut lands. Philip flares.

"You speak boldly, Elizabeth. You know nothing of my burdens. This union is policy, not love. The fire in your voice—that is conviction...useful to know."

The air freezes. Elizabeth flushes with anger.

"What drives you, Your Majesty, is only policy. Just policy. Do not call me sister. I had one brother, and he is gone. I am not the prize for your failed ambition. My sister is queen, and I will stand loyal to her—faults and all."

Philip lowers his voice.

"I mean no insult."

Elizabeth's temper breaks.

"You dare insult her while she lies broken. You dare think I would betray her? You run from the world you made. The world does not revolve around you, my lord."

He recoils, pride and hurt plain. He straightens.

"I will not be lectured. My duties call me. In time you will see I had no choice."

He turns for the door. Elizabeth's voice follows.

"Go then, Your Majesty. Know this. You leave a legacy of weakness. That is how they will remember you."

He does not turn back. His steps fade. Elizabeth stands with a heaving chest. She clenches her fists.

"Men like you," she whispers. "Too proud to see the truth."

From the next room Mary cries out.

"Philip!"

Elizabeth wipes her eyes.

25 August 1555

A great fire climbs the Privy Council Chamber chimney at Hampton Court. Mary sits rigid in a carved chair, hands white on the arms. Philip stands near the window and stares at the gardens. The air between them crackles.

Mary's voice comes thin with desperation.

"Philip, must you leave so soon? We have had so little time."

Philip rubs his face and turns.

"My father is stepping down. The empire is splitting apart. Spain and the Netherlands will come to me. My uncle Ferdinand takes what remains. There are oaths, ceremonies, and claims that must be secured in person."

Mary rises. Silk rustles.

"But I am your wife. Must his empire outrank your duty here? Am I not enough for you?"

The door bursts open. Old Will Sommers, King Henry's and Queen Mary's court fool, ambles in with a tired grin and a faded cap. A young fool who calls herself "Jane Foole," not her real name, in motley tumbles after him, bells chiming.

Jane leaps to a stool.

"Leaving already, Your Majesty of Spain and not yet of England? Was it our weather or our roast beef that soured you?"

Will adds dryly, "Or our ale?"

Philip's face closes. "Do you think my leaving is a jest?"

Jane leans to Mary and stage-whispers.

"Good Cousin Mary, do you think he runs from us? Or from our women?"

"Enough!" Philip's voice cuts. The fools still. Will lowers his head.

Mary lays a trembling hand on Philip's arm.

"They mean no harm, my lord. If you leave now the people will take it ill. They already whisper that you care more for Spain than for England. Or for me."

Philip brushes her hand away with care.

"You have to understand. I do not have a choice. My father's abdication is not just a private matter—Christendom itself hangs in the balance. The Netherlands are already stirring with rebellion. I have to go."

Tears rise yet she holds them.

"And what of me? What of plots? Must I face them alone?"

Jane cannot resist. "If he must go, give him a map. Or a faster horse."

Philip turns on her.

"Do you think it is easy to leave my wife and a realm I swore to aid? I am a king, not a fool."

Mary flinches, then steps close.

"If you leave, I fear my enemies will rise. I fear for my throne. I fear for my life."

His face softens.

"You are stronger than you think, Mary. You have my support even from afar. I must go."

Jane and Will trade a look and fall quiet. Mary drops her eyes.

My darling.

Philip lowers his gaze and turns for the door. The fools follow with a soft jingle. The door shuts. Mary presses a hand to her chest.

26 August 1555

Rain hangs in the air like a rumour as the procession forms in the Base Court at Hampton. Trumpeters lift their instruments. The notes cut clean through the damp. Mary mounts the royal barge at the King's Stairs, her veil pinned tight against the river wind. Philip gives her his hand, gloved, precise. Grooms release the mooring lines. Oars bite. The barge slides into the brown muscle of the Thames.

They sit beneath a canopy edged with gold fringe, side by side and not quite touching. Behind them: Gardiner, Paget, the Earl of Pembroke, faces set to official neutrality. London gathers along the banks—apprentices on wharves, fishwives with baskets, Spaniards in dark velvet standing apart, Englishmen with their eyes thin and measuring. A muted cheer rises from a few Londoners.

"Whitehall first," Philip says, a statement more than a plan. "We dine. Then Greenwich."

Mary nods. "Yes." She watches the reach ahead, calculating the length of the river and the length of days ahead. He will go. She will stay. *'Tis arithmetic. How it hurts!*

***

At Whitehall they disembark to a brief blaze of ceremony—salutes, lowered halberds, a rush of stewards. Mary eats little. The meat dries on her tongue. She toys with a crust of manchet bread and leaves the rest. Philip speaks of winds, pilots, packets of letters already sealed for Brussels. He is courteous, alert, impossible to catch with the hand of need.

Back on the water, the tide carries them east. Warehouses slide past, then the open bends where the river widens and begins to taste of the sea. Spray freckles Mary's sleeve. She gets comfortable and presses her palm flat on the bench to steady herself.

"Your people watched you," Philip says, gazing at the north bank—tilers, coopers, whole families perched on ladders to see.

"And yours watched you," she answers. "We are both on trial."

He turns at that, just enough. "I do not take you for granted, Mary."

"I would rather you did not take me for temporary."

Silence takes the space between them. Below, the oars keep time like a sober drum.

Greenwich rises ahead—pale stone, green lawn, the towers of the palace like open hands. As they draw in, the great clock tolls the quarter. Courtiers line the landing. Mary stands. Philip offers his arm. For the watching crowd they are pageant-perfect: Queen and King, matched, unassailable.

But when they step onto the wet stone of the river stairs, Mary's grip tightens once. Not for balance. To keep the moment from slipping.

"Three days," she says under the heralds' noise. "Stay those to me."

"They are yours," he answers, and the promise is honest, because it is small enough to keep.

29 August 1555

The day breaks hard and clear, as if the sky has been scoured clean. The Thames runs bright with sun. Mary has done what a queen can do: Mass at dawn, petitions signed, orders laid down for the Council, and a private hour with her chaplains. None of it touches the single fact that waits by the water.

In the Privy Chamber she pins on a collar of pearls and takes it off again. She chooses plain black with a narrow border of ermine—no need to gild a wound. Lady Margaret Clarenceux brings her gloves. Mary forgets to put them on.

Philip enters at the quiet knock reserved for him. He is travel-dressed: black velvet, short cloak, the Garter at his knee. A sword he will not draw in England. He bows, then crosses the space between them with that measured stride that reads as certainty to the world and distance to a wife.

"Winds are fair to Dover," he says. "If they hold, I embark within days. I will write from Calais. From Brussels. Regularly."

"Write, yes," Mary says. "But look at me now."

He does. For a moment the polished surface cracks. Behind it, fatigue, duty, the map of Europe laid like a burden across his shoulders.

"This is not refusal," he says, low. "Nor escape."

"It feels like both."

He takes her hands. His palms are warm. "I go to hold what must be held—for you as well as for Spain. War grinds, treaties fray, and your cousins in France watch every silence, every delay," he says. "I will not give them one."

"Do not sell me policy," she cuts in, not sharp but final. "Give me a husband."

He breathes once, deeply. "Then hear a husband: I will return."

They walk together to the riverside. The palace opens before them: bright gravel, green sward, the long façade throwing back sunlight. The court has learned its lesson and stands well away—to give privacy the appearance of state. At the water, the royal barge waits, and beyond it, a smaller craft for the King's quiet passage downriver, less pageant, more speed.

The river smells of tar and salt and iron. The cry of gulls tilts the air.

At the top of the landing-steps Mary stops. The whole court halts behind her like a diagram of power: Gardiner steady as oak, Pembroke stone-faced, Paget counting futures, Spanish grandees grave and inward. The only sound is water licking stone.

Mary turns to Philip. Her voice is firm now. The tremor has burned off in the clarity of loss. "Go do what you must. I will do what I must. But know this—that I do not love you as a cipher or a treaty. I love you as a woman loves a man she has chosen. Come back to me not as a duty, but as a desire."

He does not kiss her quickly this time. He takes her face in his hands and sets his mouth to hers, deliberate and long enough that the court must look down. When he draws back there is colour in his cheeks, and something like hunger that he masterfully locks away.

"Mary," he says, and the single word carries more than the speeches he has made all week. "Pray for me."

"I do. And for England. Bring me news I can bless."

He descends the wet steps. The bargemen shift weight. The craft touches and eases off. Philip stands at the stern, hat in hand. He does not wave. He holds her in his gaze until the angle of the river takes him.

Mary does not move. The small boat narrows to a black stitch on silver water. Bells in the palace chapel strike the hour. Each stroke lands like a nail driven sure. At last she lifts her chin.

"To council," she says to no one and to everyone. "There is work."

Only when she turns does the court breathe again. The river keeps its counsel and runs on towards the sea. Somewhere beyond the bend, oars bite deeper, carrying Philip towards troubles not yet openly declared.

Mary stands fast, already a widow to the crown she wears.

2 September 1555

Salt wind whips the crowded quays at Dover. On the quay, sailors roll casks of dried peas and barrels of biscuit, and heave salted beef and cod and red wine towards the holds—the same grey fare that will follow Philip to the Low Countries. He stands on the *Espíritu Santo's* deck as men haul lines and the cables creak. Cargo thuds. Orders crack through the din. He watches the horizon with a mix of relief and bitterness.

Close confidant Gómez Suárez de Figueroa, the Count of Feria, joins him and studies his face.

The captain approaches and bows.

"Your Majesty, we stand ready to weigh anchor."

"Weigh anchor at once."

"At your command, Your Majesty."

The captain turns and shouts.

"Weigh anchor! Loose cables!"

Philip keeps his eyes on the white cliffs.

"Don Gómez, I cannot leave England fast enough."

Feria raises a brow and waits.

"This land is a barren field to me," Philip says. "I pour in effort and reap nothing. Even the fools scorn me as a foreigner."

"I felt no warmth either, Your Majesty."

Philip pulls a letter from his pouch.

"Our countrymen are robbed and hated. Listen to this report: 'Your Majesty, the English hate us worse than the devil. They rob us on the road and in town. No man dares ride two miles.' Highwaymen fell on a company of Spaniards and beat them. The Council knows and says nothing."

"I have heard the same, Majesty."

"I did not expect such loathing. Many return to Spain or flee to the Low Countries. But did I not stay for the peace of Spain and England? Even princes do not enjoy freedom."

He draws breath and lets it go.

"If only things were different. I misjudged the Princess Elizabeth."

"She, Your Majesty?"

Philip nods. "For a moment I thought she might be an ally—sharp as the Channel winds. She has a spirit that could steady a crown. But I had her sister. The contract named policy, not love."

"She is clever, Majesty. Clever—and dangerous. Do not mistake spirit for loyalty."

"I married because of my father's policy. To stand with England against France. Survival. Yet even now I measure what part she may play if she comes to rule."

"I am sorry, Majesty."

Philip's shoulders sag.

"I hoped for a child at least. An heir for England to make this endeavour worth the cost."

Feria's gaze sharpens.

"Your realms are rich and many. Spain. The Netherlands. Naples and Sicily. The Indies. They need you more than that island. England is a piece, not the board."

Philip looks out to sea.

"Yes. Naples and Sicily with grain and stone. The Netherlands, rich and restive. The Indies with metals that feed all. Spain the heart. There they love me. In England, I am tolerated or despised."

Feria's voice stays steady.

"Let England sulk. The empire is your work."

Philip's eyes sharpen.

"You are right. My father's empire is my charge. Let England keep its rain and fog. I will shape a greater dominion elsewhere, and return to Mary in my own season. I know my duty."

Feria nods.

"Yes, Majesty. Spain will stand long after England's troubles fade."

4 September 1555

Wind fills the topsails. The *Espíritu Santo* heaves north and east. Below, the bell for the noon mess sounds; the men line up for stewed peas and salt fish over broken biscuit, washed down with watered wine, while their king broods at the rail.

Feria stands with Philip at the rail.

"If we keep the weather gauge, we will make Flanders soon."

Philip watches the swells.

"When we first came up the Channel, I remember a place named for a creature. A crawling one."

"That was the Lizard, Sire. In Cornwall."

"The Lizard. A strange name. Yet we need such 'reptiles' to defend Spain against France."

Feria laughs.

Philip nods towards the fleet.

"That is why I told the Queen to strengthen her Navy Royal. United with Spain, it stands against any foe."

Father Alfonso de Castro, Philip's confessor, and Ruy Gómez de Silva approach.

"A fair thought, Sire," Castro says. "I trust you keep well."

"Yes, Father. At least at Mass, with the Blessed Eucharist, I feel at home. But England—England wears me down. I never fit in there. Even the Catholics kept their distance. Gardiner could barely hide his dislike. They do not want a foreign king."

Castro folds his hands. "Sire, the English love their nation fiercely. Yet be assured many Catholics stand with us against heresy. Praise be to God and the Blessed Virgin that the Queen purges the realm."

Philip's reply is quiet.

"As a son of the Church, I cannot abide heresy. Not with fire if it can be helped. Martyrs breed more martyrs. I choose tact where I can."

Feria cuts in.

"Elizabeth will be trouble, Sire. A Tudor in blood, but one who draws the Protestants like moths. She has not renounced."

Philip's voice stays mild.

"She had poor teaching under her father. She told the Queen as much."

Castro lifts a brow.

"You speak kindly of her, Sire. Yet she mocks our rites and our Pope. That is the truth of her."

Philip looks back to sea.

"Perhaps. Yet she has wit enough to bend, given the right guidance."

11 October 1555

Philip's chamber in his palace in Brussels is cold though the hearth hisses. Bells toll across the city. Papers lie strewn with figures of war and debt. The weight of a crown presses on his shoulders.

He rubs his neck and thinks of England. A cup of dark Rhenish stands cooling by the inkstand. Mary's face comes to him with raised eyes and hope for a child. He hears the hollowness in her voice when they parted. He knows how tongues gnaw at her.

A courier waits outside. Philip draws clean parchment and dips the pen. Words resist him. Duty demands them.

He writes:

"*Most High and Excellent Lady, and most dear and beloved Wife. Though miles divide us, my thoughts remain with Your Majesty. I pray for your health and beg frequent word of it. Though absent, I am no less your husband. My father's abdication is at hand. Many kingdoms now claim my labour. Yet your name and welfare are ever in my prayers. I trust God will soon grant you the blessing of children for England's good and for your contentment. Hold firm in council and beware the practices of France. Rely upon my love and faithfulness. Your most faithful husband, Philip.*"

He sands and seals the page.

"Send him in," he calls.

The courier comes, kneels, and takes the letter. The seal glows red in the firelight.

"Ride hard," Philip says. "England awaits."

Bootsteps fade. Papers wait. His thoughts linger on the road and the Queen whose hands will break the seal. He lifts the next sheet and does not write—only stares at the blank as if it might absolve him. Outside, the bells keep counting, and with each toll the distance to England sounds less like miles than judgment. He sets the quill down, palms flat on the table, and lets the cold room have what the letter will not: his doubt.

28 October 1555

Afternoon light fades at Whitehall Palace. Mary sits in her Privy Chamber with a prayer book open and unread. She has sent daily to Brussels and heard nothing.

The door opens. A courier enters, dusted from the road. He drops to one knee and holds out a letter sealed red. Her heart leaps. She dismisses the room with a glance. The courier backs out, silent, and the door shuts. A small cup of hippocras—spiced wine left by an anxious lady—rests beside her prayer book.

Her hands tremble as she breaks the seal.

"*Most High and Excellent Lady...*"

The words swim. She presses the parchment close as if it might give back his touch. "*I trust in God that He will soon grant you the blessing of children.*" Her breath catches. Tears sting. She has prayed the same.

She reads on. "*Hold firm in council. Beware the practices of France.*" Politics intrude as always. Duty presses between them. She is wife and queen. Duty threads between each line of his hand.

She traces his name. *Philip*. She mouths it like a prayer. She presses the letter to her breast and closes her eyes. For a moment she believes the distance bridged.

The fire sinks. The courier is gone. Only the letter remains, a thin thread between her longing heart and the cold miles of Europe. She lifts the cup at last and only wets her lips; even the sweetness cannot steady her.

Chapter 5
Philip's Marriage Scheme

20 March 1556

Morning spills over the palace heights in Brussels, washing the stone and slate of the Coudenberg. The wind moves cool along the terrace. Below, the city stirs—bells, carts, a far clatter of hooves—while Philip, now ruling as King of Spain in his father's stead, holds a folded letter in Mary's handwriting, its seal already broken. His cup of watered red wine sits on the terrace rail. A faint smile touches his mouth, then fades as duty reclaims him.

Don Gonzalo Pérez, Philip's secretary, and Don Diego de Mendoza, a royal diplomat, wait nearby.

Philip turns to Mendoza. The ambassador produces a second letter—in Simon Renard's hand from Brussels—and unfolds it.

"Your Majesty," Pérez says, "Renard urges a marriage for Princess Elizabeth—with Emmanuel Philibert, Duke of Savoy."

Philip's mouth hardens. "My cousin? They call him the Ironhead."

"He writes: '*Set the Lady Elizabeth in the Duke's house and you bind her inclination to ours. You also take from France the hope of her person.*' He urges speed while Paris looks elsewhere."

"Ironhead."

Philip paces towards the balustrade, then back to the table, the letter crackling once in his hand.

"A Savoyard marriage secures more than fleets or armies. And Elizabeth..." He pauses, the name lingering. *And Elizabeth.* For an instant his eyes soften, as though recalling her fire, her wit—qualities he cannot dismiss. A flicker, gone as quickly as it came. His voice steadies. "...Elizabeth will see reason. Our strength will serve to her advantage."

Ruy Gómez de Silva, one of Philip's closest confidants, advances in measured steps. "Majesty, Elizabeth is no Mary. She smiles like a courtier and thinks like her father. If she bends, it will be because she chooses—not because you command."

Philip halts, pivots. Irritation sparks, then fades as he resumes his pacing. "She understands alliances. England is never united—give that realm a Catholic duke and we anchor her court. The Protestant fire cools. Through her, England is ours—not by force, but by bond."

Mendoza folds his arms. "Or we provoke revolt. Pressing her too hard may weaken Mary before her own council."

Philip stops at the table, fingers drumming once, then moves again to the terrace. His tone steadies, edged with resolve.

"Mary's position is firm enough—for now. This plan strengthens her. Place Elizabeth in loyal hands, and the French lose their purchase—not in some distant season, but now, while Paris looks elsewhere. Savoy does not merely anchor England; he bars France from the gate. That is the future."

Pérez inclines his head. "Renard is right, Majesty. If Elizabeth takes Savoy, we secure England for a generation."

Mendoza lowers his eyes, unconvinced. "I submit to your wishes, Sire. But the risk remains."

Philip turns to the river, the sun flashing on steel waters far below. He lifts his chin, every inch the King.

"It is settled. We advance Renard's plan. The Duke of Savoy is the key."

Wind tugs at his cloak.

"This is the path," he says now, not softly. "No one stands in our way."

15 April 1556

A clear falsetto carries "Pastime with Good Company," once made famous by her father, through the Great Hall at the Royal Palace of Hatfield, Hertfordshire. Lutes and viols lift warmth into the room. At a side table, Elizabeth, her fiery red hair tucked beneath a delicate French hood, sits with Lady Anna von Kleve, better known as Anne of Cleves, former wife of King Henry VIII, a visitor received in quiet privacy. She had come down to Hatfield to pay her respects and speak without ears at court. Gilded cards lie between them for a round of "Maw."

With a thick German accent, Anne clears her throat before reading aloud, adopting the tone of a child to mimic the letter's flowery language.

"'*Permit me to show, in this billet, the zeal with which I devote my respect to you as queen, and my entire obedience to you as my mother. I am too young and feeble to have power to do more than felicitate you with all my heart in this commencement of your marriage. I hope that Your Majesty will have as much goodwill for me as I have zeal for your service.*'"

She sets the letter down and sighs. "I have always treasured that letter."

Elizabeth studies the cards in her hand. "I was six then," she says.

"Precocious you were, Your Highness," Anne says, drawing a card.

Elizabeth lays a sly one and taps the board.

"Lady Anne, they say my father rejected you because you were plain. Not true. I have seen Master Holbein's portrait of you—you were not plain."

Anne smiles, then lowers her voice and chuckles briefly.

"I remember New Year's at Rochester. New gown. Jewels. All to please. He fooled me. He came dressed like a courier and gave courtesy with guarded eyes. After he left the room, I heard him—plain enough: 'That Flanders mare? I like her not,' he told Master Cromwell."

Elizabeth's mouth tilts.

"That sounds like Father. Blunt as a hammer and careless who hears. He judged faces like he read hearts. Wrong, often enough. You were not the first."

Anne spreads her hands, amused and unbothered.

"I did not fare badly. Because of your father, I am well kept. Pensions. Houses. I am the King's Sister by law now." She sets down her cards and puts her hands to the sides of her head. "I kept my head because I agreed to what he wanted. I am a reasonable woman, you see? I agreed to the annulment. *Ja, ja, ja zu allem.* Then I was free."

She takes her cards and Elizabeth plays another card.

"A free woman. My sister's mother should have done the same."

Anne lifts a brow and plays.

"I learned from Catherine. I am blessed, child. I am sorry I cannot say the same for your sister the Queen. I do not know which is worse—losing a child or losing a child you never had."

Elizabeth's face darkens. She gathers the trick.

"I may never bear a child. I fear neither will my sister. I saw Philip looking at Mary. His eyes said 'I like her not,' without a word."

Anne leans closer.

"*Ja.* Still, I have seen him watch you. His eyes said, 'I like.'"

Elizabeth lets out a breath and touches the cards without seeing them.

"I know—charm is not lost on me. But I am my sister's subject first. Whatever nonsense flitted through my head is gone."

Anne draws another card.

"Has the King spoken of his return to England?"

Elizabeth places one with care.

"Nay. It matters little. He found in England a trusty ally against France. That was our purpose."

Anne nods.

"And the game has changed. The Emperor abdicated, and your brother-in-law is the Most Catholic King."

"Game of kings. King of games," Elizabeth says, a hint of a smile held in check. "His empire fills his mind more than his wife. He may even inherit your Duchy of Cleves."

Anne shrugs.

"It makes no difference to me. England is my home. Had I returned to Cleves, my brother would have lorded it over me for life."

Elizabeth laughs lightly.

"No lords. No masters. Lady Anne, I take your lesson. My sister is queen, yet her husband's wishes bind her. That is a weakness. If I ever wear a crown, I hold the winning cards. Always."

She lays her last card and smiles. "Who shall me LET? I win!"

Anne laughs and gathers the deck. "A true Tudor. You play to win."

"I never lose," Elizabeth says.

Anne's tone softens. "I heard whispers of a proposal from the Duke of Savoy. It may be most advantageous."

Elizabeth's fingers still for a breath. She meets Anne's eye.

"No lords. No masters, Lady Anne. I keep my own course."

Anne smiles, knowing.

"Wise. Still, the Duke is not easy to overlook."

Elizabeth does not look up.

"Then he should mind his steps. I can crush small things without so much as rising."

27 February 1557

Winter grips the gardens at Hampton Court Palace. Frost silvers the gravel. A bitter wind cuts through bare branches.

Queen Mary walks with her ladies, heavy in black velvet and winter-white fur. She insists on the air and the rhythm of her step on the path.

Hooves break the hush. A rider comes on a dark horse, cloak snapping. Sir Robert Rochester, the Queen's trusted Comptroller, swings down and bows.

"Your Majesty, a letter."

A lady in burgundy sable steps forward, receives it, and places it in Mary's gloved hands. Mary breaks the seal.

Her face changes as she reads. Blood warms her cheeks. Her mouth parts.

"God is good. God is good—He has heard me at last!"

Her joy rings over the cold beds and hedges. Yet wary eyes trade whispers.

***

Inside, fires burn but give little heat. Courtiers drift in low talk beneath heavy tapestries. A draft runs along the stones.

Heels strike the flagstones. Mary enters bright with an emotion long starved from her face. The court turns and bows.

"Anon, my husband the King returns," she calls. "Make ready! Prepare victuals! Send for Sir Thomas Cawarden—Master of the Revels!"

Approval stirs. Applause breaks into a cheer. Dark winter garments flash with sudden purpose. Lists begin. Orders fly.

Mary's step quickens. Her ladies keep pace. Behind her the palace wakes and breathes with work.

Hope glows in the letter. The fog of winter thins.

"He is gone more than a year," one says.

"He returns now," answers another. "It lifts her and stills the Council, for a time."

An older man lowers his voice.

"Spirits rise. Will they hold once he stands under this roof? Or will we drown in Spaniards and quiet looks behind fans?"

"Best keep such thoughts," a younger man warns. "He is her husband and our king. Oaths bind."

"I forget nothing," says the elder. "I remember how silent she grew when he left. She was heartbroken."

Servants hurry with silver. Stewards call for fresh rushes. The palace hums with life. Not comfort. Expectation.

1 March 1557

Ale, woodsmoke, and sea-salt mingle thick in a tavern near Dieppe, France. Laughter spikes over dice. A bawdy song tumbles from a corner. From the common room beyond comes the smell of onion and beef stew, thick and cheap, carried on the steam.

At the bar sits Monsieur Jacques de Brissac, a French crown agent with a quick smile and a quicker tongue. Thomas Stafford enters, cloak tight against the damp.

De Brissac tosses coins to the keeper. "Your back room."

They step into the small chamber. Firelight throws moving shadows across the table. A jug of red wine waits between them. A wooden platter with a hunk of coarse rye bread and a wedge of sharp goat's cheese sits between their elbows.

De Brissac smiles, but his eyes measure Stafford the way clerks measure coin.

Stafford does not waste breath.

"I did not come for pleasantries, Brissac. Speak."

De Brissac pours into his cup and Stafford's. "Straight to the point, Master Stafford. I appreciate a man who values his time. Very well. But take some wine first, my friend."

Stafford drinks and sets the cup down. "Thank you."

De Brissac leans in. "France knows your quarrel with Queen Mary and her Spanish husband. We know your loyalty to a truly English course. We stand ready to help you restore England."

Stafford studies him like an enemy across a field.

"Why should France involve itself? I know full well how little you care for England's freedom."

De Brissac's smile deepens.

"Because Spain is our enemy, and Mary chains your realm to Philip's designs. We will not see England as a Spanish pawn."

Stafford's hand rests on his dagger. His other hand gestures towards the Frenchman.

"What does France propose?"

"With our ships, arms, and coin, you can raise a rebellion and bring her down," de Brissac says. "We want the same thing. Mary's faltering. The people are restless. You are a Stafford—your name still pulls weight."

Stafford's grip tightens at his side. He grabs the wine, takes a long pull, and sets the goblet down with a soft thud. The name Stafford had once meant power, but his family's fortunes had waned. Under Mary's reign—and under Philip's shadow—his own ambitions had soured into resentment.

Stafford drinks again. The jug thuds softly against the board. "And Elizabeth. Would France support her claim if I move?"

De Brissac shrugs. "Elizabeth is intriguing. She is not our concern. Our concern is you. Lead, and we bring success. Who sits after—that we may discuss."

Stafford's eyes go dark. "You expect me to trust a Frenchman in the final count. You are as duplicitous as the Spaniards."

De Brissac's warmth cools. "You have no time to be proud. The people tire of phantom heirs and foreign hands. If you do not seize the hour, another will, and you are forgotten."

Silence holds. The fire cracks. De Brissac waits. Stafford speaks at last.

"I lead on my terms, sir. I am not your puppet."

De Brissac inclines his head.

"Of course, Thomas. France wishes only for your success."

Stafford stands and presses on his dagger hilt. "Then ready your ships and your gold. But understand—England rises for itself."

De Brissac rises with a thin grin.

"As you wish."

Stafford steps into the cold night, the weight of ambition and doubt pressing in equal measure. Yet a new heat brightens his gaze, something honest beneath the bravado.

16 March 1557

In the afternoon at Hatfield, the corridors fall quiet as the light thins. In the music chamber Elizabeth plays a pavan on the virginal. Calm notes fill the room, yet her face says otherwise.

Kat Ashley sits nearby, mending a lace collar and watching.

The last chord fades. Irritation rises in Elizabeth's voice.

"Do you know, Kat—I am a bird in my sister's cage: pretty, clipped, and watched."

Kat sets the work aside. "Your Highness, you are heir presumptive. Caution is natural."

"Caution," Elizabeth says, and presses the keys into a brief discord. "Every move watched. Letters seized. Eyes in every corner."

Kat answers gently.

"Wyatt's uprising left wounds. Mary fears plots."

Elizabeth stands. The bench scrapes. She paces.

"How many times must I say I was not in it? Yet I remain a prisoner."

"It is not forever," Kat says. "Your time will come."

Elizabeth stops at the window. "Must I bear the insult until it does? Spies in my own house. Who reports to Mary? The stablemaster? The cook? Some maid with quick eyes?"

Beyond the door, Sir Henry Bedingfield's measured tread goes by and fades. Elizabeth does not look towards it, but her fingers still on the keys.

Kat shakes her head. "Not I. Not Master Parry. Not any who love you."

"I know," Elizabeth says. Her hand rests on Kat's shoulder. "You are my anchor."

Kat smiles faintly and covers the hand. "You are stronger than you think. They will not break you."

Elizabeth sits again but does not play.

"And now Philip. Mary commands me to greet him with all due show. The foreign king I must address as my brother-in-law."

"Be wary," Kat says. "He is courteous and calculating."

"Oh, I am wary, very wary," Elizabeth replies. "Of him. Of Mary. Of all who see me as a threat. But what choice do I have? If I refuse the part, I am lost. If I play it, I lose pieces of myself."

Kat kneels a little to catch her eye.

"Play it so well they never spy the truth until the hour has passed. Do not lose yourself. Keep your head high."

Elizabeth's eyes glisten. She nods and lets her fingers find the keys again.

A knock breaks the music. Thomas Parry enters and bows.

"Your Highness, a messenger from court. A letter with the Queen's seal."

Elizabeth takes it. The crack of wax is small and final. She reads without a flicker, sets it down, and meets Kat's eyes.

"My sister demands my presence."

Kat frowns as if she is weighing something heavy.

"Is it safe?"

"Safe or not, I go," Elizabeth says. "Let them mark it well. I am no marionette for a master's string. If I must sing in a cage, the song is mine."

19 March 1557

In the English Channel crossing to Dover, the sun drops towards the haze. A royal convoy of Spanish ships drives west-northwest from the Low Countries towards the Downs and Dover. Topsails fill. Hulls shoulder the sea in an ordered line.

On the flagship's deck, Philip stands with the Count of Feria, Gómez Suárez de Figueroa. The captain watches the rim of water, a finger at his lip as if keeping time with the swell.

Philip breaks the quiet.

"Don Gómez, the English call that reach the Downs. Strange names for tricky waters."

Feria nods, then takes in a deep breath.

"Fitting names, Your Majesty. These narrows hide teeth. We fared them when we brought you for your wedding. Little has changed."

Philip's look turns flinty.

"England is cunning and proud. Although it is useful to us, I will not let it rule me."

Feria chooses the edge of his words.

"This country answers only to strength. Firm discipline brings obedience."

Philip's mouth tightens, then eases.

"They are not hounds to thrash," Philip says. "It is their pride that makes them useful. We can turn it to our ends. England is not dripping with gold, but there is gold enough to matter. The Queen already yields—near as a subject. She will shake out the money, find the ships, and open her ports."

Feria inclines his head.

"England and France have never loved each other. It suits us."

"Then we do not make England an enemy. We keep her as a useful friend."

Feria glances aside. "Wise policy, Sire."

Philip rests his hands on the rail. "There is one thing I look forward to."

Feria looks over.

"Your Majesty."

"Elizabeth. She did not take kindly to my departure. She called it a failure of duty. Her fire was...overwhelming."

"They say her red hair marks a fiery soul, Sire."

Philip's voice softens.

"Her father Henry burned. Mary burns. Yet there is good fire in Elizabeth."

Feria allows a faint smile.

"She has a sharp tongue and a will to match. Do not underestimate the Lady Elizabeth, Sire."

"I do not. She bears the weight of power in her mind. She is both a rival and a kindred spirit."

Feria turns his eyes to the water.

"Winds change, tides turn—and so do allies," Feria says. "Be careful whom you trust at your elbow. She is a heretic. If she takes the crown, our bond may not hold."

"Not if she marries my cousin Savoy," Philip says. "They call me prudent—with cause. Mary weakens—I dare not trust miracles. Elizabeth stands next: wed her to Savoy, let her bear him a son, and the bond endures."

"Sire, the Queen hates her sister's creed. She will not brook a Protestant heir."

"Better a heretic queen bound to us than a Catholic regent who leans to France. Mary will be pressed to name Elizabeth. I will see to that. And I will have Mary talk to Elizabeth about marrying the Duke."

"And if Elizabeth refuses marriage?"

"We chart the course and stand to it. God favours only the true faith. He overrules her stubborn mind. If England drifts from Rome, we send the tide to fetch her."

Feria inclines his head, though the set of his mouth remains guarded.

Behind them, a boatswain passes with two deckhands, speaking low as they tend a line. The wind snatches the words and carries them aft.

"—the English tides don't answer prayers," one mutters.

The other hushes him sharply.

Philip does not turn. His hands stay firm on the rail as the ship presses on, the water darkening beneath the bow.

Chapter 6
Whispers of War

20 March 1557

Dawn. Dover's harbour heaves with voices and rigging as King Philip's convoy drops anchor. Spanish officers disembark with drilled precision. Standards lift and snap in the salt wind.

Philip steps ashore with practiced dignity. Whatever stirs beneath his composure does not reach his face.

Waiting at the quay, Sir Thomas Cheyne, Lord Warden of the Cinque Ports, bows with the town's officers at his side.

"Your Majesty, welcome to England. Her Majesty regrets that she cannot greet you here. She awaits you in London."

Philip inclines his head. "I understand. Her health must take precedence."

A ripple passes the local dignitaries—dutiful, not warm. Philip's gaze lingers a beat too long on their fixed smiles before he looks away.

He mounts his horse. A chill wind lifts off the chalk. He speaks low to Gómez Suárez de Figueroa, the Count of Feria, riding at his flank.

"Even now England finds a way to be cold."

Feria gives the faintest smile.

"And yet, Sire, it is the warmth of her treasury and her men that we seek."

Philip exhales and says nothing more. The cortege turns from the harbour and takes the London road, Spanish colours bright against the iron sky. Behind them, Dover's quay goes back to its work. Fishwives hawk baskets of salted herring and fresh whiting. A pie-seller shouts over his mutton pasties, and sailors hunch over pots of eel stew and black bread with cheese.

***

The Queen's apartments at Greenwich are dim and close. Queen Mary sits near the hearth, hands folded, face pale with weary lines. Her ladies move quietly across the carpets.

She cradles Philip's letter like a relic, its edges worn thin by the pressure of her hands. Each crease tells of nights she has unfolded it, lips moving in silence as if the words might answer her prayers.

"He comes," she whispers. "But does he come for me?"

Lady Jane Dormer kneels beside her, laying a gentle hand over Mary's clenched fingers as if to steady both queen and letter alike.

"Your Majesty, he is your husband. He returns to England and to you."

Mary shakes her head. Tears brim.

"I fear he comes for war with France, not for his queen. He comes for Spain—not for me."

A knock sounds, sharp against the silence. Dr John Caius, her physician, steps inside and bows. His face is solemn. His eyes go straight to the Queen, as if he can read her condition in her pallor.

"Your Majesty, I urge rest. Do not let the strain of his arrival weigh on you."

Mary straightens and gathers herself.

"I will not rest until I see him. I must speak with my husband. Perhaps...this time will be different."

Dormer and Caius trade a glance and keep their counsel.

***

By late afternoon—after hard riding—bells begin to ring across the city of London. Greenwich stirs like a hive. Messengers hurry. Servants take their posts. Courtiers smooth their sleeves and murmur.

Hooves ring on cobblestones. Philip's party enters the courtyard. Spanish banners gleam sharp against the English guard.

Philip swings down in a single smooth motion. Boots strike gravel. He brushes dust from his doublet and lifts his eyes to the palace without a flicker. Then he mounts the steps. Each footfall sounds in the chill.

At the far end, Princess Elizabeth stands with a small knot of attendants. Her posture is straight, her face carefully composed. She wears deep crimson silk that seems to hold its own light, the rich fabric catching the glow of torches as though it were kindled from within.

Her red hair, framed by a French hood, gleams beneath the hall's high beams, making her presence impossible to overlook even in silence.

The doors open. Philip enters with Spanish grandees and a handful of English lords. His stride is confident.

His gaze finds Elizabeth at once. Warmth edges his mouth. He checks himself—immediate, practiced: temper the tone. Elizabeth is a piece on the board; courtesy the instrument, nothing more.

"Your Majesty," Elizabeth says, curtsying low. Her tone balances respect with distance. "England is honoured by your return."

Philip inclines his head and does not look away.

"Princess Elizabeth, your welcome is balm to a weary spirit. It pleases me to see you again."

Elizabeth rises, her hands clasped, her voice even.

"We feared you might not return. England has missed Your Majesty's presence."

Philip lets a soft laugh escape. He hears the edge beneath her courtesy.

"And yet England is as vivid as ever. I see it in its people. And—I see it in its brightest jewel."

He smooths the seam of his glove with a thumbnail before he lifts his eyes to hers.

"You flatter me, Your Majesty. Was your crossing easy?"

"As easy as the sea allows," he says, stepping closer. "When England's coast rose out of the haze, the worst of it passed. Princess, I am eager to set things right after this time apart."

"It is good to hear. My sister will find comfort in your presence, as will the realm."

Something unguarded shows in his face, then retreats. "Mary—of course. I have hurt her by staying away, and I hope to mend it. How do you fare, Elizabeth?"

"Absence leaves wounds, Sire. Yet my sister's love for you does not fail."

He winces and recovers. “And you, Elizabeth. Has my absence left its mark on you?”

Elizabeth’s brows lift. Her smile cools.

“I am your subject and your sister by marriage. Your Majesty, I make no claims upon you.”

Philip lowers his voice. “No claims, yet I have thought often of you. Your wit. Your fire. Rare qualities.” His cordial mask slips a fraction.

“My only fire is loyalty to the Queen and to England.”

He studies her, confidence flickering. “I do not mean offence. I was hoping we could repair what was strained between us. We said hard things before, you know.”

She fixes him with a steady look, her tone edged like steel.

“Strain comes of deeds, not speeches. England remembers what has been done. So does my sister.”

Philip retreats, bowing his head slightly. “Then I have misread the moment. Forgive me.”

“There is nothing to forgive. I desire my sister’s happiness and England’s safety.”

“Then we see both,” he says.

Footsteps approach. An attendant from Mary’s household bows.

“Your Majesty, the Queen awaits you.”

Philip looks once more at Elizabeth.

“Until we speak again.”

“Until then, Your Majesty.”

He follows the attendant. Elizabeth watches after him, her thoughts quickening into shapes too dark to speak to others.

“Kings and their games,” she whispers, and turns towards the light from a high window.

***

In the Presence Chamber, Mary sits beneath the canopy of state, her hands clenched in her lap. The great doors open. Philip enters, straight and austere, his black cloak trailing behind him. The sound of his boots strikes the flagstones in steady rhythm. Her ladies sink into curtsies as he passes, their silks rustling in the stillness, their eyes lowered yet watchful.

He comes before her. For a long breath, neither speaks. He stops at the foot of the dais. They only look—Mary pale and trembling with longing, Philip composed, his face a mask of dignity.

At last, he extends his hand. The gesture is formal, almost ceremonial, but his grip is gentle, lingering.

"Madam," he says, his voice low, unexpectedly tender. "It is an honour to see you again."

Her lips part, unsteady. "You came," she whispers.

"As I said I would."

The silence swells—not heavy, but full. Tears glisten in her eyes, and her mouth quivers as though words might shatter her.

"Must we be so...formal?"

Then, with a sudden burst of courage, she rises and throws her arms around him. The ladies gasp softly, their eyes flicking up in astonishment. Queens do not embrace so before a chamber full of witnesses. But Mary clings to him with the desperation of a drowning soul, pressing her cheek against his chest.

"My lord...Philip." Her voice falters. "I have longed for you!"

A murmur ripples through the court. It sharpens. A few courtiers look quickly away, as if burned; others lean together, already weighing what they have seen. Lady Jane Dormer stiffens half a step behind the Queen, colour rising in her cheeks.

For a heartbeat, Philip stiffens, startled by her unguarded passion. Then, visibly moved, something in him breaks. His arms enfold her tightly, protective and sure. He bends his head until his cheek rests against her hair, his eyes closing as the iron mask slips away.

"Mary," he murmurs, his voice roughened with emotion. "My dearest Mary. Forgive me. I should never have left you so long."

Tears wet the velvet of his doublet, but still she holds him, trembling with relief. "You are here now," she whispers. "That is all I ask."

Her ladies exchange furtive glances, their astonishment plain. They had expected ceremony, perhaps distance, but not this—not a king visibly shaken by his wife's embrace.

Philip cradles the back of her head in one hand, his thumb brushing her veil as though it were fragile silk. His breath comes deep and slow, steadying himself. And in that moment, before politics and war reclaim them both, husband and wife stand locked in each other's arms—two sovereigns, yet simply man and woman, holding fast as her fingers dig into his doublet and his breath warmed the crown of her head.

At last, Philip eases back, though his hands linger at Mary's arms as though reluctant to release her. He bows his head, recapturing the solemn composure of a king, yet the softness in his eyes betrays what has just passed.

"My time in England is brief," he says, the words formal but touched with regret. "But not without meaning."

Mary's fingers tighten once more on his sleeves, unwilling to let go. Her voice trembles. "Brief or not, you are here. And for me, that is enough."

He lifts her hand and presses his lips to it, lingering. He releases her hands at last. "I must make myself ready for the evening, madam." He bows and withdraws.

Then, with a last glance at her face, he turns and strides from the chamber, his cloak sweeping behind him. The doors close with a heavy thud, leaving silence in his wake.

Mary sinks back into her chair, her chest rising and falling as though she has run a long race. She presses her cheek where Philip kissed her with trembling fingers, tears streaming unchecked down her face.

Around her, the ladies-in-waiting dare at last to move. They exchange quick, astonished glances, their low talk spreading through the court.

"Did you see?" one breathes. "He held her—as if he loved her."

Another, younger, shakes her head in wonder. "I thought he was made of iron. Yet his face...there were tears in his eyes."

Lady Jane Dormer clasps her hands to her breast, her eyes shining. "God grant it is true. For if he loves her, then perhaps her strength will return."

A silence falls again as all eyes turn to Mary. She sits beneath the canopy, clutching her hands together, her gaze fixed on the door through which Philip has just vanished. In her face burns something none of them have seen in months—hope, fragile but alive. Only when the chamber begins to breathe again does she remember where she is.

The chamber remains hushed after Philip's departure, the fire snapping in the grate as though reluctant to intrude upon the Queen's silence. At last Mary stirs, rising from her chair with effort, her face wet but glowing.

"Jane," she whispers.

Lady Jane Dormer steps forward at once, adjusting her French cap and bowing her head. "Your Majesty."

Mary seizes her hands suddenly, clinging to them with surprising strength. "Did you see him? Did you see how he held me? There were tears in his eyes. Tears."

Jane's own eyes brim as she nods. "Yes, madam. I saw."

Mary draws her close, almost desperate. "I prayed so long for a sign, Jane. For some spark of love, for proof that my marriage was not only chains and politics. And tonight—tonight I felt it." Her voice lowers to a fervent whisper. "It was as if my soul clutched his, and for a breath he clutched mine. I will not doubt again."

Jane squeezes her hands gently. "Then hold on to it, Majesty. Let it give you strength. The court gossips will whisper, but they cannot know what I saw tonight. It was not a pretence. He meant it."

Mary releases a shaky laugh that turns into a sob. She folds against Jane, her arms going around her as though she were a daughter. "Oh, Jane...if I could only give him an heir. If I could only bind him to me forever."

Jane strokes her back soothingly. "Perhaps God will yet grant it, madam. You are His servant. You are England's mother still, even if no child rests in your arms."

Mary pulls back, her face solemn but alight with renewed fire. "Yes—I will not despair. God has shown me mercy. Philip still loves me—of that I am certain. And while that love lasts, I will endure whatever is asked of me. In time, England will see. They will see their Queen is not forsaken."

Jane bows her head, hiding her own tears. "Amen, Your Majesty."

Mary lifts her chin, wiping her cheeks with the back of her hand. She looks again at the great door through which Philip had vanished, her eyes shining with fragile hope.

"Brief, he said. But brief is enough. For in that briefness—I have life again."

She takes Jane's hand and smiles.

Love in a king is not only tenderness—it is leverage. And every eye that flicks to the door Philip has taken is already weighing what it might mean, who it might raise, who it might ruin.

***

Candles flood the great hall with gold. Silver gleams across the board, and the air hums with talk and toasts. Platters of roast beef and capon, venison pasties, lamprey pies glossed with rich sauce, trenchers piled with manchet bread, and dishes of stewed prunes and marchpane roses crowd the tables. Red Gascon wine and sack run freely for those bold enough to drink to Spain. At the high table, Mary and Philip sit side by side. A consort of musicians plays pavans and galliards in measured courtly rhythm, the soft strains threading through the chatter.

The dishes are rich, the feast abundant, yet under the glitter, unease stirs.

Mary leans towards him, her voice low, tender with hope. "You look well."

Philip sets his goblet down and turns to her, his dark eyes searching her pale face. "I am well. And you, Mary—how fare you?"

Her breath catches. The words escape fragile, trembling. "As a queen without an heir. As a wife without her husband."

He is still for a moment, then folds his hands, steadying himself. "I do not wish to hurt you. Duty to Spain and to the empire pulls me from your side."

Her eyes glisten. Her voice lifts before she can stop it. "And your duty to me?"

The hall falls into sudden hush, the courtiers startled. Mary forces a smile, her tone bright for those watching. "Attend to your feast, my lords and ladies."

She hears her own voice rise—and hates herself for it. Then, lower—aching: "And your duty to me? Am I not your wife? Have I not borne all for you?"

Philip leans closer, his tone gentled. "You are my wife, Mary, and I do honour you. But the crown I wear costs more than either of us can bear. You know that—you have lived it, you feel it as I do."

Tears slip down her cheeks. She turns her face, but he reaches for her hand beneath the table, closing it firmly within his own. His thumb presses lightly against her knuckles, steadying her.

"I wanted so much to give you an heir," she whispers. "To keep England safe, to make you proud. But I could not. Tell me I have not failed you."

His gaze softens, and the sternness in his face eases. He leans close enough for only her to hear. "You have not failed. The world is hard—even for a crown. Yet you, Mary, have borne it with a courage most could not."

Across the hall, guests cast wary glances, then quickly look away, sensing the intimacy between them.

Mary's eyes search his, desperate, childlike in their pleading. "Do you really love me, Philip?"

The question stills him. For a heartbeat the mask of kingship falters, and his reply comes softer than the music, stripped of formality.

"I love you as a man loves the woman God has bound him to. You are my queen. And more—you are my Mary."

The words, imperfect yet tender, break her. She turns to him with wet eyes, her hand still clutched in his, holding on as though his warmth alone keeps her from slipping into despair.

Across the floor, Princess Elizabeth draws quiet attention. Crimson and gold catch the candlelight. Her laughter is bright. Men lean in to hear her. Philip's gaze drifts.

Mary sees it. She always sees.

Elizabeth leans forward, her eyes bright.

"Did you hear what was said of my father when he kept Lent? One courtier whispered he was the strictest man in Christendom, for he fasted from nothing but patience. Another replied that it was a miracle indeed—that he had so little patience to begin with."

She pauses, her lips curved in a sly smile, letting the ripple of laughter spread. "I daresay my father would have found the jest less holy than the preacher intended."

Philip smiles. Elizabeth's eyes flash with mischief.

Mary's knuckles blanch around the stem of her goblet. She sets it down very carefully.

"Does she never cease to preen?" she whispers.

Philip turns. "What was that, madam?"

"Nothing, husband," she says, staring into her goblet. "Only that the evening is lively."

The music quickens. A galliard. Elizabeth rises with a flare of skirt.

"A galliard, I think. Who joins me?"

There are murmurs. Master Robert Dudley, a tall, well-proportioned and strikingly handsome courtier, steps forward and bows. She laughs. "Shall we, Robin?"

They move to the centre. Elizabeth leaps and turns with effortless grace. He keeps pace. The court claps time.

Philip smiles without guarding it. "She dances well," he tells Mary.

Mary's jaw tightens.

The smile she forces for her guests cannot hide the ache spreading through her chest. Weariness drags at her, her heart already skittering in her chest. Envy burns within, sharp and raw. When she shifts in her chair, her foot searches for the rushes as if the floor has moved a fraction. She pushes herself to her feet. A stitch bites under her ribs when she draws breath. The chair scrapes loud against the floor, but she scarcely hears it. Faces turn, her ladies start at her side, yet the hall fades to nothing. All she can see is the younger woman at the centre of it all, lit as though the world itself conspires to make her shine brighter with every step. I am not yet defeated. She wipes her eyes with both hands.

"Husband," she says, clipped. "If a galliard is the fashion, then I shall join."

Philip blinks. "Mary, are you certain? You need not—"

"I am certain."

She descends the dais. The music falters. Elizabeth and Dudley halt.

Mary takes the floor. She points to a tall, dark-haired knight of her household.

"You. I choose you."

The musicians look at one another.

"Play," Mary commands. "And faster."

They begin. Mary dances. Her steps land like edicts—exact, hard—more iron than grace. She drives herself forward, leaping, turning, pushing her body past its limits as though each motion were proof that she still reigns. Her skirts flare, her jewels rattle, her breath comes sharper with every beat.

Her partner struggles to match her pace. He stumbles, rights himself, then stumbles again, the effort plain on his face. The courtiers clap in rhythm, but their eyes betray their unease—watching not a queen at play, but a queen testing the strength of her very body before them.

Philip watches from the high table. At first his lips curve, proud to see his queen command the floor. But pride curdles quickly into unease. Her movements are too fierce, too forced. He leans forward, his gloved hand pressing against the table's edge.

"Mary..." he murmurs under his breath, unheard over the music.

Elizabeth retreats to the edge, face tight with alarm.

"Faster," Mary calls. Breath shortens. Colour rises. The tempo climbs. Her partner reaches to steady her. She waves him off.

Philip leans forward, his chair scraping back.

"Mary, enough!" he calls, his voice carrying above the music.

But she does not hear him—or will not. Her face burns with colour, her breath ragged as she drives herself through one more turn. Then the figure falters. Her slipper skids on a stray rush. She sways once—and her strength fails. Her vision washes white. The floor tilts. She folds and crumples to the floor.

A sharp gasp tears through the hall, spreading from mouth to mouth like a wave. Courtiers surge to their feet, their applause forgotten. The musicians choke the music into silence.

Philip is already moving, his cloak flaring behind him as he descends from the dais. "Make way!" he shouts, his Spanish accent hard and commanding. Attendants drop to their knees beside the Queen, hands fumbling to lift her.

Whispering breaks out in the corners of the hall, anxious and fearful, only to hush again as Philip kneels beside his wife. His hand presses against hers, warm against cool fingers. Her head lolls, her crown slipping askew, jewels catching the candlelight with a cruel glimmer.

"Fetch the doctor," Philip orders. The command cracks like a whip across the chamber.

Dr Caius already pushes through the press.

The hall seethes with murmurs, fear coiling into speculation. Some weep openly, others avert their eyes. A queen has fallen, and with her, the fragile hope she carried.

Elizabeth comes near. Her gaze fixes on her sister, pale and still against the stone, and for an instant something flickers—fear, sorrow, perhaps even pity. She lets it show only for a heartbeat before smoothing it away.

As darkness presses in, Mary holds to the knowledge that crowns were not won by dancing nor kept by wit alone. She had paid for hers in blood, sickness, and faith—and she would not be unseated by grace, nor eclipsed by youth.

"Her Majesty is unwell," Elizabeth says, her voice calm, carrying over the whispers. "Attend her with care. See that nothing disturbs her rest."

"Take the Queen to her bedchamber at once," Caius orders.

They bear Mary out. Philip looks up sharply, his eyes locking with Elizabeth's. For a moment the hall holds its breath. Then Elizabeth inclines her head, the perfect image of a dutiful sister, before turning aside.

"This evening should not have ended so," Philip says.

Elizabeth holds his gaze. "Indeed, Your Majesty. My sister's spirit is stronger than her body."

He says nothing and follows the attendants.

Elizabeth turns away. Her thoughts run hot and fast.

"Musicians, play. Dancers, dance," she says to the room, and then exits quickly.

Behind her, the court resumes its borrowed cheer.

***

In Mary's bedchamber an hour later, when the worst of the faintness passed, a grave-faced Dr Caius stands at the foot of the bed. He detects a lingering tremor. On the bedside table a silver cup of warm posset—milk thickened with ale and honey, scented faintly with nutmeg—sends up a gentle steam that does little to clear the sour smell of sweat and fear. Philip hovers close, his hand braced on the carved post. The Count of Feria lingers behind, rigid as iron. Elizabeth stands at the bed.

Mary stirs. A faint groan breaks from her throat as her lashes tremble. Slowly, she blinks, her sight struggling through the haze. At first, shapes blur together—the dark physician, the tall figure of her husband, the stern Spaniard. Then, beyond them, she sees a glimmer of red silk.

For a moment Mary cannot breathe. The sight of her sister—composed, upright, watching—sends a stab of fear through her chest, followed at once by a pang of yearning. *Why must it always be her?* Mary wonders, even as some fragile part of her aches for the comfort only family can give.

Elizabeth's lips part, her voice a rasp. "Sister..."

"Madam, I give you your leave," says Mary in a small voice.

Philip cuts in at once.

"Mary, if your sister leaves, I leave. I am in earnest."

He looks to Elizabeth. "Pray stay, Princess."

Caius faces Mary.

"Your Majesty, you are not as young as you were. I prescribe rest. Music in your chamber. Light work in the garden. Needlework. Nothing more."

"Doctor, tell me the truth. Can I bear a child?"

He does not soften it.

Philip's eyes flick to Elizabeth—warning—then back to Caius.

"Your Majesty, your years and ailments weigh against you. If you conceive now, the danger to you and the child is grave."

Mary weeps. Philip glances at Elizabeth.

"Doctor—Princess—my lord. Leave us," he says. "I will speak with the Queen alone."

Caius, Elizabeth, and Feria bow and withdraw. The door shuts heavily.

Philip stands without moving. He shifts, steps forward, stops again. His hands hover and fall. At last he draws breath.

"Madam. Mary. Affairs of state weigh like iron. I am King of Spain, King of Naples and Sicily, Lord of the Netherlands. I can scarce name all the titles I carry. I made peace with the King of France, and he deliberately broke the peace. Now Spain and the Empire must stand at war with France. The burden is mine and my uncle's."

Mary keeps her eyes down. She knows the weight. She knows the hunger of titles.

She speaks a little louder. "Yes, my lord." She takes a deep breath. "The enemies of Spain are the enemies of England," she says. "Yet there is a treaty that forbids England to fight Spain's wars. Do you remember the articles we swore before Parliament?"

Frustration marks his face.

"That is scratching on parchment, madam. Do you take it so seriously? Henry of France and the Pope make war on us. Guise eyes the Pale of Calais. He seeks to dispossess us of it."

"Calais," she repeats, and the word carries a century of care. "Calais is ours."

Philip presses. "Up north, France and Scotland move as one—enemies above and below. How long do we stand idle? Invasion is a threat. We must declare war on France now."

Mary lowers her gaze. The crown feels heavy. She swallows.

"We have lost much to France. Calais is our last bright jewel. I must bring this to the Council."

Philip reaches and takes her hand. His voice falls.

"Men. Money. Ships. I urge something more. Use your influence with Elizabeth. She is powerful. If she marries the Duke of Savoy, our position strengthens in England and beyond. He is a soldier first, ruler second, the perfect Catholic anchor."

Mary's hands still.

"Elizabeth's still a girl, Philip. She gives her heart to no one. Proud. Pushing her for policy may drive her away."

"She may not understand now. You know alliances. Savoy is not only a match. He is a Catholic ally. If she marries him, she strengthens England and, by that, your reign. It is an opportunity for us."

Uncertainty crosses Mary's face. She has fought for her own place. Now Philip asks her to lift Elizabeth into greater power.

"I do not doubt your logic," she says. "But she is stubborn. She may never see sense in marriage for Spain. She may even come to hate it."

"This works in your favour," he answers. "With Savoy as her husband, she must work with us. The tie to Spain grows. You are the Queen. She will have a greater part, but a part that serves your reign."

Mary nods slowly. She sees the sense and the risk.

"I will do what I can. Know this. She values her own sovereignty above all."

Philip kisses her brow.

"I know. Our duty is to secure England's future. In time she will understand."

Mary says nothing. Thought turns and turns. She hears the truth she does not like. Europe shifts. Alliances must hold. Even if it means pressing Elizabeth towards a match she will resist.

Philip's breath leaves him in a single, controlled exhale. For a moment the mask slips. "I did not cross kingdoms, or bury my youth in crowns and altars, to watch England drift into chaos," he says quietly.

At last, Mary looks up, the tremor gone from her hands. Her eyes are rimmed red with strain, yet steady now, like steel tempered in fire. "I will speak with her. I will try."

Philip's mouth shows quick satisfaction. "Thank you, Mary. Together we will surely secure England."

***

Later, in his chamber, Philip stands at the window. London lies sodden beneath a smoky sky, its streets glimmering faintly with torchlight. He rests one hand against the cold glass, feeling the weight of the realm pressing back at him.

The door opens. The Count of Feria bows with quiet formality. "How does Her Majesty fare?"

Philip does not turn at once. A jug of dark Spanish wine stands open on the table beside him, two cups set but only one stained; he has poured for counsel, not for company.

"Fragile. In body and in spirit. She clings to me as though I were her salvation, and I—"

His voice tightens, then steadies. "I am her husband, yes. But I cannot give her what she desires. Not a child. Not permanence. England will not have me. To them I remain the foreigner, whatever crown I wear."

At last he turns, his eyes shadowed. "And yet I love her, Don Gómez. God help me, I do. Her devotion humbles me. But love cannot guard an empire. Spain requires more of me than England ever will."

He knew the love was real—and that reality made duty harder, not easier.

Still, when the reckoning came, he knew which claim would yield—and it would not be the empire.

Feria's face is stern. "Majesty, kings do not rule by love. The Queen's longing unmakes your resolve. England drags at your feet like an anchor. You must use her, not be used by her."

Philip steps forward, a flare of anger crossing his face. "You speak of my wife. Whatever England is, she is my queen—I will not have her mocked by my own men. Do not mistake tenderness for blindness, Don Gómez. I see this country well enough: cold, divided, stubborn—I may loathe it. But her? I will not treat her with contempt."

Feria bows his head, half-subdued. "As you command, Sire. Still, the question remains: does she understand England must march with us against France?"

Philip's jaw hardens. "She does—for now. She holds to the treaty, but it costs her dearly with her people. Every step towards Spain drains her." He turns back to the window, his reflection wavering in the black glass. "We will take what we need. We will break France." His hand presses to the pane, eyes fixed on the night beyond. "And when it is finished—then we go home."

The last word lingers, heavy with longing. Home—Spain, the empire, the sunlit courts where he belongs. A home Mary can never truly share. The thought twists in him, leaving the victory he names already tainted with sorrow.

***

Later that night, in her own chamber, Mary lies awake though the candles burn low. The fire settles to embers. Her ladies doze in corners, but Mary cannot close her eyes.

She remembers Philip's touch that evening—warm, tender, almost gentle. It should have eased her heart. Instead, it troubles her more. For even in his kindness, she felt the drift, as if part of him already looked beyond her, beyond marriage, and beyond England.

Her fingers tighten around the worn edges of his last letter, the one she keeps close. She lifts it again, though she knows every line by heart. "My dearest wife...my beloved queen..." The words blur as tears gather.

"Do you still write them with feeling, Philip?" she whispers into the empty room. "Or only because a husband must?"

The thought stings. She presses the letter to her chest, clutching it as though the parchment itself might anchor him to her. For a moment, she imagines Spain—the brilliance of its sun, the grandeur of its palaces, the home he longs for more than England's cold stones. A home that will never be hers.

Her breath hitches. She sits forward suddenly, wrapping her arms around herself as though she might keep her body from shaking apart. She whispers to the darkness:

"I will not lose him. I cannot."

The embers spit once, then settle into silence. Mary wipes her eyes, straightens her shoulders, and lies back. She forces herself to believe the words she had spoken before. *He loves me still. England will see. I am not abandoned.* But even as she closes her eyes, the loneliness of the chamber presses in, vast and merciless.

Somewhere beyond these walls, he is already turning toward other duties, other kingdoms. And in the dark, faith strains beneath the weight of what must be endured alone.

22 March 1557

Dusk slides along the shuttered fronts of Dieppe. Fish, tar, and the sour reek of cheap wine cling to the harbour wind. Inside a dockside tavern, Sir Peter Carew sits hunched over a half-drained mug, torchlight carving hollows in his tired face. French sailors mutter over dice. Someone tunes a lute badly. The room is small, smoky, worn.

The door slams wide.

Thomas Stafford strides in—tall, coat embroidered with the Plantagenet rose as if daring anyone to challenge it. Talk falters mid-word. Days ago his swagger was theatre. Now it has hardened into something colder, a certainty that burns behind his eyes.

He goes straight to Carew, drops a hand on the table with a thud, and sits. A pot-boy rushes to bring wine. Stafford drinks deep, wipes his mouth with the back of his hand, palms open as if showing the tavern he fears no one.

"You've sulked long enough, Peter," he says, breath warm with wine but voice steady. "An hour past, men in Rouen swore to me. Rouen, mind you. Not beggars or zealots—men with arms. Do not you see it yet? England tilts. And I intend to be standing when the rest begin to slide."

Carew looks at him, blinking as though trying to reconcile two different men in the same face.

"Slide?" he echoes. "Thomas...what are you saying?"

Stafford leans back, adjusting his gloves as if preparing for a portrait. His smile is thin, triumphant. "The court frets over dangers," he murmurs, "but dangers bend to the will that calls them forth. The future moves towards me, Peter. And a wise man does not strain against the tide."

Carew's fingers loosen on his mug. Wine spills over the rim onto the table. He sets it down slowly, as if testing whether the wood's truly solid. "You speak like a man bewitched," he says quietly. "Since when are you the wind?"

Stafford's grin widens, cold as steel. "Since I remembered what I am," he says. "Plantagenet blood. Royal blood. They took the crown by a bastard's sword and called it God's will. I have not forgotten."

Carew stiffens. "Yours? Thomas...have you lost your wits? I thought we laboured for Elizabeth. For England against Spain. Not for your vanity dressed as destiny."

Stafford leans forward, his voice dropping to a low, dangerous murmur. "I do not serve Elizabeth. I endure her. France and Spain will never fear a Tudor girl. But a Stafford—ah, that they understand. I must take the helm. She may keep her throne so long as it suits me, but the crown answers to me by right."

The room seems to tilt. Conversations die. Dice stop mid-roll.

Carew pushes back from the table, pale. "You're mad," he whispers. "You dream crowns in tavern smoke."

Stafford's pride flickers—then calcifies.

"Do you call me deluded?" he says. "You—who hides in France because you lack the stomach to shape England's fate?"

Carew stands abruptly; his chair skids, biting the floor. Men glance over warily.

"I see a fool drunk on himself," he says, voice raw. "I will not follow you into treason dressed as destiny."

Stafford rises in one smooth motion, looming, heat rolling off him like forge-fire.

"Then go," he says. "I have men enough who don't tremble at shadows."

Carew searches his face—once friend, once comrade—and finds only a stranger crowned in air.

He turns and shoulders through the watching crowd, out into the night where the sea wind hits sharp as betrayal.

Behind him, in the dim tavern light, Thomas Stafford lowers himself slowly to the bench, his eyes bright with grand designs no one else can see. He traces the crest on his coat with two fingers, as if touching a future that answers only to him.

The tavern returns to its murmurs—but a few men keep glancing his way, uneasy.

For Stafford sits alone, shaping a future that will never be his, yet believes utterly that the kingdom waits for his hand.

25 March 1557

In the Privy Council Chamber at Whitehall, the long table is cluttered with papers gone soft at the corners from too many hands. Wax crumbs dot the wood. Ink blots mark hesitation. Voices rise, overlap, fall back again.

Henry FitzAlan, Earl of Arundel, lets his signet ring strike the oak once—not loud, but final.

"The marriage articles are plain," he says. "England does not fight Spain's wars. Yet we are pressed to march against France. Are we to break the safeguard that lets the marriage stand at all?"

Edward Stanley, Earl of Derby, leans forward, palms flat, shoulders tight.

"The King's will is clear enough. But the people mutter. They remember the oath taken in Parliament. They remember it very well."

Sir William Paget snorts, a short, ugly sound.

"You prate of parchment while France sharpens knives. Do you think words stop cannon? Do you think vows plug a breach in the hull?"

FitzAlan turns on him.

"And you would have England row wherever Spain steers? The articles promised neutrality. Shall we tear them up because Philip grows impatient?"

William Herbert, Earl of Pembroke, speaks evenly, but there is steel under the calm.

"The danger is not Spain's quarrel alone. It is the breach of faith. Break the treaty and we lose the people's trust—and our credit abroad. Philip may ride away when it suits him. England will be left to count the cost."

Sir John Mason rubs at his jaw.

"Her Majesty's honour is bound to her husband. To refuse him too bluntly risks offence to the Queen herself."

Pembroke turns, voice sharpening.

"Is honour served by beggaring the realm? Our loyalty to Mary is not in question. But loyalty to England must come first."

William Paulet, Marquess of Winchester, brings his cane down once. The sound snaps the room to order.

"England is not a Spanish province. I will not see our fleet burned for Philip's inheritance."

Mason's colour rises.

"Inheritance? He is our king. Refusing aid edges close to disloyalty."

Paulet does not blink.

"To squander England for Spain's wars is treason to England."

The table hums with assent and dissent in equal measure. No one smiles. The treaty sits among them like a corpse they cannot agree how to bury.

***

In the Presence Chamber, Mary sits beneath the canopy of state, robed in crimson, the weight of it heavy on her shoulders. Philip stands at her side in Spanish black, rigid, contained. The councillors line the chamber's edge, waiting.

Philip speaks without ceremony.

"France conspires now. It stirs your north. It comforts your Protestants. Will you wait for the blow, or strike with allies? A treaty does not shield a crown. Steel does."

Mary lifts his hand and presses it to her cheek. Her eyes remain lowered.

"My lords say the people trusted that treaty. If I cast it aside, what faith remains in me?"

"Quite true, Your Majesty," FitzAlan says at once.

Philip's voice cuts across him.

"Faith without force is wind. Your councillors count coins. I count armies. If France gains the upper hand, no oath will keep England safe."

Mary looks towards the men gathered at the chamber's edge.

"What say you? Do we stand by the oath—or stand with Spain?"

Silence answers her. Long. Uncomfortable.

Mason clears his throat.

"Majesty, the treaty is plain. Yet France gives comfort to English rebels. If they aid sedition within your realm, are we still outside their quarrel?"

Mary's fingers tighten in Philip's sleeve.

Paget steps forward, eyes hard.

"This is peril, not parchment. France whispers to exiles and sows doubt at home. If they feed rebellion, peace is only ink. Better to take the field by choice than be dragged into it at France's hour."

Mary hesitates. The chamber watches her measure the cost.

"The people will say I betray them," she says quietly. "They clung to the written promise that England would not bleed for foreign quarrels. They trusted me."

Philip answers at once, cold and unyielding.

"This is survival, not sentiment. France arms your enemies within and mine without. Delay does not save you."

The room murmurs again. Mary does not move. Then she speaks.

"I cannot break the law. We abide by the treaty until France threatens our shores in deed. It is the law of the land. I am bound to it."

"Wise decision, Your Majesty," Paulet says.

Mary turns slightly towards Philip and lowers her voice.

"I am sorry, Philip."

For a heartbeat he says nothing. Then a curse slips from him, sharp and foreign, and he turns on his heel and leaves the chamber without another word.

The doors close hard behind him.

He had once believed love made duty heavier. Now he knew better: duty made love expendable.

Chapter 7
Scratches on Parchment

28 March 1557

Morning light filters thinly through the bedchamber hangings at St James' Palace, painting pale lines across the floor. Mary lies propped among pillows, her face drawn but luminous in the glow. Philip stands close by, his robe drawn about him. The firelight flickers across his features.

He steps nearer.

"Mary, I know I have not been the husband you deserve. I am more fitted to crowns and councils than to love."

She lifts her gaze, forcing a small smile through her weariness.

"In time, you could truly love me as a husband would."

Philip's hand hovers, then settles gently upon hers.

"My heart is yours, Mary. As much as I could, I have tried to give it wholly. But politics is the life thrust upon me. My duty to England, to Spain, to the Empire. It stands above all. And we must face the truth." His eyes lower. "We may never have an heir."

Her composure breaks. Tears slip down her cheeks.

"I know. I have thought of that. My cousin Margaret Douglas, the Countess of Lennox, could serve as Queen. Renard advised it, and I saw his wisdom. She would preserve the Catholic realm when I am gone. I have given her lodging at Westminster, to prepare her."

At this, Philip's expression hardens, fire flashing in his eyes.

"Madam, your lawful heir is Princess Elizabeth. That is by the law your father himself had signed."

Mary's voice sharpens.

"Lady Elizabeth!"

He leans closer, firm but not harsh.

"Princess Elizabeth, madam—she is the daughter of a king. The Succession Act—and your father's will—place her next in line."

Mary lets out a brittle laugh, more pain than mirth.

"My, my, husband. Now you praise English law—scratches on parchment—when it serves your cause."

Philip straightens.

"And you name Margaret against the very law you claim to honour." He does not blink. "Law binds when it bites us both. First remove the beam from your own eye."

The words strike her. Mary shudders, her lips trembling.

"My sister is a heretic," she whispers. "A whelp of a heretic witch."

Philip bends and places his hand gently on her shoulder.

"Elizabeth will succeed you, Mary. Under you—and under her—the realm must stand against enemies without and within."

Mary closes her eyes, drawing a long, ragged breath. "Yes, my lord."

Philip does not let the silence end there. He sits on the edge of the bed and takes her hand firmly in both of his, his face softening. For once, the mask of kingship slips—though the habit of command still holds his jaw tight. She sees not a sovereign but a husband, moved. He bends, pressing a kiss to her brow, lingering as though to seal the words he cannot find.

Mary exhales shakily, clutching his hand with surprising strength.

"Do not leave me, Philip. Not yet."

He draws her carefully into his arms, her frail frame trembling against his chest. His chin rests lightly on her hair, and his voice, when it comes, is hushed and unguarded.

"I will not leave you, Mary. Not tonight."

She clutches him, as though the embrace itself keeps her alive. For that fleeting morning, duty loosens its grip—not from surrender, but from exhaustion. The crown does not yield; it simply sits heavier on the same shoulders.

***

Morning light breaks hard and pale over the harbour in Dieppe, flattening colour into iron and chalk. The tide creeps in slowly and grudgingly, thick with weed and refuse. Masts knock softly together. Ropes creak. Nothing moves with urgency.

Thomas Stafford stands on the quay, boots planted wide, cloak snapping in the salt wind. He watches the water as if it might yet be shamed into obedience.

"It should have been yesterday," he says. "Or today at the latest."

Giles Darcy stands beside him, hands tucked into his sleeves, eyes narrowed against the glare. "The sea does not care what should be."

Stafford rounds on him. "Nor do merchants, it seems."

At the edge of the pier, two ships lie moored bow to stern—lean, serviceable craft, neither warship nor fishing tub. Their hulls are sound, their decks crowded with barrels and coils of rope, but they sit heavy in the water, unfinished in spirit if not in timber.

Monsieur Le Guern, their owner, approaches with careful steps, counting planks as he walks as though the ground itself might betray him. He is a narrow man with a weathered face and eyes that flick constantly from Stafford to the ships and back again.

"You were told," Stafford says before the man can speak. "They were to be ready."

"They are ready," Le Guern replies, spreading his hands. "As ready as Providence allows."

Stafford snaps. "Speak to me of wind."

Le Guern gestures towards the open water. "North-easterlies. Unsteady. They rise, then die. A false promise. If you sail into that, you will crawl, not cross."

Stafford laughs once, sharp and humourless. "I do not need speed. I need departure."

Monsieur de Brissac joins them, immaculate despite the wind, his gloves clean, his expression mild. "You need arrival," he corrects. "Preferably with men who can still stand."

Stafford turns on him. "Every day we wait is a day Mary breathes easier."

"And every day you drown in the Channel is a day England laughs at you," de Brissac says evenly.

Darcy shifts his weight. "What of the men?"

"They drink," Stafford says. "They dice. They grow soft."

"They grow bored," Darcy replies. "Bored men talk."

Le Guern clears his throat. "It is not only the wind."

Stafford fixes him with a stare. "Then finish it."

"Provisions," Le Guern says. "Salt meat came in spoiled. I will not load sickness aboard my own ships."

Stafford steps closer, close enough that the man smells of pitch and fear. "You took French coin."

"And I intend to live long enough to spend it," Le Guern answers, more firmly now. "I will not send you out crippled."

De Brissac watches this with interest, like a man observing a blade tested for flaws.

"How long?" Stafford demands.

Le Guern hesitates.

"How long," Stafford repeats.

"Around two weeks," the shipowner says at last. "Seventeen April. No earlier. The tide will favour you then. The winds should settle. You will cross in six, seven days."

"Seventeen April," Stafford says, the word bitter on his tongue. "By then—"

"By then," de Brissac cuts in smoothly, "Mary's court will still be whispering about phantom heirs and Spanish councils. Nothing decisive will have changed. Delay is not always defeat."

"Delays frustrate," Stafford remarks.

Stafford looks back to the sea. A gull wheels overhead, crying, then drifts away on the wind. The harbour remains stubbornly still.

"In Spain," de Brissac continues, almost conversational, "great fleets sit idle for want of the right wind. Kings stamp their feet. Admirals pray. The sea answers when it chooses."

Stafford's jaw tightens. "I am no admiral."

"No," de Brissac agrees. "You are a man betting everything on timing."

Darcy glances at Stafford. "Better to strike clean than arrive broken."

Silence stretches between them. Somewhere a hammer rings against iron. A sail flaps once, then falls slack again.

Stafford exhales, long and controlled. When he speaks, his voice is steadier.

"Seventeen April," he says. "We sail then. No excuses."

Le Guern inclines his head. "You will have ships that carry you across. I give you my word."

Stafford turns away, eyes hard, already measuring days like rungs on a ladder. He sighs.

"England waits," he says, more to himself than to any of them.

Behind him, the ships remain moored, patient and immovable—while history, unseen, gathers its wind.

29 March 1557

Pale spring light filters through the shutters of St James' Palace, gilding the tapestries and glancing off polished silver. The air feels less heavy, as though the whole household breathes easier.

Mary rises from her bed with help from her ladies, but today there is colour in her cheeks, a spark in her eyes. She clasps Jane Dormer's hand and smiles with rare warmth.

"Do you see, Jane? God has not forsaken me. The King was with me through the night. He held me as though I were his only care. My heart is lighter than it has been for months."

Jane, moved by the change, bows her head. "Your Majesty, it gladdens me beyond words to see you so. You shine as though years have fallen away."

Mary allows herself a laugh, thin but genuine, startling in its brightness. "I feel it too. Hope, Jane—that I am not forgotten. That love has returned to me."

***

In the Presence Chamber, courtiers murmur as the Queen enters with measured steps, her rosary glinting at her waist. She greets them with a voice steadier than any had heard in weeks. Some courtiers exchange astonished looks, whispering of a revival, a rekindling.

Philip arrives soon after, sombre in black, yet when Mary turns to him the severity in his face softens. Before all eyes he takes her hand—simply, without flourish. Gasps ripple through the hall at the uncharacteristic display, but Mary beams as though the gesture were worth more than all her crown jewels.

As they sit together at the Privy Council table, clerks clear away the remnants of breakfast to make room for the piles of warrants and petitions. Mary leans close, whispering with a secret smile, "See how they watch, husband? They wonder at you—and at me. Let them. For today, I am their queen and your wife, and no sorrow troubles me."

The other Council members sit nearby, faces schooled to neutrality.

Philip nods, though the weight of letters from Spain lies heavy before him on the table. War, money, alliances—all wait to reclaim his thoughts. Yet for this moment, he lets them rest—though his hand tightens once on Mary's before his gaze drifts back to the sealed letters from Spain, as if answering a summons already given.

Mary lifts her chin, eyes bright with brief triumph. *I am not yet defeated.* She lets none of it show. To the members of the Privy Council, she says, "Well, gentlemen. What is our first order of business?"

Later, all items of business having been addressed, the Council disperses, papers gathered and voices subdued, yet the Queen remains radiant. Mary lingers by the window, Philip at her side, their hands still loosely joined. Courtiers bow as they withdraw, murmuring behind the sweep of their cloaks.

Mary does not follow them at once. She remains by the window, issuing two quiet instructions to a waiting clerk—measured, precise, the Queen unmistakably present beneath the glow.

Even so, she had worn a crown before Philip ever dreamed of England. She would not be ruled as a patient, sedated by affection.

In the antechamber, two councillors pause. Paget lowers his voice further.

"She glows as though youth's returned to her."

FitzAlan replies grimly, "A fragile light. The King's war will soon eclipse it. Affection softens, yes—but duty's iron. When Spain calls, he will not stay."

Paget glances back towards the closed doors, the muffled sound of Mary's laughter drifting faintly through. "And when he goes, her strength goes with him."

The Earl of Arundel nods, his tone heavy. "God help her then. For England must endure what her heart cannot."

They move on, their footsteps fading into the hush of the palace corridors, leaving behind the uneasy knowledge that the Queen's fragile joy cannot withstand what waits just beyond her husband's shadow.

30 March 1557

At Hatfield, the spring morning carries news faster than the horses that bring it. A messenger bows before Princess Elizabeth, delivering word of the Queen's sudden vigour. On the table beside her, a half-eaten pear and a cooled cup of ale mark a breakfast broken off for news.

Elizabeth listens without interruption, her hands folded neatly before her, but her eyes sharpen. When the man withdraws, she turns to Kat Ashley and Anne Denny, who hover nearby.

"So," she says, voice even, "my sister smiles again. And all because her husband has chosen, for a breath, to remember her."

Kat frowns, lowering her sewing. "Your Highness, if it gives the Queen comfort, perhaps it is for the good."

Elizabeth tilts her head, lips curving faintly though not with mirth. "For the good, yes—if comfort is measured in hours. But tell me, Kat—when has Philip ever set aside Spain for England? When has he ever stayed?"

Anne shifts uneasily. "They say he showed her tenderness before the whole court. That he took her hand openly."

Elizabeth's laugh is quiet, cutting. "Philip of Spain? Displaying tenderness in public? That is theatre, not truth. A king plays many parts, and my sister...my poor sister is desperate to believe them all."

Kat's brows knit, but she says nothing.

Elizabeth rises, crossing to the window. Beyond the glass, the fields stretch green beneath the paling sky.

"When Spain calls, he will sail home again—that is his duty. England's queen will be left with nothing but her tears. And when that day comes, the realm will look elsewhere for strength. Whether I wish it or no, they will look to me—because there will be no other."

Kat crosses herself softly, while Anne studies Elizabeth's profile with quiet awe and unease.

Elizabeth turns back to them, her expression smoothed into composure. "Send for my secretary. If Spain pulls my sister towards war, I must be ready."

Anne inclines her head and goes to obey. Kat gathers her sewing again, her mouth set, eyes troubled.

In the antechamber beyond, the messenger lingers just long enough to hear the summons carried down the passage.

Ready, he thinks—and understands it as others will.

By the time he is back in the saddle, riding hard for London, the story has already taken its shape: the Princess of Hatfield, alert, preparing, her eyes fixed not on Spain—but on the crown.

Chapter 8
Stafford Takes Scarborough Castle

7 April 1557

The English embassy in Paris is no palace—just a rented hôtel near Saint-Germain, its chancery records packed into two coffers and a narrow closet. Sir Peter Carew stands stiffly opposite Ambassador Nicholas Wotton. His face is taut, his expression carved by the weight of what he knows he must confess. His stomach tightens.

He has tried too long to keep faith and remain silent about Thomas Stafford's plotting. Silence has become too heavy to bear. The time for concealment is over.

"You are certain of this?" Wotton says, candlelight flickering in his dark eyes. "This is no tavern tale, Sir Peter. Stafford's ambition has long pricked us."

Carew nods.

"It is not mere ambition. Stafford is preparing to seize Scarborough Castle. He intends to use it as the base of his rebellion against Queen Mary. He believes he has a rightful claim to the throne. And he is willing to risk everything to prove it."

Wotton pushes to his feet, shoulders taut. He strides across the chamber, his irritation barely contained.

"Do you see what that means? It is treason—by a man backed by nothing but his own arrogance. He is courting the French to prop him up. If we remain idle, it will not stop at one fortress. With discontent already smouldering, England could split again."

Carew straightens. He keeps his tone level.

"I know the cost, sir. Do you think I would come without certainty? Stafford has been at this for months—writing letters, gathering malcontents. Scarborough is a beginning—a calculated strike at Mary's crown. The plans are fragile, but if left unchecked, we may face rebellion on English soil. And it would be needless."

Wotton halts mid-step. He studies Carew carefully, weighing him. His face hardens. "You said French aid. Do you mean his rebellion has touched the ears of the French embassy?"

A troubled shadow crosses Carew's face. He opens his mouth, then hesitates, measuring candour against silence. The fire crackles, yet the chamber feels colder. At last, he answers.

"It has. Rumours and whispers, but enough. The French need little excuse to meddle. They do not require armies—only a few ships, a purse of gold, a handful of mercenaries. Just enough to breed doubt. Chaos suits their ends well."

He glances towards the shuttered window, as if expecting to see sails already gliding into English waters.

"They may not intervene openly. But if Stafford raises his banner in Scarborough, it will not be stone he commands. It will be a symbol—for rebels, dissidents, those who dream still of replacing Mary with Elizabeth. Or civil war."

Wotton strokes his chin slowly, concern creasing his face. The weight of the moment settles heavily across his shoulders.

"This is more dangerous than we feared. If Stafford succeeds, even for an hour, Scarborough becomes more than mere mortar and rock. It becomes a beacon—one the Crown cannot afford."

He moves swiftly to his writing desk.

"God reward you, Sir Peter. You may have spared us great loss. I will send dispatches to London tonight."

15 April 1557

At Hatfield in the late afternoon, Elizabeth sits in a cushioned chair, needle flashing bright silk into her tapestry. Beside her, Kat Ashley works quietly. Anne Denny bends low over her own frame. From the corner, lutes thread the melancholy line of "Hélas Madame."

A knock breaks the air. A steward hurries in, bowing low.

"Your Highness, Her Majesty, your sister, has arrived. She requests an audience of you at once."

It was an uncommon journey for the Queen—undertaken only because Savoy mattered—and because Mary would trust no messenger with her request.

Elizabeth's eyes widen. "My sister—here?"

The doors swing open. Mary enters in dark velvet, her rosary glinting at her waist, attended by a small train of ladies and officers. Sir Henry Bedingfield lingers watchful at the rear. Yeomen remain planted outside.

Elizabeth rises and dips a deep curtsy. "Your Majesty honours me."

Mary forces a smile, but her eyes glisten with something rawer than courtesy. "We are sisters, Elizabeth. Forgive the surprise."

"The ride from London must have been tedious. Hatfield is your former home. It is always open to you," Elizabeth replies, recovering her composure.

Wine and sweetmeats appear. The sisters settle by the hearth. They exchange small courtesies—weather, gardens, health—but soon Mary's face steadies into intent.

"Elizabeth," she says, quiet and urgent, "the Duke of Savoy is a noble match. He is the King's cousin. A marriage would strengthen England, secure your place, and guard our family's future. He is loyal and strong. And he would stand at your side."

Elizabeth studies her, reading the fervour in her eyes. "You travelled a long way to come here. I see it means much to you, Majesty."

Mary leans closer, clasping Elizabeth's hand with sudden force. Her voice trembles. "It means everything. You cannot know, Elizabeth, how I have longed for comfort. But Philip...Philip shows me kindness now. He holds me when I falter. He speaks with gentleness when the world feels cruel. I thought love would never come, yet it comes now, slowly, as a mercy. It saves me from despair. And if I can find it—even I, so late, so battered—then surely you can find it too, with a husband chosen for both duty and devotion."

Elizabeth rises, fingers brushing the chair before falling loose at her side. Her voice is calm, but there is an edge beneath.

"Does this mean everything? I listen to you always, sister. But what of the heart? A crown can be borne. Loneliness cannot. Do you ask me to marry for duty alone, to wear the same crown of solitude you wear?"

Pain flashes across Mary's face. She leans forward, voice breaking.

"Do you think I do not know the cost? I have lived it. But Philip eases it. He has shown me tenderness—God's granted me that mercy. Desire must bow to the realm, yes. But sometimes...sometimes love follows after duty."

Elizabeth answers softly, her gaze steady.

"Perhaps. Yet I see the weariness in your eyes. Do you not long for something more than borrowed moments of tenderness? You have a crown, and you have a husband. But do you have peace? What good is a crown if the heart remains half-starved?"

Mary stiffens, then falters. She looks down, whispering as though confessing a sin. "You are right, Elizabeth. I am tired. This is not the life I imagined. I thought marriage would mend me—that love would come quickly. It has not. But even a little love is a lifeline. Without it, I would break."

Elizabeth steps close and lays her hand gently on Mary's arm. Her voice is low, but firm. "I do not wish to see you broken. Nor to see myself trapped in the same way. If I marry, and only if, it will be to one who knows me—not only my crown, but my soul."

Mary raises her eyes, her expression wavering between hope and anguish. "I dreamed of love once. I settled for duty. Now God gives me scraps of love, and I cling to them—as though they were bread. Perhaps that is enough."

Elizabeth's smile is small, real, touched with sorrow. "Perhaps. But I do not wish you to bear it alone."

For a moment Mary's gentleness breaks through. Her eyes soften, her grip on Elizabeth's hand tightening as though she might never let go. "You are right, Elizabeth. Yet what has been done cannot be undone."

Elizabeth bows her head. "Thank you, Mary. I wish you peace wherever it may be found."

The sisters sit in silence—not empty, but brimming with burden and with their unspoken love.

25 April 1557

The air is thick with salt. The timbers creak as the ships rock gently on the grey swells of the North Sea. After sailing many leagues from Dieppe, two French vessels, the *Agnus Dei* and the *Saint Michel*, close in on the Yorkshire coast. Scarborough's cliffs rise ahead through the mist.

On the *Agnus Dei*, Thomas Stafford—son of Henry, Lord Stafford, and Ursula Pole, and claiming Plantagenet blood through his mother—stands at the bow, gripping the rail, his eyes on England's shore. His jaw is set with resolve, though in the depths of his gaze burns something more desperate. At his side, his second-in-command Giles Darcy, a battle-hardened former soldier, shifts uneasily. Below deck, the crew murmurs in low tones, but above, the two men speak in whispers meant for none but each other. A tarred cask of salt beef and a barrel of ship's biscuit stand open by the mainmast; a boy hacks off lumps with a knife and hands them round, but Stafford has waved the food away since dawn, feeding on anger and the throne he thinks awaits him. He had spent years nursing the fantasy that England owed him more than what he called exile.

"I am certain Scarborough Castle will fall."

Darcy nods cautiously. "If the gate is unguarded, we are inside in two minutes. If not, we lose ourselves among the market folk and re-embark. No banners until the powder's inside."

Stafford does not seem to be paying attention. He keeps looking up at the coast.

"Thomas, are you listening?"

"Every word, Darcy."

"Three days at best before Lord Westmorland hears and rides. He will have his reinforcements. We must copy the proclamation, post it in the town, and send riders north and west *today*. If the townsmen do not flock by nightfall, we spike the guns and go back to sea."

Stafford steps closer.

"We will take it. I will take it. If we hold Scarborough, we prevent other castles from bowing to Philip's grasp. One by one, Mary and Philip will see where true loyalty lies."

Darcy narrows his eyes. "Other castles? That is if we rouse enough support from the people. If not, we retreat to fight another day."

"Yes," Stafford replies quickly, averting his gaze and rubbing the back of his neck. "We will get that support. They will support the true King of England."

"Thomas, you make no sense—"

"I have royal blood," Stafford cuts him off, eyes bright with it. He digs into his cloak and produces a folded parchment—an escutcheon sketched in ink, the quarterings crowded with names.

"Look," he says, thrusting it towards Darcy. "My mother was Ursula Pole. Her mother was Margaret Pole—Margaret Plantagenet—daughter of George, Duke of Clarence."

His finger taps the line as if striking a match. "Yorkist blood. The sort that men remember. No Spaniard can manufacture that."

Darcy stares, stunned. His breath catches. "You...would claim the throne?"

"Not would. I do," Stafford says, coldly. "England will never rest under a foreign king. No, not under Philip's papist hand. I will return her to God's word—set before the people without priestly veil or papist gloss—under a monarch of their own. Under me."

Darcy looks away, torn between admiration and dread. His scarred cheek catches the sun. "Thomas, we must be realistic. Philip commands more than words. He commands armies. And Mary lends him strength. Do you think you can match them?"

"King Henry of France knows the danger," Stafford replies. "He sends aid for the same reason we rise—to break Spain's grip. Together we'll undo Philip."

Darcy exhales. "And Mary?"

Stafford laughs bitterly, the sound carrying across the water. "Mary's no queen—she is Philip's pawn. She cannot stop what is coming. I carry the blood, the right. The throne is mine, and I will take it."

Darcy studies him, heavy doubt in his gaze. "You'll stir the wars of York and Lancaster again, Tom. You risk everything."

Stafford smiles faintly, a dangerous light in his eyes.

"The time is now. When we seize Scarborough, the kingdom will feel the tremor."

Wind snaps his cloak like a banner. He plants his boots wide on the damp planks, eyes locked on the looming cliffs. The ship groans, men murmur and adjust their weapons while Stafford stands silent, sharpened by the cold. He leans slightly forward, the way a man does when he is on the verge of a decision.

"Let them see me coming," he mutters—more to the sea than to anyone nearby. "Let them hear the return of a name they tried to forget. Prepare yourself, Darcy," Stafford says quietly. "The future of England will change soon enough."

Darcy watches him, torn but intrigued. "Perhaps you do deserve the throne, but only if the people want you to rule. And we have three days to find out."

To Stafford, the danger ahead is not merely of nature but of power; in his mind, everything he feared and desired seemed, for once, to lean his way.

As the two ships edge towards Scarborough, timbers creak. Mariners shout while preparing to dock. No flags fly. Their purpose remains wrapped in heavy fog.

The ships drop anchor. The gangplank thumps to the quay. Men move quickly and in order. Muskets and swords are kept wrapped and close. Determination hardens their faces.

On the rocky shore, captains oversee unloading. Stafford strides to a boulder and climbs. His dark cloak snaps in the wind. One hand grips his sword hilt. He plants his boots and lifts his voice.

"Fellows!" He raises his sword high. "Today we strike against the tyranny that strangles our realm. Spain drags England into foreign wars. A queen forsakes her people. Mary Tudor and her Spanish consort bring us ruin. She is more loyal to Spain than to England. Philip would empty our coffers and spill English blood for Spanish ambition. Mark me well. Scarborough was to be handed to the Spaniards. Not only here. Other strongholds face the same betrayal. Spanish garrisons will seize them."

A gust snaps his cloak hard against his legs. One of the men shifts his grip on a musket. The wind carries Stafford's words down the line, uneven but hungry.

Giles Darcy glances up at him, askance. He knows it was a charge chosen for its fury, not its truth. Stafford drives on.

"The queen means to sell this kingdom brick by brick until we are but a province of Philip's empire. No more. We take Scarborough Castle in the name of English liberty. I call on all true-born Englishmen to rise, to cast off the Spanish yoke, and to restore our nation to her own rule."

He lowers the sword, pointing towards the ground.

"Let all who would subjugate us learn that this land is England's—no man else's."

The men cheer. Stafford gestures towards the boats.

"We have muskets and powder—steel enough for any man willing to fight. Scarborough shall be our stronghold. From here we'll rally those who are discontented with Mary's rule."

Behind the cheers, men eye the sacks of salt fish, rye loaves, and small kegs of ale being hauled up from the boats; if they are to hold a lonely rock against the Queen, they mean to know how many days' victuals stand between defiance and hunger.

Another cheer. Stafford's voice rises once more.

"If the Queen's forces come, let them come. We will answer with match, musket, and blade. Our loyal English people will rise when they see our banner flying over Scarborough."

He sheathes his sword with a flourish.

"Onward to Scarborough Castle. Today we make history! Tomorrow we reclaim England."

They hide weapons under their cloaks. Disguised as country folk and market-goers, they move in a tight knot towards the cliff path. The wind carries the hush of their steps and the faint clink of steel beneath cloth.

***

Within the gates, Captain Lovel, the officer in charge of the castle garrison, stands with eleven guards at the main gate.

"The gate is open. There will be no violent confrontation," Lovel says. His voice is steady, though his eyes are grave. "We've been warned—our task is to buy time and to spare blood."

The soldiers nod. Loyal. Weary. Ready.

They have expected this ever since Westmorland's riders recently brought word north. Stafford means to seize Scarborough. The garrison is ready for the worst and something else. They will not fight. They will surrender on entry.

A lieutenant steps forward, jaw set.

"We give up the castle without a fight, sir? They are rebels. Traitors. Should we not make them bleed for it?"

Lovel meets his eyes.

"There will be no bloodshed, Lieutenant. London's command is plain. Preserve lives. Give them the show of victory. Westmorland's militia will come on their heels. Prepare the gates. Let them think they have won."

The men bow to the inevitable.

On the damp stone path outside, Stafford's boots drum towards the barbican. Swords close at hand. Muskets ready under cloaks.

"Thomas," Darcy murmurs, slowing his pace. He scans the walls. "Where is the garrison? Why no banners? Why no shouts from the towers?"

Stafford laughs and draws his cloak tighter.

"All in the privy, I suppose."

He presses a palm to the iron-bound door. It groans and yields. No challenge. No cry. Only emptiness.

Darcy stops short.

"Why are the gates not defended? Why unlocked?"

Stafford flashes a triumphant grin.

"They hand us a gift. Perhaps they fear us more than their queen."

They step inside. The courtyard lies still. The wind keens through broken battlements. In the shadow of the Great Tower, a cluster of soldiers stands waiting, as if they have already lost.

"Ho you there! I am Lord Protector Thomas Stafford," he calls. "I claim this castle. Put down your swords."

Captain Lovel steps forward, posture straight, gaze unwavering.

"So that is it—you mean to pen us like cattle, 'Lord' Stafford?"

Darcy notes the man's cavalier tone. The looseness of the soldiers' faces. Slight smiles almost rising. Something is wrong. This is too easy.

Lovel unbuckles his belt, draws his blade slowly, and offers it hilt first.

"Here is my sword."

"No resistance?" Stafford asks.

"None," Lovel says, lips tight. "You outnumber us. We will not resist."

Stafford waves a hand, scarcely looking at them.

"Ha! Search them for weapons and drive them down and lock them in the Great Tower's cellar. There is no steel among sheep. Give food and water when needed. Give them bedding and buckets as well."

The rebels herd the guards towards the belly of the Great Tower. Lovel turns a fraction and gives a small nod to his sergeant. Down they go, docile as lambs. The prisoners are shoved into the cellar and given only a cursory pat-down for weapons. Stafford is too eager to secure the walls to waste time on a full search. Once inside, Stafford had the firearms carried to the chapel armoury and locked away.

In the cellar, a thick iron door slams shut. The lock clacks. Later, the key is given to Stafford.

Lovel shifts his weight. His hand settles on the broad dagger sheath at his belt. The leather is worn smooth. A thin dark strip runs its length where a clasp should be. He touches it and feels the truth. Not a clasp. A key. Blackened, filed flat along one edge to match the warding, carried in plain sight.

"Overconfident fools. They did not even search well," Lovel quips.

A sergeant whispers.

"We are locked in. What now?"

Lovel's smile barely shows.

"Locks are made by men. Men forget keys come in pairs."

He shows the sergeant the hidden key and hides it in straw bedding. The lock behind them stands—for now.

In the yard, Stafford throws his voice across the stone.

"They think their castles are secure. They think their Spaniard king is secure. Hear me. Soon England's main strongholds will fall away from Spain's grip. Soon Philip will cease to be king in favour of a proper Protestant English king."

His men cheer.

"I, Thomas Stafford, stand forth as Protector of this realm by blood and by God's ordinance—until England is restored to her own. I will free England from Spanish and papist corruption. The crown shall return to true English blood. In time, I will take up the style of my house and lead you as Duke of Buckingham and Protector, to restore what foreign influence has stolen. Many thanks to the King of France. He will send ships and soldiers. We will not let this or any castle be taken by the Spanish King of England."

His little army howls back.

"Boo! Nay! Not our king! A pox on her! Fie on her! Spanish strumpet she is! A curse on her crown!"

The proclamation rides the wind over the headland. Stafford's heart swells. Darcy hears the borrowed title and winces, as if the saying might make it true. For a moment, ambition feels like destiny.

28 April 1557

This was the third day since the landing. Thirty men in all—mostly French mercenaries with a few exiled Protestants with nothing to lose. The castle fell without a drawn blade. The muskets had been locked in the chapel armoury as soon as they seized the keep. Stafford's banner hangs limp above the gate. A handful of proclamations from France cling to church doors and market posts along the roads nearest the coast.

Nothing comes of it yet—no answer swift enough to save them.

No villagers rally. No Protestant lords send word. Scarborough closes and whispers prayers. The sea takes the rest.

Giles Darcy folds his arms near the hearth. Flames paint the scars on his cheek. He stays because turning back now means death—from Stafford's men or the Crown's. Better to stand with the devil he knows.

"It has been near three days," he says at last. "What now?"

Stafford blinks as if waking. His face is pale. His eyes are hollow from sleepless nights and failed hope.

"They have heard," he says. "The flame is lit. All it needs is breath."

Darcy scoffs and shakes his head.

"Breath? You have had three days of silence. You thought Yorkshire would rise because a half-forgotten noble hung a banner on a crumbling keep and cried treason?"

"It is not my name they rise for," Stafford snaps. "It is England's. We are ruled by a Spanish puppet and still they sleep? Philip will bleed this land and hang our faith from every gibbet. I told them Scarborough was to be handed to Spain."

"You lied," Darcy says. "There was no plan to hand the castle to Spaniards. That was your invention."

"A necessary invention," Stafford growls. "War is deception. Fear rallies faster than banners. If men believe their towns will be filled with foreign troops, they will act."

He goes to the arrow slit and stares into the mist.

"I needed a fire. So I lit one."

"You tried to light one. I see no fire."

Stafford turns in a tight circle, arms wide.

"That proclamation is nailed on every road we can reach, from here to York. Not only do the words spread. The doubt. The fury. The will. I carry royal blood. I did not come to play outlaw."

He gestures at the cold stone and the hunting wind.

"This is what we have. One castle. One banner."

He lets the truth sit.

"It is a beginning."

Darcy does not move. Sparks spit in the grate.

"You would burn the truth to light your cause?"

"If that is what it takes," Stafford says. "Let them hate the marriage. Let them fear the Spanish boot. Let them remember that once, someone stood."

"Then you should have prayed for a miracle," Darcy answers, weary. "They knew we were coming before we landed. I knew it was too easy. No man is coming to you, Thomas. Only the Queen's soldiers. We are in their trap. If I quit now, I hang beside you anyway."

Silence settles. Outside, a low horn call floats over the cliffs. A cold wind from the north answers.

"If they come, we fight," Stafford says at last. "Bar the barbican. Man the tower. If the country will not join us, let them at least see we did not kneel."

"You will die for nothing," Darcy says.

"Better than living for silence in submission."

Darcy stares into the fire, then back at Stafford.

"No," he says. "You will die for being remembered wrong."

***

Earlier that day, thin pale light lies across the old Norman walls. Cold clings to the earth. Below the headland, ranks of local militia and the Queen's regulars wait in ordered lines—pikes grounded, muskets slung, eyes fixed on the rock-crowned keep above.

Canvas snaps in the wind.

Inside the command tent, Henry Neville, Earl of Westmorland and the Queen's lieutenant in the North, stands over a map weighted with stones. His cloak is heavy wool; his jaw is set. Opposite him, Captain John Talbot tightens his sword belt, helmet tucked under one arm. On a low chest nearby sit a cold collop of beef, coarse bread, and a jug of small beer—touched only when there is time, which is little.

"Stafford is no common thief," Talbot says, nodding towards the dark outline of Scarborough. "He dresses treason as righteousness. Speaks of freedom from Spanish chains."

Neville snorts. "Freedom? He rebels against his lawful sovereign and calls it liberty. How many men does he truly have?"

"No more than forty," Talbot answers. "Likely fewer. But he holds stone and height. A blind assault costs us blood—and gives him the martyr he wants."

Neville taps the table once. "I will not answer to Her Majesty for wasted lives. Your plan."

Talbot leans over the map, tracing the outer works. "His men are green—French hirelings and exiles. He expects us at the gate. So we deny him that. At dusk we loose fire over the curtain—hay, scaffolding, anything dry. While they scramble to save their keep, the ram takes the barbican. Then we drive straight up the causeway and strike the Great Tower."

Neville folds his arms. "Chaos from two sides. Good. Take Stafford alive if you can. His death must be public—axe and scaffold, not smoke and rubble."

Talbot nods once. "He boasts loudly. He will not die well."

Neville allows himself a thin smile. "Let him boast. He will soon have no tongue for it."

The tent wall snaps again. Talbot turns towards the door. "I ready the archers. By nightfall, they break."

Neville looks once more towards the grey crown of Scarborough. "Godspeed, Captain. The Queen's wrath rides with you."

***

As the light wanes and the wind sharpens, Talbot stands at the edge of the encampment. Men move with purpose now—checking match cords, setting rams into their frames, tightening straps.

"They are few," Talbot tells his second, "but they hold stone. We breach before full dark."

"They have the sea at their backs, Captain," the younger officer says. "Already caged."

Talbot's mouth curves thinly. "Good. Smoke them out. That gate is their throat. We take it tonight—or bleed for it tomorrow."

***

Inside Scarborough, the wind prowls the corridors, threading through arrow slits and broken joints in the stone like a restless animal. It carries the smell of salt and wet rope, of damp wool and cold iron. The great hall breathes with it—smoke-stained rafters exhaling old fires, stone flags sweating beneath boots that have not moved in hours.

Thomas Stafford sits slumped in the governor's chair, its carved lions dulled by age and neglect. His fingers clutch the arms so tightly the knuckles blanch, as though the wood itself might steady him. He does not look like a conqueror now. He looks like a man holding ground against a thought he cannot banish—that the kingdom he came to claim has already begun to close around him, silent and implacable, like the stone beneath his feet.

On the table before him lies a trencher: a few leathery strips of salt fish, a heel of oat bread gone grey at the edges. The fresh joints, the white loaves, the ale poured too freely on the first day—gone. Spent on cheers and certainty. On the belief that hunger would be brief and glory swift. Now rebellion tastes of brine and dust, and it dries the mouth even as it fills it.

He does not eat. The food has cooled, stiffened, lost even the pretence of comfort. His stomach knots anyway, not with hunger but with waiting.

The fire at the hearth sinks lower, its glow retreating into a crust of red embers. No one moves to feed it. Smoke hangs in the air, thin and acrid, stinging the eyes. Somewhere deeper in the keep, a door creaks, then settles. A man coughs. Boots scrape stone and stop.

Stafford leans back, the chair groaning beneath him. The wind presses again at the walls, and for a moment it sounds like voices—distant, accusing, or perhaps only imagined. He stares into the dying fire, jaw tight, as if daring it to flare again.

It does not.

***

As evening falls, mist lifts off the sea.

On the barbican, four of Stafford's men stamp their feet and curse the cold, muttering about French ships that never come.

Then one of them freezes.

A dark line emerges from the trees.

It lengthens as it comes, resolving into ranks—too many to count at a glance.

Steel glints dully where torchlight catches pikeheads and helm rims.

The ground itself seems to answer them, a low tremor carried up through stone and bone.

Torches flare. Pikes rise. Two columns march in step, disciplined and silent. At their head ride two figures—one in dark livery with an upraised hand, the other beneath a plumed helmet, a red cloak snapping hard in the wind.

Lord Westmorland. Captain Talbot.

Behind them, battering rams roll forward on oxen-drawn frames.

"They've brought half of York," Miles Carter whispers, backing from the parapet.

"We are ghosts," Ned Whittle mutters.

None of the four carry muskets. Stafford has locked them all in the chapel armoury, fearing betrayal more than assault. These men are eyes only.

"Inside!" Carter barks. "Barricade the gate!"

They bolt down the spiral stairs. The outer doors groan shut. The cross-beam drops. Loose masonry is shoved into place. It will not hold long.

They sprint across the ward towards the Great Tower.

Stafford looks up as boots thunder in. "What is it?"

"They're here," Carter gasps. "Hundreds. Rams."

A hush falls.

Stafford crosses to a narrow slit and looks out.

"So," he says quietly. "The Crown comes to collect its ruin."

He draws his sword.

Outside, a hiss cuts the air.

Flame blossoms.

One burning arrow strikes a hay cart. Another bites into the chapel scaffolding. Dry timber flares at once.

Panic ripples through the yard. Buckets slosh. Smoke thickens.

A horn sounds.

The Queen's soldiers advance in tight order, arquebusiers and pikemen closing behind the ram, its iron head wrapped in chains.

"Now," Talbot breathes.

The ram strikes.

Oak shudders. Splinters fly. A second blow cracks the beam. The third bursts the door inward.

The Queen's banner surges through the arch.

Trumpets sound. Soldiers flood the ward.

Stafford's men break—some casting down their arms at once, others running for the keep.

At the tower stairs, a smaller ram is unpinned.

"Drive it," Talbot orders.

Iron thunders on oak.

***

Deep below, in the cellars, Captain Lovel lifts his head.

He has listened for days to footsteps and wind through the murder holes. Now the sound is different—deep, deliberate.

Another blow. The tower shakes.

Lovel smiles. "At last."

He draws the hidden key from the straw and jams it into the lock. It sticks. He twists harder. The bolt gives.

"To your feet," he snaps. "The Queen's men are here."

Locks turn. The garrison spills out. They run for the armoury.

Inside wait arquebuses, muskets, powder, match, pikes—forgotten by rebels, waiting.

They arm fast.

"Up the stairs," Lovel orders.

***

Smoke drifts through the tower slits. Shouts echo. At the Lord's Hall door, Lovel halts.

"In the Queen's name," he calls. "Open."

Inside, Darcy's face drains of colour. He slides the bar back.

Lovel's men pour in.

At that instant, the tower doors burst open under the ram.

"Forward!" Talbot roars.

The Queen's soldiers flood the hall. Westmorland enters with sword drawn.

Across the chamber stands Stafford, ringed but uncut.

"Take him alive," Talbot says.

Westmorland steps forward. "I will."

Stafford meets his gaze. "My Lord Westmorland?"

Neville's eyes are stone. "Master Thomas Stafford."

Stafford looks down at the sword in his hand.

He releases it.

The blade clatters on stone.

A murmur moves the hall as the sound echoes and dies.

Westmorland signals for irons. Stafford is taken by the arms, his head still high, his eyes unreadable. Smoke curls along the rafters. Outside, the shouts soften into order.

Near the door, a clerk stoops to gather the torn proclamations pulled from the gate and chapel doors. One catches his eye. He smooths it as he walks, lips moving once as he reads.

"*England betrayed to Spain. By the aid of France, England may yet be freed.*"

The clerk exhales through his nose and folds the paper away.

By morning, that will be the story carried south.

Chapter 9
England at War

28 May 1557

Grey sky presses low on Tower Hill, beneath the Tower of London's shadow. A chill wind runs across the stones. The crowd gathers in tight ranks, nobles in velvet, commoners in wool, soldiers in steel. Pie-sellers weave through the press with trays of hot beef-and-onion pies and eel pasties. Savoury steam mingles with the sour tang of sweat and wet wool. Apprentices hoot from windows. A preacher near the steps cries that England must be purged of traitors. A child on a man's shoulders sobs. All eyes rest on the wooden scaffold at the centre of the open grounds. A steel axe gleams on the block.

Thomas Stafford emerges from the White Tower between two guards. His hands are bound before him. His back is straight, his head high. He carries himself as a man who still believes in his cause. He passes through the gate and approaches the scaffold.

A bell tolls. The crowd parts. He climbs the steps. Each fall of his boots sounds sharp in the cold. The executioner waits, silent.

An official lifts a parchment and reads.

"Thomas Stafford. For treason. For conspiring with the King of France to depose Mary, the rightful and lawful Queen of England. For attempting to install yourself as Lord Protector of the Realm and for attempting to usurp the Crown. By English law, you are to be executed on this twenty-eighth day of May in the year of our Lord fifteen hundred and fifty-seven."

He lowers the warrant and hands it to the executioner.

"Master Executioner, here is your warrant. You are guiltless of murder. Thomas Stafford, have you any last words?"

Stafford turns to the crowd. He searches the faces. Some are hard. Some curious. Some look away. He draws a breath.

"People of England," he calls. "I meet my end not as a traitor, but as a man who sought to free this realm from tyranny."

A murmur ripples through the crowd—not assent, but confusion. Some cheer. Others mutter prayers. A few look away, already weary of speeches.

"I am condemned for rising against a queen who has tied this noble land to a foreign power. My actions were born not of malice, but of love for England. If that is treason, then I stand guilty."

He lifts his gaze to the sky.

"I go to my death with a clear conscience. I acted in the name of freedom. Though my body falls, my spirit remains with all who yearn for a free realm. Call me what you will. Let no man say I was Spain's pawn. God save England."

Silence settles. Cloaks stir. An old woman coughs. Stafford turns to the executioner and nods once.

He looks at the crowd one last time. He lifts his chin. "Remember me."

After a moment, he says quietly to a guard, "Bring me my purse."

The guard places it in Stafford's bound hands, the cords loose enough for his fingers. Stafford tips it towards the executioner.

"For you."

The executioner takes the purse with a brief nod and gestures. Stafford kneels and lowers his head to the block. He murmurs a prayer. He stretches his bound hands forward.

The executioner says, "Are you ready, sir?"

Stafford replies, "Ready. Jesus receive my soul."

The axe flashes and falls. The crack of the blow and the thud that follows roll across the yard. The crowd gasps. The body slumps.

The executioner lifts the severed head for a moment, then lowers it into a basket.

A herald steps forward and unrolls a new parchment.

"Let it be known that Thomas Stafford has paid the price for treason against the Crown. May this serve as a warning to all who would rise against Her Majesty Queen Mary and the authority of the throne."

7 June 1557

Morning light filters through tall windows. Lavender lingers in Queen Mary's private chamber at Whitehall. She sits at her dressing table in deep crimson. The mirror shows a face resolute and worn. Lady Frances Baynam adjusts the folds of the Queen's cloak.

On the table by the window, a silver trencher holds a slice of manchet bread, a little quince marmalade, and a cup of warmed hippocras. Mary has only torn the bread once, more from habit than hunger. Behind the chair, Philip rests a hand on the carved back, his face a calm mask. By the window, Reginald Pole, Archbishop of Canterbury, clasps his hands as if in prayer.

"Your Majesty," Pole says softly. "This moment demands clarity. War with France must be seen as a necessity, not a choice. It is a holy task. Without it, the faith suffers. England's sovereignty suffers."

Mary touches the small crucifix at her neck.

"France harbours traitors like Stafford," she says. "It insults our crown. It threatens Christendom's unity. Yet I fear my people do not see what I see, cousin."

Philip's gaze fixes on her. His tone is calm and firm.

"They must be reminded of their loyalty. You are anointed. They will follow if you lead with conviction."

Mary meets his eyes. Her voice is anxious.

"I fear they do not love me as they loved my father—do not see me as their Henry."

Philip steps closer and rests his hands more solidly on the chair.

"You are not your father. You are Queen Mary. England will stand with you because you stand with God. You have me, and through me, Spain. Together we defend Christendom."

Frances Baynam fastens the clasp.

"Your Majesty looks every inch the warrior queen," she says. "Parliament will see your resolve, even if they grumble."

Mary rises and smooths her skirts. Her hands quiver.

"Resolve must be enough. For England. For the faith. For Spain. We will remind them what it means to stand against heresy and treason."

***

In the corridor towards the Lords' chamber at the Palace of Westminster, Mary turns to Pole and asks, "Is Parliament ready?"

"They await Your Majesty," he answers.

Philip offers his arm. She hesitates for a breath, then takes it. As they walk, he speaks softly for her ear alone.

"Let them see not only England's queen, but a daughter of royal Spanish blood. You are more powerful than you know."

They pass guards and ushers. At the doors, William Paget, Lord Privy Seal, bows.

"Your Majesties—Lords and Commons are assembled. The time has come."

An usher slips an aniseed comfit into his mouth to sweeten his breath; the sharp sugar reek mingles with beeswax and the faint stale ale smell rising from the Commons below.

"Then we waste no time," Mary answers.

Lord Chancellor Nicholas Heath steps forward and places a sealed scroll in her hands.

"The words are strong," he says. "You will command the room."

"I do not seek to command them only," Mary replies. "I seek to unite them."

The chamber is packed. Robes rustle. Voices murmur in an uneasy tide. At the far end, the carved dais waits like a stage before the last act.

Silence falls. Mary enters. Shoulders square. Chin high. Pale, yet steady with the grace of one who knows the weight she bears and bears it still. All eyes follow as she mounts the dais.

She turns to face them. Velvet and chains shine among the Lords. Sober black lines the Commons. Loyalty and doubt move like a current through the hall.

She unrolls the scroll. Her hands tremble slightly.

"Lords and Commons of England," she begins firmly. "We stand before you not only as your queen, but as a servant of Almighty God. This realm has a history of defending the true faith and of resisting those who would destroy it. We also have a rich history of defending our soil. Today that duty calls us again."

She lets the words settle.

"France gives haven to traitors to this Crown. France acts in open hostility to England, to her allies, and to the unity of Christendom. As your queen, it is our sacred duty to safeguard this realm and to honour the alliance with my husband, King Philip of Spain. Together we stand against those who threaten God's order."

A murmur runs the benches. Some assent. Some hold back. Mary's gaze hardens.

"We do not choose lightly. War brings charge and travail, yet honour and surety may come of it. We defend our honour and safety. We maintain the honour of this crown and realm. We require your support, not for our sake, but for England's future."

She draws breath and speaks to the point.

"King Henry of France favours pirates who despoil our subjects. Nothing has turned him from his methods. Last April he abetted the traitor Thomas Stafford, sending ships and succour—whether by order or by French malice matters little. He abetted the brief seizure of Scarborough Castle before he was brought south to answer for his crimes. That king has long sought Calais. He has sent an army to invade Flanders, which we are bound to defend. We therefore proclaim to our subjects that the King of France is a public enemy to our person and our nation. Let every Englishman regard the King and his vassals as open enemies of this realm, and let us render them harm wherever possible."

Philip's face brightens with approval.

Mary looks out over the Lords and Commons.

"Let us do our duty before Almighty God, and let England not fail in it. Let us show them we stand firm in faith, courage, and resolve. We are at war."

The hall holds its breath. Then applause breaks and grows. Mary stands composed, though her hands tremble behind the parchment.

As she and Philip leave the chamber, her counsellors draw near.

"Well done, Your Majesty," Heath says. "They will follow your lead."

"They must," Mary answers. "England's future depends on it."

***

In a Whitehall corridor later in the afternoon, Philip and Don Gómez Feria meet Elizabeth at a turn, unexpected but not improper in the crowded corridors. Surprise flickers across their faces. Elizabeth curtsies.

"You have your war, my lord," she says. "Harass the enemy well. Good day."

She quickly exits.

Elizabeth is not a temptation, Philip reminds himself, but a variable—unsettling precisely because she does not yield.

"Don Gómez," Philip says quietly. "We prepare for Calais. We have the French to break."

Elizabeth's words linger longer than he liked. They follow him into silence and refuse to loosen their hold.

4 July 1557

Dover's harbour is alive with clamour. Gulls cry over rigging that creaks against the masts. The King's flotilla gathers, the galleon *Espíritu Santo* among them, readying for sea. Sun breaks through low mist and washes the quay in thin gold. Despite the bustle, sombre tension grips the royal party on the dock.

At the foot of the gangplank, Philip stands with his face composed, every line of his bearing regal. Yet the stillness in him contrasts with the restless motion around. Porters strain as they shoulder heavy chests, their boots thudding on wet planks.

The slope of the gangway groans under the burden of pay chests, arms, and baggage. Barrels of salted beef and biscuit roll past, marked for the voyage, and a cooper shouts for care—one cracked cask means hungry weeks in the Narrow Seas. Shouts of mariners cut across the air, sharp with command. The rhythm of loading is brisk, almost frantic, as though the tide itself urges haste. Banners snap in the sea wind, and the scent of tar and salt clings, thick and unrelenting.

Queen Mary holds tightly to Philip's arm. A veil hides only part of the tears that slip unchecked down her cheeks. Beside her, Princess Elizabeth keeps her expression smooth, though her fingers knot in her skirt. In the weeks since their fraught meeting at Hatfield, loneliness and strain have worn at Mary, softening her anger towards Elizabeth.

"Must you leave so soon, my lord?" Mary whispers.

Philip turns to her, his voice softened.

"Mary, you know my duty. Spain's enemies are many and her allies few. My duty now includes defending England. Your people are my people," he says—the words delivered smoothly, without warmth. "You are never far from my thoughts. Never."

Mary's hands tremble as she clutches his sleeve.

"Will you come back to me?"

He takes her hands and holds them.

"You are England's heart, Mary, and I am your servant. If God wills, when peace returns, I will come back to you. Trust God's plan for us."

She nods, lips parting, but no words come. She does not let go, as if one more heartbeat might change fate.

Elizabeth steps forward, the sea wind tugging a loose strand from beneath her French hood. Grace on the surface. Steel beneath. She gathers it behind her ear without haste and dips in a measured half-curtsy, low enough to honour rank, not so low that it concedes more.

"My lord," she says, voice smooth, unhurried. "England bids you God-speed. May your voyage be swift—and may thoughts of this realm keep you company when nights grow long."

She lifts her eyes to his, the hint of a smile touching her mouth, courteous and unreadable. "You are remembered here, as King of Spain and as our sister's consort. We are grateful for such remembrance as you bestow on England in turn."

Philip inclines his head. "Princess, your words do you credit. I trust you will stand by your queen as faithfully as I have."

Elizabeth lets the words pass through her, then responds with careful grace. "I stand by the Queen, as I have ever done. All England does. We pray your successes lighten her burdens, for they are many. You know how heavily they fall, do you not?"

Her tone never hardens, yet the line hangs between them with the weight of truth. She adds, almost lightly, "When you write, my lord, your letters will cheer her. And when you return, you will find England as you left it, loyal, watchful, and patient."

She dips again, a fraction shallower than before. "God keep you, Your Majesty."

Philip's smile is faint. He turns towards the gangplank.

Mary grips his arm again.

"Promise me," she pleads. "Promise you will write."

He brushes her cheek and takes her hand.

"I will write, Mary. You have my word."

He kisses her and mounts the gangplank. Each step sounds too loud in the morning air. At the top he turns. Mary reaches out as if she might call him back across open space. Elizabeth stands unmoving beside her, a sentinel to her sister's grief. Only the tightening of her jaw suggests she feels anything at all.

"Farewell," Philip calls, raising a hand to wave. "May God watch over you and keep you, Mary."

The ship's bell rings. Ropes fall away. The sails climb and fill. The galleon eases from the pier.

Mary's knees fail. Elizabeth catches her.

"Steady, Your Majesty," she whispers. "Do not let them see your weakness."

Mary hated showing weakness before her sister—it had never been her way.

Mary clutches Elizabeth's arm, gaze fixed on the ship.

"My heart goes with him, Elizabeth."

Elizabeth keeps her eyes on the dwindling ship. Her fists close at her sides.

"It is you and England now, Mary," she says. "I hope that is enough. And there is also me."

They watch the *Espíritu Santo* slowly move into the Channel. For Mary, the moment marks the beginning of living with loss.

She turns to see Elizabeth's face.

"Sister!" she breathes.

They lean into each other and weep. For once, grief makes them sisters before it makes them rivals.

7 July 1557

After days of foul winds, convoy delays, and foul tides, the sea proved unkind. The narrow waters of the English Channel churn with white-capped waves, a reflection of the sky above. Wrapped in a dark, fur-lined cloak, Philip stands on the deck of his flagship, the *Espíritu Santo*. The salt spray stings his face, but Philip does not flinch. His mind is elsewhere—on France, on the war that awaits him, and on the woman he leaves behind. Mary had wept at his departure, her tears a mixture of longing and desperation. She had clutched his hand in their final moments, her voice trembling as she begged for news of his swift return.

But as the waves carry him closer to France, Mary does not unsettle him. Elizabeth does. Her presence had been subdued at court, always in the shadow of her sister, yet she was impossible to ignore. Her sharp mind, her quick tongue, her calculated restraint—these haunted him in a way he could not explain. He was used to bending others to his thoughts. Elizabeth had not bent at all.

Elizabeth's last words returned, unwelcome but precise. He had dismissed them, thinking they were a mere jest. Now, as he sails towards the French coast, he finds himself turning them over in his mind. He allows the thought only long enough to assess it, then presses it back beneath preparation, where distractions are buried before battle.

***

Out in the Channel, the horizon is a canvas of deep blue. The Spanish and English fleets, laden with soldiers, sail side by side, their masts cutting into the clear sky. They join Philip's flotilla as an escort, steering for Calais and the Flemish coast. The red cross of St George flutters proudly from the English ships, while the red cross of Burgundy snaps sharply in the wind. The sight is both majestic and foreboding—a testament to the unity forged between Queen Mary's England and King Philip's Spain.

At the helm of an English ship—the *Golden Lion*—is Admiral Edward Fiennes de Clinton, smartly dressed in a dark-blue doublet, ruff, and maroon cloak. He looks at the Spanish galleon, the *La Loba,* one of the principal Spanish escorts, its deck bustling with activity as sailors prepare for its arrival in France.

The Spanish captain and friend of King Philip, Álvaro de Bazán, in a dark uniform trimmed with gold braid, steps to the rail of his ship and salutes. Clinton, with a grin that betrays both camaraderie and the competitive spirit of a sailor, returns the gesture with a sweeping motion of his feathered hat.

"Fine weather for an alliance," Clinton says, turning to the ship's master, who chuckles.

"If only matters of state were as smooth as the seas, my lord."

Across the waves, sailors from both fleets exchange shouts of greeting, their voices carrying over the spray. Cannon muzzles gleam in the sunlight, a reminder of the violence that awaits them once they reach France. Clinton leans against the rail, his gaze shifting to the horizon.

"Let the French see this," he murmurs. "An Englishman and a Spaniard, sailing in league."

The fleet cuts across a darkened blue, sails bellied hard, rigging groaning as spray salts the decks—a union of masts and flags that looks solid from afar and feels brittle up close.

***

At last, the sharp cry of gulls pierces the thick coastal air as Philip's fleet approaches the harbour of Calais. On a grudging clear afternoon, the late sun hangs low, casting a haze over the narrow streets and weathered ramparts of the English garrison town. Philip, in his gilded armour for ceremony, stands on the deck of the *Espíritu Santo*, his expression grim. Around him, the crew works in tense silence. The rhythmic creak of the ship's timbers underscores the anticipation that hangs like a storm cloud.

Philip descends the gangplank, each step striking the cobblestones with crisp finality. A contingent of Spanish and Flemish guards snap to attention, their halberds gleaming. Behind them, banners bearing the twin symbols of Spain and the House of Habsburg flutter in the coastal breeze. Waiting for him is Don Fernando Álvarez de Toledo, the Duke of Alba, his face stern, his armour streaked with dust from the campaign. Behind Alba, a tired English officer wipes grease from his fingers with the corner of his cloak, the remains of a cold beef pasty and a heel of manchet on a nearby trestle—a poor soldier's breakfast snatched between alarms.

"Your Majesty," Alba says, bowing, "the French are mustering their strength near St Quentin, but they grow restless. With your arrival, their resolve may falter."

Philip inclines his head slightly, revealing nothing. "We waste no time. Prepare the escort. I will press on to St Quentin at once. Don Fernando, we will harass the enemy."

14 July 1557

The roads from Calais to Picardy are a miserable sight. The once-fertile fields lie trampled and barren, their crops sacrificed to the relentless passage of armies. Villages stand silent, their charred remains bearing testimony to the conflict's reach. As Philip's carriage rattles along the uneven path, he sees survivors huddled by the roadside, their faces gaunt and hollow. The war has not spared them, and its shadow stretches far beyond the battlefield.

At every stop, commanders gather to greet their sovereign. Makeshift tables are spread with maps, ink-stained and worn, showing the positions of the armies like tokens moved by a hard hand. A pewter flagon of thin wine, a trencher of coarse rye bread, and a lump of hard cheese sit pushed aside, forgotten by men who have talked more than they have eaten.

Philip listens intently, holding his gloves and tapping them lightly against his palm as the generals speak of troop movements, supply shortages, and the enemy's fortifications. Each report carries the press of looming violence, yet also the flicker of hope that victory could soon be theirs.

"Your Majesty," one officer says, pointing to a cluster of markings on the map, "the French have fortified their lines here, but their flanks are vulnerable. If we press them hard enough, they will break."

Philip's eyes scan the map. "We will break them," he says in a cold and deliberate voice. "But the cost must not outweigh the gain. Hold the English forces in reserve. Their presence strengthens our alliance."

As the carriage presses towards St Quentin, the distant rumble of cannon fire grows louder. It is not yet the crescendo of battle, but an ominous prelude that sets the soldiers on edge. Smoke smudges the horizon, mingling with the evening mist. Philip orders the procession to halt and steps from the carriage. His boots sink into the mud as he surveys the scene before him—a rolling expanse of churned earth and makeshift trenches, the grim geometry of war.

The Duke of Savoy, Emmanuel Philibert, rides up to greet him, dismounting with a bow.

"Your Majesty, we await your command. The French forces are entrenched but show signs of strain. The days ahead will decide the fate of this campaign."

Philip places a hand on the Duke's shoulder. "You have done well, cousin. We move with precision, not haste. Let the enemy think us hesitant while we ready the hammer blow." He nods, his gaze fixed on the distant horizon. He speaks quietly, yet his words are resolute. "We will force the enemy to scatter. Harass them well."

The phrase echoes in his mind, and for a fleeting moment, he sees Elizabeth's face as clearly as if she stood beside him. Philip's lips twitch, the faintest hint of a smile breaking his composure. Her words had seemed a forced pleasantry at the time, but now, as he watches his forces press the advantage, he realises their wisdom.

He thinks of her again. He does not deny it and hates that it stays with him. She is not his wife, nor his ally, yet she occupies his thoughts with a persistence that unsettles him.

"Your Majesty?" The Duke of Savoy's voice pulls him back to the present.

Philip straightens, his expression sharpening. "Ensure the men press their advantage. Do not allow the French to regroup."

The Duke bows. "At your command, Sire."

As the Duke rides off, Philip climbs into his carriage and heads for the command tent, where dispatches, battle charts, and a much-needed flask of wine await. His men raise their swords in salute as he passes, their voices ringing with cries of victory.

Yet even amidst the triumph, his thoughts wander back to Elizabeth. The memory irritates him. He forces it aside—not in longing, but in discipline. She belongs to a board already played, a path no longer open.

He leaves his carriage and enters the tent. The cheers of his men fade into the distance, leaving him alone with his maps and his plans.

***

That night, in the dim glow of lanterns, Philip sits in his field tent, penning a letter to his wife, Queen Mary.

"*My dearest heart,*" he writes, the words flowing steadily despite the weariness in his eyes, "*we are on the cusp of a great confrontation. I feel your prayers across the distance, strengthening my resolve. Anthony Aucher in Calais begs me to assure you he will hold our fortress for England. Pray for Spain, for England, and for the triumph of our cause.*"

He pauses to sip from a pewter cup of sour Gascon wine and breaks a strip from a length of smoked sausage left by a Flemish captain, the simple soldier's fare at odds with the duty of the crowns on his head.

A faint smile crosses his lips, but it is a fleeting smile. The battle ahead requires all his focus. With one last glance at the map, he extinguishes the candles and steps out into the night. Camp sounds greet him—a chorus of preparation and anticipation. The final clash at St Quentin looms. Spain is ready.

10 August 1557

At St Quentin, the Duke of Alba stands atop a hill, his sharp eyes scanning the battlefield. Within sight, the English contingent under William Herbert, the Earl of Pembroke, and other commanders form a resolute line. The Duke's voice booms over the din of cannon fire.

"Stand fast, men!"

Below, the French forces surge forward, their banners waving defiantly. The ground shakes with the thunder of hooves as cavalry charges, lances glinting in the midday sun. Spanish arquebusiers fire in disciplined volleys, cutting down waves of attackers. A handful of English bowmen—old levy work beside newer shot—send arrows in high, hard arcs down upon the French ranks. Some of the English chew on scraps of salt pork or stale biscuit between volleys, jaws working as steadily as their bowstrings, knowing they may have no time for any other meal that day.

Amid the fray, Robert Dudley and his brothers Ambrose and Henry fight with valour on the battlefield, their swords gleaming as Robert rallies the English troops.

"Steady, lads! Show them what an English heart is made of!"

A French knight breaks through the line, his warhorse trampling the bodies of fallen soldiers. Herbert lunges forward, his blade striking true and unseating the knight. Around him, English pikemen surge, driving the French back with shouts of triumph.

Meanwhile, the Spanish infantry, clad in their distinctive breastplates and morions, press forward with unwavering determination. The Duke of Alba, his scarlet cape billowing, barks commands to his officers.

"Flank them! Drive their cavalry into the marsh!"

The French forces begin to falter under the combined pressure. A breach in their left flank allows the Spanish *tercios* to sweep in, their pikes devastating the French foot soldiers. The English, emboldened by the Spanish advance, surge forward, their cheers ringing out as they push the French into retreat.

A French cannon fires from a distant ridge, the ball carving a deadly path through the English ranks. Herbert narrowly dodges the blast and pulls a wounded soldier to safety. Gritting his teeth, he calls for the English artillery to return fire.

"Take that battery down!" he shouts. "Show them English iron!"

The cannonade thunders, earth shaking with each explosion. Spanish cavalry charge the French rear, their swords flashing as they cut through the panicked enemy. The French forces, overwhelmed and disorganized, begin to withdraw, their standards dipping and scattering.

As the sun lowers, the battlefield falls silent save for the groans of the wounded. Spanish and English soldiers stand together, bloodied but unbowed, their alliance proven on the fields of St Quentin.

On the ridge overlooking the battlefield, the Duke of Alba clasps William Herbert's forearm, a rare smile crossing his stern face.

"You fight well, Englishman."

Herbert, still catching his breath, smirks.

"And you Spaniards know how to win a war."

The two men stand together, their shared victory a testament to the strength of their alliance. Below, the soldiers tend to their wounded, their faces marked by exhaustion but also by pride. The war is not yet over, but the fields of St Quentin bear the scars of battle. They also bear the seeds of a partnership that will turn to enmity and reshape the balance of power in Europe.

25 August 1557

In a shuttered chamber off the courtyard of St Quentin, the air still smells of powder and sweat, the echo of victory fading into a harsher quiet. Pigeons wheel above the shattered rooftops, their wings clattering like a drumbeat of unease. A camp cook tips a cauldron, pouring out the last of barley-and-beef pottage into wooden bowls for wounded men propped against the walls, the steam briefly masking the stench of blood.

Philip waits in the shadow of a stone archway, his black doublet absorbing the heat, his hands clasped behind his back. He feels the charge of many crowns pressing at once—Spain, Naples, Sicily—and in all of them the same truth: France will not stay beaten for long. And in the weeks after St Quentin, victory hardened into calculation.

His gaze fixes on the Duke of Savoy as he approaches. The Duke's cloak is streaked with dust, his boots worn from the march. A soldier's bearing, yes, but Philip sees more: hesitation in his stride, doubt flickering at the edges of his resolve—the same caution Philip had marked in Savoy's letters. A man who courts Elizabeth with courtesy, when what is needed is iron.

As Savoy draws near, Philip's expression stiffens, all warmth stripped from his face. He measures him already against Elizabeth's pride, against her Protestant leanings, against France's reach. A match of kingdoms, not hearts—yet here stands a man still thinking as a suitor.

Savoy halts at the edge of shadow and bows, the grit of the courtyard crunching beneath his knee. Philip does not move, his eyes cold and steady, already pressing the weight of his expectations down upon him. With Mary childless and England's future uncertain, Philip feels time narrowing.

Philip speaks first, his tone clipped. "St Quentin was only a beginning. France will rise again. That is why England must be bound to us—through you. Elizabeth cannot be allowed to drift. Your marriage to her is not a sentiment. Your marriage is survival."

Savoy shifts uneasily. "I have made my suit, Sire. She listens, but gives no answer. She guards her independence."

Philip's jaw tightens. "Independence? This is not about her moods. France will not wait. You must press her—make her see what delay will cost. Without England, our cause falters. With her, we decide the future of Europe."

Savoy lowers his eyes, voice cautious. "I will try, but too much force may drive her away. She is not easily swayed by pressure."

Philip leans in, voice low, urgent. "This is not about winning her heart, Emmanuel. It is about securing her crown. England torn between Catholic and Protestant, France at the door—do you think she can stand alone? Make her see the truth. If persuasion fails, we will find another path."

The words hit hard. Savoy straightens, face set with reluctant resolve. "I understand. I will do what I must."

Philip's expression does not soften. "Good. Remember—this is no courtship. This is the future of Christendom. Go, and do not fail."

Savoy bows deeply, then departs, the load settling heavily on his shoulders. Philip remains beneath the arch, unmoving, his eyes on the horizon as if already measuring the battles to come.

Chapter 10
A Soldier Returns to a Changing Princess

7 September 1557

The grand stone walls of Hatfield seem to hold their breath as Elizabeth paces the long hall, her eyes cast downward in thought. Outside, the late-summer sun filters through the trees. The peace of the house feels fragile, as if one wrong word might shatter it. It had been a long time since she had seen Robert Dudley, her childhood friend and confidant.

As the heavy wooden door opens, Dudley enters the room. His face is weathered from months of campaigning, his eyes weary from the brutality of the French wars. His coat is streaked with dust, his features set like stone. He stands still for a moment, taking in the sight of Elizabeth, who had grown into a woman of immense strength, yet in his eyes he still could see the spark of the girl he once knew.

"Elizabeth."

"Robin."

Her heart had not fully let go of what they had shared—those dark months when both were prisoners in the Tower. The years had made them both more guarded, more aware of their roles in the world. She gestures for him to sit.

"It is good to see you back, despite the grim reason you were away. How are the wounds of France?"

A maid sets down a small table with a silver flagon of claret, two cups, and a plate of marchpane and spiced quince slices between them. Elizabeth pours for him herself, the wine dark as dried blood in the cup.

Dudley's thin smile fades as he sinks into a chair across from her. "The wounds of war? They are many, and some run deeper than others. We lost many good men. Some of the battles were relentless."

He lifts the cup, only to wet his lips, then lets it rest untouched—fingers tight around the stem.

"Tell me, Robin. Did you see much bloodshed? Were you in the thick of it?"

Dudley pauses. "I was in it, yes. St Quentin."

His mouth tightens. "They pressed us without mercy. We stood, because there was nothing else to do. In the end we prevailed—but at a price I still reckon with."

"Robin, I am sorry you had to witness it. I know how heavy the weight of battle can sit on a man. How did your brothers fare?"

He glances at her, then looks down. He blinks hard once, then wipes a tear from his eye. She pretends not to see. Gently, as if offering him firmer ground, she asks, "And Amy? How does she fare?"

Dudley's expression hardens, his gaze briefly drifting away from hers.

"Amy? She is well enough, I suppose. She has been in the country, away from court. You know she has never quite taken to the bustle of the palace."

"Is it as you expected? The life you both chose?"

"I suppose I did what I was expected to do. And Amy, well, she has her own life, far removed from my duties. I wonder sometimes if we truly know each other anymore."

"I have asked you here, Robin, because I need your advice on something important."

"What is it, Elizabeth?"

"It is about the Duke of Savoy. I am not blind—I know Philip wants me to marry him. To bind us tighter to Spain, to shore up England's place in Europe. He thinks it is the only way to keep us safe, the only shield we have against France."

The words hang between them.

"Philip? This would be one of his schemes."

Elizabeth looks away. "I have my doubts, Robin. But I cannot just dismiss what this marriage would mean. I know my brother-in-law's mind—he is convinced it is the only way to secure England's future."

Dudley rises from his chair and paces the room. "Of course he wants to secure Spain's future. Can you not see, Elizabeth? You are being used. This is not love or loyalty—it is Philip grasping for more power. To him, you are just a piece on the board. And this marriage? It is the move that puts England in his hands." He shakes his head and goes silent.

"Pray, go on."

"I know what is at stake—but listen to me. Your heart and your freedom are not coin to be spent. This marriage will not save England—it will chain you to Philip and his ambitions. And once you are bound, there is no breaking free. You are more than a means to an end."

Elizabeth's eyes search his face.

"I will make the decision. But I needed to hear your thoughts. I trust you, Robin. More than anyone else."

He nods. "Then, choose wisely, Elizabeth. The future of England—and your own heart—depend on it."

1 December 1557

On the Devon coast, the wind knifes in from the Channel, sharp with brine and iron. The *Falcon's Wake* pitches under a leaden sky, her sails sagging slightly as the crew adjusts course. Frost clings to the rigging. Ropes stiffen like frozen veins. The world smells of wet timber, tar, and salt. Below decks, a mess of salt cod and onions stews in a blackened pot, the fat thin and the smell strong; a boy breaks ship's biscuit with a mallet, knocking the weevils out before dropping the crumbs into the broth.

Francis Drake, not yet eighteen, stands at the tiller.

The master's hands are numb with cold. The boy fills in without complaint. Drake's raw-knuckled hands grip the worn wood with the tenacity of someone who understands how quickly life can shift underfoot.

He is small for a sailor, still coltish in build, but there is no mistaking the authority in his movements. His grey-green eyes, the colour of Channel water in fall to winter, scan the horizon with calm intent—and then, with a flash of something hotter, scan the world as if it ought to make room.

"Ease the foresail!" he calls over his shoulder. "We're dragging the leeward line. We bear two points to larboard and ride the swell smoother."

An older crewman grumbles, but the command is obeyed. No one argues with Drake anymore—not for rank, but because the boy is rarely wrong.

Beside him, Master Reeve, a broad-shouldered mariner with a wool cloak soaked through at the collar, casts him a sideways look.

"You'd make a fine mate if you learned to keep your mouth shut," he mutters, spitting over the rail. "Most lads your age think of women or dice. You look like you've buried both."

Drake does not answer at once. He pulls biscuit from his pouch and breaks off a piece. He chews it down hard, as if grinding his temper with his teeth.

His gaze stays fixed on the horizon, where a faint smudge marks the silhouette of a high-riding galleon, inching westward.

"Spanish," Drake says, more to the wind than Reeve. "Too heavy for Channel trade. She's fat with something—plate, coin, or men."

Reeve snorts. "Every sail puts you on edge these days. Ever since rumours started up about the French mustering near Calais, you've been watching the horizon as if it owes you rent."

Drake's eyes narrow. "It does," he says flatly. "It owes England rent."

Reeve lets out a short laugh that's swallowed by the wind. "Hear him. The Channel's been your tenant since you were in swaddling."

Drake's mouth twitches—almost a smile, almost a challenge. He shifts his weight, shoulders squared against the cold, and raises his voice again.

"Stand by to trim! If she comes closer, I want her in clear view. No hiding in mist. Not today."

A few men glance up from the rail, wary. The master starts to speak—then bites it off. Drake is not captain. Drake is not even a mate. But Drake speaks like a man who expects the sea to answer.

Reeve's voice drops, edged now. "She's not our business."

Drake keeps the tiller steady. "Everything afloat is our business," he says. "The sea doesn't belong to Spain because they pray louder."

Reeve leans nearer so the wind won't carry what follows. "And if she is Spanish, what then? You'll whistle her to stop? You'll board her with a prayer book and a knife?"

Drake turns his head just enough to meet Reeve's eyes. There is mischief there, and pride, and the first hard glint of appetite.

"If she strays close enough to count her guns," Drake says, "it would be rude not to count her cargo too."

Reeve's jaw tightens. "That's piracy."

Drake's gaze returns to the galleon, tracking her like a hound tracking scent. "It's practice," he answers. "And one day, it'll be policy."

For a moment the wind seems to sharpen around them. The *Falcon's Wake* rises, falls, shudders through a cold swell. Drake rides it with a sailor's instinct and a gambler's calm.

Below decks, someone begins a low, tuneless hum over the stewpot—old habit against hard weather. Above, Drake lifts his chin, tasting the brine like it's a promise.

Reeve watches him a beat longer.

"You keep talking like that," he says quietly, "and one day you'll shout your own name from a quay as if the world ought to clap."

Drake's lips part—something almost boyish, almost pleased.

"Why shouldn't it?" he says. Then he adds, without looking away from the mist-hung galleon: "If men are going to fear me, they may as well learn how to cheer too."

Reeve's expression flattens. "Cheering makes noise."

Drake gives a small, reckless shrug. "Noise is useful. It makes cowards move. It makes kings listen."

The galleon slips slightly in the mist. Drake tracks it, grip on the tiller sure and silent—then, as if he can't help himself, raises his voice again, louder than necessity.

"Keep your eyes up! Let her see us watching!"

Reeve flinches, just a fraction, and spits again. "You're going to get us killed for pride."

Drake's knuckles whiten on the worn wood. "Maybe," he mutters. "But if I go, I'll take a mast or two with me."

The mist thickens as they veer towards the Plymouth inlet. A bell tolls faintly from the harbour mouth. Drake's gaze stays fixed across the sea—towards Calais, towards Antwerp, towards the smudge of Spain moving like a dark thought on the water.

"Someday," he murmurs, as if confiding it to the wind alone, "they'll hear my name and the docks will fill. Churches will empty. And every man will swear he saw me first."

Reeve does not respond—or chooses not to.

The *Falcon's Wake* cleaves through the cold water in rhythmic strides, but Drake's mind is already ashore: a quay, a crowd, a story told too loudly, and the dangerous sweetness of being believed.

21 January 1558

A rare winter storm hits Hampton Court Palace like an omen. The wind shrieks down the Thames, rattling window panes and slamming rain against the glass in sheets. Queen Mary sits not upon her throne, but in a plain, high-backed chair near the hearth—pale, jaundiced, and swaddled in layers of velvet, though her skin feels cold as stone beneath it. On a small table by her elbow, a silver cup of spiced wine has cooled beside a little bowl of thin capon broth and two slices of manchet bread gone hard at the edges. Even warmth in a cup turns her stomach now.

Her eyes, once sharp with resolve and now rimmed with fatigue, stare into the fire as if hoping the flames might burn away her sorrow.

Her hands tremble in her lap. Her knuckles are yellowed, her cheeks sunken, and the rings on her fingers no longer fit her. The physicians called it a "distemper of the liver" or dropsy, or melancholy—but she knows better. What had begun as swelling months ago now is claiming her breath. She is dying. Bit by bit. And England, her England, dies with her.

The door creaks open. Lord Chancellor Nicholas Heath enters, removing his cap. His expression bears the weight of too many messages like this.

"Your Majesty," he bows. "Although we and our Spanish allies prevailed at St Quentin last year—we lost Calais on 7 January. The news reached us only days ago."

Mary's breath catches. A sharp gasp escapes her as her hand flies to her chest to grasp her crucifix tightly. She turns towards him, stunned—as if slapped. The thunder outside seems to crash in time with her heartbeat.

"No," she whispers while shaking her head.

"The Duke of Guise took the fortress," Heath continues reluctantly. "Lord Wentworth surrendered the town. The keys of Calais are in French hands once more. Sir Anthony Aucher died of his wounds shortly after."

Mary shuts her eyes as if darkness might dull the ache she dare not name. She leans back into the chair, not with ease but with the weight of someone seeking to vanish into it, to fold herself into the wood and velvet and be forgotten. Her hands grip the carved arms and her jaw tightens—not from physical pain, though that too had become a constant companion—but from the deeper wound festering inside her.

It is not the ache of flesh that breaks her—it is the silence after hope has gone. The child that never came. The husband who never stayed. The prayers that never rose past the ceiling. Something in her chest twists, and she bites the inside of her cheek, forcing the sorrow down where no one could see it. Not now. Not ever again.

"Calais—my father's jewel," she whispers. "Held since the days of Edward III. Lost under my crown."

Her breath is short, as if the air refuses to enter her lungs.

"Is there anything left?" she murmurs, more to herself than Heath. "Anything that still belongs to England?"

"Yes, Your Majesty. Faith still belongs to England. And the memory of a queen who would not bend to her enemies."

The storm outside still rages.

He continues, "The land still holds her churches. Her prayers still rise. And your courage—your example—will endure, long after borders change hands."

He pauses, then adds more gently, "A crown weighs less than a conscience, Majesty. And yours remains unburdened by cowardice."

The fire crackles, throwing orange light over her waxy skin. She looks not like a queen but a ghost.

"I am shrinking," she says. "My limbs swell, but I grow smaller each day." She pauses. "My face." She touches her cheek with trembling fingers. "My skin—it yellows like old parchment. Even the mirror flinches."

Heath shifts uneasily but says nothing. What comfort could words give now?

"I shall never see Philip again," she says suddenly.

"Majesty—"

"He no longer writes. No more than what duty demands. And even those are stale. There was a time I clung to his every word like scripture. But now, silence. Spain has claimed him, and England has nothing left to offer him—not land, nor son, nor youth."

She turns her face towards the window. Lightning flashes across the pane.

"I gave him everything. And when that failed, I gave him my body—twice swollen with false hope. My womb lies empty as my court."

She falls silent for a long moment. Rain pounds the windows like fists. Mary's shoulders sag.

"I will always love him," she whispers. "I no longer know whether I loved a man—or a promise."

The fire hisses as another log collapses into ash.

Heath remains still. There are no proclamations to draft, no edicts to announce. Just a queen fading, and the crown growing heavier by the day.

He bows, not as to a monarch, but as to a woman who had lost more than history would remember.

4 July 1558

The summer heat barely penetrates the high stone walls of the Coudenberg Palace in Brussels. Inside the audience chamber, the air is still, shadowed, and cool—like a crypt awaiting its revelation.

Philip, draped in sombre black velvet, sits beneath a carved canopy. His posture is precise, but his silence bears weight: the iron stillness of a monarch tempered by empire, war, and solitude.

Before him stands Thomas Thirlby, Bishop of Ely, envoy of Queen Mary and a man visibly strained. Sweat clings to his brow—not from the climate, but from the pressure. Thirlby fears what may come for England if Protestant hands seize the crown.

"Your Majesty," he begins, voice taut, "Her Majesty bids that you know her strength wanes. She has not risen from her bed in over a fortnight. Her physicians speak of fever and wasting. She coughs blood."

Philip does not move, though his fingers press slightly into the carved wood of the armrest.

"The court at St James' Palace is anxious. The Lords measure each breath. And now—" Thirlby hesitates, "...there is open talk—dangerous talk—of the Lady Elizabeth."

A flicker crosses Philip's gaze.

"Princess Elizabeth. Has she been named successor?"

"Not formally. But her name is no longer whispered. It is spoken aloud—even among the Queen's own household."

Silence folds around the chamber.

Philip leans back slightly, voice quiet, contemplative.

"She is her father's child—not her sister's. Elizabeth owes no blood to Spain, no sacred bond to me. That is the danger—not her heresy, but her independence."

Thirlby nods, uneasily. "She is not openly hostile to Your Majesty," he says.

"Hostile, nonetheless," replies Philip.

"But she is cautious. She sees foreign crowns as threats, not partners. And she remembers the fires of Smithfield."

"As do I," Philip murmurs. "That chapter is closed. Yet if England must turn from Rome, let it not also turn from reason."

He rises, slow and deliberate. The room stirs around him, as if his very movement bends the atmosphere.

"If Elizabeth ascends the throne unmarried, we lose her to the winds. She will make her own course. I know her. And England will drift with her—perhaps irreversibly."

He walks to the tall windows overlooking the rooftops of Brussels, where the tiles burn gold in the low country sun. Somewhere in the distance, the Angelus bells toll.

"I had hoped the Duke of Savoy might secure her hand. A Catholic prince, loyal, and of my family. Not to control her, but to steady her. But she delays. She has doubts."

Thirlby lowers his eyes. "She delays all suitors, Your Majesty. Spanish, French, suitors from the Empire. She plays the clock like a queen already."

A dry smile touches Philip's lips. "She plays her game well."

But it fades quickly, replaced by steel.

"And yet, when Mary dies, Elizabeth rises. That much is clear under English law. If that must be, then I would rather she rise with Spain's goodwill than with France's cunning."

He turns to face Thirlby fully now, his voice deeper.

"You understand this better than most. If England becomes a Protestant stronghold again—and joins hands with France—it could serve as a base for enemies of the faith, and worse, a port for rebellion."

He steps forward.

"Already, Calvinist heresy stirs in the Netherlands. Already, my governors plead for more men, more ships. If England, untethered, becomes a haven for rebels and heretics, the Netherlands will burn. And Spain will bleed. We will not tolerate that for one minute."

Thirlby swallows hard.

"I fear it too, Majesty. May God help us if she makes an alliance with France or gives harbour to the enemies of Rome."

Philip nods once.

"Then we must act with caution. Support her? Perhaps. But only if she understands Spain comes as a friend, not foe. Let her know that Philip of Spain does not seek her throne—but he does seek her trust. And that trust may yet be built—perhaps through marriage."

"To the Duke?"

"If not him, then someone else, a prince who answers to both altar and crown. One who can keep England anchored in the right winds."

He pauses.

"Tell your Lords: Spain does not fear Elizabeth. But it does fear a queen unbound—adrift, dangerous, and determined to chart her own world."

He gestures to the chamberlain.

"Wine for His Excellency. He has earned it."

"Many thanks, Your Majesty."

"Take it with you. You have my leave, Your Excellency."

Thirlby bows. As he is led from the room, the weight of the world follows him.

Philip remains behind, still in the golden shafts of sunlight. He turns to the window again. His voice is quiet—meant only for the stones.

"Mary is dying. And with her, the last thread tying England to me."

He presses his signet ring against the table's polished wood, leaving a faint indentation. Then, with deliberate gravity, he makes the sign of the cross and lowers himself into the chair. A single candle burns beside him. Beside it stands Don Diego de Ayala, one of his most trusted secretaries.

"Don Diego, write a letter."

Ayala fetches a parchment, quill and ink. He sits, then dips the quill in ink, nodding once in readiness. He holds the parchment steady as Philip begins to dictate.

"*To the Princess Elizabeth Tudor,*" Philip says softly. "*Daughter of the late King Henry, and sister to Her Majesty Queen Mary, sovereign of England.*"

Philip stares into the flickering candle flame. His voice holds the chill of diplomacy—controlled, and carefully precise, much like a man placing pieces on a distant chessboard.

"*It is with a heavy heart that I write, knowing the afflictions that now beset Her Majesty. Though she is my wife, I cannot be blind to the whispers in her court, nor deaf to the name that is spoken with growing clarity—yours.*"

He pauses. Ayala waits.

"*Should the hand of Providence raise you to the throne, I write not to flatter, but to counsel. Spain has ever sought peace with England—not as master to servant, but as brother to sister. It was my hope that the bond forged by my marriage to Her Majesty would hold—and that this loyalty might extend even to the Duke of Savoy, even after Her Majesty's days are ended. I would advise you to consider the Duke as a suitable King Consort. England must not forget the order I offered. The peace I preserved."*

Ayala's quill moves with practiced silence. Philip's gaze drifts beyond the flame, towards shadows only he could see.

"*The world shifts swiftly. France stirs again. The heretics grow bold. But alliances are not always written in blood. They may yet be written in ink.*"

He rises and walks to the shuttered window. The Brussels dusk is quiet, but the wind carries Europe's tension through the creaking panes.

"*You are young. You are clever,*" he continues. "*And though we are of different minds in faith, we are not of different minds in governance. You value order, as I do. You understand the cost of rebellion, as I do.*"

He turns from the dusk, back towards Ayala.

"Don Diego, this letter may take time to reach her, but if she opens it, she will know one thing: that I am watching. She will know that I am not her enemy—unless she makes me so."

He returns to the desk, takes the quill from Ayala's hand, and in his own script signs the bottom:

"*Philip.*"

He presses his ring into the soft wax. A clean seal. A careful offering. Only then does he reach for his cup, taking a slow mouthful of watered Spanish wine, more to rinse the taste of decision from his mouth than to slake any thirst.

"Deliver it through Antwerp," he says. "Use a merchant of Antwerp if you must. No Spanish sigils. No court markings."

"At your command, Your Majesty," Ayala replies. He bows, then withdraws—gloved hands cradling the letter like a secret flame.

Philip stands alone again in the chamber, one candle flickering low behind him, and all of Europe in play before him.

2 August 1558

Late afternoon. The summer heat clings to the high walls of Hatfield like a wet cloak. In the private solarium, the windows stand open, but the breeze is dry—carrying the scent of scorched grass, lavender, and distant thunder. Inside, Princess Elizabeth stands by a long oak table, reading the same parchment for the third time.

On the table lie the leavings of a light collation: a trencher with a crust of manchet and a silver cup of cooled hippocras. Her fair red hair is pulled back from her brow, her fingers trembling not with fear—but with fury bound behind the mask of restraint.

At her side, her friend and adviser Master William Cecil, thirty-eight, waits in silence. His hands are folded behind his back, his posture still, though his eyes flick once to the broken seal on the floor—a letter from a king to a woman not yet crowned.

Elizabeth lowers the letter.

"So," she says. "He dares write to me?"

"He is a king," Cecil replies. "He dares what he pleases—even when it is unwise."

She turns away and paces, the parchment still clenched in one hand. The wax—plain, discreet—lies broken at her feet. Her free hand strays to the cup by habit; she lifts it, tastes the spiced wine gone warm and dull, and sets it down again with a faint look of disgust that has nothing to do with the drink.

"He calls me '*clever*,'" she says, voice clipped. "As though I were a favored dog for not biting the hand that once burned my country in war."

Cecil allows himself the faintest of smiles. "That may be the most honest sentence in the letter."

She whirls on him, eyes flashing.

"He cloaks it in diplomacy, but every line drips with warning. '*England must not forget the order I offered. The peace I preserved.*' As though his Spanish peace ever sat comfortably on English shoulders."

"Your Highness," Cecil says, calmly, "this is not an alliance—it is a maneuver. He knows the Queen is dying. He senses the court shifting. This is his opening move in a new game."

"A game with me as his piece?" she snaps. "He thinks I might be handled—if not through fear, then through flattery. But he forgets I am no Mary."

She turns again.

"He writes of the Duke of Savoy. Still pressing that tired match. A Catholic prince, cloaked in reason, sent to anchor England once more beneath the Pope's heel."

"And yet," Cecil replies carefully, "he does not threaten. Not directly. That alone is telling."

"It tells me he fears what comes next," Elizabeth says. "He fears me."

"He fears what you represent," Cecil corrects. "A Protestant sovereign. An English crown untethered from Rome—and from Spain. And should you rise unmarried, he sees the danger multiply. If you ally elsewhere—France, or worse, no one at all—Spain loses its footing entirely."

Elizabeth stops pacing. She turns towards him, calmer now.

"What would you have me do, Master Cecil? Send him thanks for his ghostly overture? Assure him that I will be good and gentle and obedient?"

"No, Your Highness," Cecil says. "I would have you do nothing. Not yet. Let his message go unanswered. Let him wait with bated breath as England awaits. Your silence is your answer—for now."

Elizabeth regards him for a long moment, then moves to the hearth, stirring the embers with the tip of the poker, sparks flaring as her thoughts turn inward.

"He remembers Mary as his ally. He forgets Mary bled for him. Lost Calais for him. She is dying with his cause wrapped around her like a winding sheet. And now he expects I will step into her place."

She looks down at the letter. Then folds it, carefully, and slides it into the cover of a leather-bound book on the table.

"Let it be recorded. That while I wore no crown, kings still sent me warnings in the dark—because they knew the light was coming."

Cecil bows his head.

Elizabeth continues, "And may they tremble all the more when it arrives."

17 November 1558

In the wee hours of the morning, Mary's bedchamber at St James' Palace is dimly lit, the heavy curtains drawn against the cold, grey light of the London autumn. A fire crackles in the hearth, its warmth failing to chase away the pervasive chill. The smell of beeswax candles burning at all hours pervades the air, mingled with vinegar and herbs used by physicians to ward off pestilence.

Quiet footsteps echo on the boards as ladies-in-waiting move about in hushed tones, adjusting linens or offering her sips of broth or cordial. At the foot of the bed, a priest keeps vigil, ready to murmur prayers for her soul.

The Queen of England lies in her grand bed, propped against pillows. The ornate canopy and layers of embroidered blankets swallow her small gaunt frame. Her face, pale and drawn, is marked by the ravages of illness and sorrow. In her hands she clutches a rosary.

Beside her stands a worried Dr Caius as he checks her pulse, his long, scholarly fingers moving with a deliberate calm.

Mary's breath comes shallow and uneven. Her voice is faint but clear, still carrying the resolve of a queen who had spent her life navigating the tempests of faith and faction. Her eyes, sunken yet sharp, are fixed on a gilded frame propped on a small table near the bed. The portrait of Philip, her absent husband, stares back at her, his painted features as distant and cold as the man himself.

Her voice, barely more than a whisper, carries her words: "I should have sent for my sister." She pauses, her breath catching as though each word costs her strength. Her eyes remain fixed on the portrait, fingers feebly clutching the rosary. "I did not want her to see me. I wanted her to remember me as I was...not this pale echo of a Tudor queen."

Dr Caius leans closer, his voice gentle. "Your Majesty, shall I summon Lady Elizabeth?"

Mary's lips tremble, a ghost of a bitter smile crossing them. "No. I must make peace with God alone. She will be queen after I am gone," she murmurs, her tone heavy with resignation. "That is my command. She will need guidance, though I fear she will not heed it."

One of the ladies-in-waiting, emboldened by Mary's rare display of reflection, steps forward.

"Your Majesty, you have done all you could for the faith. The Lord will judge you kindly."

Mary's eyes flick towards her, glassy yet piercing. "Judge me kindly?" She lets out a weak laugh, little more than a dry rasp. "The fires I lit. Will they count as salvation or as damnation? I shall find out soon enough."

Her gaze returns to Philip's portrait. Her fingers reach towards it, trembling with weakness. "I loved him," she whispers, her voice breaking. "More than he deserved. He only loved the idea of me." Her words falter, her breath becoming more laboured.

Dr Caius places a hand on her wrist, his expression grave. "Your Majesty, you must rest."

Mary shakes her head, a rare flash of determination flickering in her sunken eyes. Her voice softens, as though speaking to herself. "When I am dead and opened," each word laboured yet deliberate, "you shall find Philip—and find Calais—engraved in my heart."

***

The morning mist lingers in the Great Park at Hatfield, clinging to the bare branches of the trees and the dew-laden grass. Beneath a great oak tree, its twisted limbs reaching towards the heavens, Princess Elizabeth sits alone. Wrapped in a dark coat, her hat perched at a jaunty angle, she reads a Latin book, her lips silently forming the ancient words. An apple in her hand gleams with morning dew as she takes a deliberate bite, her gaze drifting momentarily to the horizon.

The stillness is broken by the sound of hoofbeats. From the distant path, five men approach, their horses kicking up soft clouds of dirt after a hard ride from London. At the front of the group rides William Cecil, already carrying the weight of responsibility in his sharp eyes. His riding mantle lifts in the breeze as he guides the party forward.

Elizabeth, hearing the approach, looks up, shielding her eyes from the pale sunlight filtering through the branches.

"How now, Master Cecil?" she calls.

The riders halt a few yards away. Cecil dismounts first. He draws near, his features composed and careful. He bows and, from within his cloak, withdraws a small object. The half-eaten apple sinks slowly in her hand, the bright flesh browning in the chill air as the weight of the object presses into her palm.

Elizabeth's fingers curl around it instinctively. She recognises it immediately: Queen Mary's coronation ring. Her smile fades as her mind grasps the unspoken message. She looks up into Cecil's eyes, and he gives a single, sombre nod.

"Dead," he murmurs, his voice barely above a whisper. "Your...Majesty."

Elizabeth freezes, her breath catching in her throat. Her fingers tighten around the ring, her gaze dropping to the ground. The weight of the moment is on her, but only for an instant. Slowly, she rises to her feet, her voice trembling.

"I am queen," she whispers, testing the words. "I...am...queen?" Then, stronger: "The Queen! I am the Queen!"

The realization sweeps over her like a wave, and something breaks open in her. With sudden vigour, she hurls the apple into the distance, watching it tumble into the wet grass. It lands with a dull thud among the fallen acorns, a common fruit cast aside at the moment a crown, at last, is offered. Then, with a laugh that carried both triumph and relief, she pulls her hat from her head and flings it into the air.

"WHO...SHALL...ME...**LET**!" she cries, her voice echoing throughout all of the Great Park.

The men behind Cecil exchange glances, some startled, others moved by the display of passion. Elizabeth turns and drops to her knees, her arms outstretched towards the heavens. Her face, illuminated by the pale sunlight breaking through the trees, is a mixture of joy, humility, and awe.

In a voice both reverent and commanding, she proclaims, *"A Domino factum est istud et est mirabile in oculis nostris!"* Her Latin rings out with clarity. Then, switching to English, she declares, "This is the Lord's doing, and it is marvellous in our eyes!"

The men remove their hats, bowing their heads in deference to the woman before them. Cecil approaches, kneeling beside her.

"Your Majesty," he says softly, his voice steady. "England has her queen. And England shall have her future."

Elizabeth rises slowly, brushing the dirt from her knees. She turns to Cecil, her eyes bright with determination.

"Come, Master Cecil. There is much to be done."

She quickly strides forward towards the manor house, the great oak standing sentinel behind her as if bearing witness to her transformation. The men mount their horses and follow, the horses' hoofbeats quickening to match the pace of England's new queen.

1 December 1558

The winter dusk presses against the high windows of the Coudenberg Palace, muting the last streaks of light over Brussels. Inside Philip's audience chamber, the air is close and solemn, warmed only by a brazier glowing near the hearth. Candleflames tremble along a carved walnut table where Philip sits motionless, his black velvet sleeves pooled like shadows at his wrists.

Before him, a marble chessboard lies mid-game, the pieces frozen in quiet opposition. Across from him, a hooded cleric studies the board, his face veiled by the fall of his cowl. Neither man speaks. Only the faint crackle of the brazier and the distant toll of St Gudula's bells disturbs the silence.

Philip's hand hovers over the chessboard, his sharp eyes locked on the intricate arrangement of pieces.

The heavy oak door creaks open, breaking the stillness. Don Gonzalo Pérez, a royal secretary, enters the room and bows. His face is solemn, his hands clasped tightly before him.

"Your Majesty," Pérez begins, his voice heavy with sorrow. "I regret to tell you that your wife, Queen Mary...is dead. I am sorry."

Philip's hand freezes above the chessboard. He sits back slowly, his blue eyes squinting as the weight of the news settles over him. For a moment, the room is silent save for the crackling fire. He exhales, his tone devoid of passion, laced instead with calculated detachment.

"I...feel a reasonable regret for her death, Don Gonzalo," he says at last, his gaze falling on the chessboard. "She was a faithful wife, and she fulfilled her duty. May God receive her soul." He crosses himself. Then the clergyman and Pérez do likewise. A servant, thinking to offer comfort, moves towards the wine; Philip stays him with a slight movement of his hand and does not drink.

He pauses, his lips tightening before he continues. "Now Elizabeth is queen." A faint smirk plays at the corner of his mouth. "Not married, but queen. I am satisfied."

Philip reaches for the chessboard, his fingers closing around the queen piece. He holds it up, examining its intricate carving in the flickering light. The hooded clergyman leans back, his face still shrouded, remaining silent.

Philip rolls the piece between his fingers, his gaze fixed somewhere far beyond the board.

"The Queen is dead," he murmurs to himself with a slight smile. "Long live the Queen. The...Queen."

Chapter 11
The Coronation of Elizabeth

15 January 1559

Westminster Abbey stands washed in winter light, its great Gothic vaults lifting like stone wings towards the heavens. Sun pours through stained glass in bands of red and gold, breaking across ancient pillars and the bowed heads of peers, prelates, and citizens packed tightly into the nave. Incense hangs heavy—sweet, resinous—mingling with wool, candle smoke, and damp January cloaks.

The great bell tolls. Once. Twice. The sound rolls through the Abbey like a verdict.

At the heart of the crossing, upon the raised dais, Elizabeth sits on the Chair of Estate set before the Coronation Chair. It is the seat for the opening rites—near enough to be seen, not yet the ancient chair that waits behind her. Beneath it is the ancient Stone of Scone, a mute witness to centuries of kingship. The regalia awaits in solemn order—orb, sceptre, crown—golden weight poised to become burden.

Near at hand stands Owen Oglethorpe, Bishop of Carlisle, robed for the rite as Canterbury's see still stands vacant.

A hush tightens as the first public question is put—not poetry, not confession, but law and vow.

Oglethorpe's voice carries, formal and unwavering.

"Madam, will you grant and keep, and by your oath confirm to your people of England, the laws and customs to them granted by the Kings of England, your lawful and religious predecessors—and namely the laws, customs, and franchises granted to the clergy and to the people by King Edward, your lawful predecessor?"

Elizabeth's head lifts. Her face is composed; her voice, when it comes, is clear enough to reach the far arches.

"I grant and promise so to do."

A second question follows, the shape of it as old as the Coronation Chair.

"Will you keep peace and godly agreement entirely, according to your power, to the Church of God and to all the people?"

"I will keep it."

And then the third—hardest, because it binds her not to applause but to judgment.

"Will you to your power cause law, justice, and discretion, in mercy and truth, to be executed in all your judgments?"

"I will."

No flourish. No personal homily. The Abbey does not want a speech; it wants a sovereign bound.

Elizabeth rises and goes to the altar. Before the sacred table she kneels, and there, with her hand set to the book, she swears the oath in the sight of God and the realm. The words are not for drama. They are for record—for the day her enemies will insist she never meant them.

She rises to sit in the Coronation Chair. There she is to be anointed and clothed, hidden for a time beneath the canopy. The liturgy moves like a river cut deep into stone: prayer, blessing, the solemn anointing that makes even a crowned head feel suddenly human. When she is vested, the cloth of gold and the stole settle on her shoulders with a quiet finality—like a door closing behind her.

Then the Crown of State is lifted.

For a heartbeat, all of Westminster seems to forget to breathe.

The circlet descends onto her flame-coloured hair. The Abbey holds the moment as if it might crack. The sceptre is placed in her hand; the orb follows—weighty not only with gold, but with expectation and the long memory of England.

"God save Queen Elizabeth!"

The cry breaks forth—first near the dais, then rolling outward from choir to nave, from stone to street.

"God save the Queen!"

Bells answer bells. Beyond the west doors, London takes up the sound. In Westminster Hall, spits turn; the smell of roasting beef and capons rides the damp air.

As the choir lifts the *Te Deum*, Elizabeth settles in the chair. The crown sits steadier now—not lighter, never that, but fixed. Her gaze goes forward, not seeking anyone's face for reassurance.

Below the dais, Robert Dudley remains head bowed, still as carved oak—present, but careful not to claim the moment.

Elizabeth does not look at him.

She looks ahead, into the long corridor of days that will demand more than any fine words ever could.

23 January 1559

A private chamber in Hampton Court Palace is warm and intimate. A fire crackles in the stone hearth and tapestries hang on the walls to ward off the chill of the late evening.

Elizabeth, in a richly embroidered gown, sits on a cushioned chair near the fire. Beside her stands William Cecil, ever composed and calculating, and Master Francis Walsingham—one of the returning Marian exiles now seeking place and purpose—still more hopeful courtier than the future hardened intelligence man.

Walsingham bows before the Queen.

"Your Majesty, I am elated to be back in my home country to serve my Protestant sovereign."

Elizabeth tilts her head slightly, a glimmer of amusement in her eyes. "So long abroad—and yet you've come home. My sister would have burned you. Your diligence and your diplomatic skills are known to us. Master Walsingham, be assured we shall find you a future position in my government."

Walsingham straightens, his face alight with sincerity. "My fellow Protestant exiles were in earnest prayer for you, Your Majesty. Some even composed a song in your honour."

Elizabeth's brow lifts, intrigued. "A song? Spirit," she says to Cecil—using the pet name she so playfully gave him. "You know about this?"

Cecil stands at ease beside her, a rare smile crossing his lips. "Indeed, Your Majesty. It is not without wit."

Elizabeth claps her hands lightly, leaning forward. "Well, out with it then. I would hear this tribute."

Walsingham and Cecil exchange a glance, and then, to Elizabeth's delight, they both begin:

"The bells of England tolled with dread,
As smoke and fire rose high;
The faithful knelt, the faithful fled,
Beneath a darkened sky.
The pyres burned, their prayers grew faint,
Yet hope was not bereft,
When they with violence were burnt to death,
We prayed to God for our Elizabeth!"

Elizabeth laughs. "A witty tune indeed! That is a tune I can follow." She rises to her feet and, with a playful twirl, sings in a lilting voice, "We prayed to God for our Elizabeth!"

She stops abruptly, her tone turning solemn as she adds, "Walsingham, I shall call you—if you'll bear it—my 'Moor,' and Cecil, my Spirit, pray for my subjects and myself."

Elizabeth turns, and with deliberate grace kneels on a richly embroidered cushion by the fire. Folding her hands, she raises her eyes to the heavens, her voice soft but fervent as she begins to pray.

"Stretch forth, O Lord most mighty, defend me from my enemies, that they never prevail against me. Give me, O Lord, the assistance of Your Spirit, and comfort of Your grace, truly to know You, entirely to love You, and assuredly to trust in You. Grant this, O merciful Father, for Jesus Christ's sake, our only Mediator and Advocate. Amen."

Walsingham and Cecil, moved by the moment, bow their heads and reply in unison, "Amen."

The room falls silent for a beat, the crackling fire the only sound. Then Cecil, ever practical, speaks with a hopeful smile. "Surely God will never let our enemies prevail! And may God send our mistress a husband and by him a son, that we may hope our posterity shall have a masculine succession."

Still kneeling, Elizabeth stiffens. She lowers her gaze from heaven to the fire, its flickering flames reflected in her piercing eyes. Rising slowly, she turns to Cecil, her face a mask of calm.

"Master Cecil," she says coolly, "pray let us not burden the Almighty with too many requests at once."

26 January 1559

Candlelight flickers in the corner, throwing uneven light across the stone walls of Philip's private chamber at the palace in Brussels. The room is plain—just a desk stacked with letters and a table holding a chessboard mid-game. He paces the room. The fire crackles softly in the hearth.

Philip pauses in his pacing. His right foot gives a muted throb—sharp enough to make him halt, faint enough that he wonders if he imagined it. He shifts his weight, dismisses the sensation, and resumes his slow circuit of the chamber, his brows drawn in thought.

He reads the letter again.

"*Your Majesty's favour towards me has ever been a matter of the greatest honour...*"

It is Emmanuel Philibert of Savoy, still pressing his suit for Elizabeth. Philip exhales through his nose—half sigh, half irritation—and moves to the firelight to read more clearly.

"*...the silence of that court leads me to fear that my suit is little regarded...*"

Another jolt stabs the joint of his big toe—hot, sudden, needling. Philip stiffens, glances down with a frown. His boot feels tighter than it did this morning, as though some invisible hand were squeezing bone against leather.

He forces himself to continue reading, but his eyes flick briefly towards the empty wall where Charles V's cane once hung during the old emperor's convalescences in Brussels. A memory surfaces—his father grimacing as he lowered himself into a chair, muttering about "the cruel little devils that gnaw at a king's feet."

Philip sets his jaw and pushes the thought away.

He puts the letter aside and looks at the chessboard. His hand hovers over the king piece, its golden crown catching the light. Slowly, he lifts it from the board. His gaze shifts to the queen piece—dark wood, intricate, elegant. He picks it up as well, holding both between his fingers as though weighing two nations.

A flicker of intent passes across his face.

Then—another spike of pain. Sharper. He inhales sharply, the pieces clacking together in his grip. He holds still, ignoring the sudden warmth blooming in his toe. He will not limp. He will not sit.

England must be bound to me.

He sets the king and queen together on the same square, their bases touching. For a moment he regards them, immovable, composed—everything he himself must appear to be.

With a sharp breath, he moves to the writing desk. The pain follows him, pulsing like a tiny ember trapped beneath his skin. Pulling a sheet of parchment towards him, he dips his quill. The scratch of the quill fills the room as he writes.

Bound to me.

He adjusts his foot under the table. The motion sends a shock up his leg. He clenches his jaw until the ache subsides.

When he finishes, he holds the letter to the candlelight. His voice is low as he reads his draft:

"*My dear friend Elizabeth, it would be for the stability of Christendom if our former amity were strengthened...I beseech you to consider me as your devoted...husband...*"

His voice trails off. A tremor of uncertainty flickers in his eyes—whether from the words or the sudden, traitorous flare of heat in his foot he cannot say.

His glance drifts back to the chessboard. The paired pieces stand like a prophecy. Yet beneath the table, his toe throbs again, harder, humiliatingly alive. A king's body should obey him. Not betray him.

He ignores it, dips the quill again, and signs with controlled flourish:

"*Your friend forever, Philip.*"

The ink is still drying when the next jolt of pain forces him—just once—to grip the edge of the desk. He inhales, steadying himself until the room settles. No servant must ever see this. Not yet.

He sands the letter, folds it, seals it.

"Check," he murmurs, though the word comes tight. He stands—carefully, deliberately—and calls for a courier. Even that small movement sends discomfort spiraling up from his foot.

He straightens his spine and lifts his chin. The candlelight catches the determination in his expression.

"Perhaps, my dear Elizabeth," he whispers, "this time, it shall be...mate."

But as the courier departs, Philip remains standing a moment longer than needed, eyes fixed on the chessboard—king and queen joined—while beneath his boot a slow, burning ache gnaws with the promise of many years to come.

2 February 1559

The audience chamber in Hampton Court Palace is colder than it looks. Though the hearths are stoked and tapestries line the walls, a winter damp hangs in the air, settling into the joints of the older courtiers and making the younger ones all the stiffer. Still, the room is packed—nobles, ambassadors, and ministers gathered shoulder to shoulder, speaking in low tones while waiting for the Queen.

Pages move quietly among the press with tall cups of warmed hippocras and little trenchers of candied almonds and caraway comfits, but most of the courtiers are too intent on the Spaniard's errand to do more than pick at the sweets. The steam from the spiced wine hangs faintly in the cold air, a thin comfort against the February damp.

The hush tightens as Elizabeth enters. She does not sweep in theatrically, but walks with controlled grace. The crown rests atop her red hair like it belongs there. She ascends the dais and takes her seat without a word, her posture straight but not stiff.

Her eyes move across the hall—calculating, calm, not unkind, but never casual. She knows how to hold a room. Her hands rest lightly on the arms of the throne as she nods once towards the waiting figure before her.

Don Gómez Suárez de Figueroa, Count of Feria, the Spanish ambassador to England, advances. He bows with practiced elegance, his cloak brushing the polished floor. His heavily-embroidered black doublet with a laced, stiff collar accents the unmistakable opulence of the Spanish court. He does not look up immediately—he knows the weight of ceremony here, and he uses it well.

"Your Majesty," he begins, his English words tinged with a Castilian accent, practiced like a courtly blade. "I bring the warm regards of His Catholic Majesty, Philip of Spain, and assurances of continued amity between our crowns."

Elizabeth's face remains composed. Only the faintest tilt of her head suggests curiosity—or calculation. "We are always pleased to hear from His Majesty. Though I confess, your arrival is...timely."

At the far side of the chamber, William Cecil stands with arms folded. Beside him, Master Nicholas Bacon watches even more closely, saying nothing, but noting everything.

Feria straightens, offering a respectful nod. "It is an honour to stand once more in Your Majesty's presence. England is fortunate to be guided by such grace and resolve at a time when so many thrones across Europe sit uneasily."

He pauses, as if weighing his next words carefully.

"His Majesty sends not only his greetings, but his admiration—and his confidence in your rule. Rest assured, Your Majesty, His Most Catholic Majesty King Philip supports you in every way, and he will maintain your right to the Crown of England."

Elizabeth's eyes tighten with amusement, a faint smile playing at the edge of her mouth. Rising from her throne, she steps forward, her voice cutting through the murmurs of the court like a blade.

"Indeed! Is that what His Majesty thinks? Rest assured, Your Excellency, I thank my people, and not your master—my royal brother-in-law—for the crown I wear!"

A murmur of approval ripples through the gathered courtiers. Elizabeth's sharp gaze silences them as she raises a parchment high for all to see. She flattens the parchment with her palm, then lifts it again—her claim, not Spain's—before the court.

"And now, Your Excellency, I have an announcement to make which you shall carry to my royal brother-in-law."

The court falls silent, every eye fixed on the Queen.

Elizabeth holds the parchment, the letter from Philip, aloft. "My lords, this letter says my brother-in-law, the King of Spain, has a notion to marry me and so become King of England again."

A gasp ripples through the room, but Elizabeth's wry smile deepens.

"England and Spain have a peaceful relationship that I hope lasts for decades, even centuries. But I marry Philip?" She lets the question hang in the air.

Elizabeth raises her voice, her tone playful yet pointed. "Yes, did not my father, King Henry, claim it was a sin to marry his late brother's wife? What example do I set in marrying my late sister's husband?"

The laughter swells as she pauses for dramatic effect.

"My lords, my dearly beloved spouse is England. Look at this coronation ring." She raises her hand, the light catching the gleaming band on her finger. "Does allowing a man to be my husband mean I must divest power to him, obey him, and have him rule over me?"

Her expression hardens, and her voice rises with conviction. "Nay! I will have no lord, nor master, nor duke, nor prince, nor even Pope rule me, save God Almighty! I have learned well from my sister's error. This crown is my bond. I am married to England." She extends her right arm stiffly and raises her hand, the coronation ring catching the light, holding it aloft for all to see.

The court erupts in cheers and applause, her words striking a chord of patriotic pride. Elizabeth walks to her throne, her smile triumphant but her eyes sharp as they flick to Feria. He does not flinch, but the stiff set of his shoulders betrays what his face will not.

As the final cheer fades into a low murmur, Elizabeth settles into her throne with practiced grace, the hem of her gown whispering along the dais. The courtiers begin to disperse into pockets of hushed conversation, some still chuckling, others exchanging wary glances.

Feria bows low, slower than before. As he straightens, his gloved thumb smooths the cuff once—then stills.

"Your Majesty, your message shall be delivered faithfully."

Elizabeth nods, her smile cool. "Good. See that it is, Excellency."

He stands motionless for a breath, his gaze steady but opaque, then with a slight bow, turns and steps away. One of the Queen's pages escorts him towards the exit.

Behind her, Cecil leans towards Bacon and mutters under his breath, "That will sound sweet enough in Antwerp."

Bacon does not smile. "And rile well in Madrid."

Elizabeth says nothing more. She rests one hand on the arm of her chair, the other still lightly touching the coronation ring—subtle, but unmistakable. The point had been made. And the whole room knew it.

Across the hall, a court musician nervously plucks a note on a lute, then a second. A ripple of uneasy laughter follows. The spell is broken.

The Queen has spoken. Let Spain chew on it.

17 March 1559

Philip sits in Brussels at a carved wooden table in his dimly lit private chamber. The mingled scents of polished wood, ink, and candle grease permeate the room. From the far side of the chamber, Pérez, Philip's secretary, enters silently and approaches with a folded letter in hand.

"Your Majesty," Pérez says, his voice low, "a message from England, from the Queen."

Philip looks up, his face expressionless. He takes the letter at once, unfolds it, and begins to read. His eyes scan the page, his lips tightening as he absorbs its contents.

He finishes with a defeated look on his face, then exhales sharply through his nose, folding the letter with care. Without a word, he turns to the flickering candle on the table. He touches the corner to the flame, watching as the edges begin to blacken and curl.

The fire consumes the letter, and Philip drops it onto a metal tray, his gaze fixed on the curling ashes as they disintegrate. For a long moment, he says nothing, his features illuminated by the dying glow of the flame.

At last, he speaks, his voice heavy with restrained frustration. "Elizabeth," he murmurs while shaking his head, the name hanging in the air like a challenge.

He leans back in his chair, his hands steepled beneath his chin, and watches the last embers fade. The ashes of the letter mirror the smouldering remains of his ambitions in England. *Elizabeth.*

20 March 1559

The Privy Council Chamber in Whitehall Palace hums with the scrape of chairs and the shuffle of parchment. A page moves along the panelled wall with a jug of small beer.

Candles sputter in the draft, their light flickering across tapestries of English saints and conquerors. Elizabeth sits at the head of the long table, a coronet gleaming faintly in her hair, her crimson gown stiff with embroidery. She looks smaller than her throne, yet the tilt of her chin fills the room with command.

William Cecil, Secretary of State, rises, his hand resting on a sheaf of bills.

"Majesty, the settlement must heal, not wound. If we enforce uniformity too quickly, we risk revolt in the shires. We should allow some measure of latitude—a prayer book firm enough to restore order, but not so sharp as to drive your Catholic lords into open defiance."

Before he sits, Sir Francis Knollys leans forward, voice rough.

"Half measures invite contempt. If England is to be Protestant, let it be so without disguise. Strip the altars, ban the Mass, and silence Rome's whisper. A weak faith is no faith at all."

Elizabeth raises a hand, stopping the rising murmurs. Her eyes sweep the table, catching each man's gaze before it dares to fall away. "Gentlemen, I have heard priests thunder obedience from pulpits, and I have heard rebels cry liberty with swords in their hands. I was born in neither Spain nor Rome. I am Queen of England. And England shall have neither chaos nor tyranny while I live."

Her voice hardens, though her smile lingers like frost in sunlight. "We will have a prayer book in English—plain enough for the ploughman to follow, yet reverent enough that no honest man calls it heresy. The altars will stand, but not as shrines for idols. The sacraments will be given, but without papal licence. And as for Rome—tell His Holiness this queen keeps her own keys to her own kingdom."

A stir ripples down the table. Cecil bows his head, satisfied. Knollys scowls, muttering to Pembroke, but Elizabeth ignores them. Knollys takes a long pull of his small beer instead of answering, the thin, yeasty drink doing little to cool his temper.

She leans back in her chair, her voice turning silk over steel. "I will not turn England into Rome's province, nor will I see it torn into pieces by zealots. The crown is mine by law, by blood, and by God's providence. Let no man mistake me for a reed to be bent. This settlement will pass, and England will breathe again."

The councillors bow, some with relief, some with resentment, all cowed by the certainty in her tone.

***

Later that night, the Spanish ambassador to England, the Count of Feria, dictates his report to the King to his secretary, his voice low and troubled.

He finishes with "*Sire, she is a woman, yet she rules like a king. With a word she silences her council. With a smile she makes enemies bow.* Philip must know this: Elizabeth is no Mary. She will not be bent. She plays for herself—and for England alone. If we are not careful, she will make herself the very banner of heresy in Christendom."

He seals the letter with a firm hand, the wax hissing in the candlelight.

***

At the Palace of Westminster, the chamber of the House of Lords is close with bodies and wool, the air heavy from river mist clinging to cloaks brought in from the Thames. The scent is damp cloth, ink, wax, and old wood warmed by too many men. Lords Spiritual and Temporal sit ranked beneath the cloth of estate, while at the lower end of the chamber the Commons stand summoned, packed together, restless and watchful.

The business of the session has been ground out over weeks—bills read and reread, clauses sharpened, softened, struck through and restored. Yet the argument has never truly settled. It mutters still, carried in glances and half-whispered remarks, sharpened now by the knowledge passing from mouth to mouth that the Queen herself is coming to address both Houses of Parliament.

A Lord Temporal leans towards his neighbour, voice pitched low. "This settlement is a rope of sand," he mutters. "Bind it too tight and it snaps. Leave it loose and it strangles us later. I would have law enough to keep the peace, and no more."

A bishop's ringed hand lifts slightly, as if weighing the air. "Peace," he answers, "and reverence. If you make the church a plaything of each reign, you teach the people that faith is only policy."

From the Commons' end a burgess, standing on aching legs, shifts his weight and whispers back, sharper. "And if we leave the Pope a finger in the door, he will take the house. We have had fires in Smithfield. We have had men hanged for praying in English. Shall we call that reverence?"

Another, older, more cautious, pulls his cloak tighter. "I have had enough of blood in the streets," he says. "Call it what you like—Pope, Prayer Book, Supremacy—I want my market open and my sons alive."

A low laugh moves through a few men—quick, humourless. Someone answers, "Then pray for a queen who can keep both Rome and Geneva from tearing the roof down."

Near the woolsack a lord in black velvet shakes his head, his mouth tight. "You speak as though conscience were a dog to be leashed. There are matters that do not belong to Parliament."

"And there are matters," another murmurs, "that do not belong to any foreign prince—spiritual or temporal."

The noise is not loud yet, but it is everywhere: small eddies of opinion, currents meeting and clashing. Faces turn towards the doors, then away. Papers are smoothed. Knuckles rap once against benches and stop. Each man listens for footsteps that will end the argument, or condemn it.

Before the officers can call the chamber to order, a Catholic lord rises, his voice steady but strained.

"This Act sets the governance of Christ's Church beneath temporal authority. It strips the Bishop of Rome of his ancient jurisdiction in this realm. By what warrant does Parliament make a woman supreme in causes sacred as well as civil? These matters were entrusted to Peter, not princes. This settlement overturns the order received from our fathers."

A low stirring runs through the benches. Some incline their heads in assent. Others sit rigid, displeased.

William Cecil rises from his place, papers neatly aligned before him.

"My lord, this realm has never acknowledged any foreign prince—spiritual or temporal—as sovereign here. The crown of England answers to God alone. Her Majesty claims no power to preach nor to minister sacraments. She claims only that governance which by law and inheritance belongs to her office. That is no novelty, nor usurpation."

Before the murmurs can subside, a Protestant voice cuts in—too sharp, too eager.

"Then let us not halt halfway. Let the Mass be abolished outright, and Rome named for what it is—a sink of corruption. Leave no root that may grow again."

Another voice answers from the Commons' end, louder still.

"Aye—purge the realm of popery, lest it return to plague us!"

The old quarrel flares openly now, victory pressing one side to arrogance, defeat driving the other to defiance. The chamber trembles with it.

Then the doors at the upper end are thrown open.

"The Queen!"

All rise and bow.

Elizabeth enters beneath the cloth of estate, robed in white damask edged with gold, the light catching on the fabric as she advances. She mounts the dais with unhurried grace and takes her seat. The chamber stills, and the members take their seats. When the Serjeant-at-Arms commands silence, it falls at once.

Elizabeth stands up.

"My Lords, and you of our Commons," she begins, her voice clear, measured. "You have travailed long in our service, and with no small care. We thank you for your diligence in matters touching both the peace of this realm and the ordering of our laws."

She lets her gaze pass over them—nobles, bishops, burgesses alike.

"Concerning religion, we do not require that any man's conscience be forced. God alone makes the heart, and to Him alone each soul must answer. Obedience is owed to the Crown in outward things; faith itself rests elsewhere."

A few heads lift. Others remain guarded.

"We seek not," she continues, "to peer into the consciences of our subjects. Let there be one rule of order, that the realm may stand in quietness, and no man take upon himself to disturb the peace under colour of zeal. Our purpose is not to press belief, but to preserve unity."

Her voice firms.

"We are your queen. Though a woman, we bear the charge that belongs to a king. By lawful inheritance and the will of God, this crown is ours. We will acknowledge no foreign jurisdiction within this realm. If others call us what they will, England knows us for her sovereign—and so we remain."

The words settle heavily over the chamber.

"Return now to your counties and boroughs," Elizabeth concludes, "with our thanks for your service, and with our prayer that Almighty God will grant this realm concord, obedience, and peace."

For a heartbeat, the chamber is silent.

Then a murmur rises—measured, restrained, yet unmistakable. "Hear, hear. Well spoken!" Some incline their heads. Others bow stiffly, submission given if not freely, then by necessity. The arguments that burned moments before fall quiet beneath the authority of her presence.

Elizabeth inclines her head once.

Regal. Controlled. Unchallenged.

***

In Brussels, Philip reads Feria's dispatch, his signet ring tapping once against the table before stilling—his face betraying nothing. Candlelight sharpens the hollows of his face. The ambassador's words are stark:

"She bends her realm without breaking it. She speaks as her father once did, with charm masking iron. England has chosen her creed—and it is not Rome's."

Philip folds the letter, his jaw tightening.

"So be it," he murmurs. "The heretic Protestant queen sets her course. Then I must set mine."

12 April 1559

Whitehall Palace's Council Chamber smells of damp wool and smoke. Rain has been falling since dawn, steady and unrelenting, drumming against the leaded windows like a reminder that England is an island whether she wishes to be or not. A small fire works at the chill but does not defeat it. Cloaks steam on pegs near the hearth. Water beads on the stone floor where boots have tracked it in.

At the head of the table, Elizabeth sits motionless, both palms laid flat against the polished wood as if steadying the room itself. She has not yet spoken. At twenty-five she holds her posture well—straight-backed, controlled—but the strain is there, etched faintly at the corners of her eyes. The crown has settled. It is already heavy.

William Cecil clears his throat as he finishes reading aloud a dispatch from Sir Nicholas Throckmorton in Paris and lets the parchment fall quiet in his hands. The sound seems louder than it should. No one moves.

"The articles between England and France were concluded on the second of this month," he says at last, carefully precise. "Our commissioners at Le Cateau set their hands to them. Calais is to remain in French keeping for eight years. Thereafter, it is to be restored to your crown—or France is to forfeit five hundred thousand crowns."

A pause. The words hang, uncomfortably complete.

"And Spain?" Elizabeth asks. Her voice is calm. Too calm.

Cecil lifts his eyes. "Spain and France signed their peace the following day. The wider accord is sealed. Savoy restored. Frontiers settled. The marriage agreed in principle. His Catholic Majesty has his quiet."

Elizabeth's fingers tighten once against the table. "And England?"

Cecil does not evade it. "England was not foremost in their reckoning."

"So Philip has finished his war," she says. "And laid us aside."

Nicholas Bacon shifts in his seat, the movement stiff with age and irritation. "Laid aside politely, Majesty. With parchment and promises. France keeps

Calais now. Spain keeps its peace. And England is invited to trust that eight years of continental goodwill will not fracture."

Elizabeth exhales through her nose. "Eight years." She tastes it. "A term long enough to forget—and short enough to betray."

A low murmur runs the table, quickly stilled. The Earl of Pembroke taps one finger once against the wood and stops. Maps lie half-unrolled beside Cecil's elbow—Calais ringed in ink, the Channel traced and retraced like a wound that refuses to close. The room understands what no one quite says: the war ended without England's consent, and the peace has been made above her head.

Elizabeth lifts her chin. "So we bow to French possession because Spain has grown weary?"

Silence answers her. It is not defiance. It is arithmetic.

At length Cecil speaks again. "Your Majesty, without Spain we cannot prosecute a continental war. Calais was lost under Queen Mary. To recover it now, alone, would beggar the realm."

He hesitates—just long enough to mark that what follows matters more.

"And Calais is not the sharpest edge of this peace."

Elizabeth's eyes do not leave him. "Go on."

"France emerges unbound," he says. "No Spanish pressure. No Italian distraction. The Guises turn their sight north."

A shift, perceptible but real, passes the table.

"Scotland," Bacon says flatly.

"And beyond it," Cecil continues. "Mary Stuart is both Queen of Scots and Dauphine of France. Her uncles rule her councils. In their correspondence, they do not style you queen."

Elizabeth's composure fractures. "They dare—"

"They style her," Cecil says quietly, "*the rightful Queen of England.*"

The words land like a blade set carefully on the table between them.

Elizabeth rises so quickly her chair scrapes stone. "Rightful?"

"The phrase appears more than once," Cecil replies. He does not apologize for it. "The peace frees them to speak it aloud."

Bacon leans forward, grim. "She is sixteen, Majesty—but she is married to the heir of France. And the Guises govern in his name. One papal instrument. One stroke of fortune. And her claim becomes a rallying cry for every Catholic grievance left unresolved in this kingdom."

Elizabeth's voice is steel. "I will not be ruled by Spain's convenience nor unseated by a French girl's ambition. They mistake restraint for weakness. They forget whose daughter I am."

No one contradicts her. No one reassures her either.

At last she draws a breath, measured, deliberate. "We accept the terms. We swallow the eight years. But we do not sleep."

Her gaze sweeps the table. "I want eyes on France. On Scotland. On Mary and her uncles. I want our ambassadors reminded that England has a queen who listens—and remembers."

Cecil inclines his head. "It shall be done."

Chairs scrape back. Cloaks are gathered. The council disperses, the machinery of the realm already turning toward the next necessity.

Cecil remains behind a moment longer. He folds Throckmorton's letter with habitual care, his expression composed, his hands steady.

Before he slips it away, his eyes return—once more—to the line he did not want to read aloud.

"*Rightful Queen of England.*"

The fire crackles on, obedient and bright.

It does not warm the room.

Chapter 12
No More Rome

8 May 1559

The bells of St Paul's peal throughout London, their jubilant notes rolling through the smoky air. From Cheapside to the river, people pause to listen. A few cheer, throwing caps in the air. Others cross themselves hurriedly, muttering as though the sound itself were dangerous.

In a tavern by Fleet Street, a young printer wipes ink from his fingers, grinning.

"Did you hear? It's proclaimed—English service is coming. English prayers in every church! No more mumbling Latin we can't follow."

His neighbour, a cooper, claps him on the back.

"Amen to that. They say the new book'll reach the churches by midsummer. My boy shall learn his catechism in the tongue he speaks. God save the Queen!"

But at the next table, an older man slams his mug down. His accent still bears the north.

"God save 'er, tha says? She spits in Rome's face an' calls it peace. Mark me, lads, nowt good'll come o' this. The Pope'll not bide quiet, ye'll see."

The tavern falls still for a beat before the talk turns again, some siding with him, others spitting on the floor at Rome's name.

In a narrow lane near Whitefriars, a procession of Catholic priests in plain cloaks moves silently, their faces set. They smell faintly of onions and stale black bread from their noon meal, the scant fare of men who have already begun to taste exile in their own city. One mutters a prayer for the Queen's soul. A crowd of apprentices jeers, chanting, "No more Rome! No more Rome!"

By the river, two women kneel together outside St Bride's. One clutches a rosary, the other an English Bible, kept hidden through Mary's reign. Both pray aloud—but to different rhythms, in different words—yet side by side, their voices rise into the same grey sky.

***

From the palace windows at Whitehall, Elizabeth hears the bells ring. She steps closer to the glass, the city sprawling below in smoke and spires. Behind her, Cecil bows low. "The settlement holds, Majesty. Parliament obeys. The people—most of them cheer."

Elizabeth does not turn, her gaze still on the streets beyond. "Most of them, William. But not all. And not forever. I have given them peace in law. But peace in hearts? That is another matter."

She toys with the stem of an untouched glass of Rhenish wine on the window ledge, then lets it be, unwilling to sweeten the taste of the choice she has just forced down the country's throat.

Her reflection in the glass is pale, her crown gleaming faintly in the dim light. She lifts her chin, her eyes bright with resolve. "Let Rome rage. England has chosen."

12 May 1559

Royal Apartments, Greenwich. The chamber is still, save for the muted ticking of a small table clock on a shelf above the hearth. On a nearby table sits a silver ewer of cool well water, a flagon of pale sack, and a dish of sugared orange peel from Seville—an expensive courtesy laid out for the Spanish envoy. The peel glistens, but no hand has dared reach for it yet.

Outside, the Thames gleams under a soft afternoon sun. Inside, Álvaro de la Quadra, Bishop of Áquila, King Philip's newly arrived envoy, stands with composed formality, holding out a sealed dispatch. Queen Elizabeth accepts it delicately, as though it were made of glass, her silence more pointed than any words.

William Cecil, beside her, clears his throat slightly. "From His Majesty Philip?"

De la Quadra bows.

"It is a most respectful communication, Your Majesty. His Majesty sends warm greetings and prays for your wisdom in these early days of your reign. He also entreats your aid in maintaining the balance of Christendom in these dangerous times."

Elizabeth's brows rise. "Aid?"

"A gesture of amity between sovereigns," de la Quadra replies smoothly. "He asks that England remain a friend to Spain in its trials with France. That you uphold the legacy of cooperation Queen Mary established."

"Cooperation?" Elizabeth's voice remains calm, but sharpens slightly. "My sister's cooperation nearly cost this realm its peace. And its soul."

There is a pause. The envoy does not respond. He only inclines his head with studied courtesy.

Elizabeth moves to the window, hands folded before her. Behind her, Cecil watches the ambassador with open suspicion.

She speaks without turning. "Tell me plainly, Your Excellency. Does His Majesty request an alliance?"

De la Quadra chooses his words carefully. "No formal treaty, Your Majesty. Only that England not act against Spanish interests. That your court maintain civility—and that you reassure him of your goodwill."

Now she turns. "Then he fears I will support France."

"He fears...instability. France watches closely. Others will take their cue. His Majesty only wishes for clarity in these uncertain days."

"Clarity, is it? Then carry this: England keeps her own counsel."

Elizabeth looks to Cecil, who nods slightly. She returns her gaze to de la Quadra.

"You shall have your answer, my lord. But let His Majesty know that I am neither France's pawn nor Spain's subject. England is ruled by no foreign power. Nor ever shall it be."

The envoy bows again, offers a final pleasantry, and exits.

As the door closes behind him, Elizabeth exhales.

"I know what Philip wants," she murmurs. "He wants quiet. He wants no war with us while he is bleeding in France. And he wants to know if I am still pliable."

Cecil steps forward. "Then give him what he wants—enough peace to keep his armies busy elsewhere, and enough steel to remind him who you are."

Elizabeth nods. "I will write to him myself. He may have married England once. But I am not my sister."

She looks out at the river, the sun low over the water.

"This is not just diplomacy, William. It is a warning."

17 May 1559

At Greenwich Palace, Queen Elizabeth sits at her writing desk. She reads the words again, each line measured with the precision of a monarch walking a diplomatic tightrope:

"*Most Serene King Philip, I trust this letter finds Your Majesty in good health. It is with respect and care that I reaffirm my intentions now that I have assumed the English throne. Though the times have changed, I hope the peace between our nations shall not. I acknowledge the deep responsibilities before me and seek to preserve the cordiality once shared between Your Majesty and my late sister, Queen Mary. I will strive to prevent anything that might disturb that harmony. Our kingdoms differ in religion—this I do not deny.*"

She stretches and yawns. Then she continues.

"*But differences need not breed hostility. I assure you that England, though Protestant, seeks no quarrel with Spain, nor with the Catholic faith you so devoutly uphold. I recall the wisdom and diplomacy you exercised during my sister's reign, and I hope to continue in that spirit. The challenges of Europe remain—France presses ever forward, and the balance of power shifts like sand. Let us address such matters with patience and mutual respect. Know, dear King Philip, that I hold you in high regard. I will defend England's sovereignty, but I seek peace and understanding between us. With sincerity and goodwill, Elizabeth R.*"

She exhales and leans back in her chair, the weight of the crown settling again on her shoulders. The creak of the chamber door breaks the quiet. William Cecil enters and bows.

"Your Majesty," Cecil says, "is that the letter?"

Elizabeth looks up from the letter. "It is. The letter goes to Philip tonight. It is a gesture of peace—and a line drawn in diplomacy."

Cecil steps forward, tone cautious. "May I read it, Your Majesty?"

She hands it to him and he reads.

After a few moments, he hands it back to her and says, "The sentiment is noble, but we must be clear-eyed. Philip is not a man to be dissuaded by words. His pride, his empire, his faith—they leave little room for diplomacy from a Protestant queen."

Elizabeth examines him for a moment, then asks, "You think he will see this not as strength, but as weakness?"

"Not weakness," Cecil replies, "but opportunity. He may not question your legitimacy, but he questions your religion and your governance. A courteous letter will not unmake his suspicions—or his ambitions."

He pauses. "Yet if we say nothing, we risk provoking him further. This letter may not win him over, but it may buy us time—time to prepare, to fortify, to shape alliances of our own."

Elizabeth stands and walks towards the window, her voice low but resolute.

"I will not pretend Philip is a friend. But neither will I hasten enmity. He bleeds from a war that has only just ended on paper. He cannot afford a second front. If we offer him peace, he may take it—if only to delay."

She shifts back to him, her gaze cool and calculating.

"But we will be ready. If he treats us as pawns, he will find a queen, not a girl, staring back. I will not be manipulated as my sister was."

Cecil's face tightens. "We must chart our course wisely. Philip may accept your words—but he will test your strength."

"Let him," Elizabeth says. "This letter is no surrender. It is our first move."

She returns to the desk and places the quill beside the parchment, her decision sealed.

In the quiet, the tension lingers like smoke. The letter would cross the Channel—but what follows would shape the fate of England. Elizabeth had chosen peace—but made no promise to kneel.

12 June 1559

In Brussels, the midday heat clings to the walls of the royal study, its thick silence broken only by the ticking of the tall clock and the faint rustle of parchment. King Philip sits behind a carved walnut desk, his eyes on a sealed letter bearing the unmistakable hand of Elizabeth Regina.

Across from him, Don Juan de Silva, the Marquis of Montemayor, a trusted member of his council, stands with arms folded.

"I see it is from the English Queen," Philip says without looking up.

"Yes, Majesty. Delivered through her English envoy in Brussels this morning. Marked personal and bearing her own hand."

Philip breaks the wax and unfolds the letter. His eyes scan the lines in silence, lips tightening at the familiar language of diplomacy—measured deference, guarded reassurance, veiled assertion. Elizabeth is clever. He knew that. But this was something else. Calculated restraint. Beneath her courtesy lies cold steel.

When he had finished, he laid the parchment flat and stared at it for a long moment, as though the ink itself offended him.

"She writes like her father," he says at last. "A flatterer with a dagger beneath the smile."

Silva shifts. "And yet she offers peace, Majesty. An olive branch."

Philip's voice is low. "She offers peace, yes—but on her terms. Protestant terms. She dares to speak of 'sovereignty' and 'mutual respect' while her bishops strip the altars and her ministers preach rebellion against Rome. She keeps Cecil and other Protestant councillors close—men whom Rome paints as eager to burn every Catholic in England if left unchecked."

He stands and moves to the hearth, stirring the ashes with a poker. Sparks flare, then die, like his hopes for England—bright under Mary, now dimmed under her sister's rule.

"She is not Mary," he mutters. "There is no devotion in her, only resolve. She smiles, and yet I feel the door closing."

Silva approaches. "She does not provoke, Majesty. Not yet. And her words are cautious. She offers the appearance of respect."

Philip turns, his tone sharper now.

"The appearance of respect is not obedience. Elizabeth knows she cannot stand alone—not against France, not against the Empire. This letter is not friendship. It is delay. She wishes to breathe while we decide whether to crush her."

He returns to the desk and taps the parchment once with a gloved finger.

"But she is not without foresight. She knows France watches as well. She fears pressure from two sides at once."

Silva nods. "And she is not wrong to fear it."

Philip pauses, considering. Then, in a quieter voice, "She is young, but she governs like an old fox. If she thinks I will be soothed by words, she underestimates me."

He hands the letter to his secretary.

"Draft a reply. Cold, respectful. Say I welcome her desire for peace, that I look forward to further correspondence. Make it distant. No warmth. She will read between the lines."

"And what of action, Majesty?" Silva asks.

"We wait. Let her believe she has bought time. We will use it to secure the Netherlands and test her alliances. If she stumbles, we will not need war. Her throne will collapse beneath her."

He turns towards the window, his eyes now fixed on the western horizon, where the sun begins its descent.

"The lion's cub believes she rules alone," he murmurs. "But even queens bleed, when the hour comes."

27 June 1559

In the Queen's Privy Council Chamber in Whitehall Palace, the heavy wooden doors creak open as William Cecil enters, his face grim and shadowed in the dim candlelight. Elizabeth, seated at the head of a polished table adorned with correspondence, looks up from the letter she had been reading.

Cecil pauses to bow. "Your Majesty."

Elizabeth says briskly, setting the letter aside. "You look as though the very devil himself has chased you here. Speak plainly."

Cecil crosses the room, his boots clicking softly. "I have received word from my sources in Spain, Your Majesty. The proxy marriage to Elisabeth of Valois is now beyond question. The contract is sealed by all reports."

Elizabeth raises an eyebrow, a faint smirk tugs at her lips. "Married? Already? It seems our dear brother-in-law wasted no time finding a new queen to replace me." She laughs.

Her tone is light, but there is an edge beneath it, sharp as the jewelled rings on her fingers.

Cecil hesitates only a moment before continuing. "The French king means to use his eldest daughter as a tool of policy."

Elizabeth stiffens, her smirk fading. Her fingers tap lightly on the edge of the table. "Elisabeth of Valois," she repeats slowly, the name lingering on her tongue. "How fitting. A French Elizabeth to replace the English one he lost. And his new father-in-law will not make war with him. He plays the game of crowns well."

Cecil speaks with a wry smile. "It seems the Spanish king has a preference for women named Elizabeth. He once wanted one to be his queen in England, and now he will have another to sit beside him in Spain."

Elizabeth turns her sharp gaze on him, her lips curving into a faint smile that does not reach her eyes. "And what do you think of this new Elizabeth, Master Spirit? I dare say. Will this new Elisabeth prove as...tro ublesome...to King Philip as the old Elizabeth?"

Cecil inclines his head. "It is Philip who is troublesome, Majesty. We must watch him, not his bride. This marriage binds Spain and France together—a troubling alliance for England. The French have ceded much to Spain in this match, Your Majesty. Philip grows stronger."

Elizabeth rises from her chair, the rustle of her gown filling the room as she moves to a nearby stand where dispatches lie waiting, lifting one absentmindedly as though hoping for a distraction from her thoughts. She gazes out of a window at the grey sky, her reflection faintly visible in the glass. "Philip may have gained a wife, yet he also gained a country in his bedchamber for a rival. Let us not forget that France does not easily yield its pride. And Valois or no, this new queen will find Philip's ambition as cold as the crown he places on her head."

Cecil moves to the front, hands clasped. "Your Majesty, this union changes the balance of power in Europe. England cannot stand idle. We must strengthen our alliances, particularly with the Protestant states."

Elizabeth turns back to face her advisers. "And what would you have me do, William? Sell myself to the highest bidder in the name of diplomacy, as Philip and his Valois bride have done?"

Cecil hesitates. "Not sell, Your Majesty. But choose wisely. Your hand remains the strongest instrument of treaty in Christendom."

Elizabeth's lips curl into a sardonic smile.

Cecil runs a hand down his face, trying to tame the frustration tightening in his chest. He exhales—sharp, not soft—then strides forward. "Your Majesty, your clarity is a strength—not many monarchs see the game so plainly. But Philip...He plays for all. He does not tire, he does not forget, and he does not forgive. This marriage of his—it is not about companionship or even diplomacy. It is a lever. Another footing. He is tightening his grip on the continent, one crown at a time."

He pauses, meeting Elizabeth's eyes. "We may not see his soldiers on our shores, but his influence is already here—quiet, calculating, and watching. We would be fools—"

"Fools, you say?" she interjects.

"Yes, fools, Majesty. To treat this as anything less than the next move in a long campaign."

Elizabeth's eyes narrow, her voice cold. "Then let him play his games. I will play mine, and mark my words, I will play them well. England has weathered Spanish storms before, and we shall weather them again."

She glances at Cecil, her gaze sharp and commanding. "Strengthen our defences. Renew our ties with the Protestant princes. And as for Philip and his new queen—let them know, quite subtly, that England is not a pawn in their chess game."

Cecil bows. "As you command, Your Majesty. Spain will watch us. Let us ensure they see our strength."

31 December 1559

The air in Elizabeth's Privy Chamber at Whitehall is thick with tension on the eve of the New Year. In the outer rooms, musicians tune for the night's revels and servants carry in trays of spice-cakes, marchpane crowns, and jugs of mulled wine for the court, but in the privy chamber itself a single goblet of clove-studded ale sits on a stool by the hearth, its steam fading as her temper rises.

The flames in the hearth crackle loudly, echoing the fire that burns in the Queen's heart. She paces the chamber in short, sharp turns, the letter clenched so hard the parchment creases in her fist. She reads it again. Colour rises in her cheeks—disbelief giving way to a clean, burning anger. With each line the heat climbs higher in her chest, every sentence pressed like an insult against her sovereignty and her freedom.

The letter from Philip is, as always, a polite demand masked in pleasantries. But this time, his arrogance is more than she can bear.

The letter reads:

"I do not approve of your determination to delay your marriage, and think it would be better for yourself and your kingdom if you would take a consort who might relieve you of those burdens better borne by a husband. If you should decide

on Charles, Archduke of Austria, my cousin, it would be most pleasing to myself and beneficial to your kingdom."

The audacity of it—Philip's presumption to dictate her life, her choices, her kingdom's future—is more than Elizabeth can stand. She has bent the knee to no man. Her reign, her sovereignty, is hers alone, and she will not tolerate being treated like a child in need of a husband's guidance.

With a sharp motion, she tosses the letter onto the table, her hands trembling with rage. Her fingers leave faint smudges of ale on the parchment where she had gripped the cup earlier, trying and failing to let the warmth soothe her before the words undid her restraint.

She turns to William Cecil, who had been standing in the corner, observing the scene quietly. His face is impassive, but he knows well the turmoil rising within the Queen. He had never seen Elizabeth so consumed by fury.

"Does my brother-in-law presume to be my lord and master?" Elizabeth's voice rings through the chamber like a bell, harsh and unforgiving. "Does he presume to be Emperor of the World with me as his viceroy in England? My sister allowed him to tread on her as if she were a mean Flanders carpet under his boots, but not so with me!" Her eyes, usually so controlled, blaze now with the intensity of her anger. "I told him once to his face the world does not revolve around him!" Her voice shakes with emotion. "I will not be bullied into marriage by any man, least of all by him! He presumes to command storms. No man commands the storm. I am the storm!"

She turns back to the table and slams her fist down three times, the papers shaking with the force of her outburst. Her breath is quick, shallow, as she struggles to regain control. But this insult is too great. The King of Spain dares to question her sovereignty and her choices so brazenly.

Cecil, ever the steady adviser, advances, trying to calm her, but he knows better than to push too hard when she is like this. "Your Majesty, I understand your anger. Philip's letter is an imposition, and we know the stakes of the situation. We must not reveal the whole game at a stroke. His displeasure is not something we can ignore, not entirely. We must move carefully here."

Elizabeth turns sharply on him, her gaze as cold and sharp as a dagger. "Carefully? Carefully?" she repeats, her voice rising again. "I have been careful my entire life! I have been careful in my choices, careful in my reign. And look where that has gotten me—treated like a pawn with no voice! But no more, Cecil! I am Queen of England, am I not? I will not let Philip or anyone else dictate my path!"

Her fingers curl into a fist again, but this time she holds it at her side, taking a steadying breath. Philip has no right to assume he could control her decisions. His kingdom, his empire, is vast, but that does not give him the right to push her into marriage, much less a marriage where he chooses her spouse. No foreign prince or king will manipulate her into a decision before she is ready. She will decide her future...on her own terms.

Elizabeth says, "Philip does not make this a happy new year for me."

3 January 1560

Privy Council Chamber, Whitehall Palace. The heavy oak doors thud shut, sealing the warmth and gravity of power inside. Within, the hearth sputters beneath a ceiling heavy with tension. Queen Elizabeth sits at the table in a fur-lined mantle of deep crimson. She holds a goblet loosely in her hand but does not drink. The pale sack within has long since lost its warmth; she lets it rock once in her fingers, then leaves it untouched.

Her eyes scan the room—Cecil, Lord Keeper of the Seal Nicholas Bacon, Sir Nicholas Throckmorton, Lord Admiral Edward Fiennes de Clinton, and Sir Thomas Parry—arrayed around a table cluttered with maps and missives.

Cecil breaks the hush. "Your Majesty, dispatches from Scotland and from Lord James Stewart confirm the French entrenchment at Leith. Mary of Guise has strengthened the garrison. The Lords of the Congregation grow desperate."

Elizabeth's voice is calm, deliberate. "And what is it they ask of us?"

"Assistance," Cecil answers. "They require coin, powder, arms—and they hint that men would be welcome too."

The Queen's gaze falls to the edge of a sealed letter. "And if we were to oblige them, what would England stand to gain?"

Lord Keeper Bacon leans forward.

"A Protestant Scotland. A buffer between you and the House of Valois. If we do nothing, France will own our northern flank."

"They already prepare the ground, Majesty. Coins bearing Mary Stuart's face and the arms of England circulate in France. Her claim is no longer whispered—it is minted," adds Throckmorton, the Queen's diplomat, still travel-worn from France.

Elizabeth's knuckles whiten around her goblet. "So they aim to crown her Queen of England before I am buried?"

"Not just that," says Admiral Clinton, his voice gravel-thick. "If Mary returns to Scotland with French support, it will not be to mend fences. France will press the Auld Alliance to its fullest reach. A dagger in the north—and one held to your throat."

Elizabeth turns to him, brow raised. "Lord Admiral, is our fleet prepared for such a storm?"

Clinton bows slightly. "We can patrol the Firth of Forth, Your Majesty, but not hold it if France sends her full strength. The Channel is still ours—but the Scottish coast? That may slip through our fingers like Boulogne did."

Sir Thomas Parry, long her loyal servant, clears his throat. "Your Majesty, the matter is not only military. We must be seen to uphold Protestant brethren without inviting Catholic wrath. If you aid the lords too openly, Philip may accuse you of inciting rebellion across Christendom."

Elizabeth replies, "So Philip waits for me to trip, while Mary's claim is paraded across the Alps and the Pyrenees alike. And if I blink, I wake to find her claiming her crown in Edinburgh—and half the realm wondering if she wears the right crown."

Cecil states, "Then we must make Scotland unwelcoming to her return. Split them before France sets its claws too firm. Quiet aid to the lords may fracture Mary's path before she sets foot on it."

"She will come with lilies and the cross," Clinton mutters, "but beneath her train will ride soldiers."

Cecil nods. "Not war, but preparation. Support them with coin and munitions. Let the Protestants in Scotland fight their battle—with our whisper behind them."

Parry adds, "And send word to our envoys. France must not think us blind, nor the Pope think we will bow."

Elizabeth turns, her expression hardening. "I wear the crown of England without Rome's approval. And I will not sit idle while my enemies sharpen their knives."

Her hand sweeps over the maps. "Give the Lords of the Congregation what they need—but quietly. A powder keg is no place for trumpets."

She finally lifts the goblet, only to brush the rim against her lip and set it down again, the wine untasted; there is no comfort strong enough in any cask to soften what she has just loosed towards the north.

As the council murmurs assent and rises, Elizabeth remains still.

The room waits on her breath. She feels the familiar weight settle—the old knowledge that crowns are not defended by innocence, only by perception and force. England is ringed with cousins and claimants, each convinced God leans their way. But Mary Stuart is something more precise—and more dangerous—than a rival queen.

France does not need Mary to challenge Elizabeth outright. It needs only to hold her up.

Mary is young where Elizabeth is seasoned; Catholic where England is fractured; crowned by dynastic certainty where Elizabeth's title is still argued by lawyers and priests. In French hands, Mary becomes a comparison—silent, gleaming, unavoidable. A living question placed before every court in Europe: *Which queen looks more ordained? Which rule appears settled?*

Mary Stuart is not the blade at Elizabeth's throat. She is the mirror France holds before the world—polished to show England's doubts, angled to make Elizabeth's crown look provisional, dangerous precisely because it reflects without striking.

To answer that mirror with hesitation would be to let others decide what it shows. To act is to risk war. To delay is to invite it on terms chosen elsewhere. Elizabeth knows this as she knows her own name.

Scotland is the fuse. France is the hand steadying it. And whether she strikes first or not, the spark is already burning toward England's border.

***

Later that night, the palace's council chamber was empty. A cold fog curls at the windows. Only the low crackle of the fire remains as Elizabeth sits alone in her Privy Closet. Outside, a bell strikes the tenth hour.

A soft knock at the inner door.

"Enter."

William Cecil steps inside, his face taut. He bows. "You summoned me, Majesty."

He smells faintly of smoke and kitchen herbs, dragged from a half-finished trencher of boiled beef and parsley root in the council buttery the moment her message reached him.

Elizabeth does not look up immediately. She still peruses a map made of vellum on her writing desk—one not shown to the Council. Scotland. Every burgh, crossing, and coastal inlet marked in fine ink.

"I trust the Council will speak nothing of our discussion tonight," she says at last.

"They know discretion, Your Majesty."

Elizabeth's lip twitches slightly, though it never becomes a smile. "Discretion is useful. But not always enough."

She stands and moves to the fire, making her tone sharp. "You spoke well today. But words are one thing. Outcomes are another. If this Mary Stuart sets foot in Scotland, France will not need her to march south. Her *presence* will do the work for them. Every Catholic lord will see a crowned answer to my rule. Every foreign prince will begin to weigh alternatives."

Cecil nods. "Then we must ensure she finds no ground firm enough to stand upon."

"Exactly."

Cecil nods slowly. "What do you require of me?"

Elizabeth turns, her eyes hard now. "Begin communications with Lord James Stewart in secret. Not through couriers from Berwick. I want a man I can trust—your choosing. Someone who knows the terrain, and who will speak plainly."

"Shall he go with money or only words?"

"With both. There are still men of the old religion who would sell their silence. I want to know their names. I want to know where they kneel, and to whom."

Elizabeth turns to the fire. A coal collapses inward with a sharp crack, sending sparks briefly up the grate.

"And if France moves first?"

"Then we must move faster." She returns to her desk and slides a sealed letter across it. "This is for our agent in Paris. He is to shadow anyone in the French embassy that leaves for Scotland. If Mary boards a ship, I want to know the tide she sails on."

Cecil takes the letter and tucks it into his cloak.

"I will have men in place within the week."

Elizabeth's voice drops. "And Cecil—no fanfare. I do not wish Philip to see my hand. Let him think I am hampered by courtly scruple."

She approaches, so only inches stand between them.

"If Mary seeks my crown," she says, "then let her find that the ground beneath her feet has been cut away."

Cecil bows. "As Your Majesty commands."

He leaves without another word.

Elizabeth remains by the fire, staring down at the flames as if they held the shape of the future.

"She would steal my name," she whispers, "but I will bury hers before she crosses the border."

Chapter 13
The Young Queen in France

17 April 1560

It is evening in the Queen's Apartments at Château de Fontainebleau, France. The fire snaps in the marble hearth, scattering embers like restless thoughts. Rain drums faintly on the leaded windows, but the greater storm is within.

Seventeen-year-old Mary Stuart, Queen of Scots and Queen Consort of France, stands near the casement, wrapped in a silken robe embroidered with the *fleur-de-lis*. Her face, radiant with youth, is pale with fatigue and worry. Letters from Scotland lie folded on the table behind her—one from her half-brother, Lord James Stewart, another from her mother Mary of Guise, Regent of Scotland. Beside the letters sits a small Venetian glass of hippocras, long since cool, and a silver plate with three sugared violets and a half-bitten marchpane rose she had forgotten to finish earlier.

Behind her, King Francis, sixteen years old and half a head shorter than his wife, paces the chamber in agitation, wringing his hands.

"You are too quiet, Marie," he says. "T-tell me what is wrong. Say something."

She turns slowly to face him, her dark-brown eyes shining, tears held back and something heavier: dread.

"It is my mother, François. She is failing. Every letter from Edinburgh sounds more desperate than the last. Doctors say she can barely leave her bed now. She does not even rise with the sun anymore."

Young Francis flings up his hands with frustration.

"Then let the soldiers bleed for it! That is why we have generals. To fight, to hold the line! Your mother may be regent—but you wear the crown. You are the Queen, M-Marie. Make them remember it!"

Mary's shoulders relax as if confessing something she has only just admitted to herself.

"Yes. I am queen," she says, almost with a trace of irony. "Crowned before I knew what a crown was. But Scotland—I know Scotland is not truly mine. Not in the way people think."

She looks away for a moment, eyes searching the middle distance. "It is not the land I remember. It is not the place I know. France is my home. I was raised in its courts, shaped by its language, its music, its light. I dream in French, not the Scots tongue. I am French in heart and tongue."

She pauses, the weight of the thought settling in her chest. "When I hear the Scots speech now, it is strange in my ear—so raw, so rough. Like a language that does not belong to me anymore. And when I speak it, I sound like a foreigner. And to them? I am one."

Her gaze drops. "What kind of queen returns as a stranger to her own people?"

She moves to the table, picks up her mother's letter, and folds her arms tightly, crushing the letter against her.

"And they expect me to return?" she says, eyes shining with frustration. "The Catholics at least. They write as if I am their hope, their answer—as if I will just sail in and everything will fall into place. Rule. Unite. Be their queen."

Mary lets out a short, brittle laugh—more pain than amusement. "They do not know me, François. Not really. How could they? I left Scotland when I was five. I was a child in a cradle, and they called me queen." She pushes on. "Since then, I have grown up in courts dripping with perfume and Latin verse, where disagreements are settled in whispers behind fans—not with steel in the heather."

She glances towards the window, though the glass shows only shadows. The letter is still clenched in her fist. "And I do not know them either. Not the men with names older than the hills. Not the lords who still count clan feuds like heirlooms. I know the sound of the lute, not the bagpipe. I speak French like a native, and Scots like a stranger."

Her voice falters as she looks down, fingers tightening around her sleeves.

"How am I supposed to lead a country that listens more to the sword than the crown? That tears itself in two at every whisper of religion?"

She takes a shaky breath, then speaks more softly, as if saying it aloud makes it more real.

"And the worst of it—some would sooner follow the heretic John Knox or the demon Jean Calvin. Geneva's pulpit, not Rome's. They call it 'reformation.' I call it rebellion."

She finally looks up again—wounded, but resolute.

"How can I be queen to a country that might already have stopped believing in what I was born to be?"

A flicker of irritation crosses Francis' face. He stops pacing and stands before her, his youthful face twisted in frustration.

"You c-cannot go," he says. "You will not go. You are my wife, Marie—France's queen. The Scots will rip you to pieces there. They say those knaves in Edinburgh throw dung at priests. You are safer here, with me."

Mary gives him a small, sad smile. "I made a vow at our wedding, François," she says. "Until death do us part. And I meant it. I just fear a strong current that could drag me beneath the tide of court and kingdom."

Francis reaches for her hands and clasps them, as if afraid she might vanish if he lets go. His voice cracks with a mixture of fear and urgency.

"Then do not go," he pleads. "Stay here. Rule Scotland from France if your mother cannot. We will send more soldiers—better led, stronger ones. More gold, whatever it takes."

He swallows hard, searching her eyes.

"You are a Valois now. You are my wife. You belong here—with me."

She lets the letter fall back to the table, then draws her hands away—gently, not out of anger, but out of duty. Her fingers linger for a heartbeat before slipping free. Her voice is quiet, almost breaking, but every word carries weight.

"I love you, François. You know that. But it is not only you. I am yours, yes—and, whether I like it or no, I am also theirs—the Church, the crown, the people who still call me queen, even if I feel like a stranger to them."

She turns slightly, glancing out towards the window as if she could see across the sea to the hills of Scotland. A silent shake of her head is all she allows herself.

"If my mother dies—and the doctors say she is slipping by the day—if I just sit still, say nothing, do nothing—the Protestants will take Leith, and with it threaten Edinburgh. Then they will take the rest. They will set new lords in my place. But I am torn."

Her voice lifts, more urgent now. "And if that happens, France does not just lose me. France loses her place in the north entirely. All those years, all that blood, for nothing."

She turns back to him then, eyes wet but burning with resolve. "So I cannot pretend I am just a girl in love. I am a queen. And my time runs out."

Francis blinks rapidly, his pride struggling to shield his heart.

"And the English throne?" he asks. "D-do you still dream of that?"

Mary hesitates. The storm outside rattles the panes.

She draws in a slow breath, her eyes drifting for a moment—as if weighing old dreams. When she finally speaks, her voice is low, but clear, and edged with something deeper than pride.

"It is mine by right," she says. "By every measure of the Church—by the blood of my grandmother Queen Margaret Tudor—by law older than Henry VIII's whims." Her gaze sharpens. "Elizabeth sits there because men fear disorder more than they respect truth. But let us not pretend—she was born of a marriage Rome never recognised, and her mother died condemned. They can call her queen all they like. It does not make it so."

She pauses, then sighs, and the fire in her eyes dims a shade.

"But I have no hunger for that fight—not now. England may wear gold, but that crown is dipped in thorns. And I have bled enough for two kingdoms already."

She turns back to the window. Raindrops streak the glass like tears.

"I do not wish to leave France," she murmurs, her hand brushing his cheek. "I do not ever want to leave. Yet the thought tugs at me. If I delay much longer, I may lose Scotland altogether. And once a crown slips from one's grasp...it rarely returns."

Francis comes beside her, trembling now—not from cold, but fear.

"I cannot lose you," he whispers. "I cannot. I am king in name, but without you I am no one. You make me strong, Marie. You make me brave."

She reaches up and touches his cheek, softly, the way one might soothe a child after a bad dream. Her thumb lingers just beneath his eye, where the frustration still burns.

"And you," she whispers, "you make me feel cherished—more than a queen, more than a crown. I do not want to leave you, François."

Her voice wavers, yet her gaze stays fixed on his. A long silence falls between them as thunder rumbles in the distance.

7 May 1560

The tiltyard at Greenwich is alive with noise and colour. Trumpets blare from the gallery, drowned in turn by the roar of the crowd as hooves strike the packed earth like rolling thunder. One can smell horses, oiled leather, and the faint sweetness of trampled rushes strewn to keep down the dust. From the rails, pie-sellers weave through the press crying their wares—hot mutton pasties, eel pies, and trenchers piled with spice cakes—while boys pass leather jacks of ale and small beer from hand to hand along the benches. Above the field, bright pennons snap in the wind, the royal arms embroidered in gold thread catching the spring sunlight.

Within the railings, two destriers wheel and stamp, their iron-shod hooves striking sparks as the knights take their places. The armour of each gleams, polished to a mirror sheen, crested with plumes that sway as the men lean forward in their saddles. Pages scurry to adjust straps, while the heralds cry their names in formal cadence, the words echoing off the timbered stands.

From the gallery, the Queen's ladies murmur behind their fans, their eyes fixed on the favourites. None draws more attention than Robert Dudley, Elizabeth's Master of the Horse, whose figure is marked by confidence as he lowers his visor. His opponent salutes, lance raised in ritual courtesy, and Dudley mirrors the gesture with practiced grace. The salute complete, they settle into readiness.

The Master of the Lists, standing at the tilt barrier, raises his staff. A drumroll thrums like a heartbeat, the tension drawing silence from the crowd. Then the staff falls, and with it the horses spring forward, muscles straining, nostrils flaring white in the charge.

The field blurs—dust rising, banners snapping, sunlight glancing off steel. The lances meet with a crack like a cannon. Shards of ash wood scatter across the barrier. Dudley's lance slides wide on his opponent's shield, missing the clean strike, while his rival's weapon bursts against Dudley's cuirass in a spray of fragments.

The crowd erupts, cheering Dudley's flourish as he lifts his visor, grinning as though a missed strike were no more than part of the sport. He dismounts smoothly, sweat streaking his brow, his armour gleaming in the sharp sunlight. Around him, the tiltyard rings with trumpets, the clash of steel, and the relentless roar of the people. But Dudley's eyes are already drawn to the royal box where Cecil and Sir Nicholas Throckmorton stand, watching not only the joust but the man himself.

He strides towards them, a smile still upon his face though tempered now with a graver cast. A female admirer gives him an apple.

"Well struck, Dudley!" Throckmorton calls as he approaches, his voice rising over the din. "None in the lists rides with such grace."

Dudley gives a playful bow, his smirk quick and cutting. "If only the same could be said for the aim of my opponents. Their shields seem forged of iron, not wood."

Cecil's mouth twitches, his tone dry as ever. "Not iron, but stout enough. Still, better a broken lance than a broken treaty. A fine display, Master Dudley—but we both know politics bite harder than any splintered ash."

The jest slides away. Dudley's face sharpens, and he leans closer. "Perhaps. Yet I doubt France could best England—in war any more than at sport."

Throckmorton's gaze darkens at the name. "Let us hope your words prove true. France makes no sport of this. They parade Mary Stuart's claim as if it were already hers to wield—and each week her partisans dig deeper at Leith. Their fortress grows. Their soldiers multiply. Scotland is not a neighbour at peace, but a knife at our border."

Dudley frowns while tossing the apple in the air and catching it. He digs a thumb into the skin at last, releasing a brighter spray of juice than his mood deserves, then takes a slow, thoughtful bite, the crunch of it loud against the muffled roar of the crowd.

"Mary is still in France. What matter her titles here?"

"Her titles are not the danger," Throckmorton replies. "It is the French guns pointed from Scottish walls. If Leith holds, the Tweed is no barrier. Their cannon would face us directly."

Cecil speaks then, low but certain. "Mary of Guise governs in name, but the French rule in fact. If Elizabeth waits too long, she may find the gates of Scotland are France's gates, and her own crown the next prize."

From behind them comes a voice, the cadence unmistakably Castilian, calm yet commanding.

"Well jousted, Master Dudley!"

They turn. Bishop de la Quadra, Spain's ambassador to England, had approached unseen. His expression is genial though his eyes watch sharply.

"I could not help but hear," he says, "your talk of Leith, of France. Spain observes events with great interest. My king is pleased to see England stand firm against such designs and that you defend your border. France in Scotland is not only your peril, but ours."

His thumb worries the signet at his finger, but his gaze fixes past Dudley to the royal box—speaking to one man, aimed at another. He pauses, letting the words linger. "The siege at Leith is no small matter. With your army under the leadership of Lord Winton—"

Throckmorton interjects, "That is Wilton. Lord Grey de Wilton, sir."

De la Quadra says, "Pardon me. Lord Wilton, yes. With his leadership, you defend more than England—you defend the cause of order itself."

Dudley's smile returns, thin and wary. The apple in his hand weighs heavy, forgotten. "A generous speech, Excellency. But tell me—does Spain delight more in England's strength, or in her dependence on Spanish favour?"

De la Quadra's smile does not falter. He bows slightly, his tone silken. "Independence is guarded best by strength, my lord. And strength—true strength—is never found in standing alone."

The trumpets blare again, summoning fresh riders into the lists. The crowd's roar swells, but at the rail another contest begins—one without lances or shields. Cecil's face betrays nothing, while Throckmorton's gaze sharpens with wary thought. Dudley, at last lifting the apple to his lips and taking a bite, stares northward past the tiltyard dust, already hearing the drums of war.

The sport was done. The real joust had yet to begin.

16 June 1560

The low tap of boots against polished oak echoes softly through the Privy Gallery at Whitehall Palace. Heavy velvet curtains deaden the sound of the outer court.

William Cecil, Elizabeth's "Spirit," moves like a man bearing storm clouds. At his side, Nicholas Bacon clutches a sealed letter, the wax broken but the message still fresh with peril. Both men pause before the antechamber doors. Inside, the Queen awaits.

Cecil knocks once, sharply. "Your Majesty?"

Her voice comes cool and clear: "Enter."

The chamber is dim, save for the warm circle cast by a silver candelabra. Elizabeth stands before it. Her eyes snap to them before they bow.

"Well, Spirit and Master Bacon?" she asks without ceremony.

Bacon steps forward, handing her the letter. "Your Majesty, intelligence has arrived from Scotland. Mary of Guise, the Regent—is dead."

Elizabeth does not move. Her eyes flick from Bacon to Cecil.

"When?"

"Five days past," Cecil answers gravely. "Eleventh of June. She had been ill for weeks—dropsy, they say—but none expected her to go so swiftly."

Elizabeth walks slowly to the hearth, holding the letter as if it might burn.

"Who...rules...now?"

"No regent named," Bacon says. "Not officially. The Guise faction has suffered a blow. King Francis and Queen Mary Stuart remain in the Paris court. But Mary Stuart...she is now queen with no regent between her and the realm. And I reckon she will not let that power lie dormant for long."

Elizabeth folds her arms—not in defiance, but to still the tremble in her hands. Her shoulders are set like iron. The chamber falls silent.

"Ruling Scotland from France?" she says, her voice low but flint-edged. "That is a fiction—and a danger." Her eyes lock on Cecil. "You cannot effectively govern a land you do not walk on. You cannot bind rebels with letters written in another tongue, sealed with another crown."

There is a pause. The fire pops in the hearth.

"And what of the Lords of the Congregation?" she presses. "They will not wait much longer before they take Scotland for themselves—by sword or sermon. And if they do, will France not respond? Will the Guises not send more ships, more soldiers, more banners with Mary's face beside mine as if we are equals?"

Cecil exchanges a glance with Bacon.

Elizabeth's voice sharpens. "No. France must be made to own its choice—peace or provocation. But we must be ready for either."

"The Lords of the Congregation hold the north, and the coast," Cecil replies. "Leith is in French hands. But they are wary. With no regent and no French reinforcements, they press for influence—but they know Mary will return eventually."

Elizabeth turns to face them fully. "Then the tides of events shift. Scotland may soon be ruled not by an aging French widow—but by my young cousin, the would-be Queen of England."

Bacon says darkly, "Though she has never worn the crown here, her supporters grow louder. In France, she is styled Queen of England by Catholic tongues—and her arms bear the quarter of your kingdom."

Elizabeth's nostrils flare. "Then she marches with stolen banners. And if she returns to Scotland, she does so with fire at her back."

Cecil steps closer. "Your Majesty, if she comes home, she will be nearer to your throne than ever before. The Scots may be torn, but she is their rightful queen. Her presence there—if unchecked—may rally not just Catholics, but disaffected nobles. France may have lost its grip, but Mary is young, clever, and still a bride of France."

Elizabeth turns to the window. Dusk falls across the Thames. "Send word to our agents in Paris. I want eyes on every gate and every courier. I want to know not only what gowns Mary chooses, but who stitches the hems, how many pins fasten her veil, and what prayer she mouths at dawn—and what ships load at Le Havre. Scotland must be watched like a tinderbox."

She turns back, her voice lower now. "And Dieppe? Keep the channel of letters open. Quietly. I want news of every whisper from court. If Mary makes one move towards returning, I want to know before she sets foot on a gangplank."

Cecil bows. "It shall be done."

Bacon follows suit. "I will double our presence in Edinburgh as well. The Lords must not stand alone. If she returns, England will stand prepared."

Elizabeth's hand drops to the hilt of her small ceremonial dagger at her waist, fingers tightening. "I will not be made a scene in her masque. Watch them all—France, Scotland, and Mary herself. She may wear a crown, but I wear the realm."

17 June 1560

At Château de Saint-Germain-en-Laye, France, the scent of lavender still lingers in the corners, but it does nothing to calm the breathless silence that hangs over the Queen of Scots.

Mary sits alone on the cushioned bench beneath the tall window, her fingers twisting the edge of her sleeve. A letter rests beside her—creased, tear-stained, sealed in black wax.

From across the room, the door creaks open.

"Marie?" comes the soft voice of her teenaged husband, Francis.

He steps in, his slight frame swallowed by velvet, curls damp at the edges from the June heat. He looks hesitant, unsure whether to comfort her or stand in awe of her stillness.

She turns her head towards him slowly, her face pale but composed. Her eyes are red-rimmed, but dry now—dry as though no more tears could be spared for duty.

"She is dead," Mary says, voice almost too calm. "My mother is dead."

Francis steps towards her. "I know. My council received the messenger last night. The physicians...they said it was the swelling sickness, but too far gone."

Mary lowers her eyes.

"Dropsy. A slow drowning is what they called it."

She pauses, swallowing hard before continuing.

"She died alone—surrounded not by friends or family, but by men who hated her. Not even a priest of her choosing. Not even a daughter to hold her hand."

Mary looks up, her eyes shining but dry.

"That is how the Regent of Scotland died. Mother. Dying by inches while they watched and waited for her to fail. And I was here—wearing pearls, dancing in silks—when I should have been there. They served sweetmeats last night," she says bitterly, "sugar-plums and quince pastes while my mother fought for breath across the sea. I could not force down a morsel without tasting ashes."

She looks down at her hands. "The Catholics there will expect me to return. They will want a queen. The Protestant nobles, however, have no use for me."

Francis frowns, confused and pained. "But you are queen. Here. You are my queen, and through me, Queen of France. Let someone else—your uncle, perhaps—let him rule Scotland. You are needed here."

Mary shoots to her feet, her voice cracking with raw frustration. "Needed here? Needed—here?" She paces a short step, hands trembling as they ball into fists at her sides. "In this court where every whisper speaks of Guise plots and Protestant devils lurking in every chapel?"

She turns sharply towards him, eyes glistening now. "In this palace where I cannot breathe without feeling watched—even by your family?"

Her voice catches. "They hate me, François. You know they do. They say nothing, but I hear it in their silence. And your mother—" Her breath hitches. "Your mother looks through me like I am some foreign burden she must endure. Do not pretend otherwise."

She presses a hand to her chest, as though trying to hold herself together. "I am not blind. And I am not secure."

Francis steps back as if struck, hurt flickering across his face. "I love you, Marie," he says softly, his voice unsteady, almost boyish in its sincerity. "I have always loved you. Not because you are a queen, or because they said I must—but because you laugh like no one else and cry like the world is ending and speak as if your heart is on fire."

He reaches for her hand, hesitant now. "I know this court is cruel. I know my mother eyes you like a hawk waiting for weakness. But you know I am not them. I do not care about their whispers or alliances or cold silks and rules. I care about you."

When she does not speak, he presses on, his voice growing firmer. "If you go, they will tear you apart. Scotland is angry and broken and full of men who only understand war. Here...here you are at least alive. Here I can still hold your hand, even if the whole world hates me for it."

He pauses, swallowing hard. "Please do not shut me out, Marie. You say you are not safe here—but you are safest with me."

She softens, but does not move. "I do love you, and I meant my vows. But Scotland cannot be ignored. My title is no longer symbolic. If I delay too long, others will move to fill that space—and I risk losing not only that throne, but any standing I have in England as well."

At that, Francis' face clouds. "You...speak of England again."

Mary turns to him, trembling. "It is mine by my Tudor blood, François."

He shakes his head, childlike in his pleading. "But Scotland—Marie, it is full of rebels, of heretics who hated your mother. You do not even sound like them."

She smiles faintly, bitterly. "In their eyes I may never be wholly theirs—but they are still my people. And without me they may tear each other apart."

Francis grabs her hand, his voice breaking before the words even form.

"Do not go. Please, Marie. Let someone else deal with Scotland—anyone else. I cannot lose you. I do not care about crowns or thrones. I care about you."

He squeezes her fingers tightly, desperate now.

"Scotland's cold. Very cold. It is hard. They will not love you—not like I do. You promised me you would not leave."

She swallows hard, then looks into his eyes.

Her voice breaks slightly. "I told you I would not leave you, and I meant it, François. Every hour I have spent by your side has been more joy than I ever imagined this world could give me. Just help me to fight the current."

Mary looks at him then—truly. Her child-husband, stuttering and trembling with emotion, ruled in name only, a boy dressed in crowns. She loves him, but she sees the boy, not the King.

His thumb brushes her cheek. Tears well in his eyes. She kisses his hand.

Outside, a mourning bell tolls in the courtyard below—for a queen regent lost, and perhaps, for the quiet end of childhood.

27 June 1560

The noon sun bakes the pale stone of Toledo, and within the Alcázar, silence presses close despite the cool shadows of the King's study. Philip stands at the tall window, his prayer book open but unread in his hands. On the table behind him lies a letter, its seal broken, its contents gnawing at his thoughts.

The servant who had brought it lingers nervously until dismissed with a flick of Philip's fingers.

The door opens again. Trusted councillor Gómez Suárez de Figueroa, Count of Feria, who has lately returned from England, enters quietly and bows. "Your Majesty."

Philip does not turn. His voice is flat.

"She is dead."

Feria pauses. "Yes, Sire. Mary of Guise. She passed away in Edinburgh."

The King's hand closes around the prayer book and he crosses himself. "I cannot say I grieve for her as Guise is our enemy. However, as a Catholic, she was the last pillar of the Holy Church in Scotland. Now the heretics will take what is left."

Feria moves closer, his voice low but edged with frustration. "The Lords of the Congregation waste no time. They preach rebellion in God's name and seize the towns. And the French have let it slip from their fingers. They promised to keep Scotland Catholic, yet their soldiers rot behind Leith's walls while England bleeds heresy into the north."

Philip turns sharply, his eyes cold. "Yes. France falters, as always. They spend their strength chasing King Henry II's quarrels in Italy, and meanwhile the Gospel of Luther and Calvin spreads under their very nose. They cannot even hold the Queen Regent's ground."

He goes to the table and taps the letter with two fingers.

"Now will Elizabeth step in, parading herself as self-appointed guardian of Scotland? France fails and England fills the void. A realm once Catholic now drifts into the hands of heretics."

The muscle in Feria's jaw hardens. "Should we move, Sire? Troops, gold, a fleet for the Catholic nobles? The Queen of Scots still lives. Her claim is not extinguished, and she is not well-liked by the French king's family. If she returns, there may yet be a standard to rally behind."

Philip stands silent a long while, the weight of decision in the air. Then, slowly, he shakes his head.

"No. Not yet. France must feel the shame of this loss. Let them see what comes of neglect. If we strike too soon, we fight their war for them. Better to let the Scots rip themselves apart. When the dust settles, Mary Stuart may need Spain more than France. And then we shall act."

He lifts the letter and feeds it into the fire. Philip watches it burn until nothing remains but ash. Behind him the wine in his cup has gone warm; when he drinks, it is more sour than when it was poured, a rough Castilian sting that matches the taste in his mouth as he speaks of France and her failures.

"These are my orders: To our ambassador in Paris—report each day on the girl Mary Stuart's movements, Guise counsels, and any embarkation from Le Havre or Dieppe. To Brussels—watch English aid to the Lords of the Congregation. Intercept powder moving through Zeeland—Flushing and the islands. To London—press our protest: no English protection for rebels, else trade tightens."

The fire cracks. Outside, a wind stirs from the north. Philip closes his prayer book with a snap, crosses himself, and turns back to the window, the shadow of his crown heavy on his brow.

Below, in the chapel court, a bell tolls for the noon office. The sound drifts up the stone like a reminder unanswered.

Philip does not move to join it.

He remains at the window, watching the heat lie motionless over Toledo, knowing what he has chosen not to save—and what that restraint has already cost.

The bell falls silent.

The kingdom does not.

Chapter 14
Edinburgh's Bargain

29 June 1560

The heat of the afternoon presses against the leaded glass, but inside the council chamber at Greenwich, the air feels heavy and unmoving. Queen Elizabeth stands near the great map of Europe pinned to the wall, fingers tapping on France, then on Scotland.

Just a few steps away, William Cecil holds an unsealed parchment like a question left hanging. His expression is not anxious—it is methodical, the crease in his brow the mark of a mind already three moves ahead. On the table between them, a pewter flagon of sack sweats faintly in the close air, beside two untouched silver cups and a trencher with the heel of a manchet loaf and a knife still greasy from cutting cold roast capon.

"We have received word from Scotland, Majesty," he begins quietly. "The siege at Leith is concluded. The French are ready to withdraw."

Elizabeth does not look up. "A year ago, they were swearing loyalty to the Auld Alliance. And now they creep back to France for no more than the glint of English steel?"

Cecil does not rise to her tone. "A treaty has been drawn. The Scots call it the Treaty of Edinburgh. I have a copy of the document here. I have read the terms. They are acceptable."

"I trust your judgement, Spirit."

"Thank you, Your Majesty. If all parties agree, France will abandon its garrisons. No more troops north of the Tweed, no danger on our border."

"And you want my signature."

"I want your approval," he corrects. "Your Majesty need not sign it yourself."

She lifts her gaze now. "And why not? If this is England's triumph, why should I not put my name to it?"

Cecil hesitates. "Because it names Mary, Queen of Scots, directly—and calls for her renunciation of the English crown."

Elizabeth purses her lips. "So by signing it, I would acknowledge that her claim to my throne is legitimate. As if I see her as an equal. Or worse—a rival."

Cecil lowers his voice. "And if you refuse to sign at all, it will appear you dispute the treaty's terms—or worse, that England negotiated without Your Majesty's sanction. I can sign it, as your minister. It will suffice. Legally. Politically."

Elizabeth moves to the window, pushing it open with the heel of her hand. The wooden frame groans. "You think Mary will sign it?"

"No, not personally," Cecil replies flatly. "I anticipate that she will hold on to that claim like a mastiff with a marrow bone. It is the core of her posture. She will not give it up, not even in ink."

"Then what is the use of this, William? A treaty that one party will ignore and another must pretend to endorse?"

"The use," he says carefully, "is leverage. If Mary refuses to ratify it, she exposes herself as the one who breaks with peace. It paints her as the aggressor. It paints England as the peacemaker."

Elizabeth turns, her eyes sharp. "And what happens when those French coins with her face and the arms of England quartered land in Kent? What then?"

"Then we hold them up for all to see," Cecil replies. "Let the world know who stokes the fire, and who holds the water."

A long silence settles. The only sound is the soft creak of Elizabeth's gown as she crosses back to the table. She brushes her fingers along the edge of the treaty, then stops.

"She is clever," she murmurs. "Or her uncles are. They see me as a novice. A woman alone. They think they can force my hand."

She looks up.

"Let them learn I am not my sister."

Cecil gives a slight bow. "They already have, Majesty. On 6 July, by your command, Sir Nicholas Wotton and I will conclude the terms. The commissioners will sign in Edinburgh. Lord James Stewart will sign for Scotland and France will sign by the King's commissioners."

"Yes—you sign it." She speaks quietly. "Let it be England's will, not mine. I will not give Mary the satisfaction of believing I see her as a queen of anything beyond her own quarrels."

Cecil nods. "History will read it your way, Majesty. I will see to that."

Elizabeth sits back, fingers steepled before her lips, her eyes distant.

"See that it does, William. Because the next treaty we sign might not be written with ink, but in blood."

17 November 1560

In the Château d'Orléans, King Francis sits hunched in a velvet chair near the hearth, one hand pressing hard against the side of his head. His fingers tremble. A pewter cup sits on the table beside him, the wine gone cold.

He tries to stand.

The moment he does, the floor seems to lurch beneath him. He staggers—just barely catching the arm of the chair—his legs buckling beneath the dizzy tilt of the room. A sharp gasp escapes his lips. He clenches his teeth as pain lances through the side of his skull and down into his jaw.

"Marie!" he calls.

His knees hit the floor. Sweat gathers at his brow, cold despite the flicker of the fire. His stomach turns.

Francis reaches towards the hearth for balance, but the stones feel far away, as if the world itself shifts. The flame blurs. His ears ring. Is the room tilting, or is he?

Mary enters quickly, her silk skirts whispering across the floor. "François?" she asks, kneeling beside him.

He flinches, eyes red-rimmed. "I n-need h-help," he mutters, but his voice trembles. "I cannot stand straight. There is a sharpness behind my ear. It will not stop. Like a knife...inside my skull."

Mary's brow creases with worry. She touches his temple—hot. "You are fevered."

Her glance flicks to the cup. "You have not drunk your wine," she murmurs, half to herself. "You would not touch the broth either." A king refusing his table in France is an omen enough without physicians.

"I am just cold," he snaps, then grimaces. "No—no, I am sorry. I did not mean..."

She holds his gaze. "Shall I send for Doctor Paré?"

Francis hesitates. Then, softly, "Yes. But d-do not tell Mother. She will summon half the court."

Mary rises, but her heart sinks. He was never short with her before. Not like this. Something deeper than a chill had taken root.

5 December 1560

The hour is past midnight at the Château d'Orléans. The King's bedchamber is steeped in shadows, the candlelight flickering against old stone and worn tapestries. The hearth sputters with a dying flame. On a nearby table a pewter ewer of watered wine and a cooling bowl of spiced chicken broth stand ready, the fat gathered in yellow islands on the surface where no hand has stirred it for hours.

King Francis lies in his bed propped on silken pillows, his breath shallow and uneven.

Mary kneels at his side, both hands clasped around his limp fingers. Her forehead rests briefly against his knuckles before she raises her head again, watching his face as if willing him to remain tethered to the world. Her tears brim but do not spill—her grief, for now, is silent, breathless.

Across the room, Francis' mother Catherine de' Medici stands in a shadowed profile near the tapestry-lined wall. Her black veil falls heavy over her shoulders, her gloved hands folded together in a gesture more ceremonial than maternal. She says nothing. She does not move. Her gaze remains fixed on Mary with the cool scrutiny of a woman who has survived courts, kingdoms, and too many funerals. Her silence is not born of sorrow but of calculation.

Mary glances up at her once, quickly, but Catherine's expression does not change. If there is mourning in her face, it is buried beneath layers of old distrust. The stillness between the two women stretches—uneasy, unspoken.

Francis stirs. His thin frame curls faintly towards the hearth, the instinct for warmth still in his bones even if it no longer serves him. His brows knit together, and a faint tremor runs through his hand as he grips Mary's.

"Marie..." His voice is thin, a frayed thread. She draws closer.

"I am here," she whispers quickly, brushing a damp lock from his forehead.

His lips twitch—an effort at a smile, or maybe just the pain.

"When I go, you must not stay. Not here." He wheezes. "You must return. To Scotland. And after that..." He struggles to form the words, his chest heaving gently. "You know what must follow."

She bites the inside of her cheek, saying nothing. "Do not speak of it," she murmurs. "Please."

"You must," he insists, his fingers gripping hers again, tighter this time. "Scotland was your birthright. But England—that was always your destiny. I said it before. I say it now—your claim is real. The world may not want to hear it, but it is written in your blood."

Mary bows her head, her voice cracking. "My only destiny was to love you."

Francis gives a faint breath of a laugh that dies quickly in his throat. "You were always more than a consort," he whispers, searching her eyes. "And I have always known it. But she..." His eyes shift to the darkened corner where Catherine still stands, unmoved. "She never trusted you. She never believed you."

Mary follows his gaze but says nothing.

"Not your tears, not your piety. Not your loyalty." His voice fades into a rasp. "She sees only Guise ambition, never your heart."

Mary holds his gaze as the silence folds over them again.

Catherine's expression does not change, but one hand tightens slightly on her fan.

Francis winces and closes his eyes. "Do you...hear that?" he asks suddenly, voice tinged with fear. "There is singing..."

Mary leans in, alarmed. "François? I hear nothing."

His eyes dart upward. "Voices in the rafters. Latin...monks?" His pupils dilate. His limbs grow still. A final breath slips through his lips, thin as smoke.

Silence.

Mary clutches his hand tighter. "François?" she says again, voice cracking. "François, please..."

He does not move. His fingers are already beginning to cool.

Across the room, Catherine steps forward slowly. Her gaze passes over her son's still body. Then it settles on Mary with an unreadable finality.

Mary feels it. The subtle shift. The unspoken warning: You are no longer Queen of France.

But Mary does not look away. Instead, she bends her head over Francis' chest and weeps.

17 July 1561

The Privy Chamber at Château de Saint-Germain-en-Laye is hushed, tapestries swallowing sound. Beyond the door, servants drift away on instinct, trained to know when proximity becomes peril.

Mary stands by the casement, her black mourning gown unadorned, the cut severe. Widowhood has stripped her of ornament and left only rank. One hand rests against the stone as if the walls themselves must remind her she is still real.

Catherine de' Medici does not pace. She stands near the hearth, composed, hands folded, her stillness more unsettling than motion. She wears black velvet and pearls, every line of her dress declaring control rather than grief.

"You remain," Catherine says at last. Her voice is level. "Longer than is wise."

Mary turns. "I remain where I am received."

Catherine's mouth tightens. "You are received. You are not *placed*."

Mary holds her gaze. "I am Queen of Scots."

"And dowager Queen of France," Catherine replies. "A title that commands respect, not direction. My son's court must move forward, Marie. It cannot linger in mourning."

Mary's eyes sharpen. "Nor should it forget the dead too quickly."

Catherine inclines her head, conceding nothing. "France remembers its kings. It does not arrange its future around widows."

Silence stretches.

"You draw men," Catherine continues calmly. "Old Guise loyalties. Young courtiers with too much memory and too little caution. England listens when your name is spoken. Spain listens. That is not useful to me."

"Useful," Mary repeats softly.

"This court must be orderly," Catherine says. "Clear in its authority. France cannot afford echoes."

Mary steps closer. "Then say plainly what you wish."

Catherine meets her halfway, their voices low now. "I wish you settled. With purpose. With a kingdom beneath your feet, not beneath your memory."

"And Scotland?" Mary asks. "You know what waits for me there."

"I know," Catherine says. "Protestant lords, an untested settlement, a crown that must be claimed in person or lost in absence. That is precisely why you must go."

Mary's jaw tightens. "You would send me into disorder."

"I would send you into *reality*," Catherine answers. "Here, you are a reminder. There, you are a sovereign."

Mary studies her. "And if I stay?"

Catherine does not raise her voice. "Then you will find your household thinned. Your access narrowed. Your allowances...reconsidered. Not as punishment. As necessity."

The meaning is clear. No decree. No guards. Just air slowly withdrawn.

Mary draws a measured breath. "So France closes its doors without ever touching the latch."

Catherine allows herself a thin smile. "France opens another door. Northward."

A pause.

"At your leisure," Catherine adds. "But not indefinitely."

Mary inclines her head, a queen acknowledging another queen. "I see."

Catherine turns towards the door. "I wish you a safe crossing," she says. "Scotland will require all of you."

When she is gone, the chamber feels larger—and emptier.

Mary returns to the window. Beyond the glass lies a road she has delayed too long. Beyond that, the sea. And beyond that, a crown that will not wait to be asked twice.

She presses her palm to the cold stone.

France has let her go without a word of farewell.

19 August 1561

The sea lies under a pall of mist, the grey sky pressing low as the French galleys ease into the harbour of Leith, Scotland. Their oars dip in measured rhythm, water slapping against wood like a dirge. Along the shore, a crowd has gathered—Scottish nobles in dark cloaks, burghers and fishermen craning to see the woman who is now their sovereign.

The harbour reeks of tar, salt, and the sharp oil of drying herring strung on lines behind the houses; a boy in a stained jerkin clutches a heel of oat-bread in one fist and a leather jack of ale in the other as he squints up at the ships.

From the deck of the flagship, Mary Stuart stands cloaked in black, her face pale against the veil at her brow. She is eighteen years old, a widow already, her youth marked by both splendour and grief. Behind her, French attendants cluster close, whispering in her mother tongue. But their words fall heavy, strangers in a land that feels half-foreign to her.

The anchor drops with a dull roar, chains grinding. A gangplank creaks into place. Nobles step forward, their breath visible in the cold morning air. The Earl of Huntly bows, his voice formal.

"Your Majesty, Scotland welcomes you home."

Mary inclines her head, her composure perfect, but her eyes glisten. *Home*, they call it, though it feels nothing like the gilded courts of France. She tightens her grip on the rosary entwined in her fingers, a habit of solace since the day François was laid to rest.

As she steps onto Scottish soil, the crowd breaks into cries—some joyful, some guarded. A piper strikes up a mournful tune that winds through the harbour mist, sharp and alien to French ears. Mary pauses, the sound cutting deep. She looks back once, towards the sea she has crossed, towards the life she has lost.

In her heart, she whispers, "France. My heart remains with you."

Then she draws herself up, spine straight, gaze fixed ahead. Her French-accented voice carries, clear and firm.

"Lords of Scotland, I am your queen. I come not as a stranger but as a daughter of this realm. May God grant me wisdom to govern you with justice and with love."

The nobles bow again. Behind their obedience lurks calculation—Huntly's ambition, John Knox's fury, and the Earl of Moray's patience.

The mist thickens, curling around her like a shroud and a crown all at once. Mary steps forward, her attendants trailing behind. She carries not only her baggage ashore, but the weight of a kingdom—and the first faint shadow of a cousin's crown across the border in England.

22 August 1561

At Whitehall Palace, Elizabeth sits alone at the centre of the chamber. Her eyes—sharp, usually steady—now glimmer with something rawer: alarm.

William Cecil enters swiftly. Nicholas Bacon follows, slower, quieter, the seal of a ciphered dispatch still in his hand.

Cecil bows, but does not wait for pleasantries.

"Your Majesty, the news we feared has been confirmed."

Elizabeth turns to him sharply. "Speak plainly, Cecil. My patience is thin."

Bacon opens the paper. "From our agent in Dieppe. Mary Stuart departed Calais on the fourteenth of this month. She landed at Leith in Scotland on the nineteenth."

Elizabeth blinks once. *Landed at Leith on 19 August.*

She goes silent.

She bites a knuckle. A tremor ripples through her. She sways. For a moment, it looks like she might fall. Cecil lunges forward—but she steadies herself, one hand braced against the table.

She whispers, "She is there...in Scotland?"

"Yes, Majesty," Bacon confirms softly. "Returned at last to her throne."

Elizabeth's hand clenches into a fist.

"That woman...that woman would have my crown, my throne!" Her voice rises, ringing like iron on stone. "She sets her feet on Scottish soil, and already I feel her shadow crawling towards my chair."

"She travels with only a modest company," Cecil offers gently. "No army, no banners—"

"No army? She needs none," Elizabeth snaps. "She has her French family behind her in blood, the papists in Rome behind her in creed, and half my enemies behind her in hope! Hope—that I will fall, and she will reign in my place!"

Bacon speaks carefully. "We anticipated this. But now it is a fact. She is Queen in Scotland—and she is closer to England than ever."

Elizabeth's expression hardens.

"Then we watch her. Day and night. I want every whisper she speaks to be carried to this court. Every ally she greets, every letter she sends—I want it known to me before the ink has dried. Double your agents in Edinburgh, in Leith, in the Highlands if you must."

Her hand snatches up a silver cup of Rhenish. She takes a brief, sharp sip—more to wet a throat gone dry with anger than from any wish for wine—then sets it down so hard the pale liquid climbs the rim.

"Yes, Your Majesty," Cecil says quickly.

"And if she so much as utters a prayer in Latin," Elizabeth continues, pacing now, "I want the Pope's courtiers to feel our tremor. If she so much as sighs towards Spain, I want Philip's court shaken before the breath leaves her lips. Philip needs to think twice before supporting that queen against me!"

Elizabeth stops at the window, gazing across the Thames. The river moves beneath the twilight, dark and wide—like the space between two queens.

"She plays the game now," she says coldly. "Then so shall I."

She turns back to her advisers.

"Go. Prepare everything. Let her know—without ever telling her—that I see her. Every move. Every ambition. She has returned to Scotland, yes. But she is not welcome in England."

28 August 1561

Thursday morning at the Royal Alcázar, Madrid. Philip, recently come from daily Mass, sits at his desk in his private study to begin the day's work, tending to his empire. A plain earthenware cup of watered wine and a small plate with two dried figs rest at his elbow, the simple fare of a man who long ago turned from feasting to fasts and paper. He starts to write a letter. A clerk enters, bowing, parchment in hand.

"Sire, news from Scotland. Mary Stuart has arrived at Leith. She claims her crown."

Philip does not look up from the letter he writes. He pauses only a moment, dips his quill again in the inkpot, and with a flick of his wrist, signs his name. The ink glistens wet beside a dark ring where an earlier drop of wine had dried on the wood, the only sign the King has ever let his hand shake at this desk.

Then, without shifting his gaze, he says, "Good."

And he writes another letter.

7 September 1561

The long galleries of Holyrood Palace smell of damp stone and smoke from the hearths. Torches hiss against the draft. Mary Stuart stands at a tall window overlooking the gardens, her black gown trailing like spilled ink across the floor. She holds a small ivory casket open in her hands. Inside lies a miniature of her late husband, François, painted when he was still bright with life.

Her servant, Mistress Mary Livingston, hovers nearby.

Mary closes the casket gently, her fingers lingering on the latch. She exhales, then speaks softly, half to herself, half to the chamber.

"France is lost to me. My husband is gone. Scotland is my kingdom again, and yet it feels rough and strange. I went away as a child and came back as a queen, and I do not belong to these walls."

She moves to the fire, letting the casket rest on the mantle. The flames dance, casting shadows across her face. Her voice lowers, edged with something both wistful and sharp. "And across that border sits Elizabeth—my cousin, my sister in blood. A woman on her own throne. They say she is clever, proud, and loved by her people. They say she smiles with her father's boldness. Some call her a bastard, but she wears a crown. And crowns do not yield to whispers."

Livingston dares a quiet reply. "Your Majesty, perhaps she will be your friend. Two queens might bind their kingdoms together."

Mary gives a small, rueful smile. "Friendship between queens? Perhaps. But sisters often quarrel, do they not? Especially when both would claim the elder's inheritance."

She turns back to the window. Beyond, Edinburgh's spires pierce the mist, the city sprawling like a challenge beneath her. "I want her love, yet I know the world will set us against each other. Rome has its dreams of me. France watches. Spain would use me. And she—she will fear me. Already, I feel her eyes upon me, though she is far away."

Mary presses her palm to the cold glass, her reflection merging with the blur of city and sky. "If it comes to rivalry, may God guide me."

21 October 1562

In the Royal Alcázar of Madrid, the courier's boots leave a trail of dust and rain across the tiles. He drops to one knee, breath ragged. Don Gonzalo Pérez, grey and spare behind his desk, snatches the packet and breaks the seal with a thumbnail.

"From London," he says. "De la Quadra."

Philip stands at the window, the city's light the colour of pewter. He does not turn. "Read."

Pérez reads fast, voice low. "Her Majesty of England is stricken with the smallpox at Hampton Court. I am told the danger is mortal. The court is already talking about succession. There is talk that if she dies, Robert Dudley would be Protector. Of course that is only talk."

"Indeed. He is her favourite."

"Some name the Lady Catherine Grey. Others whisper 'Mary Stuart of Scotland.'"

The room tightens. Ruy Gómez de Silva—soft hands, sharp eyes—rests two fingers on the table's edge like a musician finding a note. The Count of Feria's jaw sets. He has England in his blood and an English wife, Jane Dormer, at home. The Duke of Alba is stone by the hearth, arms folded, a winter in armour. Between them, on the council table, a silver ewer of wine and a dish of black olives and almonds sit; no one reaches for so much as a nut while England's fever is weighed like another item of state.

Philip turns now. No hurry in it. "What else?"

Pérez reads the next leaf. "The Council there is divided. Cecil gathers his men. The French watch. The Scots hover. I beg Your Majesty to take steps while the matter is uncertain."

Stillness sits among them like a fifth chair.

Feria breaks first. "Sire, forgive my boldness. If Elizabeth dies, England may be ours to steady. Mary of Scotland is Catholic, and she is an heir to the throne. We should move before France does. Letters to Scotland. Money. A hand on the tiller."

He glances towards Philip—testing the king's face—before adding, quieter, "But if we hesitate, Paris will seize the moment."

"France already has its hand," Silva says gently. "Guise uncles, French bishops, a paper crown ready for the girl. If we push, we make the island a gameboard for Paris and Madrid and wake the old fears of a Spanish yoke."

Alba's voice is gravel. "Fear is useful. If the English think Spain will land at Dover, they will choose a Catholic to keep us out. Or they choose Dudley, and then we have our enemy named."

"Dudley," Feria says, bitterness slipping out, "is a swaggering Protestant who smells of the Queen's chamber." He bows his head at the memory of Mary Tudor—Philip's dead wife—then risks meeting Philip's gaze. "Your Majesty knows what the English become under bad counsel."

Philip says nothing. He moves to the chair at the table and sits. The ring Mary Tudor gave him knocks once, softly, against the wood. He does not look at it. He does not have to.

"De la Quadra says she may die," Silva presses on, "but smallpox kills and then spares in the same breath. We must plan both ways: what to do if she lives; what to do if she does not."

"She will live," Alba mutters, not as comfort but as a soldier's assessment of fate's perversity. "And then she will remember who circled when she bled."

Pérez lifts another slip. "Yet we should take seriously the rumour that she named Dudley for Protector if—if she should not recover."

Feria exhales hard. "There. The heat under the kettle. If she dies, we face a Protestant Protector who locks the door against Mary Stuart, against us, and against any Catholic settlement in the Low Countries. If she lives, the rumour alone makes England more skittish and cruel towards our friends."

Philip's fingers steeple. He hears rain spitting on the stone. *Always the island, always the island.*

"Spain does not chase rumours," he says. "We do not send armies across the Channel because an Englishwoman coughs."

Alba inclines his head. "Then we sharpen the sword and wait."

Silva tilts his head. "We can do more than wait, Majesty. Quiet measures. Write to de la Quadra to comfort and to warn—comfort, so the English do not hide their panic from him. Warn, so they know we see their factions. And a message to the Scottish queen: should Providence call her to her inheritance, she must not sell it to France. Promise nothing. Offer prayer. Keep the road open."

"Money," Feria says. "Money finds the men who sway English councils."

Philip looks up, and Feria stops. "We do not buy England. Not like a mule in a market."

A beat. Then Philip's voice softens by a hair. "But we do not leave the purse at home, either. I need a letter."

Pérez sits at the desk, his quill already moving. Philip says, "*To London: Your Excellency will express the concern of His Catholic Majesty for the health of the Queen of England, and his hope for her recovery. You will observe which lords speak for Dudley, which for Grey, which for the Queen of Scots. You will write each day by courier. You will remind the Catholics there to keep quiet tongues and steady hearts.*"

"Add this," Alba says. "*If the Protestants contrive to set Dudley over them, we will not leave the Netherlands naked. Let them hear it.*"

Silva raises a hand. "Softly. Hints, not threats. If she recovers, we must do business with her again."

Philip's gaze goes to the window, past the rain and stone. "She will recover," he repeats, almost to himself. "She is hard to kill."

He closes his eyes briefly—two breaths—and opens them clear. "*To Scotland*," he continues. "*A note for the Queen: God disposes kingdoms in His hour. Should He raise you to another burden, remember those who held you in prayer when others sought to sell you dear.* No more. No names."

Feria bows. "Sire."

"And to Paris," Philip says. "Nothing. Let them learn from the wind like everyone else."

Alba smiles without warmth. "A policy."

"A policy," Philip agrees.

Pérez pauses, pen hovering. "Your Majesty—if she dies?"

The room waits.

Philip's hands lie flat on the table. "If she dies, we move no armies. We send condolences. We watch who takes the keys. If Mary Stuart is proclaimed, we greet her as a cousin in Christ and ask only that England keep her treaties and keep her hands off the Netherlands. If they raise Dudley or Grey, we bolster our friends in the North and on the Council and hold the sea with iron. We do not give France the war it wants. Not for an island that hates to be touched."

Feria's voice is low. "And if she lives and remembers?"

"Then we send her roses," Philip says. "And we pay de la Quadra to count her thorns."

A porter knocks. The door opens a crack. "Majesty, the chapel bell—"

Philip lifts a finger. The door hushes shut.

He reaches for the wax and sets his signet by Pérez's draft. The seal blooms red, then cools. "Send it at once. Not a word to the English ambassador here."

Alba bows from the waist. "The Low Countries?"

"We keep our line, Don Fernando. No new fires while the wind is wrong."

"At Hampton Court," Feria says, gentler now, "they pray for Elizabeth the way we prayed for—" He stops himself.

Philip's mouth is a straight line. "The way we prayed for Mary. Pray for them all," he says. "Pray for the island that never learns peace. And pray that we do not learn pride."

He stands. The men stand with him.

"Go," he says, and the room empties fast—Alba to the map room, Feria to the scribes, Pérez with his packet, Silva last, quiet as a cat.

Philip remains a moment longer. He touches the ring he never wears in public now, remembers the steady hand that placed it there, and releases it.

Then he turns for the chapel, where he will sit without moving and ask God, not for the life of Elizabeth, not for her death, but for a path that does not drown Spain in another country's fever.

Chapter 15
The Thirty-Nine Articles

10 February 1563

By the light of a single candle, Ambassador de la Quadra bends over his writing table in the embassy house near the Strand in London. The air is cold enough to thicken the ink. He warms the nib over the flame, dips his pen, and begins. His script is fast and tight, each line written with the knowledge that it will be weighed in Madrid.

"*To the Sacred Catholic Majesty, the King my Lord. Sire, from London this tenth day of February, I kiss the royal hands of Your Majesty and give account of matters now in motion in this realm. In these days the clergy in Convocation have set forth certain Articles of religion, which they number thirty and nine, to be held for the doctrine of their Church. If the Queen's ministers press these Articles towards full authority and drive men to subscription to them, the breach with the Holy See will be hardened beyond easy remedy, and there will remain no soft place for Rome to press.*

"*The chief points are these. They proclaim that man is justified by faith alone, without the works of the law, citing Saint Paul as their witness. They deny the true presence of Our Lord in the most Holy Sacrament, affirming that bread remains bread and wine remains wine. They strip away the jurisdiction of the Pope, whom they name Bishop of Rome, and set the Queen in his place as Supreme Governor of the Church. In this way they overthrow the order that has endured since the first preaching of the Gospel in this land.*

"*The bishops who remained faithful, Bishop Watson of Lincoln and Thirlby of Ely, endure their punishments with courage. Though stripped of their sees and kept under guard, they do not bend to the new order. They are few and sore pressed by the Queen's ministers, especially Secretary Cecil, who directs all. The party of the new learning grows bold, having many in the Commons with them and the Queen's favour behind them. Sire, if these Articles stand with force,*

England will not only be lost to the true Church, but will become a fortress of heresy upon Your Majesty's flank. The rebels in the Low Countries will look to this kingdom as a refuge and encouragement. Already the merchants of this realm traffic with the French of the new sect and spread their contagion.

"Thus the injury to Christendom is grave, and to the service of Your Majesty no less. It seems to me that unless remedy be found, the Catholic cause in this island will be reduced to silence. Yet I see that many still cleave to the old faith in secret. If they be aided and strengthened, there is hope they may endure. Without such aid, they will be crushed, and England will be altogether turned to heresy.

"Our Lord guard and prosper the royal person of Your Majesty with increase of realms and dominions. Of Your Majesty, the most humble servant and vassal, who kisses your royal feet and hands, Álvaro de la Quadra."

He sands the page, folds it, and seals it with wax. Outside two miles away, the bells of Westminster toll the hour. Inside the city, argument, preaching, and rumour move through the streets like smoke, and he sends his words across the sea as one sends a warning flare from a dark shore.

11 February 1563

Westminster and London do not speak with one voice this day. The distance between them is measured not in streets, but in power.

In Westminster Palace, the Lords are crowded and restless. Benches creak as men lean forward, voices low at first, then rising—the sound swelling beneath the timbered roof like pressure in a closed cask.

At the high table sits Nicholas Bacon, Lord Keeper, broad-shouldered and immovable, his heavy-lidded gaze fixed ahead as though carved from oak. Beside him William Cecil bends into the lamplight, quill poised over parchment, recording not sermons, but outcomes.

A clerk reads aloud from summaries carried in haste from St Paul's—reports of doctrine debated in Convocation and of the temper hardening among the clergy: *against transubstantiation; against papal jurisdiction; for the supremacy of Scripture; for the Queen's governance in causes ecclesiastical.* Each phrase lands like tinder.

Murmurs ripple the benches.

Thomas Howard, Duke of Norfolk, wary and cold, rises as though he would steady the room by force of rank alone.

"This course sunders England from Christendom," he says. "The Pope is no foreign tyrant but Peter's successor. Will you now have a woman as governor of the Church? Is it fitting that sacred mysteries bow to mortal skirts?"

Shouts answer him—approval and outrage braided together.

Anthony Browne, Viscount Montagu, pale but resolute, adds his own weight, driving Scripture like a nail into a door.

"'*Itaque, fratres, state: et tenete traditiones, quas didicistis, sive per sermonem, sive per epistolam nostram* — Therefore, brothers, stand firm and hold fast to the traditions you were taught, whether by word of mouth or by our letter' (2 Thessalonians 2:15). Cast away the fathers, and you tear Christ's seamless robe."

Cecil writes steadily. His hand tightens as the noise rises; he blots the page, keeps his face still, and measures not who wins a sentence, but what can be passed, what can be enforced, and what will break if pressed too hard.

***

Across the city, beneath the vast stone vault of St Paul's Cathedral, the arguments at the Convocation of the Clergy cut deeper and strike harder.

The Articles lie open on desks and lecterns. Quills scratch. Clerks copy carefully, knowing that what they write today will bind oaths tomorrow.

John Watson, Archdeacon of Surrey—not Bishop Watson of Lincoln—thickset and scarlet-faced, rises among the conservative clergy, his voice carrying the anger of an altar being unmade.

"This is blasphemy written in ink," he declares. "Article after article tears down the altar and mocks the Sacrifice of the Mass. You would tell Christ's flock that His Body is not upon the altar?"

He raises his voice, Latin ringing against stone.

"'*Sicut scriptum est: qui manducat meam carnem, et bibit meum sanguinem, habet vitam æternam, et ego resuscitabo eum in novissimo die* — He that eateth my flesh, and drinketh my blood, hath everlasting life: and I will raise him up in the last day' (John 6:54). So writes the Evangelist. Yet your English turns the sense. To deny transubstantiation is to deny Christ Himself."

A growl of assent moves through the Catholic remnant.

Dr Henry Cole, grey-haired and measured, follows, his tone steadier but no less severe.

"My brethren, England's faith stood firm for a thousand years. This doctrine is no ancient truth, but a novelty sprung from Germany. Saint Peter wrote: '*Hoc primum intelligentes, quod omnis prophetia Scripturæ propria interpretatione non fit* — Understanding this first, that no prophecy of Scripture is made by private interpretation' (2 Peter 1:20). The See of Rome has ever been the guardian of unity. Cast it off, and you cast England adrift."

From the reforming side rises James Pilkington, Bishop of Durham, answering Scripture with Scripture, as though the cathedral itself were his pulpit.

"My brethren, it is not novelty, but Paul himself. As the Great Bible says plainly: 'Therefore we conclude that a man is justified by faith without the works of the Law' (Romans 3:28). And again: 'Know that a man is not justified by the works of the Law, but by the faith of Jesus Christ...because by the works of the Law no flesh shall be justified' (Galatians 2:16). Will you bind England to works and ceremonies when Christ has set us free?"

The arguments grind on—precise, relentless, written down line by line as doctrine is sharpened into rule.

***

In the House of Commons at Westminster, the air is hotter, the language plainer.

Sir Francis Knollys, the Queen's kinsman, rises among the benches and speaks without ornament, his voice carrying across the chamber.

"Brethren, the matter before us is neither novelty nor rebellion, but the Gospel itself. 'For by grace are ye saved through faith, and that not of yourselves: it is the gift of God, not of works, lest any man should boast himself' (Ephesians 2:8–9). This is the foundation stone upon which no human authority may improve."

He turns slightly, as if addressing not only the House, but the nation beyond its walls.

"And again the Apostle teaches us: 'Not by the works of righteousness which we had done, but according to his mercy he saved us' (Titus 3:5). These are not German novelties, nor English inventions, but the plain words of Scripture."

Fists strike wood. Voices cry assent. The sound rolls upward, pressing against the chamber like a rising tide.

***

By evening, the streams have joined again.

At Whitehall, Elizabeth sits with Dudley, Cecil, Bacon, and Knollys, reports from Lords, Commons, and Convocation spread before them like stones laid for judgement. Her hand drifts to the coronation ring, the gold warmed by her skin. She turns it once, twice, the stone pressing into her thumb.

"They think me too slight a reed to bear the weight of Christ's Church," she says. "Yet Deborah judged Israel. Esther saved her people. Shall Elizabeth be less?"

Cecil answers carefully. "Majesty, the Commons hunger for reform, and the clergy in Convocation press their doctrine into shape. Resistance holds strongest among great lords and those who fear the speed of change. They argue theology—but they also argue your sex, and your right to govern the Church."

"The Scriptures support Your Majesty," Knollys adds. "Many look to you as the instrument to free England from Rome's yoke."

Bacon speaks last, steady as seasoned timber. "Zeal must be tempered. Too sharp a cut drives the unsure into the arms of your enemies. Authority lasts longer when it looks like order."

Elizabeth rises in a sweep of silks, jewel-light catching along her breast. She sets both hands upon the table and leans forward.

"My crown suffers no partner, least of all the Bishop of Rome. Let them snarl and thunder. Let them cite and threaten. I will have order in my Church and obedience in my realm. If Parliament and Convocation give these Articles force, then they shall stand. By God's will I govern, and by His hand I will not yield. England shall not kneel to Rome again."

Her palm strikes the table. Inkpots tremble. The torches crackle like dry tinder.

"England's soul is mine to guard," she says, "and I will guard it."

Dudley smiles faintly, pride bright in his eyes.

Elizabeth says, "Then let them see the lion's heart that beats in this woman's breast."

She meets the room, one face at a time. "Then let them look well," she says quietly. "They will find no weak heart here."

23 June 1563

Philip stands at the table, the papers laid before him squared with deliberate care. Sermons from London. Articles agreed in Convocation, not yet law. Extracts marked in a Roman hand. He has read them all before. He reads them again.

"Justification by faith alone," he says quietly. "The Sacrament denied. Obedience severed. The Bishop of Rome named a foreign tyrant." His mouth tightens. "They call this settlement."

Near the hearth stands Bernardo de Fresneda, hands folded in the wide sleeves of his Franciscan habit. He has served the King long enough to know when silence is counsel.

"They dress rebellion in law," Philip continues. "Mary—my wife—gave her life believing England might yet be restored. And now Elizabeth undoes it with statutes and sermons."

He turns at last, the chain of the Golden Fleece catching the candlelight as he moves. "Tell me, Father. Can the Church recognize a woman—once condemned by Rome—as governor of sacred things? Can a crown command the altar?"

Fresneda lowers his eyes a fraction. "No, Majesty. The Church has never granted such authority. What England claims is not governance. It is usurpation."

Philip nods once. "Then it is blasphemy sealed with wax."

He steps to the crucifix on the wall—not tearing it down, only laying his palm against the wood, fingers pressing hard as if to steady himself. The candles stir. Christ's shadow lengthens across the plaster.

"They say this is an English quarrel," Philip says. "It is not. Heresy crosses water more easily than armies. In the Netherlands they read her proclamations. They listen. They wait."

Fresneda speaks now, low, careful. "Majesty, God does not require haste to prove devotion. England may yet undo itself. I have observed that error often collapses under its own weight."

Philip draws his hand back and crosses himself, slowly. When he speaks again, the heat has gone from his voice, leaving resolve in its place.

"If she will not stand with the Church, she stands against it. I will not rush England into martyrdom—but neither will I allow it to become a beacon."

He looks to Fresneda. "Pray for me, Father. That I do not mistake wrath for justice."

The friar inclines his head. "I pray that Your Majesty remains the Church's shield," he says, "and not merely its blade."

Philip gathers the papers at last, aligning them into order.

"Then let God judge the hour," he says. "I will be ready when He calls it. I am His battleaxe and weapon of war."

21 July 1565

The Whitehall Palace Council Chamber is draped in black hangings. The rushes crackle faintly underfoot. A hush falls as Elizabeth enters, her face pale, her eyes swollen from weeping. At her side walks Mistress Anne Denny, steady and solemn. The councillors glance at each other in surprise. Elizabeth halts before the table, her hand resting on Foxe's *Actes and Monuments*, first published in 1563, open to a page of flames and martyrs.

Cecil clears his throat softly. "Majesty, shall Mistress Denny withdraw?"

Elizabeth fixes him with a gaze sharp through her grief. "No, Spirit. She will remain. Katherine Ashley—my Kat—is gone, and I will not stand before you stripped of every woman who loved me. Anne was Kat's companion, as faithful as she. If the Council may hear my words, it may hear hers also."

No man dares object. Anne bows low, then steps back by the Queen's chair, silent sentinel.

Elizabeth lays her palm against the woodcut of Latimer and Ridley. Her voice cracks.

"This book. Many of these in Foxe's book were my sister's victims. She thought she did God a service, yet she sent them to the flames—Cranmer, Ridley, Latimer. Hundreds of humble souls besides. They would not bow to Rome, nor confess the papacy, and for that, their bodies were consumed like kindling."

She sinks into her chair of estate, her hands shaking. "And now Kat—my Kat—is gone. She taught me letters when I was still a child, and guarded me in the Tower when the axe hovered. She loved me as her own, when I had no mother but the grave. I am robbed of her, and I am undone!"

Her voice breaks into sobs, heavy and raw. The councillors look down, moved yet uncertain. Anne Denny steps forward, kneeling at her side, daring to clasp her hand.

"Majesty, Kat spent herself so you could wear this crown. That was her martyrdom. I hold to Doctor Luther—faith alone. Kat believed it, even if she never named it. She would not have you falter. She would have you rise."

Elizabeth leans on her hand as if it were the last firm ground in the world.

Cecil speaks gravely. "Your Majesty, we stand against the papacy. Yet if Spain seeks a quarrel and gains a conquest, more Protestant blood shall flow. Their Inquisition would see to it. We must be resolute."

Knollys adds, his voice hard, "If England bows, the stake and the scaffold return. We will not bend our necks."

Elizabeth lifts her head, tears running but her eyes afire. "Then hear me, by Kat's memory, by the martyrs who would not yield, England shall not crawl again to Rome. Popery shall never rule this realm while I breathe."

With sudden force she slams Foxe's book shut, the sound ringing through the chamber. The councillors bow deeply, even Cecil's lips trembling.

Anne Denny rises beside her, still holding the Queen's hand. For a moment the grief of a daughter and the defiance of a sovereign are one and the same.

14 February 1567

At Whitehall Palace, the news arrives without ceremony.

No trumpet. No flourish. Just a sealed packet, damp from the road, thrust into a clerk's hands and carried—too quickly—through the corridors of Whitehall. By mid-morning it is on the council table, its seal broken, its contents read once, then read again in silence.

Elizabeth stands apart from them, near the tall windows that look out over the river. The February light is pale and hard. It does not flatter.

Cecil hesitates.

"Your Majesty," he says, carefully, "the report comes from Edinburgh by way of Berwick. It is...confused. But the substance is this."

He clears his throat and reads: "*Henry Stuart, Lord Darnley—King of Scots by marriage—has been found dead in the orchard below Kirk o' Field, outside the city walls. Not in his bed. Not in the house. Out of doors. Half-clad. Wearing only his nightshirt. No wound. No blade mark. No shot. No blood. Beside him, the body of a servant. The house in which Darnley had lodged—newly repaired for his recovery from illness—has been blown apart in the night. Stone scattered. Roof gone. Walls torn open as if by thunder. Yet the bodies lie apart from the wreckage, as though placed there."*

Cecil lowers the paper.

"No author of the crime is named," he says. "No arrests reported. No particulars beyond that."

For a moment, no one speaks.

Elizabeth turns from the window slowly.

"In his shirt," she repeats. "And unmarked."

Walsingham is already thinking aloud, unable to help himself.

"Then the blast did not kill him."

"No," Dudley agrees. "Nor did steel."

Elizabeth's eyes sharpen.

"Strangled," she says flatly. "Smothered. Or poisoned earlier and removed."

"Possibly," Cecil replies. "Though poison leaves its own questions."

"And questions," Elizabeth says, "are all we have."

She moves towards the table. The councillors step back slightly, instinctively making space. She reads the letter herself now, her finger tracing the lines.

"A house blown apart," she says. "Yet the bodies outside. Untouched by stone or flame. That is no accident. That is design."

Walsingham nods.

"It speaks of forethought," he says. "And of access. Whoever did this knew where he lay, how he was guarded, and how to remove him without raising alarm."

"And wished," Cecil adds, "for the manner of death to be unclear."

Elizabeth looks up sharply.

"Unclear to whom?"

Cecil does not hesitate.

"To all. To the law. To Europe."

A silence follows that answer.

Darnley was no loved figure—vain, violent, unreliable—but he was a crowned king. His death is not a private matter. It will be read in every court in every kingdom in Christendom.

Elizabeth's voice lowers.

"And my cousin," she says. "What of the Queen of Scots?"

"No word yet of her movements," Cecil replies. "Only that she was not in the house."

"But she placed him there," Dudley says. "Kirk o' Field was chosen for him. Repaired for him. Guarded for him."

"And guarded poorly," Walsingham adds.

Elizabeth turns on him and replies, "Careful, Moor."

"If the house was blown apart," he says, "then powder was laid. Powder requires time. Access. Men. Keys."

"And silence," Dudley says. "From servants. From guards."

Elizabeth closes her eyes briefly.

She knows the thought forming in the room. All of them do. None of them want to say it first.

"At the very least," Cecil says at last, choosing each word as if it might later be read aloud in Parliament, "the Queen of Scots will be suspected."

Elizabeth opens her eyes.

"Suspected," she repeats. "Yes. And suspicion alone may be enough to ruin her."

She walks back to the window. Outside, the river moves steadily, indifferent.

"If this is murder," she says, "then Scotland is already in peril. If it is conspiracy—if it reaches into her bedchamber—then she is undone."

"And if she is undone," Dudley says quietly, "others will rise."

"Mary's half-brother Moray," Walsingham says. "The Lords. The preachers."

"And beyond them," Cecil adds, "those who would use this chaos to press her claim—here."

Elizabeth's hand tightens on the window frame.

"Do not say it lightly," she snaps. "A murdered king is one thing. A murdered king whose widow claims my crown is another."

She turns back to them.

"No word," she orders, "is to go out from this court beyond acknowledgment of the death. No judgment. No sympathy beyond what is proper. I will not be seen to rejoice, nor to condemn—yet."

"Yes, Majesty," they answer.

Elizabeth looks once more at the letter on the table.

"In his shirt," she says again, softly now. "As if dragged from sleep. As if made helpless. As if meant to be seen."

She straightens.

"Whatever hand did this," she says, "intended the world to look—and not to know."

The councillors exchange glances. They understand.

This death will not end in Edinburgh. It will travel—through rumour, through accusation, through rebellion—and sooner or later, it will knock at England's door.

Elizabeth already hears it coming.

9 June 1567

The counting-house on the Scheldt in Antwerp smells of ink, sweat, and raw silver. Merchants crowd the benches, their ledgers open, while porters outside call out in Dutch and Spanish as wagons creak under the weight of coin bound for Philip's soldiers in the Low Countries.

At the centre of the room stands Sir Thomas Gresham, cloak cast aside, his collar embroidered with the English lion, though dulled by the dust of travel. He holds his hat beneath his arm, speaking in his clipped, careful cadence.

"Gentlemen, I am not here to meddle. England honours her debts and respects Spain's contracts. I stand only to assure His Majesty Philip's officers that no English merchant will obstruct the movement of bullion. My Queen desires peace, and I am here to prove it."

Opposite him, Spanish treasury agent Don Francisco de Vargas narrows his eyes, his fingers resting on the ledgers.

"And yet, Sir Thomas, Spanish silver disappears. Antwerp whispers that English hands divert it, that rebels in Holland line their purses with coin meant for His Majesty's soldiers. If you are her Majesty's man, why should I believe you are not part of this?"

Some of the silver was lost to smugglers, some to private hands, and some—no one could say to whom—vanished entirely. Gresham draws a steady breath. He spreads his palms over the table, not in defiance but in earnest appeal.

"Because I deal in truth, Señor Vargas, not rumour. I have accounted for every ingot that passed through my factor's hands. Yes, there are smugglers in Zeeland—men who serve neither England nor Spain but only their own gain.

I would see them punished as swiftly as you would. But do not mistake me for one of them."

A Dutch merchant at the edge of the table smirks faintly. The Spaniard beside him scowls. Gresham notices but presses on.

"England gains nothing by feeding the Dutch revolt. My Queen hates trouble on her doorstep as much as His Majesty does. She wants trade steady and the realm quiet. If I can do anything here, it is to plug the silver leaks—not open them."

He places a sealed packet on the treasurer's desk.

"Here are my accounts, signed and sealed. Every coin under my watch has gone where it was due. If you doubt me, send them to Madrid. I will answer before the King himself if I must."

There is a moment's silence. Vargas takes the papers. He scans them briefly, frowns, then nods curtly.

"Very well, Sir Thomas. I will send these on. But be warned—if even one bar of silver's found in rebel hands, it will be your queen, not you, who must answer."

Gresham inclines his head.

"Then let the truth speak for us both."

As he turns to leave, the murmur of voices swells behind him—Spaniards muttering suspicion, Dutchmen whispering in amusement. Gresham steps into the Antwerp street, the heavy air thick with smoke and the smell of river mud. He pauses at the threshold, hat in hand, and looks north—past the forest of masts towards Zeeland's flat line. Trouble is already moving there: Alba's men on the roads, creditors tightening terms, sailors whispering of "Beggars" in the shoals. He runs the sums in his head—bills due at Middelburg, exchange stiffening in Bruges—and sets his jaw. If silver's leaking, it will not be by his hand. He turns into the crowd, already planning which door to knock on next.

16 June 1567

The bells of Onze-Lieve-Vrouwekerk toll Vespers, their sound rolling over the river. Inside the Spanish treasury offices, the shutters are drawn against the glare, but the air is close and heavy with the stink of tallow and damp parchment.

Sitting at a broad table is Francisco de Vargas, his ledger open, Gresham's neat packet of accounts beside it. He flips the sealed folio in his hands. The

Englishman had stood in this very room not two days past, plain and earnest, speaking of honesty, of peace, of Elizabeth's good faith. Vargas remembers the steady cadence of his words, the calm with which he spread his palms across the table. Too calm. Too even.

From the courtyard below come the voices of merchants—Spanish, Flemish, and English alike—their arguments a babel of suspicion. Vargas hears the whispers even now: bullion gone missing, rebels in Zeeland buying powder, English ships unloading coin in the night. Each tale is more venomous than the last, but none without the stench of truth. He had figures, not proof—yet.

He dips his quill. He smooths his glove along the page's edge, then answers the empty room in a voice a touch too quick—as if rehearsed. He scratches the first line across the parchment: "*To the Sacred Catholic Majesty, the King my Lord...*"

The ink runs, black and precise, as he frames the report. He writes of Gresham's protestations, of the sealed accounts laid before him. Yet his quill does not soften. The words fall cold. "*His protestations were strong, but perhaps too strong.*" He pauses, studying the phrase. He hopes Philip will see the danger in that.

He listens to the scratch of the nib, the rise and fall of the words he shapes—suspicion dressed as prudence, concern laced with warning. He adds, "*Sire, I submit this to Your Majesty's wisdom: if Spain is to secure the treasure that sustains the war in Flanders, then England's hand in this matter must be shown openly and checked with firmness. The Queen's agent is clever, but not beyond Your Majesty's sight. May Our Lord guard and prosper the royal person of Your Majesty with the increase of realms and dominions.*"

At the margin he makes a small note in cipher, for his eyes alone: "*The Englishman is clever, but Elizabeth profits still.*"

A clerk enters with a bundle of ledgers, bows, and withdraws. Vargas sands the page, folds it, seals it with his ring.

He lifts the sealed letter, weighing it in his hand as if it were silver itself.

"Madrid must know," he murmurs, his voice low, almost a prayer. "If the King doubts England, let it be through my hand he learns to doubt them more."

Outside, the bells fall silent. The letter is dispatched by courier before nightfall, carried down to the waiting barges on the Scheldt. Within weeks, it will lie on Philip's table in Madrid, ink still sharp, the seeds of mistrust already sown. What silver could not yet prove, the letter would begin to make true.

1 July 1567

At the Royal Apartments in Madrid, the summer sun presses like a brand against the shutters. Inside, the King's study is close and airless, the heat held like a threat. Philip sits rigid in his carved walnut chair, one hand on a sealed dispatch from the Low Countries, the other worrying the great ruby ring at his finger until the stone creaks in its setting.

Before him stands Dr John Man, England's ambassador, travel-dust still in the seams of his black gown. He keeps his cap in both hands, knuckles pale.

Philip does not bid him sit.

"Doctor Man," he says at last, the words trimmed to the bone, "your Gresham juggles silver in Antwerp."

Man swallows. "Your Majesty, rumours multiply in a market city. Sir Thomas—"

"These are not rumours." Philip snaps the seal with his thumb and flicks the parchment flat with two fingers. "Here it is in a treasurer's hand: bars marked for my *tercios* vanish on the Scheldt and reappear in Zeeland, where heretics buy powder by the barrel. English factors touch the coin. English hulls carry it. English courtiers wink and call it trade." He leans forward, voice dropping to a blade's edge. "My silver arms my enemies. And you come to me speaking of friendship?"

Man forces a breath, schooling his voice to evenness. "Your Majesty, England seeks no quarrel with Spain. If any money's strayed, it is without my Queen's warrant. She is innocent of—"

"Innocent?" Philip rises abruptly. He throws one shutter wide open. A sheet of Castilian light flares across his shoulder like drawn steel. "Then your mistress is no sovereign, if merchants rule in her stead." He turns, eyes like hammered iron. "Tell her this: if one more ingot meant for Flanders goes astray, I will shut my ports to every English keel and I will command seizures, especially of English cloth. Any Englishman found carrying powder to rebels shall be taken as a pirate and hanged as one. Do I make myself clear, Doctor Man?"

Man's lips part, close. He wets them, choosing a safer hill. "Sire, I beg you—do not take offence for the deeds—"

"Do I make myself clear, Doctor Man?"

"Yes, Your Majesty. Please do not take offence at men who profit in the shadows. I promise you my queen desires peace and commerce between your realms. She will punish any subject found—"

Philip cuts him again, flat and final. "See that she does. Or shall I teach her where power lies?" He taps the dispatch once with two fingers, the sound small and hard in the heat. "I am weary of English assurances. Give me English compliance."

A beat. Man bows from the waist. "I will write to London at once."

Philip holds him in silence long enough to make the bow ache. Then, without softening, "See that you do. You have my leave, sir."

Man backs towards the door, finds the latch, and is gone.

The chamber breathes again. From the shadow by the writing desk, Don Antonio Pérez steps forward, bowing the bow of a man who knows when to keep his teeth behind his smile.

"Well, Sire," Pérez says lightly, "England will have heard a thunderclap."

Philip does not look up at once. He stares at the broken seal, thumb grinding a crescent into the wax. *She sends a merchant to juggle bullion while my provinces burn—and expects me to believe her hands are clean.*

Pérez's tone is silk over wire. "Gresham is clever. He leaves as few prints as a cat. But even a cat leaves dust." He nods at the dispatch. "The treasurer names the wharf and the night. We can pull the thread."

Philip sets the letter down, ringed hand now steady. "Write to Brussels: the Regent's to lay hands on any English cloth found without perfect warrant, and to weigh every chest that passes to the camps. Write to Seville and Cádiz: no English hull takes victual or licence until I say so. And send our mind to the Genoese—quietly. If they lend London so much as a sneeze, they will find Spanish harbours deaf to their ships."

Pérez inclines his head, eyes half-lidded. "And the Duke of Alba?"

"He rides," Philip says, a grim satisfaction tightening his mouth. "When he reaches the Low Countries, let him understand: English meddling's to be treated as mutiny in a magazine." He closes the shutter slowly, the room falling again into its hot dimness. "Let the woman in London count the cost. If her merchants touch my silver once more, I will touch her kingdom—in its purse first, and later where it bleeds."

Pérez allows himself the smallest breath of a smile. "I will put it into letters that even an Englishman can read."

3 August 1567

The midsummer sun beats down on the green of Whitehall, dappling the archery field in gold. Queen Elizabeth stands at the line, bow raised, her crimson mantle moving in the breeze like a banner. Under a striped awning nearby, a page keeps watch over a small table with a flagon of cool ale beaded with sweat and a trencher of cherries and marchpane knots dusted with sugar, laid out for the Queen and her favourites, though she has not so much as glanced at them.

She looses her arrow. It thuds cleanly into the red ring of the target.

Applause ripples from the watching courtiers. Robert Dudley, now Earl of Leicester, strolls to her with a practiced smile.

"Your Majesty never misses."

Elizabeth gives a faint smile but says nothing.

A hush falls as William Cecil approaches from the periphery. He bows.

"Your Majesty. I crave a word."

Elizabeth lowers her bow. "Speak."

Cecil's tone is low, but the tension in his eyes betrays him.

"Mary Stuart has been compelled to abdicate. She is held at Loch Leven Castle. The Lords of Scotland have placed her son on the throne."

Elizabeth stiffens. The bowstring slips from her fingers.

"Abdicated?" she repeats, voice edged and cool. "She has surrendered her crown?"

Cecil nods. "Under duress. At threat of the sword. Moray is to be Regent. And already, there are whispers she may seek refuge abroad."

"France is weary of her. Scotland's turned on her. There is only one realm where her claim has teeth."

A beat.

"She must not come here."

Cecil hesitates. "Majesty...she is likely to. Her friends in Scotland are few. The House of Valois in France distrusts her. England is her strongest card."

Elizabeth turns away, staring across the long lawn where noblemen laugh without listening.

"And what now?" she asks quietly. "Shall we commend a rebellion against an anointed sovereign?"

"That is the danger," Cecil replies. "If it may be done to her, some may dream it may be done here. Her fall gives hope to malcontents."

Elizabeth's lips tighten. "A queen cast down by her own subjects...it is a very abominable precedent."

"Yes, ma'am," Cecil says. "And one our own Catholics may read too eagerly."

Elizabeth hands her bow to a page, ignoring the cup of ale he offers with it; her thirst now is for news, not drink.

"She has lost her throne," she murmurs. "But she has not lost her use. A dethroned queen is a rallying-cry. They will make a saint of her suffering."

"Some already do," Cecil admits. "In certain houses, they call her the rightful Queen of England."

Elizabeth's jaw sets. "I will not have that said within my realm!"

Cecil bows his head. "Shall I strengthen the watch in the north?"

"Do it. Increase the search of letters. Gentlemen too devout, too silent—I want their names. And keep our eyes in France. If the Guises stir, then we will know Mary still has champions."

Cecil inclines his head. "At once, Majesty."

Elizabeth glances again towards the target, but the red ring blurs. Her thoughts are elsewhere. She sees not the painted circle but the shadow of a fallen queen, carried now not by a realm but by the hopes of those who would test England's crown.

Mary Stuart had been stripped of her throne—and in losing it, had become far more dangerous.

Elizabeth reaches for the bow again. Habit steadies her hand; the field lies unchanged.

She looses.

The arrow flies clean—then the wind lifts at the last instant. It strikes just outside the red, close enough to count, far enough to matter.

No one speaks.

Elizabeth lowers the bow slowly, eyes still on the target.

"Enough," she says at last, and turns away, knowing the next shot will not be offered so openly.

Chapter 16
News and Leverage

9 August 1567

The great halls of Philip's palace in Madrid echo with silence, broken only by the soft rustling of parchment and the occasional murmur of servants. He sits at his desk, his brow tense with focus as he reviews documents. A sharp knock comes at the door.

"Enter."

The door creaks open, and Don Cristóbal de Moura, a trusted Portuguese gentleman of his household, rising in favour, steps in quickly, his face tight with urgency. He bows. Philip glances up.

"Sire," Moura says, his voice laced with unease. "There is news from Scotland."

Philip thinks at once of Mary, Queen of Scots. He considers her a useful Catholic claimant whose very presence checks Elizabeth should England stray too far. He has encouraged her when it served him; to him she was an instrument more than a queen.

"What news?" Philip's voice is low and controlled—quiet that conceals the force gathering beneath it.

Moura hesitates, a flicker of concern passing across his face. "It is...grave news, Your Majesty. Dispatches some weeks old say Mary has been compelled to abdicate her throne in favour of her infant son. They say she signed under guard and is held at Loch Leven Castle."

For a heartbeat, Philip does not seem to breathe.

"Abdicated?" The word comes out almost as a whisper, cut with iron.

Moura nods gravely and steps closer. "Yes, Sire. The Scottish nobles forced her hand. They have proclaimed the child King James, with her half-brother, the Earl of Moray, as Regent. Their rebellion carried the day."

Philip rises abruptly. The chair legs scrape stone. He turns half away. Mary—lawful, anointed, Catholic—dragged down by her own lords. The strongest line to Tudor blood pushed aside for a baby and a heretic.

"She signed?" he forces out. "Put her name to it?"

Moura's voice softens. "It was not free will, Sire. She is held, threatened, surrounded by enemies. They made her choose between her crown and her head."

Philip's hand closes around the chain of the Golden Fleece at his breast until it bites. "And her friends?" he demands. "Huntly, Lord Fleming, the rest? Did they simply stand by?"

"Her friends have fled or made their peace," Moura answers. "Dispatches say Huntly skulks in the north. Lord Fleming lies low. Bothwell is disgraced and gone. Edinburgh is held by the Protestant lords, with the Kirk's blessing. The preachers cry that the boy-king is God's judgement. And the English..." He hesitates. "The English do nothing. Cecil and Elizabeth will not raise a finger to restore her."

Philip lets out a slow, harsh breath. "That I do not find surprising."

He turns to the window, looking out over the baked hills beyond Madrid, though he sees only islands and northern mists in his mind's eye. Behind him, the wine thickens in the heat, souring slowly in its cup. "Mary was our strongest card," he murmurs, more to himself than to Moura. "A lawful Catholic queen in my enemy's shadow. Now Scotland wears a Protestant child, and England a Protestant woman."

For a moment the weight of it all presses down—Mary Tudor's failed restoration, Elizabeth's stubborn survival, Scotland slipping away. The hope of an easy Catholic settlement in the north shrinks to a pinprick.

Then he straightens. When he turns back, the raw hurt in his face is gone, buried under something colder.

"No," he says quietly. "This is not an end. It is a change of shape."

Moura observes him carefully. "Sire?"

"They have not merely deposed her," Philip says. "They have made her suffer. They have turned a crowned queen into a prisoner. That does not erase her right—it inflames it." His voice hardens. "They think they have solved the problem. They have made a standard."

He begins to pace, not with agitation now, but with purpose.

"Let Elizabeth think herself safe with a babe on the Scottish throne," he goes on. "Let the rebels boast that they have tamed their queen. The more they boast, the more sympathy she will gather in every Catholic court. They have turned her into a story that can be told in every chapel from Lisbon to Vienna."

He stops before Moura, eyes bright with a grim light.

"Set the ambassadors to work. Rome must be made to *see* what has been done in Scotland—that a crowned Catholic queen has been broken by heretics and held by force. Let the Holy Father be urged to *maintain her right*, even if he will not yet proclaim it aloud. And in France, stir the Guises. Let them feel the dishonour to their blood, the injury done to their house. Speak to them of injustice, of lineage trampled underfoot—quietly, patiently—until outrage ripens into purpose."

Moura nods slowly. "You would have her case proclaimed?"

"Her case, yes," Philip says. "Not because I love the woman, but because her wrong gives us ground. A queen forced from her throne, a lawful heir kept under lock and key—this is cause. Righteous cause. If we must one day move against England, let it be with such a banner before us."

He half turns away again, voice dropping.

"She is no longer only a queen," Philip says. "She is a testimony. A wound. They think they have buried her. They have planted her."

He looks back to Moura, decision set.

"Prepare the letters," Philip orders. "In honeyed Latin to Rome. In cipher to Brussels and Paris. We will not speak of Mary as finished. We will speak of her as wronged. Let the world decide what such wrong demands."

10 August 1567

Late sun leaks through the heavy curtains of the Privy Chamber at Hampton Court and dies on dark wood. The air is close. A clerk's quill scratches like an insect. Elizabeth sits high in her chair of estate, pearls cold along her throat, eyes fixed on the three men before her.

Sir Thomas Gresham stands first—travel-worn, hat crushed between his palms. Dr John Man waits beside him, grave and still. William Cecil holds a folded paper at his fingertips, in the quiet posture of a man who counts consequences before they hatch.

Elizabeth taps her signet against the arm of the chair—one, two, three—and stops.

"Well? Out with it."

Gresham exhales through his nose. "Your Majesty, the King of Spain rages over Antwerp. He claims English hands—mine, if you believe his councillors—divert Spanish silver towards rebel powder."

"And do they speak truth, Sir Thomas?"

"No, Majesty. I move credit and funds to hold England's name firm, not to imperil it. If Spanish bars drift astray, it is by smugglers in Zeeland who answer no crown. Yet Madrid hears 'Gresham' and smells treason in a ledger line."

Man's gaze flicks towards him, cool. "Because, Sir Thomas, your ledger lines touch half of Europe. Mere presence smells of participation."

"Doctor, I answer to Her Majesty's purse—not to Philip's temper. Without brisk work in Antwerp, England's credit sours, and the City panics. Must I beg the King of Spain's permission to steady our name?"

Man does not blink. "You must not give him leave to call you thief while I stand in his court to say you are not."

Elizabeth's signet taps again—hard. Her voice slices between them.

"Enough. I will not have Spain call England beggar and pirate in the same breath. Sir Thomas, speak plain. Have you, by design or neglect, let Spanish silver run to the rebel magazines?"

Gresham lifts his chin. "Majesty—never by design. If any neglect is spoken of, it lies in rumour and mischief, not in my hand. I have not yielded one bar to any traitor."

Then, unexpectedly, he turns to Man. "If my trade throws you deeper into Philip's wrath, Doctor, I am sorry. I mend credit with coin, not courtesy. I would not have you share blame for what I have not done."

Man absorbs this; a small sliver of tension eases. "Thank you for the truth. I will need it where I go."

Cecil clears his throat. "Majesty, Spain's anger is a wind we cannot still—but we can set our sails to it."

Elizabeth tilts her head. "Then we set them."

Cecil steps to the great wall map. "Two points," he says. "First: your envoy must carry a firm, simple line. England denies design. England punishes smugglers. England weighs any chest that lands on her shore as strictly for Philip as for her own—unless the law says otherwise."

Elizabeth's eyes stay fixed on him. "Plain. And your second?"

Cecil's forefinger slides from the Low Countries towards the Narrow Seas. "Here lies our advantage," he says. "The silver bullion now afloat in Spanish vessels consists of Genoese loans, not Spanish property—not until the chests are delivered, received, and acknowledged in the Duke of Alba's magazines."

He taps the coast opposite Kent.

"If those chests reach Alba, he pays his *tercios* to the last maravedi. Paid soldiers dig deeper trenches, string men faster, and hire Dunkirkers till they choke our trade. With coin in hand, Alba turns the Narrow Seas into a Spanish moat."

"And if the coin does not reach him?" Elizabeth asks.

"Then Alba stalls," Cecil says. "He mutters, bargains, delays. His captains grow lean. His men recall mutiny."

Elizabeth studies him. "And the lawful ground on which we may hold such treasure?"

"By usage—by practice more than by clean law—the bullion in passage is claimed by those who advance it, not by the prince it serves. Genoese silver rides under Genoese names, and that gives us a hand. Not a clean hand—only a hand we can force into a glove, if we move fast."

"I am intrigued," Elizabeth says.

"If bullion ever lands on our shore, we may arrest it, say it is custody, not seizure, and be ready, if need be, to lay it in the Tower upon Your Majesty's credit. Spain will protest. The bankers will howl. The lawyers will argue for months. But while they argue, Alba goes hungry and the silver stays. And with it, our leverage."

Elizabeth's eyes glint. "'Arrested' sounds like a graceful veil for theft."

"We do not steal it," Cecil says. "We become the debtors. We pay the Genoese their value, as best we can. Spain is left to quarrel with Genoa first, not England. And we deny Alba the means to fire the Low Countries into our graves."

Gresham's mouth twitches—the first true sign of satisfaction. "The Genoese love a lock that does not leak, Majesty."

Man nods once, seeing the whole shape now. "Then I will tell Philip this in Madrid: England seeks peace, but England bows to no accusation unproven. Any coin landing on our shore by Providence and tide will be held faithfully while its owners and claimants argue title."

Elizabeth rises. "Good. Doctor Man, you leave at once. Philip throws thunder—meet him with civility and ice. If he calls my factors 'pirates' again, call his informers liars to their faces. In Latin."

A flicker—almost a smile—touches Man's mouth. "Assuredly, I will carry your mind, Your Majesty."

Elizabeth turns to Gresham. "Sir Thomas, return to Antwerp with clean hands and cleaner books. I want every bar you touch reckoned like a chapter verse. If any shadow falls on your ledger, I will see it before Spain does."

Gresham bows. "Majesty, you will have a ledger to shame daylight."

She turns to Cecil. "Draw the commission. And quietly send letters to our friends among the Genoese. If their silver drifts into my harbours, I would have locks—ready."

Cecil inclines his head. "Consider it done."

Elizabeth sets her palm flat on the table, voice low and decisive.

"Hear me. England will not be schooled by Spain. I will not let English coin purchase English ruin. If Philip presses us with force, we answer with law. If he sends silver, we answer with locks."

She parts the curtain with two fingers; a blade of light cuts the chamber.

"Go, Doctor Man, to Madrid. Let Philip hear our meaning from an English mouth, plainly and without ornament. Sir Thomas, go to Antwerp and Brussels. Be my eyes and ears in Brussels. Antwerp will tell Philip what the merchants fear; Brussels will tell him what the Regent's court and Alba intend. Master Secretary, to your papers. And if fortune casts a Spanish chest onto England's shore—"

Her voice hardens.

"—I will not throw it back."

"I have scarcely shaken the dust of Castile from my cloak, Majesty, and now I must face him again," quips Man.

He bows and departs. Gresham follows, pausing only long enough to murmur:

"God keep you in that furnace, Doctor. If my dealings have stoked it—"

"Then help me bank the fire," Man replies. "Send me figures that cannot lie."

"I will."

They go.

Cecil remains long enough for Elizabeth's final murmur.

"Spirit," she says without turning, "if Providence hands me Genoa in a Spanish hull, the Tower will need room."

Cecil's mouth bends at the corner. "Then we will make the Tower a counting-house, Majesty."

"Make it ready."

"With the greatest of pleasure, Your Majesty."

22 August 1567

The bells of Antwerp ring the noon hour, steady and unhurried, but the sound carries no comfort. It spreads across the quays and counting-houses like a question no one wishes to answer.

The Scheldt lies thick with traffic—hulks, hoys, river barges nudging for space—but men linger longer than they should at the water's edge, eyes turned east, towards the Mechelen road. Word in the city has come faster than any courier: the Duke of Alba has entered Brussels—some say this morning.

The name settles over Antwerp like ash. Not fire—yet—but the knowledge that fire has learned the roads.

Sir Thomas Gresham stands beneath the striped canopy of a spice merchant, his cloak drawn tight against the wind that carries grit and river-smell into the square. He does not look at the ships. He looks at the faces.

They have changed.

Voices are lower. Men speak in half-calculations, already counting what might be frozen or lost. A clerk folds his papers twice, then again, as if careful handling might keep them safe. Across the square, a Genoese factor argues in sharp whispers with a German partner, both men glancing towards the road as though expecting iron to appear at any moment.

A murmur passes through the crowd—not loud enough to name, but too present to ignore.

"Alba."

"The Iron Duke."

"God help us."

Gresham's young factor, Richard Cottingham, presses closer, his voice barely moving his lips.

"They say he rode straight to the palace," he whispers. "No speeches. No triumph. Just banners and a city taught to watch its tongue."

Gresham nods once. "That is how he works."

He has dealt with kings and creditors both. He knows which are harder to appease.

Far off, beyond the last roofs, a faint vibration reaches them—too distant to be sound, too steady to be imagined. Not drums. Not yet. The road traffic has thickened since dawn. Wagons. Couriers. Men riding hard, heads down.

Spain is moving.

A woman crosses herself at the mention of Alba's name. A brewer's apprentice drops a keg hoop; it clangs against the stones, too loud, and several heads snap towards the sound. A moment later, talk resumes—but thinner now, cautious, as though words themselves have become evidence.

Cottingham swallows. "If he has Brussels, sir—"

"He has the law," Gresham replies quietly. "The army is only there to remind people of it."

A mounted courier pushes through the square, spurs flashing. He does not slow. He does not look at anyone. The red cross of Saint James stitched on his sleeve draws eyes like a wound.

Someone says, not quite aloud, "He will ask for accounts."

Another voice answers, sharper, "First, he will ask for obedience."

Gresham watches a pair of Italian bankers step aside from their own clerks, speaking fast, hands already moving as if counting losses not yet made. Antwerp lives on credit and confidence; both have begun to drain away.

Cottingham shifts his weight. "Do we stay?"

"For now," Gresham says. "Alba does not break the table while the game still pays."

Gresham understands then how little of this he truly controls—not silver, not law, not even delay—only the order in which the blows may fall.

As if summoned by the thought, a troop of Spanish cavalry rides past the far end of the square—no fanfare, no challenge. Just order. Steel bridles. Disciplined pace. They do not stop. They are not here *for* Antwerp.

Yet.

The crowd parts instinctively, like water around a prow. Authority does not need to announce itself. It only needs to arrive. When the riders are gone, no one steps forward to claim the space they leave.

Gresham lets out a breath he had not realised he was holding.

"This city lives by ledgers," he says. "Alba will not burn it. He will weigh it."

Cottingham's face is pale. "And when the weighing is done?"

Gresham's eyes return to the road.

"Then men will learn what they owe."

And how little mercy weighs on a scale built for obedience.

Above them, the bells finish their course and fall silent. The river moves on. The ships remain moored. Trade continues—on the surface.

31 August 1567

The great hall of the Coudenberg Palace in Brussels holds the day's heat poorly. Stone walls sweat cold, and the high arches drink sound until even courtesies feel rehearsed. Men stand in small clusters, breaking off to sort papers or adjust seals when others draw near. No one settles. It is not a meeting that invites comfort.

The doors open without announcement.

The Duke of Alba enters.

There is no hurry in him. No theatre. He walks as a man accustomed to rooms giving way. Behind him come a handful of officers and clerks—no ranks drawn up, no weapons raised. The army is elsewhere, doing its work by being known to exist.

A servant sets a chair near the table. Alba does not sit. He stands, hands loosely clasped behind his back, surveying the room with the patience of a man reading a map he already understands.

"Gentlemen," he says, his voice level, almost mild. "We will proceed."

Men turn to papers—notes, memoranda, unread petitions—because speaking feels like signing.

At Alba's side stand two jurists: Licenciado Juan de Vargas and Don Luis del Río. Their robes are plain. Their faces are not. They carry themselves like men long accustomed to ink deciding fates.

"The King," Alba continues, "has charged me with restoring obedience in these provinces. Disorder has been permitted too long. Errors have been indulged too freely. It is my task to determine responsibility—calmly, lawfully, and without favour."

A few men shift. Someone clears his throat and thinks better of it.

Licenciado Juan de Vargas steps forward, unrolling a shorter parchment—not a catalogue, not a roll of doom, but a framework: articles, jurisdictions, procedures.

"This council," he says, "will examine disturbances against the King's peace. It will inquire into sedition, unlawful assemblies, iconoclasm, the harbouring of rebels, and the encouragement of heretical preaching."

He does not say *condemn*. He does not need to.

A nobleman near the front—Egmont among them, still confident enough to stand straight—speaks, carefully measured.

"My Lord Duke," he says, "the States have long governed such matters within their privileges. There are customs here—"

Alba turns his head slightly. Only slightly.

"The King's authority," he replies, "does not abolish custom. It precedes it."

The words fall without heat. That makes them worse.

"There will be examinations," Alba continues. "Some will be called to answer. Many will not. Those with nothing to fear will find this council a formality. Those who protest too loudly may wish to consider why."

A clerk steps forward with a sheaf of papers—petitions, reports, denunciations already gathered. No names are read aloud. None need be.

Someone mutters, already thinking of estates, accounts, and sons not yet written to, "God preserve us."

Alba hears it. He does not respond.

"This body," he says, "is provisional. Its authority derives from the King's commission and will endure as long as disorder endures. Its purpose is clarity."

He pauses, allowing the word to do its work.

"In time," he adds, "men may give it a name. That is not my concern."

The licenciado inclines his head, faintly. Del Río's pen scratches once, precise and final.

The meeting ends as it began—by clerks gathering papers and sealing documents, as if judgement had merely been postponed, not avoided. Men drift back, faces tight, already rehearsing explanations, already counting friends who may not answer letters soon.

At the edge of the hall, half-shadowed by a pillar, Sir Thomas Gresham observes without being observed—until he is.

Alba's gaze finds him, brief and assessing. A foreign merchant. An Englishman. A fact worth remembering.

Gresham bows—correct, minimal. Alba neither returns it nor refuses it. He simply turns away.

"There will be no haste," the Duke says to no one in particular. "But there will be thoroughness."

Outside, the bells of Brussels call Vespers. The sound spreads across the city, measured and ordinary.

Inside the palace, something irreversible has begun.

Gresham steps out into the cooling air, his factor close behind him.

"Master," Cottingham whispers, "what does this mean?"

Gresham does not answer at once. He looks back at the palace windows, already glowing with lamplight.

"It means," he says at last, "that fear has been given a desk, a seal, and patience."

He pulls his cloak tighter.

"And that patience is Spain's sharpest weapon."

The bells continue their course.

War is not declared.

But it is being organized—carefully, lawfully, and without mercy.

3 March 1568

Whitehall Palace. The council chamber is dim in the grey London morning, candles guttering in the draft. William Cecil stands at the long table, sorting dispatches into grim little piles. Elizabeth enters with a sweep of skirts, face pale but alert—the look she wears when trouble gathers.

"Your Majesty," Cecil says without preamble. "Reports from Antwerp. Alba has suspended several English accounts 'pending inquiry.' Gresham warns this is only the beginning."

Elizabeth moves to the hearth, hands clasped behind her back. "Suspended on what grounds?"

"None stated, Majesty. But the implication is clear: the Duke suspects English merchants of aiding the Dutch rebels. He means to test how far he can squeeze before we answer him."

"Then we will not squeal like a stepped-on rat. We will wait. And we will watch."

Cecil hesitates. "If we wait too long, Majesty, he will mistake restraint for weakness."

Elizabeth turns sharply—hawk-quick. "Not silence, William. Restraint. Let him imagine I am asleep. The surprise will hurt more."

She steps closer, lowering her voice.

"What of Spain's bullion shipments?"

"More than usual, Majesty. The treasury in Madrid drains silver into the Low Countries daily. Alba is building a war chest."

Elizabeth murmurs, "For the Dutch..." Then after a beat: "Or for us."

She moves to the window. Outside, the Thames glints under a sullen sky.

"Continue," she commands.

"Your Majesty," Cecil says quietly, "if Alba begins seizing English property outright, we...may need to respond."

"A measured response. Not yet open hostility."

Cecil bows his head. "At your command."

But he, like she, can feel it—the pressure tightening. The balance shifting. Something drawing closer, inch by inch.

5 March 1568

Antwerp Exchange. Sir Thomas Gresham descends the broad stone steps of the Bourse, cloak whipping in the cold wind. The air is thick with the reek of tar, river mud, and sour beer from the taverns under the arcade, where clerks gulp thin ale and gnaw at cheese and black bread between bargains. Behind him, Cottingham hurries to keep pace.

"They mean to break us, sir," Cottingham whispers. "Francisco de Vargas—Spanish treasury agent in Alba's service—has his clerks refuse every bill we present. And the *tercios* stand in the square. Armed."

Gresham stops, scanning the merchants' faces—Dutch fear, Spanish suspicion, English anxiety.

"Alba tests our nerve," Gresham says. "He squeezes a little more each day. He froze two accounts yesterday. Today, six more. Tomorrow, twelve."

He lifts a sealed letter—the one he will send to Cecil tonight.

"He hopes to provoke us into a misstep. If England strikes first, Spain claims righteousness before all Christendom."

Cottingham worries his gloves. "And if we do nothing?"

Gresham eyes the Spanish soldiers stationed at the market gates.

"Then he will take everything. Slowly. Without firing a shot."

A wagon rattles past, laden with silver bars stamped with Castile's arms—soldiers flanking it on both sides. Gresham watches it go with a face of carved ice.

"Tell the factors to hold steady," he says. "Tell them to keep English coin tight. No rash moves. If Alba wants a confrontation, let *him* strike the first blow."

Cottingham nods but cannot hide his dread.

A bell tolls. The crowd murmurs. And Gresham senses it again: a line being drawn underfoot.

He says, "Once Alba controls the flow of silver, he controls the war. And once he controls the war, he will decide who trades—and who starves."

7 March 1568

Coudenberg Palace. A thin rain streaks the palace windows. Inside, the Duke of Alba stands beside a table strewn with ledgers and reports. Francisco de Vargas reads from a parchment in his dry, venomous voice.

"Seizure of property belonging to one John Fitzwilliam of London. Confiscated on suspicion of 'dealings with the rebel party.'"

"Approved," Alba says.

Vargas continues: "Holding of funds from the house of Gresham, pending examination."

"Approved."

Another. "Inspection of English vessels in port—"

"Approved."

A younger officer, fresh-faced and perhaps too bold, steps forward.

"My Lord Duke, shall we not issue a general ban upon all English merchants? Strike decisively?"

Alba turns his head—slowly.

"No," he says. "We tighten by degrees. A rope does not kill when first thrown. It kills when it draws close."

The officer swallows.

Alba takes up a dispatch from Madrid—Philip's hand.

"*Proceed with full authority. Protect the faith. Maintain order. The Queen of England grows bold—Philip*"

Alba folds the letter.

"Madrid watches," he murmurs. "But London watches too. The Queen grows anxious. Good. Fear will make her cautious."

Treasury agent Vargas smirks. "And when she is cautious, she hesitates."

"And when she hesitates," Alba finishes, "we strike."

A moment passes, filled by the scratch of Vargas's pen and the folding of ledgers.

Then: "Continue the seizures. Quietly. Relentlessly."

Outside, thunder rumbles over Brussels—the kind that shakes shutters and unsettles horses.

Inside, Alba returns to the ledger.

The storm builds.

Not in the sky.

It builds in men.

Chapter 17
Closed Courts, Open Wars

8 March 1568

The halls of the Alcázar in Madrid hold their breath, broken only by the faint rustle of footsteps and the whisper of cloth. Servants scurry to and fro, keeping out of the way of the King's inevitable wrath. Philip, usually a man of quiet deliberation, stands near the windows of his chamber. He gazes out at the Spanish landscape below, the distant hills veiled by the grey clouds.

The door creaks open, and Dr John Man steps hesitantly inside. The sound of his heels against the marble floor echoes as he walks forward, bowing before the King. After days of silence, the summons finally came, and rumours of his sacking had already begun to circulate.

"Your Majesty," Man says, his voice respectful but laced with a note of uncertainty.

Philip does not immediately turn to acknowledge him. The weight of the moment hangs thick in the air. He thinks of Lizard Point when he first sailed into the English Channel in 1554. *An omen-name for an omen-nation.* After a long moment—long enough to hear the servants' soft hurry beyond the door—the King finally speaks, his voice low and tinged with controlled fury.

"Doctor Man," Philip begins, his words sharp like a blade. "You English..." He rubs his nose. "You are a constant vexation. I summoned you because certain matters are no longer tolerable. You are here to answer for your conduct, for your words—words that have insulted not just myself, but the very foundations of the Catholic faith."

Man's stomach drops, but he stands his ground. "I do not understand, Your Majesty," he says carefully. "I have always acted in the interests of England and Spain. I have done my best to preserve peace between our countries."

Philip finally turns to face him. "You preach peace, Doctor Man, and sow contempt. You call the Pope a 'canting little monk' and boast that the

Huguenots will win. In Catholic Spain, that is not talk—it is provocation. I will not ignore it."

Man's breath catches in his throat. He had not expected this to be brought to the forefront. The King's gaze bores into him. "I did not intend to offend, Your Majesty," Man stammers, "but I believed it was necessary to speak the truth of the French conflict. It was an observation based on the course of events. If my words were ill-judged, then I repent of the manner, not the service. I spoke as a man charged to observe, not to inflame—to report currents, not to steer them."

Philip's face hardens, his voice growing colder. "You believe it necessary to speak such heresy? To undermine the Holy See and the very faith that binds us all?" He looks down, then looks back at Man. "You do not understand, do you, Doctor Man? Your position here as England's ambassador was solely to represent your queen, not to spread poison and dissent."

Man swallows, his hands trembling slightly at his sides. "I am loyal to England and to my queen, Your Majesty. But if my words have caused offence, I beg your forgiveness."

Philip's expression remains impassive. "Your queen..." His voice trails off with an edge of frustration. "Elizabeth! I am already weary of her games. And I am weary of you with your reckless tongue."

Philip turns away, pacing slowly before continuing, his voice rising with suppressed fury. "You have not even attended any Catholic Masses, as this court expected of you. You have not just insulted me, Doctor Man. You have insulted Spain's honour, and worse, you have jeopardised what little trust we had left between our two nations."

Man's face flushes with a mixture of frustration and confusion. "Your Majesty, I have served England faithfully for years. I have always acted in good faith. I did not—"

"I do not wish to hear your excuses," Philip snaps, cutting him off and raising his hand. He turns sharply to face the ambassador. "You have brought nothing but strife and insult. You will no longer be received at my court. You will not reside in Madrid. I have ordered that you remove yourself to Barajas while your queen determines your recall."

Man stiffens. Barajas: close enough to watch, far enough to humiliate.

"This is not imprisonment," Philip adds, almost idly. "It is restraint. You will keep silence. You will provoke no further scandal. And you will wait."

Man bows, slower this time. "As Your Majesty commands."

Philip inclines his head once—dismissal. Final. Man stands for a long moment, as if the ground beneath him has shifted. When Man turns towards the door, Philip speaks again, quietly.

"You should understand this, Doctor Man. England and Spain are not yet enemies. But words such as yours labour diligently to make them so. An officer will see that you remove to Barajas. You leave Madrid not as an ambassador, but as a man who has failed both his queen and his country."

The door closes.

Philip does not watch it shut. He takes up his quill instead and begins to write—to Brussels, to Rome, to London—setting the incident into the proper channels where it will do its work.

If England chooses to wound Spain, she will discover that Spain keeps accounts.

30 March 1568

Whitehall is all taut listening.

In the Privy Chamber, the late-afternoon sun lies thin across tapestries of old conquests, and the air carries the dry sting of ink and sanded parchment. Queen Elizabeth sits high-backed and composed, her councillors arranged like silent sentries. Every man in the room knows the stakes: Spain tightens its fist over the Low Countries, and England stands in the narrowing space between caution and confrontation.

A knock. The ushers part.

A stranger is brought forward—*not* a formal envoy, but a lean, road-worn man in modest black. He is admitted at Cecil's insistence, and only because no written channel is safe. A private agent. A messenger trusted by William of Orange, for no official mission is safe yet. He produces a small packet sealed in plain wax—no arms, no flourish—only a folded hand.

Elizabeth's eyes sharpen.

"Your name?" she asks.

"Maarten van der Aa, Your Majesty," he replies, bowing. "A courier in the service of the Prince of Orange. I bring letters...and a plea."

Cecil's gaze flicks to Elizabeth—wary, calculating. No one says it aloud: this is dangerous ground. Spain watches every whisper between England and the Dutch.

Elizabeth gestures. "Speak."

Van der Aa lifts his head, and exhaustion shadows his face.

"Your Majesty, the Prince fights for the liberties of the Netherlands—for the ancient rights Philip has cast aside. Alba's terror spreads. Towns burn. Men are hanged for their creed. The Prince stands alone unless England...unless you lend some measure of favour."

Elizabeth sits very still. Her fingers rest lightly on the arm of her chair, but Cecil, watching her, recognises the tension gathering behind the mask.

"You speak boldly for a man without credentials," she says quietly. "I do not receive rebel lords as princes. Nor do I meddle in my neighbours' governance."

The courier's voice tightens—desperation breaking through restraint.

"Madam, I beg you—if Philip crushes us utterly, he will turn to you next. He will not allow a Protestant queen to reign unchallenged. Help us now, and you help your own realm."

A spark flashes in Elizabeth's eyes.

"Sir," she says, almost gently, "I am well acquainted with Spain's temper. Do not presume to instruct me on my own peril."

A stillness takes the room.

Van der Aa bows his head. "Forgive me, Your Majesty. But the Prince hopes you might show at least discreet goodwill—a harbour for the wounded, a quiet sale of powder, a place where Dutch ships may breathe free air."

Elizabeth rises.

The councillors stiffen, sensing the shift. Her voice, when it comes, is low and precise—the tone of a sovereign who has weighed kingdoms in her hand.

"You ask me to provoke Philip," she says. "To risk my throne, my people, and the fragile peace I have kept. I will not. England is not yet ready to match Spain blow for blow."

The courier's shoulders sag—but she holds up a hand.

"Yet know this. I do not turn my eyes away. If Philip's cruelty stirs storms he cannot command, should fortune shift, should the Prince stand upon firmer ground...then England may find room to show him favour. I will not strike first—but I will not be blind."

Van der Aa looks up—hope flickering.

Elizabeth's gaze softens only by a thread.

"But not now," she finishes. "Not openly. Not while Spain still pretends to keep faith with me. Take that answer back to your master."

Van der Aa bows. "I shall convey Your Majesty's words faithfully."

He withdraws. The doors close behind him.

Cecil exhales at last. "Your Majesty—"

"I know what I said," Elizabeth murmurs, returning to her chair. Her eyes lift towards the high window, where dusk spreads over Whitehall like a warning.

Between Spain and the Dutch, between prudence and conviction, England stands on the edge of a trembling Europe.

And Elizabeth, alone in her thoughts, senses the shift ahead—an upheaval she does not wish to join, yet cannot pretend is not approaching.

Courts close their doors. Letters do not.

20 May 1568

At Whitehall, the virginal's polished case catches the candlelight as Elizabeth plays, her fingers moving through "My Lady Carey's Dompe" with practiced ease. The music is measured, controlled—everything the world expects of her.

A knock cuts through the chamber.

Firm. Urgent.

Elizabeth lets the final chord die before she rises.

"Enter."

William Cecil steps inside, hat in hand, his expression grave enough to still the air. He bows.

"What storms do you bring me, Spirit?" she asks.

Cecil inclines his head. "Your Majesty, the matter is grave, and it unfolds swiftly. Mary, Queen of Scots, escaped Loch Leven Castle on the evening of the second of May."

Elizabeth turns fully now. "Escaped," she repeats. "How?"

"By stratagem," Cecil says. "Our agents in Scotland tell us that, with the aid of George Douglas, she left the island in disguise, reached the mainland, and within days gathered the lords still loyal to her."

Cecil continues, methodical.

"She rode to Hamilton territory and raised her banner. For a brief span—little more than a week—she believed the realm might yet be recovered."

"And then?" Elizabeth asks quietly.

"On the thirteenth of May, her forces met those of the Regent Earl of Moray at Langside, just outside Glasgow. She was defeated. Her army broke.

She watched the rout from a nearby height and fled the field before the fighting was done."

"So. Crown lost a second time."

"Yes, Your Majesty. She rode hard—south and west—through Galloway. By the fifteenth, she reached Dundrennan Abbey. From there, against the counsel of her remaining lords, she resolved to cross into England."

Elizabeth turns back to the virginal but does not sit.

"She *resolved*," she says. "As though England were her refuge."

Cecil's voice remains even. "On the morning of the sixteenth, she crossed the Solway Firth in a fishing boat. She landed on our shore near Workington, believing—by her own account—that Your Majesty would receive her as a fellow sovereign and restore her by mediation."

Elizabeth gives a short, incredulous laugh. "Restore her?"

"She was conveyed first to local lodgings," Cecil continues, careful. "And then—once the danger was understood—escorted under guard to Carlisle. She is now held there in what we term 'honourable custody.'"

Elizabeth's hands curl slowly.

"So," she says at last, "she loses her crown by rebellion, loses it again by battle, and then walks into my realm expecting sanctuary."

"She believes herself wronged," Cecil replies. "And believes you bound—by kinship and by crown—to take her part."

Elizabeth turns sharply. "She claims my throne in Rome. She lets herself be styled Queen of England in France. And now she plants herself on my soil and calls it trust."

Her voice drops.

"My sister once looked on me so."

Cecil says nothing.

Elizabeth moves back to the virginal and places both hands on its lid, not to play.

"As long as Mary Stuart breathes English air," she says, "she is a danger. Not only to Scotland—but to me."

Cecil inclines his head. "Then Your Majesty's will?"

"She remains where she is," Elizabeth says coldly. "Guarded. Watched. Removed from every ear that might hear her. She came seeking judgment; she shall find restraint."

Her fingers strike a single chord—hard, decisive.

"Send word to Carlisle that she is not to stir. England will not be her stage."

The sound lingers in the chamber long after her hands still.

14 June 1568

The hum of anticipation fills the grand palace of Philip in Madrid. The day's heat has already drained much of the life from the court, and yet the weight of Philip's burden seems heavier than ever. His desk is piled high with documents—matters of state, matters of faith—each one pressing in on him, but none more urgent than the news that would soon come.

Philip sits at his desk, rapt in concentration, the rhythmic tapping of his quill against the table the only sound in the room. His thoughts, however, are far from the papers before him.

The door creaks open, breaking the room's stillness. Antonio Pérez enters with a hurried step. He has the look of a man who has just borne a heavy burden and was about to deliver even worse news.

The King looks up sharply, already sensing the gravity of the moment. "What news, Don Antonio?" His voice, though composed, betrays a flicker of anxiety.

Pérez bows, but too quickly, without his usual composure. He is no longer sure of his place in a world where everything seems to be unravelling. He advances, his face pale, and Philip's stomach tightens. Something is terribly wrong.

"Sire," Pérez begins, his voice straining, "unwelcome news confirmed beyond doubt. Mary, Queen of Scots, has escaped Loch Leven Castle. She fled into England, but now she is imprisoned there."

A dark cloud passes over Philip's face. "England?" he murmurs, his voice barely audible. "She is in Elizabeth's hands?"

Pérez nods. "Yes, Sire. She was taken into custody at Carlisle Castle, under the watch of English officials."

The news is almost too much to bear. To Philip, Mary was the Catholic hope England had stolen. She is now a prisoner in the hands of the Protestant heretic Elizabeth. The thought of it sends a rush of fury through him, but it is tempered with a deep sense of helplessness. He never expected it to come to this.

"Elizabeth," Philip spits, the name searing his tongue like poison. "She holds Mary captive—Mary! It is an outrage—an affront to God and to every throne in Christendom!"

He stands and begins to pace the room. Pérez, standing by the door, does not dare to speak, watching Philip's every movement. The King's mind races with wrath, disbelief, and something deeper—an aching sense of betrayal.

"I made a mistake years ago. I urged my wife to name Elizabeth her successor. The crown of England was never Elizabeth's to take!" Philip mutters, his voice low, filled with quiet venom. "Mary Stuart is a danger Elizabeth cannot ignore—and an opportunity I cannot dismiss."

Pérez speaks carefully, his tone respectful but cautious. "Sire, I understand your anger. But we cannot act rashly. Elizabeth is no fool, and England's strength, though fractured, endures. If we move too openly, too quickly—"

"I know the dangers," Philip snaps, spinning around to face Pérez, his eyes blazing with a fire that had been absent for months. "If England must change hands, better a Catholic queen than the heresy that reigns now."

He takes a deep breath, and for a moment, the fire in his eyes dims, replaced by the cold, calculating gaze that had made him one of the most formidable monarchs in Europe. He moves slowly back to his desk, his mind already working through the next steps. The situation is delicate, but not impossible.

"We must be subtle," he says, his voice now calm. "Spain cannot act openly. We cannot be the visible hand. The world must believe that Elizabeth's imprisonment of Mary is her own doing, that it is of no concern to us. We will be the hidden hand, Don Antonio. Discreet. We will rally Mary's supporters from the shadows, and we will ensure her release, quietly, without drawing attention."

Philip's hands steady as he grips the edge of the desk, his voice hardening. "We will prepare the ground. Whether Mary ever sits in London is God's secret—but I will see that Elizabeth never sleeps easy."

He turns back to Pérez. "Make preparations. Use your contacts. But above all, be silent. The work will be done in the shadows, and when the time comes, Mary will sit upon the throne of England, and the Catholic Faith will rise again."

Pérez bows, understanding the weight of the King's words. "At your command, Your Majesty."

12 July 1568

At London's Royal Exchange, rain spatters the paving stones as Sir Thomas Gresham strides through the colonnade, ducking the crowds of merchants shouting rates in Dutch, English, and Spanish. The air smells of wet wool, tar, and the sharp briny tang of oysters sold from a barrow where apprentices gulp raw shellfish with draughts of low-priced ale. His cloak is soaked, his hat pulled low—but his eyes are sharp.

His factor meets him under the Exchange arcade, face drawn tight.

"Master, it is worse."

Gresham stops dead. "How many accounts?"

"Ten seized outright. Twenty frozen. The Antwerp houses say Alba has ordered *full disclosure*—every ledger, every cargo manifest."

Gresham swears under his breath. "He means to choke the trade itself."

"Aye. If we cannot move coin through Antwerp, the Crown cannot pay her debts. The merchants whisper of collapse."

Gresham glances at the Exchange, at the sea of anxious faces. "Collapse," he repeats, softly. "No. Not yet."

The factor lowers his voice. "There is talk that the Genoese bankers refuse to advance Philip another ducat until payment flows again."

Gresham's eyes flick upward. That...was something.

"Good," he mutters. "Let Spain feel the pinch."

***

At Whitehall, William Cecil stands before the fire, hands clasped behind his back. His friend Francis Walsingham enters, his boots rapping on the wooden floor.

"You have spoken with Gresham?" Cecil asks without turning.

"I have," Walsingham replies. "Antwerp is shutting like a trap. Alba's men pry into every English ledger—auditors, soldiers, notaries. They intend to make examples."

Cecil finally turns. "And the Queen's merchants?"

"Bleeding," Walsingham answers. "If this continues, London will scream for retaliation."

Cecil exhales slowly. "Philip wants us to make the first move."

"He may get his wish," Walsingham says. "Gresham suggests a counter-stroke: seize Spanish cargo landing in English ports. Confine it until our goods are freed."

Cecil's eyes narrow. "And provoke a war?"

"Not if we do it in the Queen's manner," Walsingham replies dryly. "Quietly. Legally. With a polite smile."

Cecil gives a faint, humourless laugh. "That is how most of our wars begin."

He turns to the map of the Channel pinned to the wall.

"Keep eyes on the Genoese galleys," Cecil says. "They will not risk Dunkirk while Dutch rebels prowl the shoals. If they run for English shelter—"

"—we take them," Walsingham finishes. "For their own safety, of course."

Cecil nods. "This year will end foully, Francis. If the winds continue, there will be blood or silver in the Thames before winter."

Walsingham's reply is quiet.

"Perhaps both."

***

Rain lashes the stone walls of the Antwerp Citadel, sluicing from the gutters in dark sheets. Inside, the council chamber smells of wet wool, tallow, and iron. The Duke of Alba strides in without pause, his boots ringing on the flagstones, his cloak heavy with rain and authority.

Two captains kneel at once.

"Your Excellency," the elder says, keeping his eyes down, "the remaining English accounts have been frozen. No transfers honoured. No credit extended. The merchants are furious."

Alba removes his gloves slowly, laying them beside a stack of ledgers as though arranging instruments. "Let them gnash their teeth," he says. "They have coddled heresy long enough. Fury is a luxury men cannot afford when their purses are closed."

A clerk clears his throat, already pale. "There is resistance, Excellency. Several Genoese houses refuse new loans until English trade is restored. They claim the risk is unacceptable."

Alba stops. Turns.

"They refuse?"

"Yes, Excellency."

For a moment, he says nothing. Thunder rolls low beyond the walls, not loud enough to startle, but close enough to be felt. Alba's gaze drifts to the windows, where rain blurs the city into streaks of grey.

"So they refuse," he says at last. "Genoese courage. It swells when it thinks itself indispensable."

He steps closer to the table, palms resting on the maps of river and road. "They forget," he continues calmly, "that silver moves only where order allows it to move. And order answers to force."

The captains shift, armour creaking.

"Send patrols to the Scheldt," Alba says. "Double them. Stop every English ship. Inspect holds. Question crews. Delay departure on the smallest fault. No proclamations. No noise. We do not close the gate—we narrow it until passage hurts."

One captain dares to ask, "And if London protests, Excellency?"

Alba's gauntleted fist comes down on the table. The blow snaps a quill and sends the inkpot skidding, black drops spattering the parchment like spilled blood.

"Then London decides whether it wishes to trade—or to posture," he says. "If they submit, they will call it accommodation. If they strike back, Philip will have the war he pretends not to want."

He straightens, smoothing the cuff of his sleeve as if nothing has occurred.

"Fear," Alba continues, almost conversationally, "is more obedient than anger. Let the merchants panic. Let their letters grow desperate. Let the Queen wonder which voice to answer first—their pleas or her pride."

Lightning flares against the windows, bleaching the room white for a heartbeat. Alba smiles, thin and without warmth.

"England believes trade protects her," he says. "It does not. It binds her."

Thunder cracks directly overhead, shaking dust from the beams.

"Let England choose its rope."

***

Later that night at Whitehall, Elizabeth sits in her Privy Closet, candlelight flickering over parchment. Her ring glints as she turns it anxiously. Cecil and Walsingham stand before her.

"Majesty," Cecil says gently, "I bring bad news. Alba has frozen all remaining English accounts in Antwerp."

Elizabeth stiffens. *"All?"*

"Every shilling," Walsingham answers. "He means to starve our trade."

Elizabeth's eyes flash.

"So Spain plays the bully again."

Cecil bows his head. "Majesty...we may need to consider a measured reply."

Elizabeth rises slowly, her voice sharpening.

"A measured reply? Spain steals from us, and we pat them like a lapdog?"

Walsingham steps forward. "Majesty—the moment may come when Spanish silver seeks shelter under English guns. If it does, we can seize it without declaring war. The Genoese bankers will wail, but they will still take payment—from us."

Elizabeth's fingers drum the table.

"And Philip?"

Cecil answers quietly: "Philip will rage. But he cannot fight France, rebels, and England at once."

Elizabeth exhales, long and slow.

"Very well," she says. "Prepare the nets."

She turns towards the darkened Thames outside her window, as if she can already hear the creaking of masts carrying silver.

"One day," she murmurs, "Spain will learn that England is no hive to be smoked at leisure."

18 August 1568

The counting-room above the Florentine silk-house on London's Lombard Street hums with muted voices and the soft scrape of quills. The shutters are drawn tight despite the warm air. A pewter jug of thin claret sweats on the table beside two cups, and a plate of figs and walnuts sits between them, scarcely touched—hospitality offered, not yet trusted.

A well-dressed Genoese factor, Signore Lorenzo Spinola, stands alone at the window, twisting a ring with nervous fingers. When the door opens, he turns sharply.

Walsingham, Cecil's agent, enters with no cloak, no guards—only a small leather ledger tucked under his arm.

"Signor Spinola," he says quietly. "You asked for discretion. You have it."

The Genoese bows with continental grace, but he cannot hide the tremor in his hands.

"Master Walsingham...Spain's seas are no longer safe."

Walsingham says nothing. Silence, in his mouth, is a scalpel.

Spinola presses on.

"The Duke of Alba seizes goods without warning. The French coast swarms with privateers. Our ships cannot promise delivery—not to Antwerp, not to Dunkirk, not even to the Basque coast without fear."

He toys with a walnut, rolling it between finger and thumb instead of cracking it, as though even breaking a shell in this room might be a kind of commitment.

Walsingham opens the ledger, but only as theatre.

"A difficult season," he murmurs.

Spinola steps closer.

"The silver for the *tercios* must sail soon. Several hundred thousand crowns. If the winds turn...if French waters are dangerous...if Alba delays clearance..."

He hesitates, breath catching.

"...we may have no choice but to steer for English harbours."

Walsingham does not smile, but his eyes narrow the way a cat's might when the bird hops closer to the snare.

"Naturally," he says softly, "we encourage lawful trade in English ports."

Spinola exhales, relief mingled with fear.

"And if such silver found temporary refuge—temporary—you would...guard it?"

"We guard what comes under our guns," Walsingham says.

Spinola's throat tightens. He understands. Perfectly.

"If the seas grow rough," he whispers, "the silver may run to you."

"And should it do so," Walsingham replies, "England will ensure it is...accounted for."

Spinola bows, a deep, desperate gesture.

"You might save us all, Signor Walsingham."

"No," Walsingham murmurs as Spinola slips out, "but we may save what interests us."

He shuts the ledger with a quiet snap. One more piece moves on the board.

Outside, Lombard Street carries on—coins changing hands, promises spoken lightly, each bargain struck as if it were harmless.

Far from the counting-room, ships are already altering course.

Silver has learned where safety lies.

And England has learned how wars are paid for before they are ever fought.

28 August 1568

At the Brussels Governor's Residence, the Duke of Alba stands at a long table strewn with maps of the Scheldt, marked with ink-black ships. Candles gutter in the drafts that haunt the old Burgundian palace. A glazed earthenware jug of sour beer and a wooden trencher with a hunk of rye bread and cold smoked eel sit at his elbow.

A courier bows low before him, holding out a packet sealed with the arms of Spain.

"From London, Excellency. From Ambassador de Espés."

Alba breaks the seal like the neck of a snake. He reads, lips thinning.

"*London grows suspicious. English customs officers make inquiries. Walsingham watches my house. The Florentines whisper that the safest harbours may be English.*"

A grunt escapes him—half contempt, half bone-deep irritation.

"These islanders," he mutters. "Always sniffing like dogs for scraps of silver or gold."

His secretary, Antonio de Albornoz, steps forward.

"Excellency, shall we delay the Genoese silver?"

"Delay?" Alba snorts. "The *tercios* starve for pay. If I delay, half of Flanders will defect to the rebels."

He strides to the map, knuckles hammering the circle around Dunkirk.

"We sail when the bankers send the chests. But double the escort. I want galleys at Gravelines, patrols near the Flemish shoals, and a warning to every master: avoid the English coast."

Albornoz hesitates. "Excellency...if storms or pirates force them to harbour—"

"Then they may run to Hell before they run to England!" Alba roars. His hand slams down so close to the trencher that the beer slops against the rim, a dark line soaking into the bread.

He grips the table, breath hard.

"Philip will blame me if the silver falls into English hands. Elizabeth will preen like a peacock. And the rebels—" His voice drops to a growl. "The rebels will live another year."

He turns away, staring at the dark windows.

"Send word to de Espés: watch the English carefully. They smile too much when they lie."

Albornoz bows. "At once, Excellency."

Alba remains still, palms flat on the map.

"Let the silver hold its course—or let every ship that bears it pay the price."

17 September 1568

At Whitehall, Dr John Man smells England before he sees it.

Coal smoke. Wet wool. The river. It clings to him as he stands in the Presence Chamber, travel-worn, hat in hand, waiting while courtiers pretend not to watch. He has been back only days, and already the air has turned cold.

Elizabeth keeps him waiting.

When she enters at last, she does not sit.

"Doctor Man," she says. "You have caused me considerable trouble."

He drops to one knee at once. "Your Majesty—"

"Rise," she snaps. "I will not have theatrics."

He obeys, face flushed, eyes bright with something between indignation and fear.

"I am told," Elizabeth continues, pacing slowly before him, "that you called the Pope a canting little monk in the hearing of Philip's court. That you spoke publicly of Protestants prevailing. And I understand you claimed surprise when Spain took offence."

Man opens his mouth.

She lifts a finger.

"You were sent to Madrid to *be endured*, not admired," she says. "You were sent to keep Spain tolerable to us, not to instruct it in doctrine."

"I believed—"

"You believed," Elizabeth cuts in, "that your tongue was wiser than your commission."

She stops in front of him.

"When I appointed you," she says coldly, "I believed you prudent enough to *hold your peace*. Philip knew what you were. I trusted you would remember it."

Man swallows hard. "I spoke in conscience, madam."

Elizabeth laughs once, sharp and humourless.

"Conscience," she says. "A fine shield for a man who forgets he serves a crown."

She turns away, then back again.

"Philip has expelled you from his court. He has written to me in great complaint. I was forced to answer for you—to soothe, to delay, to promise consideration I would rather not have given."

Her eyes narrow.

"Do you know what that costs me?"

Man lowers his gaze. "I regret the injury, Your Majesty."

"You regret being caught," she says. "Do not insult me further."

A silence stretches.

At last she speaks again, more controlled.

"You will not be sent abroad again," Elizabeth says. "You will hold no further charge in matters touching Spain. Your usefulness there is finished."

Man's shoulders sag.

"You have made yourself a problem," she continues. "And I do not keep problems longer than necessary."

She turns to Cecil, who has stood silent throughout.

"See that Doctor Man is settled quietly," she says. "No noise. No appointments. No defence pamphlets. I will not quarrel publicly with Philip over a man who could not keep his mouth shut."

Cecil bows.

Elizabeth looks back at Man one final time.

"You served me badly," she says. "Be grateful I do not say so louder. You do not know what torch you may have set to the match cord."

She turns away.

Man remains where he stands, dismissed not by guards or proclamation, but by something colder: royal disappointment, fully considered.

Outside, the court resumes its hum.

Inside, another thread in Europe's tightening web slips quietly into place.

22 September 1568

It is late evening in the Blackfriars in London. Rain falls into the Thames, turning the lane to black glass. In the Strangers' quarter, a French psalm thrums behind a thin wall. A loom clacks somewhere below like a beating heart.

Francis Walsingham waits in a narrow loft above a weaver's shop, cloak steamed dark at the hem. He writes a heading in neat French and lays his cipher wheel beside the lamp.

The door creaks. A thin Italian slips in, hat crushed in his hands, eyes shining with the sort of fear that makes men talk too much or not at all.

"Signor Walsingham?" he whispers.

Walsingham does not rise. "Close it. Sit. Speak slowly."

"My name is Matteo Velluti. I keep accounts for a Florentine house on Lombard Street. I...I should not be here." He swallows. "But London is not safe for men like me if the wind turns papist."

"What did you see?" Walsingham's voice is soft, sanded smooth.

"Meetings," Matteo says. "At the house of *il Fiorentino*—the Florentine banker in Seething Lane." He will not say *Ridolfi*. The name is a hot coal. "Two nights past, the Spanish ambassador's men came—silk cloaks, the red cross on a servant's badge. And with them a Scottish priest—tall, lean, the look of a hawk." He glances up. "They called him *il Vescovo*."

"The Bishop." Walsingham makes a mark: *il Vescovo. Bishop of Ross. Mary Stuart's agent.*

"They spoke in low voices," Matteo continues, hands worrying the hat brim to a rope. "But I heard enough: the Lady—must not despair. Friends in the north stand ready. Spain will not see her cast away. Money will come by sea if the seas are kind."

"From where comes the money?"

Matteo looks at the floorboards. "From the Genoese. The talk was of chests, of ships steering for the Narrow Seas if French waters are troubled. The ambassador says silver will find the right harbours." He risks a glance. "Says the Duke in Flanders waits only for silver and a sign."

Walsingham's pen moves, quiet as breath: *"De Espés—letters to Alba—harbour talk—Genoa—money for* tercios*—north to stir."* He shifts to Italian and writes a second set of notes with tidy arrows, as if the page itself were a street map.

"Who else?" he asks.

"A Norfolk gentleman with his cap pulled low. An Englishwoman I know from the embassy chapel—she prays loud, looks behind her louder." He gives a small, helpless shrug. "And I saw the Bishop of Ross again, at Charing Cross, speaking with a messenger from the north—mud on his boots to the knee."

Walsingham closes his book. "You have done well."

Matteo's mouth twitches. "Then keep me alive."

Walsingham meets his gaze, steady as a plumb line. "I mean to."

He gives the man a name for a baker near St Martin's, a time, a single countersign. When Matteo is gone, Walsingham douses the lamp with a breath, gathers his papers, and slips into the wet dark.

23 September 1568

Dawn bruises the sky over Gravesend. A packet-boat noses in on a falling tide on the river, its deck slick with spray. Two riders wait under the arch of the wharf—one a customs man who knows when not to see, the other Walsingham with rain ticking off his hat brim.

The master lugs ashore a leather pouch sealed with the arms of Spain. "From the Ambassador," he says. "To the Low Countries."

Walsingham's companion coughs, bored. "Routine."

"Routine," Walsingham agrees. He takes the pouch with gloved hands, notes the weight—a little too heavy for mere courtesies—and walks it into the Custom House where the clerk already has warm wax and a clean stamp ready.

In a back room, Walsingham's knife kisses the flap. Inside: two hands of cipher, the flourished signature of Guerau de Espés on the outer docket, an inner to "*His Excellency the Duke of Alba*" with a second seal. A smaller billet, Italian, from a Florentine hand he suspects before he reads it.

He does not break the inner seal, not yet. He copies the outer letter at speed, a neat clerk's hand, then his own ciphered precis in French for William Cecil:

"*De Espés encourages Mary's hope, pledges succour 'when the season is ripe.' Notes gentlemen in the north 'restive.' Requests money for agents, expects 'Genoese succour' to arrive by sea. Advises Alba to keep the Narrow Seas watched and hold himself ready to answer the trumpet.*"

He files the copies into his jerkin, reseals the Spanish dispatch with fresh wax, and watches the ambassador's pouch go back to the boat as if nothing in England had touched it.

Only when the tide is carrying the packet east does he open the Italian billet.

One line, crabbed and urgent: "*The merchants await the recall—if London offers safe harbours, the silver will obey, and Spain will feel it in her sinews.*"

Walsingham folds it twice, sharp as a blade edge, and rides for Whitehall.

***

In the afternoon, Cecil's chamber is thin with smoke and paper dust. Outside, the court hums with the day's appointments. Inside, time seems to hold. Cecil reads Walsingham's French summary once, then again, then looks up.

"The new Spaniard entangles himself quickly," he says.

"Quickly and loudly," Walsingham replies. He lays the Italian billet on the table. "Lombard Street is listening."

Cecil reads, eyes narrowing on the word *silver*. "Silver that obeys the safest key." He crosses to the wall map and taps the Low Countries with a blunt finger. "If this reaches Alba, he pays his *tercios* and buys hulls out of Dunkirk. Paid men do what hungry ones dare not. And Mary—"

"—has landed in Elizabeth's lap," Walsingham finishes quietly. "Her Bishop of Ross is busy. He meets the Florentine, he meets the Spaniard, and he writes to the north."

Cecil's mouth hardens. "We cannot yet pluck the Bishop—too many eyes. But we can blind him." He turns back. "You will keep the strangers' churches sweet and talking. Italian, French, Walloon. Names, houses, chapels. I want every Catholic who kisses the ambassador's ring known by his tailor."

"And the letters?" Walsingham asks. "You have the Custom men. I can have the ferrymen by week's end."

"Take them," Cecil says. "I want every pouch to and from Seething Lane handled as gently as you open a prayer book and as firmly as a gaoler shuts a door."

He weighs the Italian billet again, then slips it under a ledger. "And the Genoese?"

Walsingham only waits. He has learned that Cecil says the dangerous things to the air as much as to the man before him.

"If Spain's bankers run for our harbours," Cecil murmurs, "we will 'secure' their silver for their own safety and pay them ourselves. The Duke of Alba fights poorly when his chest is light."

A knock at the inner door, silence on both sides of it. Cecil gestures, and the clerk vanishes again.

"Francis," Cecil says at last, "you are not yet sworn of the Queen's chamber. You will not be thanked in public. But be patient. Patience is a weapon. Bring me witnesses who do not contradict themselves. Bring me dates. Bring me the ambassador's footprints where the mud keeps the print."

Walsingham bows, neither eager nor slow. "I will need one thing more."

"Name it."

"A warrant to question in the Strangers' French. Some magistrates in the city mistake a psalm for sedition. If they frighten my people, they will stop their ears."

Cecil takes up his quill. "You shall have it." Scratch of ink. Sand. Fold. Seal.

Walsingham pockets the paper and turns to go.

"Ah," Cecil adds, almost idly, "if you see the Florentine in Seething Lane—just smile. He likes to think of himself as Rome's ears in London. Let him hear what you would have Alba hear."

Walsingham pauses at the latch. "And what should Alba hear?"

Cecil studies the map again. "The Channel's weather is turning—and any silver that drifts beneath our guns will answer to a new master."

Walsingham inclines his head and is gone.

10 November 1568

French privateers had been the first dogs on their track, bound for Antwerp—lean lateen-rigged shapes rising out of the haze, pacing the galleon just beyond gunshot, splitting and edging to force her course while a few warning shots skipped iron across the water. The *Santa María de la Encina* ran hard, hunting shoals and weather, her master throwing her from tack to tack with the weight of soldiers' pay dragging at her bones. Then the sky itself joined the chase: wind backing, air souring, the horizon darkening until even the privateers sheered away rather than face what was coming.

The gale had chased them in like a pack of hounds.

By first light, the Spanish galleon *Santa María de la Encina* lies warped against the Southampton quay, her cables humming, her hull streaked with weed and slime. Men move stiffly on deck, faces grey with salt and lost sleep. The storm had broken her timetable and her pride in equal measure. Canvas hangs in damp folds. The great lantern at the stern gutters and goes out.

On the wharf, the town watches.

Port officers come first—quiet men, careful men—asking nothing that could not be answered aloud. The master produces his papers. Genoa. Antwerp. Soldiers' pay. All in order. Nothing to see but a ship licking her wounds.

Below decks, the chests sit lashed and sealed, heavy enough to bend the planks. Bars wrapped in hide. Sacks that ring dully when nudged. Silver that does not yet legally belong to Spain.

A courier rides before noon. By nightfall, word would reach London.

***

That evening at Whitehall, Elizabeth reads the dispatch once. Then again.

"The *Santa María de la Encina*. Storm-driven," she says. "Sheltering under our guns."

Cecil stands next to her at the table, fingers pressed to the paper as if to keep it from sliding away. "Yes, Majesty. Southampton reports her safe in port. Others may follow."

"Whose money?" Elizabeth asks.

"Genoese. Advanced for Alba's army. Pay chests, not treasure fleet."

Elizabeth smiles without warmth. "Then Philip is only the courier."

"Just so."

She folds the letter and sets it aside. "Let them lie. Say nothing. Keep the ports polite."

Cecil inclines his head. He understands.

13 November 1568

The weather softens, as if England herself takes a breath.

Low cloud lifts from the water and breaks into pale rags drifting east. The rain thins to mist, then to nothing at all. By midmorning the tide runs clean and the harbour smells of wet oak, pitch, and wrack drying on the stones. Gulls settle again on the pilings. The *Santa María de la Encina* remains where she is, her cables slackened, her wounded dignity propped against the quay.

Sailors drift ashore in ones and twos. They spend silver coppers in taverns along the quay—thin ale, salt beef, bread still warm from the oven. They swear they will sail with the next fair wind, that the Channel will be kind, that Antwerp waits. Their laughter is loud, deliberate. Each man knows he is being seen.

Below decks, the chests do not move. They sit lashed and sealed in the dim.

Watchmen come and go at measured intervals, boots scuffing the boards, halberds upright. Clerks pass through with ink-stained fingers, copying manifests, asking questions already answered. Names are written. Times are noted. The same facts are recorded again and again.

Nothing happens.

That is the point.

14 November 1568

At Whitehall, the river fog presses against the windows and thins into pearl-grey light.

Elizabeth stands at the table, gloved hands resting on the spread papers, the air faint with beeswax and damp wool. She does not pace. She does not sit. When she speaks, it is level, almost conversational.

"We will take it. Take it all. Inventory it. Secure it. Let no silver bar pass a threshold without our mark upon it."

William Cecil looks up from the draft order, the quill pausing mid-word. "Yes, Your Majesty."

He inclines his head, already calculating carts, guards, locks, ledgers. "And the protest?"

She meets his eye, steady and unblinking. "As you said before. We borrow from Genoa. We offend Spain. Write it cleanly."

The quill scratches on the page, slow and deliberate. Sand is shaken over the wet ink. The parchment is folded. Wax is warmed and pressed. The seal takes—sharp, unmistakable.

The storm, at last, finds its purpose.

Beyond the chamber, a clerk waits with the copies, ink still tacky beneath the sand. He shifts his weight, listening to a river conch-shell horn.

By nightfall, the ledgers will move. By morning, the ports will know.

And somewhere beyond the Channel, a reckoning will begin before England can name it.

Chapter 18
The Affair of the Genoese Silver

17 November 1568

The dimly lit hold of the Spanish galleon *Santa María de la Encina*, moored at a Southampton quay, is thick with the smell of bilge water, tar, and damp wood. The timbers creak.

The galleon seeks temporary refuge from pirates and storms along the coast. Her final destination is Flanders. The murmuring of Spanish voices rises and falls, each word edged with unease. At the far end of the hold, rows of heavy chests sit stacked against the wall.

"Move aside!" a voice barks, low and sharp, cutting through the hold's murmur. It is a grim-faced Admiralty officer bearing a Privy Council commission, sealed and unmistakable. A crown marshal accompanies the officer. The marshal's hand is steady on the hilt of his sword as he gestures to his men. English soldiers stand in ordered ranks, eyes locked on the Spanish sailors.

"Seize those chests!" the officer orders.

The marshal snaps, "Get on with it!"

The soldiers surge forward, moving with the swiftness of men accustomed to battle.

The Spanish crew, caught off guard and unsure of what to do, glance at one another nervously. They shift restlessly, their hands twitching towards their weapons, but they are too far outnumbered, too unsure of what will happen next.

"Not a step closer, gentlemen," the marshal says.

The Spanish sailors freeze, their gazes going between the chests of silver and the armed men before them. They know the worth of the silver—meant to fund Spain's ongoing military campaigns, especially against the Dutch rebellion. And yet, there is nothing they can do. They are outnumbered and overmatched in their own ship.

The English soldiers fall to their task with ruthless efficiency, lifting the chests and dragging them towards the gangplank. A smashed barrel nearby spills hard ship's biscuit across the floor; a boot grinds one cake to powder as the men heave treasure where food once lay.

The silver gleams brightly under the lantern light, each chest giving off a clink as the bars shift inside. A soldier wrenches one chest open, its contents spilling out in the dim light, a glittering cascade of silver that only deepens the outrage on the faces of the Spanish crew.

A Spanish officer steps forward, face flushed with fury.

He snarls. "These are royal treasures! Madrid will hear of it!"

The Admiralty officer gives a slow, exaggerated nod. "It would be a shame to take all this and not receive proper credit in Madrid." He glances at the chests. "Be sure to spell my name correctly in your complaint."

The air is tense. The soldiers move with practiced speed and precision, eyes flicking from one Spanish sailor to the next, ensuring no one dares move. The sound of boots scraping on the deck boards mingles with the metallic clink of silver being hauled away, a sound that grows louder with each passing moment.

As the final chest is dragged to the gangplank, the Spanish officer glares from the rail at the marshal, his eyes burning with a mix of fury and powerlessness.

"You think this will go unanswered?" he snarls.

The marshal, unfazed, glances at him with a cold, dismissive smile. "We will see about that. Now step back, or I will have you thrown overboard."

The Spanish sailors stand motionless, watching as their treasure is taken, pride shattered, power slipping away like the tide. The English soldiers, their muskets at the ready, haul the chests down onto the quay and make their way along it, the Genoese silver in tow.

And with that, they march off, leaving behind the stunned, silent crew of the Spanish galleon, their treasure confiscated and their fate sealed.

At the quay, William Cecil, Elizabeth's Principal Secretary, observes the operation with cold precision. Beside him stands Francis Walsingham, his face impassive but his eyes alight with the weight of calculated risk. They had travelled down with the Queen's officers and a guard detachment assigned to the bullion arrest.

"This is bold," Walsingham mutters, voice low but sharp.

Cecil's lips twitch—almost a smile. "Let them rage. The silver belongs to Genoa until it is delivered to the bankers' appointed agents in the Low Countries. We will pay the bankers ourselves. Spain can rage, but in law the chests are the bankers'—not Philip's—until delivery."

"Legally arresting the chests. Let us hope the justification holds."

Cecil turns, his voice even. "The bankers would surely prefer English honesty to Spanish greed."

He turns to the nearest guard. "Ensure these chests reach the Tower of London under guard—without delay."

Walsingham's gaze shifts to the restless Spanish sailors, their captain glaring at the scene with a face darkened by fury. "The Spaniards will not forget this slight."

"They do not have to forget," Cecil says, adjusting his cloak against the wind. "But they will have to endure it."

By lantern light, the first wagons were ordered, but the silver did not roll for London until the second tide and the third set of seals. In the weeks that follow—and into the new year—anxious correspondence would multiply.

20 December 1568

Torchlight flickers along the stone walls of the King's working chamber, casting nervous shadows over maps, account books, and the half-finished portrait on its easel. A small side table bears a pewter tray: mulled wine gone untouched, orange slices drying at their rims, candied peel stiffening into useless decoration.

King Philip sits rigid in a straight-backed chair, dressed in black velvet so severe it seems to consume the light. He has not moved in several minutes.

Before him stands Don Alonso Sánchez Coello, brush lifted with surgical precision, his posture immaculate, his face calm in the way of a man who has trained himself not to react.

Hovering at his elbow is Sebastián.

Sebastián carries too many brushes, a palette already overworked, and an expression of intense concentration directed entirely at the wrong problem.

"Do not blink, Majesty," Sebastián says, leaning in far too close. "Blinking makes the eyes look startled. Or haunted. Sometimes both. Now where is the varnish?"

Coello does not look at him. "Sebastián," he says evenly, "you are holding the varnish."

Sebastián freezes. He looks down at his hand.

"I am?"

"Yes."

A thoughtful pause.

"Oh." He switches hands. The varnish sloshes, flicking a line of pigment onto his sleeve. Sebastián stares at it. "It will dry."

Philip exhales through his nose.

Antonio Pérez steps forward, holding a folded letter. "Your Majesty. A dispatch from Don Guerau de Espés in England."

Philip does not move. "Read."

Pérez breaks the seal. As he does, Philip shifts slightly in his chair—barely an inch.

Sebastián gasps. "Majesty, no—if you move, the chin will soften."

Philip turns his head slowly.

Sebastián swallows. "Not that Your Majesty's chin is soft. Only that paint can make it...philosophical."

Coello closes his eyes for exactly one heartbeat. Then opens them.

Pérez reads.

"'Her Majesty of England acknowledges that the sum of four hundred thousand florins—valued in London at approximately eighty thousand pounds—was the property of Genoese bankers, not of the Spanish Crown. England has therefore opened negotiations directly with Genoa.'"

The room stills.

Philip rises so abruptly that Sebastián yelps and stumbles backward into the easel. It tilts.

Coello's hand shoots out and steadies it without his eyes leaving the canvas.

"Do not," Coello says quietly, "touch the easel."

Philip snatches the letter from Pérez and crushes it in his fist. "She claims it was never mine," he says, voice low. "Silver bound for my armies."

His grip tightens around the cup of mulled wine. It tips, spilling a dark stream across the table and onto the floor.

Sebastián squints. "Your Majesty is bleeding."

"I am not bleeding."

"The wine," Sebastián clarifies. "Though the color is convincing."

"Sebastián," Coello says.

"Yes, master."

"Stand behind me."

Sebastián obeys—then immediately leans around Coello's shoulder.

"Should I adjust the highlights, Majesty? Anger changes the planes of the face."

Philip turns on him.

"If you paint anything I did not commission," Philip says softly, "you will spend the winter learning fresco...underground."

Sebastián pales. "I have always respected stone."

Philip strides to the map of Europe and drags a finger along the Channel.

"She thinks herself clever," he says. "Untouchable."

Sebastián brightens despite himself. "Untouchable. That would be a powerful title."

Coello does not turn. "Sebastián."

"Yes?"

"Stop speaking."

Sebastián nods with absolute sincerity.

He immediately trips over a stool.

Pérez clears his throat. "Your Majesty. Your response?"

Philip does not hesitate. "Seize every English ship in my ports. Let her merchants learn arithmetic through hunger. Send word across Europe: Elizabeth Tudor traffics with pirates."

"Pirates," Sebastián murmurs, forgetting everything. "Very energetic subject matter—"

Coello reaches back and clamps a hand over Sebastián's mouth without breaking his line.

Philip turns toward the portrait at last. His painted likeness stares back—controlled, immovable, untouched by irritation. For a moment, the fury drains from him, leaving something colder behind.

"Finish it," he says while returning to his chair to sit.

Coello bows slightly. "As you wish, Majesty."

He releases Sebastián, who nods solemnly and—miraculously—remains silent.

The torches crackle. The brush resumes its quiet whisper across canvas. Philip's eyes return to the map, already shifting empires in his mind.

Behind him, history is being painted—not as it feels, but as it must appear.

Sebastián watches, wide-eyed, learning for the first time that kings are not most dangerous when they shout—but when they get quiet.

16 January 1569

The crisp morning air carries the scent of dew and earth as Elizabeth and her entourage finish a morning of hawking. A page rides behind with a leather jack of ale and a basket of cold venison pasties for the party, their rich, peppered smell rising each time the lid shifts.

The open field near Hampton Court Palace is alive with the flutter of wings as falcons soar and return to their masters. Elizabeth, mounted on a gleaming white horse named Mark, her posture regal, leads the group back towards the palace. Her face is striking, her cheeks reddened with a deliberate touch of rouge. A falcon perches elegantly on her gloved hand, its sharp talons gripping the thick leather.

To her right rides Robert Dudley, his dark doublet and feathered hat marking him as the Queen's undeniable favourite. To her left, another nobleman keeps pace, his own falcon perched obediently on his arm. Around them, courtiers on horseback laugh and chat, their spirits high from the hunt.

Elizabeth casts a sharp glance towards Dudley, her eyes gleaming with mischief. "Eyes," she says—her pet name for him—"since my brother-in-law has seized our ships, we owe him a response in kind, do we not?"

Dudley tilts his head, intrigued. "And what response would Your Majesty suggest?"

Elizabeth turns slightly, her falcon stirring on her arm. "Make it known that the Queen takes possession of all Spanish ships in English ports and all Spanish properties in this realm. Let Cecil put it into lawful form and let warrants be drawn."

The group of courtiers, catching her words, quiet themselves momentarily, their curiosity piqued. The nobleman to her left raises an eyebrow, and Dudley, ever attentive, leans closer.

"Spain?" Her lips quirk. "More pain than profit, whenever they knock at England's door."

A ripple of laughter breaks through the group, the courtiers delighted by her wit. One of the younger lords breaks a pasty in half and offers her the better piece with a grin; she waves it away, appetite sharpened for reprisal, not for meat. The nobleman to her left chuckles heartily, his falcon ruffling its feathers in response. Dudley grins, his admiration for Elizabeth evident.

"You have a way with words, Your Majesty," Dudley says while tipping his hat. "I shall see that your decree is carried out with all haste."

Elizabeth raises her chin, her eyes sparkling with triumph. "See that you do, Eyes. Let Spain feel the strength of England's will."

She slips the falcon's hood back into place and smiles. "If they would weigh us by silver, let them learn we also know the measure of iron."

26 January 1569

The great hall of the Royal Alcázar is shrouded in an uneasy silence, broken only by the muffled footsteps of courtiers as they avoid the King's direct gaze. The remnants of a Sunday meal—lentil pottage, a crust of coarse bread, a dish of stewed prunes—have been cleared from the high table, but the sour-sweet smell still hangs faintly in the air.

Philip sits on his throne, a towering seat carved with the symbols of the Spanish empire, his hand clenching and unclenching, the tension in his grip a reflection of his mood. Before him stands Don Guerau de Espés, the Spanish ambassador to England, freshly returned with news that the Queen of England had escalated the crisis.

Philip's face is a mask of calm. Espés bows, holding out a letter bearing Elizabeth's seal.

"Your Majesty, the Queen of England has taken her defiance further. Spanish ships, the silver destined for our army, and the property of our merchants have been seized in her ports. This is her answer to your rightful actions."

With a swift movement, Philip leans forward, his gaze fixed and piercing as he takes the letter. The seal cracks under his thumb, the sound echoing in the still room. As his eyes scan the words, a shadow of anger rushes across his face.

"The audacity!"

Antonio Pérez, standing to Philip's right, steps forward. "Your Majesty, Elizabeth's insolence cannot go unanswered. Her merchants thrive on our trade routes, yet she treats Spain as a mere adversary. Allow me to tighten our grip on the English. We can cripple their commerce in the Low Countries and seize every English vessel that dares enter our waters."

Philip's gaze remains fixed on the letter. Slowly, he folds it and places it on the table beside him. "She is reckless, yes. But she is not yet foolish enough to declare war outright. No, she toys with fire, thinking her distance will keep her from being burned."

He stands, his black robes cascading around him, and approaches the large map of Europe on the wall. His finger touches the English Channel. "The English crown sits on a throne of sand," he murmurs. "Elizabeth rules by a fragile balance of Protestant zeal and a divided nobility. She forgets that her foundations are much weaker than mine."

Espés speaks cautiously. "Your Majesty, if I may...the Queen of England grows bold because she believes she can act without consequence. Her merchants are already emboldened, violating trade agreements. And her pirates plunder Spanish vessels in the Atlantic."

Philip turns sharply. "And yet, she sends no fleet to battle. She provokes like a child throwing stones, but she fears open war."

Pérez advances again. "What are your orders, Sire?"

"We have begun; now let us tighten. We will take more than her ships. Let her merchants wail. Let her nobility see the cracks in her authority. But we will do so without haste." He turns to Espés. "Return to England. You will tell her this: Spain does not forget. Tell her that Spain's silver is the blood of its empire, and its theft is an act of treason against God Himself."

Espés bows and puts his right hand to his chest. "At your command, Your Majesty."

Philip's lips curl into a faint, humourless smile. "And while she listens to your words, we will prepare for what she fears most."

"An invasion, Sire?" asks Pérez.

Philip's voice hardens. "Yes. We consider it. The sea may yet be our stage, and her arrogance will be her undoing. For now, let the merchants of England bleed their coin, and let Elizabeth hear whispers of Spanish retaliation in every corner of her court. If the time comes, it will not be her ships we take—it will be her throne."

He mastered the anger, as he mastered everything else—by refusing it the dignity of haste.

30 September 1569

It is a wet and cold evening in London on Lombard Street. In a small room behind a Florentine bank, Francis Walsingham waits with a folded paper sealed with a strip of green silk and wax—the Privy Council's order.

Signor Roberto Ridolfi, the banker, enters. A City officer with a mace stands in the passage outside—polite, heavy, and not going anywhere.

Walsingham rises.

"Signor Ridolfi, this warrant is signed by Secretary Cecil. I am here to ask about certain letters and payments. This is a conversation, not an arrest."

Ridolfi nods. "Then let us converse."

Walsingham opens a small notebook to a blank page.

"We will start with money, not treason. Bills of exchange have moved from Antwerp to London, then London to York, then York to Durham. Clean paper makes an easy road for money. Money makes roads for men."

Ridolfi smiles with only his mouth. "Merchants move credit. Soldiers move themselves. If Customs suspects smuggling, that is their office."

"We are past Customs." Walsingham taps the wax seal and its green silk. "This is the Queen's business. Last week, a night rider came from Seething Lane to your door and left with three sealed packets. No shipping papers. No record."

"Letters are not contraband," Ridolfi says lightly.

"They are not holy relics, either." Walsingham lays down a fair copy of an intercepted outer cover: "*From Don Guerau de Espés*—the Spanish ambassador—*to Brussels. Most urgent. Bishop of Ross will confirm.*" Beneath it, a clerk's note: "'*Signor R. will advise on money for our friends.*' What does 'our friends' mean?"

Ridolfi turns his ring once, twice. "Clerks embellish. Yours are poets."

"Then help me edit the poem," Walsingham answers, calmly. "Who carries letters north to the Earls? Who serves the Bishop of Ross"—Mary Stuart's chief agent—"with routes and runners? Names, please."

Ridolfi speaks too fast. "The Duke of Norfolk is a prince of the realm. You mistake friendly talk for a plot."

Walsingham does not blink. "The Duke? I did not ask about the Duke. You offered him." He taps the page. "So now we have Spain's letters, the Bishop's routes, and—by your own mouth—Norfolk near the flame."

Silence. From the front room, an abacus clicks. Far away, a church bell thuds in the fog.

Walsingham lets the quiet work. Then, evenly: "I do not need a confession today. I need time. Two days. Signor Ridolfi—no letters, no messengers, no callers. Your servants say you are ill. All business waits. You will be 'ill' or 'busy'—choose your reason. In that time my men will walk the roads backward. If we find nothing, you have cost us only two days. If we find something...you will want to be standing on the right floor when it drops."

Ridolfi gives a short, thin laugh. "You threaten a merchant with a calendar."

"I warn a banker by Council order." Walsingham touches the green silk. "Refuse, and tomorrow I bring you before the Council, with the Lord Mayor to witness and the Star Chamber to hear how foreign packets fly through your hands. Agree, and my report will say you helped keep the peace and that you dislike violence."

Ridolfi studies paper, candles, and waiting maces. He knows the price of time.

"Two days," he says at last. "I mislay my couriers."

Walsingham closes his blank notebook. "Good. Then we are finished for tonight."

They stand. Ridolfi squints, testing him. "You play a quiet game, Master Walsingham." A brief, calculating pause. "One day you will be the Queen's shadow."

"I write notes," Walsingham says. "For Secretary Cecil."

"Ah. The man who rules by neatness."

"Neatness keeps heads attached," Walsingham replies. "Give my compliments to your chaplain. Pray for England."

Ridolfi's rings catch the flame as he bows. "We all do."

Walsingham passes the officer on the wet street. He bought two days. No more. He does not, for a moment, believe Ridolfi will waste them in bed.

1 October 1569

Fog slides along the Thames. In William Cecil's chamber, candles burn low. The room smells of warm wax and paper.

Walsingham sets a neat French summary on the baize.

"Ridolfi?" Cecil asks.

"Polite. Careful. And—for two days—harmless," Walsingham says. "He admits nothing, but he agreed to send nothing: no packets to the Spanish ambassador, none to the Bishop of Ross, none to the north."

Cecil reads and taps a line: Durham → York → London → Seething Lane. Bishop of Ross. Espés writes to Brussels about "friends in the north" and asks for ready money. Mention of Norfolk.

"The north is tinder," Cecil says. "A match and it burns." He looks up. "Norfolk?"

"Ridolfi named him first," Walsingham replies. "Too quickly."

Cecil's mouth tightens. "I will see to Norfolk." He locks the summary away, then slides a clean sheet to Walsingham. "Carry on with the strangers' churches. I want lists—tailors, goldsmiths, messengers, priests under borrowed names. Draw me the Bishop of Ross's world so clearly that if he sneezes, we can name who handed him the kerchief."

"Shall I inform Her Majesty?" Walsingham asks.

"Not yet," Cecil says, mild voice, iron choice. "She sleeps better without ghosts. When I need her anger, I will fetch it fresh."

He seals two brief notes—one to the Lord Admiral to tighten watch on the Narrow Seas and one to the Lord Mayor about "unlicensed Italian gatherings." A third paper slides across the table.

"Your warrant. In the City you will be obeyed."

Walsingham pockets it. "Ridolfi called me the Queen's shadow."

Cecil allows the faintest smile. "Shadows are useful. They show where the light is." He studies the wall map, its chalk-smeared north.

"Go on, Francis. Quietly. The loud men are already making our case."

Outside, the river moves dark towards the sea, carrying secrets with the tide.

Two days, Walsingham thinks. Enough to follow letters upstream. Enough to see whose hands reach for Spanish silver when the wind turns. He bows and goes, leaving Cecil with the fog, the map, and the neat lines that hold England together with nothing thicker than ink.

Cecil does not move at once. He listens to the river, to the soft crackle of the candles, to the imagined sound of boots on northern roads. Somewhere a spark is being struck; he cannot yet see whose hand holds the flint.

At last he draws a single line in chalk across the map, just south of the border. "If it comes," he murmurs to the empty room, "it will come here."

***

That evening the house on Lombard Street creaks in the damp. Upstairs the light from several candles throws a man's shadow against a white linen screen. A barber-surgeon presses a clove into a swollen cheek, sets a hot brick wrapped in a towel against the jaw, and rinses his lancet. The bowl on the stool blushes red. Vinegar and tallow sting the air. A small cup of warmed ale, sharp with more cloves and a shaving of ginger, steams on the table beside the bed—"for the pain"—cooling steadily as the performance goes on.

A knock. Downstairs, a maid opens to a watchman in a wet cloak.

"Master Ridolfi is abed, sir. A pain in a tooth."

She carries a wooden bowl that smells of broth and garlic; behind her, the tang of vinegar and the spice of mulled ale drift down the stairs.

The watchman looks up. The silhouette behind the screen shifts. Metal glints. A man groans. The watchman nods and steps back into the rain.

The front of the house is a stage.

The audience—Walsingham's men—see exactly what they expect: the surgeon's kit, the patient's outline, the boy trotting to the apothecary and back for "more clove and vinegar." In due course, the barber returns to "bleed the patient." If anyone checks, there is the red bowl, the slow shadow, the same bed. Perfect.

The escape plays behind the curtain.

In the garret, the real Ridolfi pulls on a plain black cloak and cap. He kisses his chaplain's brow—the chaplain wears Ridolfi's nightcap and lies still behind the screen—then tucks a small prayer book under his arm.

He eases a trap in the ceiling and slides into the neighbour's loft—two houses east. Dust lifts. Rafters complain. He stoops beneath beams, finds the narrow stair the watchers cannot see, and takes the way that does not lead to his yard but to Pope's Head Alley.

Below, the servants keep the show alive. One staggers out with a chamber pot and a face like death. Another splashes vinegar on the hearth so the sour smell crawls into the passage. A late clerk knocks, loudly lamenting that "Master is too ill to touch accounts." The watchers write what they hear: Ridolfi in bed, house awake, surgeon in attendance. Exactly right—and completely wrong.

Ridolfi ghosts through the alley to Billingsgate Stairs.

A wherryman squints at his pale face. "The barber done you in, Father?"

Ridolfi just nods and enters the boat. Oars click like a clock. The Thames takes the sound and keeps it. They cross the black water towards Southwark's lamps and the old Bishop of Winchester's riverside house.

Behind him, Lombard Street keeps acting. The shadow still moves behind the linen. The bowl still reddens. The maid still says, "The tooth." Walsingham's men close their notebooks, pleased with their vigilance, and tramp on.

The wherry kisses the stones at the Winchester House watergate. Ridolfi rises, a quiet figure in a plain cloak, and slips through the arch.

Inside, candles gutter; a prayer is murmured and swallowed by stone.

Outside, the river keeps its counsel, carrying secrets faster than horses. By dawn, Lombard Street will swear nothing moved at all.

***

Winchester House crouches over the Thames like an old confessor—its stones damp, its passages tight with shadows. In the vestry behind the ambassador's chapel, the air smells of wet wool, smoke, and the faint sourness of extinguished candles. A map of England lies open on the table, pricked not with pins but with inked dots—small, ambiguous, deniable.

Men move quietly. Robes brush benches. Rings tap wood. They have been doing so, in one guise or another, for months now. The first threads had been pulled long before the plot had a name.

Roberto Ridolfi stands at the table's head, gloves still on, hat crooked under his arm. He looks tired rather than triumphant.

"I am indisposed," he says dryly. "A toothache. And toothache, gentlemen, means I do not write letters today."

A thin smile. The joke is a veil.

Bishop John Lesley of Ross tightens his fingers around his rosary. "Aye. Master Walsingham's clerks have had their noses in your books. They poke at every Florentine account like hens."

Ridolfi inclines his head. "Which is why I asked for this meeting. If the Queen's ministers sniff at paper, we use breath instead. No letters for two days. Speak softly, remember little, and burn what you should not keep."

From the deep chapel doorway, Ambassador Guerau de Espés emerges, his eyes glinting under the candlelight—measured, wary.

"The times grow dangerous," Espés murmurs. "Cecil hears whispers through walls. Walsingham hears them before they are said. You have felt their questions?"

Ridolfi's mouth flickers. "I have felt their interest. Enough to know we must guard our tongues. Writing is where treason goes to be buried—and dug up later." He touches the map. "But talking is not—yet."

Lesley's voice frays with impatience. "Our queen has been nigh two winters' turn! And only now do the northern lords begin to stir. They will rise for her if given hope."

Espés folds his hands. "Hope is scarce. Spain watches, but His Majesty will not strike blind. He must know what strength the northern earls truly hold—and whether they mean only to restore the Mass, or to unmake Queen Elizabeth entirely."

The vestry door creaks. The Duke of Norfolk steps in, pale from sleeplessness. The air tightens.

"You sent for me," Norfolk says. "I came by river. No servants."

Ridolfi bows. "My lord, forgive the summons. Matters now move faster than letters can safely travel."

Norfolk glances at the map, then at the two churchmen. "You ask more of me than is wise. One whisper wrong-spoken and I am undone."

Lesley steps forward, earnest. "Mary needs powerful friends. If the north takes arms—if the realm sees her joined in marriage to a great English lord—"

"Marriage?" Norfolk cuts in. "Speak that word softer." He lowers his voice. "I have written to her. Letters only. No vows."

Ridolfi lifts a hand, coaxing. "No one counsels treason. Only coordination. If the earls rise together for the Mass and for the Queen of Scots, Spain may take notice—but only if the cause appears unified."

"Spain needs proof," Espés adds calmly. "Not plots."

Norfolk's jaw tightens. "I will not bring foreign steel into English fields."

"Then give Spain no cause to send it," Ridolfi says. "A show of strength. Petitions. Banners. No assault on London."

"Only freedom for our queen," Lesley murmurs.

Silence.

At last Norfolk exhales. "If I lend my name, it is as a question—not a banner. As a mediator, nothing more."

"Then we act carefully," Ridolfi says. "Soft steps. No letters. Let the north show its teeth first."

Espés nods. "Spain will watch."

A page slips in and murmurs a message into Ridolfi's ear, then vanishes. Numbers. Initials. Nothing more.

"Two matters," Ridolfi says. "First: until my toothache eases, the couriers rest. Second: the earls will move soon. If they rise confused, they doom themselves. If together..." He looks to Norfolk. "They may force Parliament to reconsider Mary's captivity."

"If I am involved at all," Norfolk says, "it remains quiet."

"Quiet is a tongue I speak well."

Norfolk pauses at the door. "What does Walsingham see when he looks at you?"

Ridolfi fastens his glove. "That the tooth troubles me. And the man is tired."

A thin smile.

"And nothing more."

Norfolk leaves. Lesley clutches his rosary. Espés glides away. Ridolfi straightens the map, wipes a candle-smudge from the margin, and checks the latch.

"Two days," Espés had said.

"Two," Ridolfi echoes to the empty room.

The Thames breathes beyond the shutters. Somewhere near Pope's Head Alley, a thin man in a low hat lingers, patient as frost—counting footsteps, noting absences, calling it prayer.

Chapter 19
Regnans in Excelsis

25 February 1570

The Papal Palace in Rome stands solemn, its vaulted ceilings and marble floors stir with the quiet rustle of robes. The low murmur of prayers exchange beneath frescoed domes. Guards shift at their posts with silent precision, while clerics glide through shadowed corridors, candles flickering in their wake. In a richly adorned chamber lined with frescoes depicting saints and martyrs, the Pope—wearing a white cassock and red skullcap, a rosary hanging from his belt—sits at a gilded desk. Candlelight illuminates his austere expression, his white robes stark against the dark wooden furniture.

Before him stands a scribe, quill poised above a parchment, awaiting the Pope's final words. The Pontiff's face is lined with the weight of divine responsibility; he speaks with deliberate clarity, his tone heavy with judgement. What follows is the substance of the bull, rendered into plain sense—its formal Latin tightened into a scribe's English for dispatch.

"*We, Pius, servant of the servants of God, in the name of Him who reigns in the highest place,*" he begins, his voice resonating through the chamber, "*declare that Elizabeth, the pretended Queen of England, has unlawfully seized the crown and has usurped the place of Supreme Governor of the English Church.*"

The scribe's quill scratches furiously as the Pope continues, his voice rising with righteous fervour. "*She has oppressed the followers of the Holy Catholic faith, instituted false preachers, and abolished the sacrifice of the Mass and the ancient ceremonies of the Church. She has ejected bishops, rectors, and other Catholic priests from their churches and benefices.*"

The Pope pauses, his piercing gaze fixed on the crucifix that hangs on the wall opposite him. He exhales slowly, then resumes, his tone laced with indignation. "*She has ordained that heretical books, according to the doctrine of John Calvin, be received and observed by herself and her subjects. We therefore declare the aforesaid Elizabeth to be a heretic and a supporter of heretics, and her adherents in the matters aforesaid to have incurred the sentence of anathema, and to be cut off from the unity of the body of Christ.*"

The scribe glances up briefly, then returns to his work as the Pope's voice grows more forceful.

"*We do deprive the said Elizabeth of her pretended title to the kingdom, and of all dominion, dignity, and privilege whatsoever. Likewise, we declare the nobles, subjects, and people of the said kingdom, and all others who have in any manner sworn oaths unto her, to be forever absolved from such oaths, and from all manner of duty, dominion, allegiance, and obedience to her. By the authority vested in us by these presents, we do also absolve them.*"

The Pope's hand, veined and steady, rests on the desk. "*We do charge and command all and singular the nobles, subjects, peoples, and others aforesaid, that they presume not to obey her orders, mandates, or laws. And whosoever shall act otherwise, or aid her, we do bind with the same sentence of anathema.*"

The scribe dips his quill in the inkwell, his hand trembling slightly as he captures the final words of the pronouncement.

"*Given at St Peter's in Rome, on 25 February 1570, in the year of the Incarnation of our Lord, in the fifth year of our pontificate.*"

The Pope leans back, his gaze piercing as he watches the scribe carefully sand the parchment to dry the ink. He crosses himself, then folds his hands in prayer and whispers, "May the Lord's will be done."

Behind him, cardinals and advisers also cross themselves and stand in sombre silence, their expressions a mix of awe and apprehension. A cardinal steps forward and bows.

"Your Holiness, this bull will shake the foundations of England."

Pius replies, "It must be so. The Church cannot abide heresy, nor can the flock suffer under a shepherd who leads them astray."

The parchment is carefully rolled and sealed with lead and silk. The Pope rises and lifts his hand in a sign of the cross.

"Take this to the world," he commands. "Let it be known that the Church stands resolute against all falsehood."

15 March 1570

The melancholic strains of viol and lute echo softly through a vaulted chamber at the Royal Alcázar. Musicians stationed in the far corner of the hall perform with delicate precision, their instruments weaving sombre tones through the thick air.

Near the hearth, Father Ruy López de Segura—adorned with a chain bearing a small gold rook pendant—and Father Alfonso Ceron sit hunched over a well-worn chessboard. The quiet clink of ivory pieces punctuates the heavy silence. Between them rests a low table with a pewter plate of candied orange peel and roasted almonds, and a tall, slender beaker of thin red wine already gone cool; López toys with an almond more than he eats, Ceron sips a little.

A burst of hurried footsteps disturbs the stillness. A young courtier, flushed with excitement, enters and bows low before the King. It had taken weeks of riders and ships for the parchment in his hand to reach Spain, but news of it had travelled faster than any courier.

"Your Majesty," the courtier breathes, eyes shining. "News from Rome. The Pope...His Holiness has at last declared Elizabeth of England excommunicated! Her soul stands under damnation! A bull has been issued—*Regnans in Excelsis*! England is dethroned, heretic rule condemned! God be praised—Your Majesty must be well pleased!"

He presents the red-sealed parchment with trembling hands.

Philip, standing beside his trusted adviser Juan de Idiáquez, accepts the document slowly. His face does not brighten—it hardens. As his eyes scan the parchment, something dark gathers behind his pallid expression. His grip tightens.

Suddenly, he forms the parchment into a ball and hurls the bull across the chamber. The young courtier recoils in confusion. The music falters. The chess pieces stop moving. Even the fire seems hesitant in its crackle.

Philip erupts.

"That man has undone us. That Pope!"

The voice—razor-sharp and echoing—slices the chamber in half. The musicians freeze. Ceron and López look up, startled, hands hovering mid-air. Even Idiáquez blinks in shock.

The King's breath comes fast and shallow. He turns his furious gaze on the young courtier, who now stands paralysed. He steps close, crowding the courtier back.

"You presume I would celebrate such reckless stupidity? You fool—get out of here!"

Philip strides across the room, retrieves the bull, and smooths it flat. He whirls back towards Idiáquez, voice blazing.

"Don Juan, Pope Pius did not consult me. Not one word, not one letter. And now I must write to my heretic sister-in-law in England, expressing how I am displeased with this action—forced to kneel diplomatically, when I should be the one commanding events!"

He slams his fist against the table near the chessboard, upsetting pieces. The two clergymen straighten them with quick, silent hands.

"He has crowned me with fire, and handed Elizabeth a sword."

Idiáquez, composed but watchful, ventures carefully, "Your Majesty, you risk excommunication yourself for such words."

Philip turns to him, slowly, eyes like steel drawn from the forge.

"Then let the Pope do it! If I stood truly under God's wrath, my kingdoms would already lie in ruin. I rule by divine appointment—not by Roman vanity."

He paces before the hearth, voice quieter but deadly serious.

"This bull is not just foolish. It is a disaster. It endangers the Queen of Scots, who Rome calls the true Queen of England, imprisoned and now more expendable than ever. Now Elizabeth has every reason to eliminate her rival permanently—and now she has justification, cloaked as self-defence."

He stops cold and points a finger towards the hearth.

"And what of the Catholics in England? It gives Elizabeth licence to purge them. Pius has turned a candle into a bonfire. We may see civil war there—Catholics calling on France instead of Spain for aid. Imagine that."

He turns back to Idiáquez.

"This cannot be allowed to spiral. We must control it. Not because it is Rome, but because it is Rome speaking out of season."

Idiáquez nods grimly. "Yes, Majesty. But the damage—"

"Must be hidden," Philip snaps. "Bury this bull. In Spain, in Naples, in the Netherlands. No copies. No echoes. No embers left for Protestant hands to seize."

He gazes down at the crumpled parchment, then—almost fussy—smooths the creases flat. He folds the parchment once, twice, and hands it to Idiáquez.

"No copies," he says. "No echoes. Let Rome play its moves with fire and Scripture," he mutters. "We play ours with silence and steel."

He turns to the chessboard again. Father López has just taken Father Ceron's bishop with his rook.

"The Church has made its move, Don Juan. Now we move—and tip the board if we must."

15 May 1570

The courtyard of Hampton Court Palace is shrouded in darkness, save for the glow of torches. A table has been set under the cloister with flagons of hot mulled wine and dishes of comfits for the courtiers, the steam from the spiced drink mingling with the torch smoke.

The night air is crisp, and a faint breeze carries the scent of the nearby River Thames. A tight knot of councillors and courtiers stands under the cloister, chosen as much for silence as loyalty. Their breaths are visible in the chill. Among them stand Sir Nicholas Bacon, William Cecil, and other prominent members of Queen Elizabeth's court, their expressions a mixture of curiosity and tension.

At the centre of the gathering stands Elizabeth, striking even in the stark firelight. Her gown of black velvet with golden embroidery catches the flickering light. In one hand, she holds a rolled parchment—a copy of Pope Pius V's bull of excommunication, newly come through Council hands. In the other, a lit torch.

Elizabeth steps forward, her eyes scanning the gathered faces, her lips curling into a mocking smile.

"Well," she begins, her voice carrying with the sharp edge of sarcasm, "the Bishop of Rome—the man some dare call the Vicar of Christ—declares me a 'heretic,' does he?"

A murmur ripples through the crowd, a mixture of indignation and restrained amusement.

"He dares to strip me of my throne," Elizabeth continues, her voice rising, "to free my subjects from their oaths of allegiance, to command that they disobey me—their sovereign, ordained by God Almighty!"

Her sharp gaze falls on the parchment in her hand. "This piece of rubbish, this bull is fit only to line privies, not bind princes. Ha! Let me show you what I think of it!"

With deliberate defiance, Elizabeth unrolls the parchment, its text glinting faintly in the firelight. Then, with a single, decisive motion, she puts the parchment to the flame until it catches, then drops it. The parchment blackens and curls. The crowd watches in silence, the words of excommunication reduced to ashes.

Elizabeth stands still, her eyes fixed on the burning remnants. The flames light her face, her expression one of cold resolve.

"Let this be a lesson to Rome," she says, her voice cutting through the night. "England bows to no pope, bows to no bishop, bows to no priest, and bows to no man who dares claim authority over this sovereign realm!"

Someone behind her raises a cup and drinks deep in rough, wordless assent, the smell of clove and wine rolling through the cold air like a second cheer.

The flames sputter and die, leaving nothing but a charred fragment on the paving stones. Elizabeth turns to her court, her tone suddenly light and biting.

"Shall I send the ashes back to him? Perhaps he will inhale them and mistake it for divine inspiration."

A ripple of laughter breaks out among the courtiers, the tension of the moment dissolving into mirth. Bacon and Cecil exchange approving glances, their queen's defiance an act of strength and theatrical brilliance.

"God save the Queen!" comes the resounding reply from the gathered crowd.

Elizabeth nods, her satisfaction evident.

22 August 1570

The Peace of Saint-Germain is only a fortnight dry, and Paris holds its breath. They meet not in the Louvre proper but in a side chamber off the covered walk by Saint-Germain-l'Auxerrois—the parish church beside the Louvre. It is close enough for a summons from Charles IX, far enough for plain speech. Tapestries are unhooked to swallow echoes; the bell tower looms like a warning.

Sir Henry Norris receives Admiral Gaspard de Coligny with the economy of a man who counts enemies by staircases. Norris stands alone, the Queen's ambassador in a city where shadows listen harder than courtiers.

Coligny—gaunt, eyes bright from too many campaigns—bows to English pragmatism rather than rank. "Monsieur l'Ambassadeur. Your Queen's friendship gives our king the courage he requires. Toleration on paper must become toleration at the gate."

Norris smiles without warmth. "Paper tears. We must stitch it with thread."

Coligny's gaze rests on the stripped tapestries. "Thread of garrisons—and towns held in surety. La Rochelle, Montauban, Cognac, La Charité-sur-Loire. If His Most Christian Majesty means the edict, he must enforce it with men, not marginalia."

Norris inclines his head. "Then we speak the same tongue. Edicts are wind unless the king nails them to the door with iron."

Coligny lets the point stand. "Enforcement follows coin. And coin sits in Brussels and Madrid. If the Duke of Alba keeps the Netherlands on a Spanish hinge, French peace turns on a foreign key."

Norris's eyes narrow. "Then a France looking north must see something other than a wall of *tercios* on the 'Spanish Road.' Spain cannot be allowed to move unopposed up the spine of Europe."

Footsteps outside interrupt: deliberate, idle—the soft tread of a Guise servant lingering in the covered walk like a rumour. Coligny's jaw hardens.

"The Guises drink Madrid's wine," he says softly. "If Spain pours more, I drown."

Norris answers just as quietly. "We know the taste of that draught. The northern lords rose last winter—and burned out just as quickly. Spain fed their courage, and Rome crowned their folly. England still carries the smoke."

He tilts his head towards the nave, where the parish bell sleeps in its cage. "You chose your ground well, Monseigneur—near enough the Louvre for the Queen-Mother's ear, near enough this church for the Guise eye. If Catherine would keep balance, she must keep your keys to those towns, and she must keep Spanish coin out of Paris."

Coligny gives the ghost of a smile. "I will take courage from that—so long as your Queen lets you speak it aloud."

"She does," Norris says. "On one condition: if Madrid buys friends here, you make them dear."

That night, Norris writes to Cecil in a hand that wastes no ink:

"*To Master Secretary. From Saint-Germain-l'Auxerrois this xxii of August. The Peace is signed, yet the streets carry tinder. Admiral C. has the King's ear by the Queen-Mother's sufferance. The House of Guise leans to Spain. The Spanish minister trafficks counsel & coin among them. If Alba be pinched of silver, the Admiral prospers. If not, the edict will bleed. The places of surety must be maintained with garrison & victual.*"

He pauses, hears the cloister's hush through the window, and adds one final line—part report, part warning:

"*We stand within the Louvre's shadow. Spain stands in the Guise's pocket. Between them, we must keep France from becoming Madrid's antechamber.*"

12 November 1570

At the Alcázar of Segovia, the chapel smells of cold stone and incense, the sort burned for long offices and longer obediences. Morning light slips through the high windows in pale bars, touching gilt, missing faces. Philip kneels where he has knelt a thousand times, his hands folded, his spine straight with the discipline that has replaced ease.

He hears her before he sees her—not footsteps, but the faint rustle of silk controlled to silence.

Anna of Austria stops two paces behind him.

She has been taught where to stand, how to wait, when to breathe. She does all of it correctly. If her heart runs ahead of her, it does not show. She has come a long way for this—Vienna to Madrid to Segovia—each mile a tightening of the future around her throat.

The confessor murmurs the last words of the office. Philip rises. He turns.

For a moment they look at one another without witnesses speaking between them. The gap is narrow. The history is not.

Anna lowers her head. Not a curtsey—this is not court—but a bow shaped by devotion. "Your Majesty."

Philip inclines his head in return. "My cousin."

They are related too closely in blood for romance to be imagined, and both know it. That knowledge steadies him. It steadies her.

The ring waits on the altar, a small circle of gold that carries more weight than iron. Philip steps forward and takes it. His fingers pause, just a fraction. He has buried a wife who believed obedience would save her. He has buried a troublesome son whose name no one speaks aloud today. The space where both once stood presses in on him now, quiet and exacting.

Anna watches his hand, not his face.

When he speaks, his voice is low, meant for her alone. "You have been instructed in your duties."

"Yes," she says. "By my confessor. By my mother. By my uncles." A beat. "By God." She crosses herself.

He studies her more closely then—the steadiness of her mouth, the absence of trembling. She is young, but not naïve. "And you consent?"

She lifts her eyes. They are clear. "I do."

There is no flourish to the words. No breathless hope. That honesty surprises him.

"You know what this requires," Philip says. "Patience. Silence. Endurance."

Anna nods once. "I was raised to be useful."

The priest begins the rite. Latin rises and falls like the tide against stone. Philip takes Anna's hand. It is cool. Smaller than he expected. He closes his fingers carefully, as if she were something that might break under careless strength.

The vows are spoken. They are ancient. They make room for no hesitation.

The priest asks, "Do you take—"

"I do," Anna says, before the question is fully formed. Philip notes this, absurdly, and lets the thought pass.

Philip slides the ring onto her finger. There is a murmur among the witnesses—approval, relief. The dynasty inhales.

The Mass continues. Anna kneels beside him now, close enough that he can feel the warmth of her through layers of fabric. She prays with her hands folded, her head bowed. He cannot see her face. He is grateful for that.

When it is finished, when the blessing has been given and the priest has stepped back, Philip turns to her again.

"You will find Spain colder than Vienna," he says. It is the closest he comes to a kindness.

"I will learn it," Anna replies. Then, because something in her demands truth, she adds, "I hope to please you."

Philip's mouth tightens. He hears in those words not flattery but resolve. "Please God," he says. "The rest will follow."

She accepts the correction. "Yes."

They walk from the chapel together. Outside, the court waits in orderly ranks—faces composed, hands folded, expectation humming beneath decorum. Philip pauses at the threshold. The sun is brighter here. It finds the gold thread in Anna's gown, the pale seriousness of her face.

She looks up at him then, really looks, and something unexpected flickers there. Not fear. Not calculation.

Trust.

It lands heavily.

"You were married before," she says quietly, as if the words have escaped before she could stop them.

He does not bridle. He has learned the cost of that. "Yes."

"She was Queen of England."

"Yes."

"Was she happy?"

The question is dangerous. Honest. Untrained.

Philip considers the courtyard, the banners, the listening stone. "She believed she was doing God's will," he says at last.

Anna weighs this. "And you?"

"I believed it was mine to require," he answers.

They stand in that truth for a moment. Then the Master of Ceremonies clears his throat. The world resumes its breathing.

Philip offers his arm. Anna takes it. Her hand is steady now, warmer. As they move forward together, the court bows as one body.

Later—much later—Philip will remember the way she looked at him in the chapel, not as a king, not as a solution, but as a man who would ask much and give little. He will remember that she did not turn away.

Anna will remember that he did not promise affection, only order. She will keep her word all the same.

For now, they walk into the light, bound not by illusion but by need—Spain's, God's, history's—while the silence of the chapel closes behind them, holding what they did not say.

24 December 1570

Frost halos the Presence Chamber windows at Whitehall. The Thames lies iron-grey beyond. Walsingham kneels, rises, and stands before Elizabeth, who wears winter layers like armour and patience like a blade.

Cecil holds a sealed packet. "Paris. Your advance baggage has already moved," he says. "You follow at week's end. Boulogne will take you if the wind is honest."

Elizabeth examines Walsingham as if weighing a coin. "Master Walsingham, you will not go to France to preach," she says. "You will go to listen. Speak to the Admiral. Show him England's hand is steady. Keep terms with the

Queen-Mother—she loves balance more than truth. Touch Norris gently. He gives offence when he means to flatter." She steps closer. "And Spain?"

"Watched," Walsingham answers.

"More than that," Cecil adds, voice flat as ledger parchment. "Paris is where Madrid spends against us; let us make them spend dearly. Note what Spain buys—favours, friends, ships, penitent priests. Since the Pope thundered against us, Spain claps to the echo. You will see who moves that echo through the French court."

Walsingham adds quietly, "The north has only just cooled."

Cecil nods once. "All the more reason to keep French powder far from English tinder."

Elizabeth's stare does not soften. "France and Spain are wolves from different dens, and both have tasted English meat. Keep them at each other's throats if you can—without letting either taste yours."

"I shall write plainly," Walsingham says, "and cipher the lines that matter."

"Do so," she replies—and, rarely, smiles. "And send me one frank sentence now and then, that I may know a man stands behind the ink."

Cecil passes the packet: urge enforcement of the peace, map the traffic between Guise and Spain, watch the Norman ports for Spanish coin and couriers. "If Alba's purse is pinched in the Low Countries, Paris stands bolder," he murmurs. "If not, it will be bought."

The seal is pressed. The moment is finished.

By Boxing Day the baggage was already on the carts—passage booked, horses ordered. By the last day of the year Walsingham was in the Channel.

31 December 1570

Night makes the English Channel a black glass. The wind scores it to a dull sheen. Walsingham's ship rides low under a scatter of stars. Spray needles his hood. Below deck the men gnaw at hard biscuit and salted beef, washing it down with sour beer that tastes more of barrel than grain. A sailor curses Spain by every saint in its calendar. Another crosses himself for a fair tide.

Walsingham keeps his stomach and his pen. His own supper—a strip of dried beef and a cup of sour wine—sits by his knee, forgotten as ink and salt spray blot together on the page. In the lee of the rigging, he scratches a line to the Queen's Secretary William Cecil:

"The passage is hard on the stomach and the rigging, but it carries us. I shall land with the year and take horse for Paris. If Norris has kept his temper, I shall keep him. If not, I shall seem to keep him while I do the needful. Coligny would draw France towards Flanders. The Queen-Mother would draw all quarrels into her rooms. Spain plays purse-strings with Guise and Spanish-backed priests of the south. If we are brisk in the Narrow Seas and chary in our speech, we may hold them long at talk."

He seals it against the damp, and adds a postscript the Queen asked for:

"Paris is where Madrid spends against us; I shall make them spend dearly."

He prays in his fashion: not to be clever, but to be accurate.

1 January 1571

Boulogne and the Road South. They make the outer mole at grey-light. Frost crusts the quay ropes. Gulls knife the air. The harbour smells of salt, tar, and horses stamping for warmth. From a nearby cookshop drifts the sharp, homely scent of onions frying in fat and yesterday's fish bones simmering into a thin broth, the only warm smell in the iron morning.

A French officer salutes without enthusiasm. "Monsieur?"

"Arrived with the new year," Walsingham replies.

A courier waits with a folded note from Norris at Paris: *"The Admiral has the King's ear. Guise grows courteous when Spaniards call. Bring ciphers. Bring patience. The Queen-Mother smiles."*

On the road between hedges laced with rime and fields gone to steel, he composes his first formal dispatch:

"To the Queen's Majesty & to Master Secretary, from Boulogne this first of January. I am safely landed & purpose to reach Paris with diligence. The court is a table with three hands upon it—Coligny's, Spain's, and the Queen-Mother's—each drawing the cloth a several way. My office shall be to keep the cloth from falling, & to note whose fingers are greased. I will cultivate the Admiral's friends, comfort the ministers, and omit no convenient kindness to those of the Old Religion who prefer France to Spain. Touching Spain: their minister at Paris feeds the Guise with hope and money. If the Duke of Alba be constrained of treasure, this court is bolder. If not, it will be bought. The places of surety (La Rochelle, Montauban, Cognac, La Charité) must be maintained with garrison & victual. I shall write often & briefly; what is weighty will go in cipher, what is urgent

by hand. In sum, I contend with Spain here, that we may not meet them in the Narrow Seas. Walsingham."

Horse-breath smokes in the cold. Paris is two days away. Work is nearer.

3 January 1571

Walsingham sees Paris at noon, roofs hoared with frost, bells tolling the new year as if to warn it. The stalls along the street steam with pots of cabbage and bacon, chestnut-sellers cry their wares beside barrels of sour wine, and the air is thick with the mingled smells of garlic, smoke, and spilled ale. He lowers his hood and looks not at the towers but at the gaps between them, the alleys where information lives.

A careful, watchful envoy enters bearing peace like a glass vessel and England's quarrel with Spain like a blade under his cloak. He will warm Huguenot hands in cold rooms, bow to a queen who smiles like a balancing scale, and mark which courtiers smell faintly of Spanish musk. He had come to keep Spain's hand out of France—and France's hand off England's throat.

That night his first notes go out in two inks: the harmless lines in Latin, the dangerous names dropped into cipher like stones into deep water.

13 April 1571

In Madrid's Royal Alcázar, the private audience chamber is cool, shadowed, its high windows throwing long bars of light across the tiled floor. Philip sits alone at a writing desk, his councillors dismissed moments earlier. Only Antonio Pérez remains, standing at his shoulder with the stillness of a trained blade.

A door opens. A steward ushers in a single man—Ridolfi's discreet courier, plainly dressed, hat in hand, eyes lowered. Not a diplomat. Not a councillor. A messenger only. Exactly as Philip prefers.

He kneels.

"Your Majesty," he murmurs. "I bring letters from Signor Ridolfi, banker of Florence, concerning certain...matters raised by Mary Stuart, Queen of Scots, and by noblemen in England loyal to the Old Religion."

Philip does not gesture for him to rise. He simply watches.

Don Antonio steps forward, accepting the sealed packet which had taken weeks to arrive. He breaks the outer seal—only the outer—glances at the superscriptions—the addresses within—and nods once.

"The letters concern," he says carefully, "the disposition of certain English lords...their grievances under the Protestant queen...and their willingness, should circumstances allow, to restore the Catholic faith."

The courier replies carefully.

Philip's voice is calm, remote, almost cold.

"Tell your master," he says, "that Spain does not traffic in fantasies. English nobles promise much, and deliver little."

The courier bows his head.

"With respect, Sire, Signor Ridolfi writes that one lord of great blood stands ready—should a favourable wind arise. He names no action. Only the hope that England may yet be Catholic again."

A delicate phrasing. *No assassination. No invasion.* Only "winds" and "hopes."

Philip folds his hands.

"And what does he ask of me?"

The courier chooses every word as though stepping across a frozen lake.

"He asks...that Your Majesty consider the plight of certain Catholics in England. And that, should the northern counties stir again—as men whisper they might—Your Majesty might...judge whether it is fitting to lend comfort to the downtrodden."

Still coded. Still safe.

Philip leans back.

"Comfort," he repeats. "Comfort is not given lightly."

Pérez inclines his head. "Sire, perhaps the courier could wait in the antechamber while I examine the letters in fuller detail."

Philip gives the smallest nod.

The courier retreats, the steward closing the door behind him.

Silence fills the chamber like gathering storm-clouds.

At last Philip speaks—not as a man tempted, but as a man weighing fate against caution.

"These English lords—do they mean to restore order, or merely replace one chaos with another?"

Pérez answers softly, "Ridolfi hints at order, Your Majesty. But he writes as a banker, not a soldier. His words must be sifted carefully."

Philip's gaze drifts to the crucifix on the far wall.

"If England's nobles truly wish to raise the Cross again," he murmurs, "they must show strength first. Spain cannot be the hand that lifts them from their knees."

Pérez bows. "Shall I tell the courier this, Sire?"

Philip's voice sharpens—still quiet, but edged.

"Tell him Spain listens. Nothing more."

A beat.

"And tell him that if these English lords crave deliverance, they must prove they are worth delivering."

Pérez puts his right hand on his chest and bows deeper.

When the courier is summoned back, Philip does not look at him. He merely speaks the single line that keeps all doors open while committing himself to nothing.

"You may inform Signor Ridolfi: Spain hears the cries of the faithful. What comes of that hearing depends on England—not Spain."

The courier bows to the ground, trembling with the knowledge that he has been neither embraced nor dismissed.

He is escorted out by guards.

Philip rises only when the door closes.

He looks at Pérez.

"Send word to Alba," he says. "Quietly. No names in ink."

Pérez inclines his head, understanding perfectly.

Spain has promised nothing.

7 May 1571

Hundreds of miles away from Madrid, in the ornate halls of the Medici court in Florence, Cosimo de' Medici, the Grand Duke of Tuscany, paces his dining room. He holds Ridolfi's letter in one hand, a golden goblet in the other. Beside him stands an adviser.

"Ridolfi," de' Medici mutters, shaking his head. "The man writes too boldly—treating bloodshed as if it were a merchant's bargain."

The adviser asks, "Shall we ignore his words, Your Excellency? Or shall we take action?"

De' Medici's dark eyes gleam with calculation. "We cannot remain silent. Elizabeth, for all her Protestant heresies, keeps the northern seas from chaos—and chaos is bad for Tuscan coin. If she falls and chaos reigns, the ripple effects will reach Tuscany."

He hands the letter to the adviser. "Send a discreet memorandum to Lord Burghley in London—this is a warning, not a favour."

***

Wax smoke hangs low in the dim hall of Winchester House in London. Spanish household guards flank the walls like carved saints, their eyes following every ripple of movement. A page slips past with a tray bearing a stoppered flask of dark Spanish wine and a small dish of olives and salted anchovies, the brine and resinous oil cutting through the chill gloom.

Captain Robert Weeks of the Navy Royal steps inside, his boots whispering on the worn tiles. One guard shifts just enough to bar the way until a steward approaches with a curt nod.

"Your name," the steward murmurs.

Weeks presents a folded slip sealed in black wax.

"From Sir Thomas Stanley."

The steward cracks the seal, skims the line, and his expression loosens by a hair. Whatever it says, it marks Weeks as trusted—vetted—worth hearing.

"Follow me, sir."

He leads Weeks through a narrow cloister into a private chamber where Ambassador Guerau de Espés sits with two clerks. Papers are arranged in perfect geometric order. Espés completes a line of cipher, sprinkles sand to dry the ink, breathes gently across the page—only when the ledger closes does he look up.

"Captain Weeks."

Weeks bows.

"Your Excellency."

"Sir Thomas writes that you are...troubled."

A precise emphasis: *a Catholic man beneath Protestant colours.*

Weeks lowers his voice.

"I have sailed in the Queen's ships since King Edward's days. I have watched the old faith hunted like vermin. I can no longer bear what I serve."

Espés studies him, weighing marrow and mask.

"Many claim such sentiment," the ambassador says softly, "yet few mean it. Testimony is wind. Proof is coin."

He toys with an untouched olive on the rim of a pewter dish, rolling it beneath his fingertip as he measures the sailor's soul.

Weeks meets his eyes.

"Then assay me."

A long beat. Then Espés gestures to a chair—but keeps his own body angled, cautious.

"Begin with this," he says. "What do England's true Catholics most fear at sea?"

Weeks glances towards the door, leans forward.

"That the Queen's navy is not what her Council pretends. Ships scattered between Medway and Portsmouth. Too little powder. Crews thin. If Spain wished to land troops..." He trails off deliberately.

Espés completes the thought:

"...England would be forced to answer faster than it prefers. Am I not correct?"

Weeks gives the faintest nod—neither treason nor denial.

The ambassador's fingers tap once.

"Captain, you came with more than fears, did you not?"

Weeks hesitates just enough to seem sincere.

"I came for guidance. If England plunges wholly into heresy, I must know where a Catholic sailor may stand—and where he must step aside."

Espés allows the ghost of a smile. Not trust—*recognition.*

"You ask the weather before you choose your course," he says.

Weeks inclines his head.

Espés turns towards the window overlooking the Thames. His voice drops, layered and careful.

"There are men in this realm," he murmurs, "who pray for England to remember her rightful obedience...for a certain imprisoned lady to breathe free air again...for certain noble houses to rise as God intended."

Weeks stands motionless. "Certain noble houses, Your Excellency?"

Espés's gaze stays on the river.

"Some speak of the Duke of Norfolk's loyalty to the ancient faith. Some whisper that England's salvation may come from alliance—within, and without."

Weeks lets silence answer for him.

Espés continues: "There is talk across Christendom—quiet talk—of co-ordinated remedy. A *design*. Let us say those who favour it believe England waits only for a spark. A rising in the north. A noble marriage. A blow struck at the right hour."

This is as close as he will come to naming the Ridolfi plan to a man on first meeting.

Weeks gives a controlled nod.

"And this design—if it moves—Spain will...assist?"

Espés turns at last.

"Spain assists when success is assured. Not before. You understand."

Weeks bows slightly.

"Aye."

"For now," the ambassador says, "observe. Listen. Carry only what you are certain of to Sir Thomas. And Captain—if you return to Winchester House, you will not enter by the front gate."

Dismissal. A test passed.

Weeks withdraws as the guards part.

Behind him, Espés murmurs to his clerk.

"Send word to Stanley. The man may yet serve—if he keeps his head above water."

Weeks steps into the fogged Southwark dusk, pulse hammering. Nothing had been said plainly. Yet everything had been said.

***

At Whitehall later that afternoon in a narrow privy chamber, William Cecil, the newly-made Baron Burghley, pores over ciphered letters. Sir Nicholas Bacon, the Lord Keeper, stands near the door, heavy brows lowered. On a small table between them rests a neglected trencher with the congealed remains of boiled beef and carrots and a tankard of ale gone flat, the sort of plain fare that marks a working day rather than a feast.

Ridolfi's codes lie open like wounds. A discreet warning from the Grand Duke of Tuscany rests atop the pile.

Cecil lifts a sheet between two fingers as though the ink itself offends him.

"Spanish forces...Norfolk's treason...Mary restored..."

He exhales sharply.

"Ridolfi weaves his web loudly enough for all of Europe. The man is a braggart dressed as a conspirator."

Bacon smiles thinly.

"He makes our work easy."

A knock. A guard enters.

"My lords, Captain Weeks awaits."

Bacon unbolts the door. Cecil raises an eyebrow.

"Excellent. Let no one interrupt treason." Then, dryly: "Except the traitor himself."

"Send him in," Bacon calls.

Captain Weeks enters—salt-stiff coat, hat under his arm, eyes alert. He sees the damning papers and the two most dangerous civil servants in England.

Bacon bolts the door.

"Captain Weeks. Before Lord Burghley, you bear one name."

He pauses.

"Traitor."

Bacon folds his arms.

"And in this chamber, Captain, that word has consequences."

Weeks says nothing. Slowly—deliberately—he lays the sword on the table. He looks to Bacon, whose hand rests on his dagger. Cecil is calm and unmoved.

"My lords," Weeks says quietly, "I surrender."

A sharp, brittle silence.

Cecil stares at the sword...then lifts his eyes, expression blank.

"What am I to do with this, Captain? Polish it for you? Or pawn it?"

Bacon snorts. The tension pops. At Cecil's nod, Weeks retrieves the sword and slides it back into its scabbard at his hip. All three men laugh—briefly, harshly.

"Well," Cecil says, leaning in, "since we are all friends now...speak."

Weeks straightens, voice low.

"I gained the confidence of Ambassador Espés. His tongue loosened like a drunkard's purse."

Cecil's eyes sharpen.

"Good. What did he reveal?"

"He spoke of a plan," Weeks continues. "A plan whispered through Christendom. A northern rising. Norfolk. Mary's freedom. A noble marriage. All needing one spark—then Spain moves, most likely from Flanders."

Bacon mutters, "Ridolfi's poison, then."

Weeks nods.

"Ridolfi—though the ambassador never named him—is clearly the courier of this scheme. Spain waits for certainty from within England."

Cecil taps the table.

"As we suspected. They hope to choke London from within."

Bacon smirks.

"The noose will tighten around the necks of traitors."

Cecil gathers the papers.

"With your intelligence, Ridolfi's loose boasting, and Tuscany's warning, the pattern is complete. Now we let them move further."

Bacon raises a brow.

"And then?"

Cecil's voice drops to iron.

"And then we close the trap. If Norfolk persists, he will put his neck where the law can find it. Ridolfi will flee or hang. And Spain will learn—once again—that Elizabeth's England is no hutch for foreign foxes."

He fixes Weeks with a steady gaze.

"And as for you, Captain...keep your sword. You may yet need it."

***

Later that evening in London, Queen Elizabeth stands in her private chambers, the letter from de' Medici in her hands. Beside her stand Cecil and Bacon, their eyes fixed on her as she reads.

When she finishes, Elizabeth sets the letter down carefully. "Cosimo de' Medici sends his regards," she says, her tone light but her eyes steely. "A pity he values stability more than my faith."

"Even a self-serving warning is a warning nonetheless, Your Majesty," says Cecil.

Elizabeth's gaze shifts to Bacon. "And what of Ridolfi?"

"He boasts still," Bacon replies. "But we have his ciphered letters, thanks to City eyes and Council hands. The plot is laid bare. Norfolk, Mary, Philip—they are all implicated."

"Norfolk, my cousin, is a traitor, as ever. Mary is a thorn in my side, but Philip—Philip—he grows bold."

"Spain waits for a domestic revolt here to justify their actions," Cecil says. "If we cut the head from this plot, the body will falter."

Elizabeth straightens, turning her signet once, twice, until the stone bites her thumb. She sets her palm flat on the table—no pounding, only decision.

"Then cut it, Spirit. Prepare Espés' dismissal and the grounds for it—let him learn it when I choose, not when he expects. Secure the evidence. Prepare the warrants. When I give the word, we move at once, and we move lawfully. Seal Mary's channels. Double the watches. Now."

Outside, the bells of London toll the hour.

Elizabeth listens until the sound fades, unaware that in Madrid the same hour is being marked—and read very differently.

Chapter 20
We Arm the Shepherds

8 October 1571

The Whitehall Council Chamber is cool, the air thick with betrayal and the threat of future plots. Elizabeth, her ginger hair tucked beneath a modest coif, briskly paces the length of the room. Her eyes burn with the frustration of a sovereign who has narrowly escaped disaster.

Her advisers—William Cecil and Sir Nicholas Bacon—watch her intently. A stack of intercepted letters and other incriminating evidence lies on the oak table at the centre of the room. Elizabeth's gaze drops to the papers. She sweeps a hand across the stack, scattering pages, then stops abruptly.

"Ridolfi's plot would have made England fall to foreign hands. My crown, my people—offered to Spain and Rome like a pawn in their holy game. Norfolk will answer for this—once the law has done its work—but what of Mary Stuart?"

Cecil answers, "Your Majesty, she must remain imprisoned. Executing her now would fan the flames of rebellion. Her supporters will see her as a martyr, a Catholic saint whose blood cries out for vengeance. Better she remains a symbol of dashed hopes than a rallying cry for revolt."

Elizabeth replies, "And as a prisoner, she continues to plot. Every letter she attempts to draft drips with treachery—even the ones we never allow to leave her custody. I am weary of this endless game."

Cecil hesitates. "It is a necessary game, Your Majesty—as cruel as it may seem. Mary, for all her captivity, remains a potent threat. But as long as we control her movements and seize her correspondence, she is a threat we can manage."

Elizabeth turns away, her hands clasped before her. "And Philip? What of him?"

Bacon replies, his tone colder, more ruthless. "He will deny involvement, Your Majesty. He will claim no knowledge of Ridolfi's ambitions, no hand in funding or supporting the plot." Bacon's lips curl into a faint smirk. "Philip is no fool. His fingerprints are faint, but they are there. Ridolfi carried the instructions. The Spanish ambassador facilitated his communications. Spanish gold was being readied. Philip's hand is clear to those who know where to look."

Elizabeth's voice sharpens. "Then why does he play coy? Why not declare open war if he so despises my reign?"

Bacon's tone grows graver. "Because Philip is patient, Your Majesty. An open war with England would strain Spain's resources and expose him to dangers elsewhere—particularly in the Netherlands, where rebellion festers like an open wound. For Philip, diplomacy and covert plots are far safer weapons. He seeks to weaken you incrementally, to sow chaos within your realm until your rule collapses from within."

Elizabeth replies, "It shall not happen!"

Cecil nods, his expression grim. "Philip's motives are as much religious as they are political. He thinks he is God's bailiff, Majesty. Philip would rather claim your soul than your ports—but he will take both if he can. To him Protestant England is a blight he cannot ignore, but he will not act rashly. He seeks certainty—an assured victory, not a gamble."

Elizabeth's hands tighten into fists. "He may be patient, but my brother-in-law underestimates me. Let him scheme, let him plot—I will not falter."

Bacon's tone softens slightly. "Even so, Your Majesty, we must prepare for the next storm. Ridolfi is not the last of it. Spain will not be satisfied. Nor Rome. They will try again, perhaps with a subtler hand."

Elizabeth's gaze turns to the scattered papers on the table. "And Mary will always be their tool."

Cecil edges forward, each word hushed but heavy with consequence. "She will, Your Majesty. But the world must see that it is her treachery that binds her, not your fear. Norfolk will be tried and surely be found guilty. His execution will serve as a warning to others who might conspire with her. Let his head on the block be a message that treason has a price."

The Queen's face stills, her displeasure held behind clenched grace. "And what of our allies? Will they stand with us against Philip's ambitions?"

Cecil's expression darkens. "The Dutch rebels may provide a buffer, but their position is precarious. As for the Protestant states of the Holy Roman

Empire, they sympathise but will not risk war to defend us. We have no shield but what we forge ourselves, Majesty."

Elizabeth exhales slowly, the weight of her isolation pressing down on her. "Then we must be stronger, cleverer. We must fight in the shadows, as Philip does. Bacon, I want every Catholic noble of consequence watched, every credible whisper of dissent traced. And if Philip sends another Ridolfi to my shores, I want to know before his ship even lands."

Bacon bows slightly. "It shall be done, Your Majesty."

Cecil adds, his tone steadier, "And Mary, Your Majesty?"

Elizabeth's gaze grows cold. "Let her rot in her gilded cage. But watch her closely, Spirit. She will not have another chance to slip the leash."

15 October 1571

The marble halls of the Royal Alcázar of Madrid are quiet, save for the soft tread of boots on polished stone. Philip faces a map of Europe. His hand hovers over England, as if contact alone might ignite conflict. His expression is calm, almost serene, but his mind is in turmoil, a thicket of calculations.

Behind him, Antonio Pérez stands silently, his head bowed. At last, Philip speaks. "Ridolfi's failure was inevitable. The man was too eager, too foolish. He shouted his plans across Europe as though they were a triumph already won."

Pérez says, "Your Majesty, the English Queen knows of your involvement."

Philip turns slowly, his dark eyes cold. "Let her suspect," he says. "She cannot prove what I have not signed—yet."

"But, Your Majesty," Pérez continues, his voice faltering, "her government grows more vigilant. The English fleet—"

Philip silences him with a raised hand. "Her fleet is not yet my chief concern. England's strength is a façade—yet even façades can hide guns. It is held together by Elizabeth's cunning and heretical arrogance. The cracks are there, even if she hides them well."

He turns back to the map, his gaze fixed on England. "She may have thwarted this plot, but she cannot thwart God's judgement. England's heresy will not endure. When the hour is right—and when England gives me lawful cause—I will answer her in a language she cannot misread. And then the world will remember that Philip of Spain does not forget an insult."

18 March 1572

The Queen's Privy Chamber is hung with biblical tapestries, their woven prophets watching like judges. Elizabeth sits high-backed in her carved chair, her hounds Pippin and Bella curled at her feet. Pippin lifts its head as the Dutch delegation enters—two men who walk not like supplicants, but like men who have buried friends.

Heer Johan van der Meer bows only as deeply as protocol demands. His eyes—cold, calculating—miss nothing. Beside him, Heer Willem de Groot, broad-shouldered and scarred from Antwerp street fighting, plants his boots as though he expects the floor itself to betray him.

"Your Majesty," van der Meer begins, voice steady as hammered iron, "we return not as beggars, but as men whose country smoulders. Spain tightens its grip daily. Our towns wither under new exactions. Our congregations scatter under threat. We come seeking alliance, not alms."

Elizabeth leans back slightly. "Alliance? Or shelter behind my crown? You ask a sovereign prince to raise arms against a king. What message do you think that sends to my own subjects?"

De Groot's jaw tightens. "Your Majesty, Philip has broken faith with us. He rules by terror, not law. No subject owes obedience to the butcher of his own people."

Sir Nicholas Bacon stands near the window, half-shadowed, arms folded. His gaze flicks towards Elizabeth.

She says, "What say you, Bacon? Shall England nurse every rebellion that cries against Spain?"

Bacon sets aside a sliver of candied orange peel he had been turning between his fingers. He bows.

"Majesty, if Spain crushes the Netherlands entirely, his strength doubles. And when he looks west, the only shore he will see is England's. Better to blunt his blade beyond the Narrow Sea than feel it hunt our harbours."

Cecil rubs the bridge of his nose—not affectation, but strain. "If we fund a war openly, we drain the treasury. And we do not yet know where the tinder lies. There are mutters along the coast, yes—exiled captains gathering hulls—but nothing certain. The cost may break us before Spain ever tries."

Dudley leans forward, eyes bright with urgency. "Majesty, Spain is already your enemy, whether he proclaims it or not. Help the Dutch now—in quiet, in shadow—or face Spain later, when he comes at his choosing. One choice spends coin. The other spends English blood."

Bella barks—sharp, ill-timed. Elizabeth waves a hand.

"Hush, Bella. Even you seem to have an opinion."

Van der Meer takes one bold step forward—nothing of meekness about him.

"Your Majesty, we do not come with empty hands. Aid us, and England will command the trade of the North Sea. Our ports will open to your merchants ahead of any. And should our people rise—as many whisper they soon may—you will have a bulwark of free provinces between England and Spain, owing their safety to you."

He gestures towards the neglected marchpane on the small table beside her. "Once our markets filled your tables: butter, cheese, linen, Rhine wine. That trade dies as we die."

De Groot adds, low and uncompromising, "Help us wound Spain now, or face Spain at the height of his strength. Neutrality will avail you nothing, Your Majesty. Philip will not spare England because she sat still."

Elizabeth rises—slow, deliberate. Every minister straightens.

She circles the table like a hawk studying uneasy prey.

"You ask me to risk my crown—to open a vein of gold that may never clot. You ask me to gamble my people's peace on your revolt. And yet—" her gaze sharpens—"you give me reasons I cannot ignore."

She taps the table once, decisive. The spiced ale beside her has gone cold; she tastes it, grimaces faintly, and sets it aside.

"Burghley, Bacon—bring me the true cost, stripped to the bone. Leicester, my Lord of Leicester—only the shadowed measures: routes that leave no footprints, hands that cannot be traced to my crown, purses that close themselves if discovered. I want papers on my table by tomorrow."

Dudley bows. Cecil inclines his head. Bacon's eyes narrow with calculation.

Elizabeth turns to the envoys.

"You shall have my answer when I am ready—neither sooner nor later. Until then, tread softly. Spain has long ears, and he listens for yours."

Van der Meer bows again, iron still in his voice.

"Your Majesty, the Netherlands will remember who aided her—and remember who looked away."

Elizabeth returns to her chair. Bella noses her hand; she strokes the dog absently, her gaze already far from the chamber.

"Spain circles us like a wolf," she murmurs. "Perhaps it is time we arm the shepherds."

15 April 1572

The oak doors close with a deep, shuddering thud, echoing off stone and carved beams as if the palace itself shared its unease. Within, Philip of Spain sits almost rigid. A brass dish beside him holds figs, almonds, and a small cup of bitter chocolate spiced with cinnamon. The drink has cooled to a skin. He leans slightly forward in his chair, one hand resting on the edge of the table strewn with charts and dispatches, the other absently tracing the worn armrest. The walls are crowded with maps—inked lines that stretch from Peru's silver mountains to the flat, restless provinces of the Low Countries—yet for all their breadth, they seem to close in on him tonight.

The brazier hisses as a log splits, throwing up sparks. Into this hush steps Juan de Idiáquez, the King's secretary, his walk careful, his gaze steady. He bows, then waits, the sealed papers in his hand a weight heavier than their parchment suggests. He knows well enough the temper of the man before him, and how news delivered here can shift the balance of kingdoms.

"Your Majesty, Don Antonio is summoned. He has news from the Netherlands."

Philip sits hunched over a map of the Netherlands, fingers tracing the rebellious provinces. Without looking up, he begins in a tone that is sharp but laced with weariness.

"I should have learned juggling when I was a lad, Don Juan. It would have given me valuable experience in politics."

"Juggling does not do justice to the burdens Your Majesty carries. The Netherlands alone would break a lesser king."

The faint smile on Philip's lips disappears, replaced by a scowl. "Take heed of the situation in the Netherlands. If my proud heretic royal sister-in-law, the Queen of England, favours the Protestant rebels, we must respond in kind. Their audacity—seeking assistance from England against their lawful, God-appointed sovereign—cannot go unpunished."

Before Idiáquez can respond, the doors open again. Antonio Pérez, the smooth-tongued secretary to the King, sweeps into the chamber, his presence immediately sparking tension. He bows with a scroll in hand. "Your Majesty."

Philip's gaze hardens. "Speak."

With a steady hand, Pérez spreads the scroll, his tone polite yet laced with scorn.

"The English pirates have struck again—raiding Spanish ships in the Narrow Seas. Their spoils include pay-chests destined for the garrisons in the Netherlands."

Philip's fist slams the table with a thunderous crack, the force rattling goblets and sending the inkwell skittering across the polished wood. Ink splashes like blood, parchment flies into the air, and both men recoil. He stills, then straightens the scattered folios, aligning edges with fussy care. "We proceed methodically," he says, voice even. Then his temper surges. "Heresy and treason sail under Protestant colours!"

He sweeps an arm towards the window. His eyes blaze—unblinking. "They infest the coasts like vermin," he snarls, "emboldened by the treachery of my so-called sister-in-law!"

Idiáquez speaks, his voice low but firm. "Sire, the Netherlands is not our only concern. Our empire's lifeblood flows from the Indies—the gold of New Granada, the silver of Potosí. These riches sustain not only our fleets but the armies that defend Christendom. Without them, our efforts crumble."

Philip reaches for an almond, snaps it between his fingers, and lets the crumbs fall onto the map of the Indies. "And yet every morsel is stolen from our grasp." He turns sharply. "And still this lifeblood is constantly under siege. English pirates plunder our treasure fleets. Francis Drake, John Hawkins, and their ilk flaunt Spanish treasure in English ports."

"Sire," Pérez interjects, "Elizabeth claims these are the acts of rogues. She denies their connection to her crown."

Philip's eyes bore into Pérez. "Do you believe her?"

Pérez hesitates, choosing his words carefully. "Her denials are convenient, sire. Yet Plymouth and Bristol grow fat with our gold and silver, and her Navy Royal flourishes with the spoils of our labour."

Idiáquez says, "Sire, these privateers weaken our grip on the Indies. Our fleets cannot cover every lane. Each loss emboldens them."

Philip walks to the hearth, tossing another log on the fire with deliberate force, watching the flames leap—his silence more ominous than words. "And the *asientos*?" he asks, his tone colder now. "Our colonies depend on labour to mine the riches that sustain Spain. Do these rebels trouble the slave traffic to our mines?"

With the familiarity of long service, Pérez pours himself a little wine from the clay jug at the sideboard—cheap local red, not court vintage—and sips to hide the smile tugging at his mouth.

Idiáquez nods. "Yes, Sire. Without those labourers, the mines at Potosí and Zacatecas fall short of their yield. The pirates and rebels know this. They attack not only our ships but the lifeblood of the realm."

Pérez adds with a sly smile, "Perhaps they understand Spain's weaknesses better than we thought."

Philip wheels on him. "Weaknesses?" His voice is a thunderclap. "Spain has no weaknesses—only enemies who will learn the price of defiance."

Pérez steps back slightly but holds his ground. "Your Majesty, retaliation is necessary, but careful discretion must guide our hand. Elizabeth is not yet an open enemy. If we drive it further—"

Idiáquez interrupts, his voice cutting. "Careful? The time for caution has passed. Every moment we hesitate, England grows bolder, and the Netherlands spirals further into chaos."

At Idiáquez's jab, Pérez's smile holds. His eyes do not.

Pérez shoots him a sharp look. "And if we provoke Elizabeth into a full alliance with the rebels? Or worse—if she allies with France? Are we prepared to face England and France on two fronts?"

Philip drives his hand down with sudden violence, sending a quill rolling and the room into silence. "Enough. Spain does not cower before Protestant queens or rebellious heretics. Elizabeth must understand that her meddling has limits."

Idiáquez presses his advantage. "Then, Sire, let us act decisively. Strengthen the convoys. Strike the pirates at their strongholds. If Elizabeth cannot control her pirates, we will deal with them ourselves."

Pérez raises an eyebrow. "And risk open war?"

Philip's glare freezes him in place. "War is coming, Don Antonio. Prepare convoys and raze the pirates' nests. We do not choose the time—we prepare for it."

Idiáquez and Pérez don masks of diplomacy, but their eyes betray the rivalry beneath. Philip turns to them both.

"Don Juan," he says to Idiáquez, "tighten the defences in the Indies. Prepare our fleets. The riches of the New World will not fall into English hands again."

"Yes, at your command, Your Majesty," Idiáquez says, bowing.

"And you, Don Antonio," Philip continues, his tone colder, "keep a closer watch on Elizabeth's court. I want to know her every move, her every thought. Coordinate with our ambassador there."

Pérez bows but cannot resist a parting jab at Idiáquez. "Of course. At your command, Sire. Perhaps some of us could learn from England's subtlety."

Idiáquez bristles but holds his tongue, his loyalty to Philip outweighing his disdain for Pérez.

Philip sits at his desk, dips his quill into ink, and prepares to write a letter. He says to Idiáquez, "The pirates, and the rebels—they will all learn the cost of defying Spain. Our patience has limits. And when those limits are reached, our justice will be swift and final."

The fire crackles as Philip begins to write, the sound punctuated by the scrape of his quill.

"*To His Excellency, Don Diego Lope de Vera, Royal Governor of Panamá. Reinforce Nombre de Dios and Panamá. Secure the Isthmus. Root out corruption. Convoy silver with heavier escort. Expend what the Treasury affords. Failure threatens the realm. Given at the Royal Alcázar, by my hand: I, the King.*"

He sands the ink and presses his signet ring into the melted wax, sealing the letter with the symbol of his authority. His dark eyes linger on the parchment for a moment before he turns to his secretary, Idiáquez, who waits nearby.

"Have this sent immediately," Philip says, his voice firm. "And ensure that my instructions are carried out to the letter."

Idiáquez takes the missive with a bow, but before departing, he ventures to speak. "Your Majesty, the viceroys in the Indies face challenges that extend beyond the pirates. The indigenous uprisings in the interior and the vast distances between outposts strain their resources."

Philip's gaze hardens. "Then they must rise to the challenge. The riches of the Indies are the sinews of our empire. If they fail in their duty, they fail Spain and God alike."

Idiáquez nods and leaves the chamber. Philip returns his attention to the map of the New World, his thoughts consumed by the endless threats to his empire. Beyond the ink and parchment lies a vast world of ambition and peril, a battlefield as treacherous as any he has faced.

The fire in the hearth flares as if mirroring his resolve, and Philip's expression remains as unyielding as the empire he seeks to defend.

Chapter 21
The Dragon Wounded

15 June 1572

The air of the tropical evening hangs heavy in Panama City. In the Royal Governor's Hall, His Lordship Don Diego Lope de Vera stands by an open window, fanning himself with a folded piece of parchment. Nearby, a glazed earthenware jug of watered red wine sweats in the heat. It sits beside a wooden bowl of wizened limes and a plate of cold stewed maize and shredded beef.

He fans himself, then stops mid-stroke—a small sign of anger edged with doubt. Outside, the distant clatter of hooves and the muffled hum of the city mingle with the rhythmic chirping of insects. In his hand, he holds a letter bearing the royal seal of Philip II, a weight heavier than the parchment itself.

The governor grimaces as he reads the letter once more by the light of a flickering oil lamp. Beside him stand his secretary, Don Pedro Ruiz, a wiry man with a quill tucked behind his ear, and two military commanders: Captain Rodrigo Vargas, a seasoned officer with a weathered face, and Major Álvaro de Guzmán, young, a heartbeat too quick to respond, his cuirass bright in the lamplight.

Pinned beneath the seal is a clerk's abstract, neat and sand-browned at the edges.

"*Extract of His Majesty's Orders, to be put in execution in Panamá.*

By order of His Catholic Majesty, it is required and expressly commanded:

• *That the fortifications of Nombre de Dios and the City of Panamá be diligently viewed, repaired, and strengthened, their platforms, walls, and works restored where decayed, and their artillery increased and kept in good order.*

• *That the Isthmus be made secure: companies to be posted at Venta de Cruces, along the Camino Real, and upon the River Chagres, with continual patrols by land and water, so that no enemy, fugitive, pirate, or malefactor pass these territories unobserved.*

• *That all treasure and mule trains proceed only under double escort, their departures regulated and made to accord with the sailings of the fleets, and that no train move without licence duly granted.*

• *That strict inquiry be made into the accounts and conduct of treasurers, provisioners, and officers, and that such as are found guilty of fraud, extortion, or neglect be removed and punished, to the terror of others.*

• *That such monies as necessity requires be drawn from the Royal Treasury, with faithful account rendered thereof to the Council of the Indies, according to established form.*

• *That a relation of all actions taken in execution of these commands be sent regularly, so that His Majesty may be fully informed of the state of his service.*

Given by command of His Majesty, by the Council of the Indies."

Vera tosses the letter onto the table, his voice tight with frustration.

"The King commands as if we have legions. 'Reinforce the garrisons at Nombre de Dios and the City of Panamá,' he says. 'Construct new fortifications,' he says. 'Use funds from the Royal Treasury, as if it were a bottomless coffer,' he says. Meanwhile, our men are stretched thin, and the silver convoys from Peru barely make it past Nombre de Dios without being intercepted!"

Ruiz adjusts his spectacles and leans forward.

"I am bound to remind Your Lordship that the King's orders are precise and binding. The garrisons must be strengthened, and the trade routes secured. If we fail to protect the treasures of the New World, Spain's empire will falter."

Captain Vargas grunts, his voice gravelly from years of shouting commands.

"Your Lordship...we are at the end of ourselves." He smashes a mosquito on his cheek with a rapid slap. Sweat pours down his temples. "We are already wrung dry. Between English privateers prowling the Main, French Huguenot corsairs who strike wherever our patrols thin, and Cimarron bands raiding our supply lines, there are scarcely men enough to watch the coast—let alone raise a wall." He kills another mosquito on his wrist. "The heat hollows the men, and the insects—God save us—do not let us sleep."

Major Guzmán cuts in, his voice tinged with youthful impatience.

"And what of the Cimarrons, Your Lordship? They know these jungles better than we ever will. There is one—an escaped slave they call Diego. He has risen among the bands and now ranges with them, striking at the mule trains, scattering the guards, and disappearing into the forest. Our silver does not reach the coast unchallenged."

Vera lets out a harsh breath and rubs the bridge of his nose, irritation simmering beneath the surface.

"Yes—Diego." The name lands heavily. "A runaway who should have been hunted down years ago, yet now he moves among the Cimarrons like a man with a purpose."

His jaw tightens.

"A slave, perhaps becoming something more. Every convoy he helps harry makes him bolder. They strip the trains and feast on what was meant for the King's soldiers—our biscuit, our dried beef, even our wine," he snarls. "They live better on our losses than some of my garrison do on their pay. The jungle shields him, and his people close around him like a court. Tell me—does anyone know his camp? His routes? Anything?"

Ruiz interjects cautiously. "There are rumours, Your Lordship—no more than rumours—that the Cimarrons have begun to speak with foreign corsairs. Some say they pass word of the roads, or guide men through the forest paths. If that is true, it would explain how the pirates strike with such confidence."

Captain Vargas scowls. "We have sent patrols after him. The jungle favours the Cimarrons, not us. Our men lose the trail—or walk straight into ambush. They fight like shadows: they strike, then vanish."

Vera presses a hand to his temple, his fingers dragging down over his cheek in weary frustration.

"And yet His Majesty demands swift and decisive action," he mutters. "He suspects negligence and corruption."

He lowers his hand and gestures sharply about the room, his voice rising.

"Tell me—who among us can be called negligent when we are pressed on every side? Pirates at sea, rebels inland, the rains, the heat—" He breaks off, jaw clenched, the list unfinished because it has no end.

Major Guzmán answers carefully. "With respect, Your Lordship, the King is not wrong to demand results. Every successful raid emboldens the Cimarrons. If we cannot hold Panama, how long before the rest of the Indies begin to slip from Spain's grasp?"

Ruiz nods. "We must choose our ground. Nombre de Dios is the hinge. Panama City must hold. Reinforcements from Lima or New Spain—if any can be spared—would stiffen the road."

Vera paces, sweat glistening on his brow. "Reinforcements?" He gives a short, humourless laugh. "Do you think I have not begged for them? Lima has its own wars. Mexico guards its fleets like a miser guards his coin. To the Crown, Panama is a coffer. To us, it is the first wall against every enemy Spain has."

He gestures towards the King's letter.

"His Majesty speaks of swift and final justice. I wonder if he understands the price of enforcing it here."

Vargas clears his throat. "Then let us send word back, Your Lordship. Tell him plainly of our condition—the raids, the Cimarrons, the rains, the sickness. Let him see how close we stand to the breaking point."

Vera stops and fixes him with a hard stare.

"And what would you have me write, Captain? That Panama—the hinge upon which the King's riches turn—is too weak to hold?"

Ruiz leans forward. "Not so, Your Lordship. But we must impress upon His Majesty the urgency of our situation. Without men and money, we risk losing everything."

Vera presses thumb and forefinger to his eyes, the weight of command pressing invisibly on his spine.

"Very well. Don Pedro—draft a reply. Assure His Majesty of our loyalty and diligence. But do not soften the truth."

Ruiz nods and begins to write.

Guzmán steps forward. "And Diego, Your Lordship?"

Vera's answer is cold.

"Find him. Use scouts. Use bribes. Use informants. Alive if it can be managed—dead if it cannot. Let the lesson carry from the coast to the Cordilleras. If this man truly draws foreign pirates into our forests, then he is no longer merely a runaway, but an enemy of Spain."

The firelight flickers across clenched jaws and tightened mouths.

Outside, thunder rolls faintly out at sea.

Vera lowers himself into his chair and unfolds the parchment fan, staring through it rather than at it—as if the solution lies beyond sight. The King's letter rests on the table before him, a stark reminder that while His Majesty commands justice, it is the men in Panama who must pay to deliver it.

Vera remains seated long after the others fall silent. The fan slows, then stills in his hand. Somewhere beyond the walls, a bell tolls the hour—thin, distant, uncertain. He listens to it fade and thinks, not for the first time, that Spain's enemies are no longer announcing themselves with banners or fleets. They come instead with silence, with guides, with patience. He reaches for the letter once more, not to read it, but to weigh it in his palm—and wonders whether the King understands that the war for the Indies will not be decided by walls or orders alone, but by men who learn faster than Spain can command.

15 July 1572

The faint crescent moonlight spills silver over the bay, broken by the quiet stroke of oars as the longboats from the *Pascha* nose closer to shore. Ahead, Nombre de Dios shows itself in fragments—a line of low roofs, the dark hump of a watchtower, the faint glimmer of torchlight wandering along the palisade.

The boats keep their distance from the surf, just near enough for sharp eyes to pick out the pattern of patrols. Men crouch low in the thwarts, muskets across their knees, watching the shoreline as hunters watch for the stir of game. No one speaks. Even the creak of oarlocks has been muffled with rags.

Not a night for storming walls—but for studying them, to learn where the Spaniards are few, and where opportunity might lie when the time comes to strike.

In the longboats, the Englishmen sit pressed shoulder to shoulder. The reek of pitch and salt clings to them, mixed with the sharper tang of oiled steel. Fingers clench tight around matchlocks and cutlasses, every creak of wood or drip of water sounding too loud in their ears. Some stare at the shoreline with the wide eyes of men imagining sentries waiting. Others mutter half-prayers beneath their breath. No one raises his voice.

Above them, a seabird wheels once and vanishes into the night, its cry swallowed by the heavy stillness. Ahead, the beach stretches black and quiet, but the men know better than to trust serenity in Spanish waters.

The frantic splashes of a lone swimmer shatter the quiet night. Diego—the runaway the Spaniards had begun to fear—claws his way through the water, his face a mix of desperation and determination, his gasps audible over the gentle lapping of the waves. Behind him, Spanish arquebus fire rings out, and shots hiss as they strike the water around him.

A burly mariner, Henry Pym, leans over the longboat's prow, squinting into the pitch-dark surf.

"Who goes there?" he calls, voice taut as another Spanish arquebus cracks from the shore.

A hoarse cry answers through the spray:

"Diego! No Spaniard! Friend to the English!"

The oarsmen stiffen. A shot hisses across the water, skipping off the waves. Jacob Worth, wiry and quick, braces himself as a dark figure splashes against the gunwale. He snatches an arm and hauls the man aboard, soaked, shivering, lungs rasping like bellows.

"Get in here, man!" Worth says.

Diego collapses on the planks. Salt water streams from his torn shirt. He lifts both hands—palms open—showing he bears no steel. One of the oarsmen shoves a cracked leather flask at his lips—stale ship's beer sloshes out. Diego coughs, swallows once, then pushes it aside, gulping air like a man who would rather breathe than drink.

"No harm...no harm," he gasps. His English is rough, the cadence learned from sailors. "I know the forest. The hills. The mule paths. Silver road. Take me to your captain."

Worth whistles low. "Bold one, this."

Pym snorts. "Or mad. Keep your hands where I can see them, lad."

Another volley flashes from the tree line.

The longboat's coxswain cuts them off.

"No talk. Row! Back to the *Pascha*—before the whole bloody garrison wakes."

***

The lantern sways in Francis Drake's cabin as the longboatmen file in, dripping saltwater.

Drake—thirty-two, compact, sea-bronzed, eyes like chips of winter glass—looks up from a rumpled chart of the Isthmus. A trencher of ship's biscuit and a wooden bowl with a few strips of salt pork sit on the edge of the table, crumbs scattered over the chart—Drake's supper, forgotten the moment the longboat hailed.

Pym gestures the dripping stranger forward.

Drake rises from his chair.

"Well then...who's this sea-wraith you have dragged aboard?"

Pym inclines his head.

"Found him swimming for us under arquebus fire. Calls himself Diego. Says he can lead us to the mule trains."

The news strikes Drake like a bell.

"Indeed."

He steps close, studying the man—trembling, half-starved, but unbroken.

"Stand," Drake orders. He nudges the trencher towards him with two fingers. "If you can keep it down, eat," he says. "Men talk plainer on a full belly." Diego only shakes his head, chest still heaving. He forces himself upright. His breath shakes, but his resolve holds.

"I want to free," he manages. "Spain take me once. Not again."

He touches his chest. "I know the paths. I know where the mules walk. Silver. I show you."

Drake's eyes sharpen—not warm, not cruel, but calculating.

"And what would you have of me?"

Diego swallows.

"Take me from here. To your land. To be free."

Pym murmurs, "Desperate men don't lie, Captain."

Drake circles him slowly, assessing the tremor in his hands, the scars on his wrists—evidence enough of Spanish chains.

"You know the guard posts? The watch at the crossings? The hours they ride?"

Diego nods fiercely. "All. I walk those roads...in irons. Now I show you in the dark."

A slow grin cuts across Drake's face.

"Then you and I, Diego..."

He taps the map with one finger.

"...may profit each other handsomely."

He pulls the chart closer.

"Show me where the Spaniards bleed their treasure—and how deep the wound runs."

Outside the cabin, the ship creaks and settles; inside, Diego nods once, slow and solemn, as if sealing a pact older than either of them, while Drake bends over the map and the road to silver begins to take shape under his hand.

Drake pauses, then looks up—not at the map, but at Diego. "Understand this," he says quietly. "I do not promise mercy, only motion. If you walk with us, you walk into fire. If you falter, you will be left behind. And if you betray us—" He lets the sentence hang, unfinished, needing no words. "But if you speak true, and if you endure, then whatever chains you wore before end here." He straightens. "Choose."

Diego does not hesitate. He places his scarred hand upon the chart, over the thin inked line that marks the Camino Real. "I already have," he says.

27 July 1572

The *Pascha* rides uneasy water, her hull working and whispering as the night closes in. In the narrow cabin aft, lantern light trembles over a rough chart spread across the table—ink-smudged, salt-stained, its edges pinned by a dagger and a pewter mug. The coast of Panama lies half-sketched, half-guessed.

Francis Drake leans over it, steadying himself against the roll. His finger rests not on a mark, but on a blank stretch of shore.

Around him stand the men he trusts.

John Oxenham, spare and sharp-eyed, listens without speaking, arms folded tight against his chest. Thomas Moone fills the opposite side of the table, thick through the neck and shoulders, a man who looks as though he was built to hold a line. Near Drake's shoulder stands his brother John—quieter, watchful, the family likeness there in the jaw and eyes, though the weight of command has not yet settled on him.

Drake taps the parchment once.

"Nombre de Dios."

The name sits heavy in the air.

"That's it," Drake says, low. "The place where the road from the South ends. What comes across the isthmus passes through that town—coin, plate, goods for the fleet—before it goes on to Havana."

Oxenham exhales. "And it is not asleep. Guns on the shore. Soldiers. A town that knows its worth."

Drake nods. "Which is why no one expects us to come at it straight."

John Drake shifts. "We are few," he says. "Barely seventy all told. If we are seen on the water—"

"We will not be," Francis says. "We land east of the town. Out of sight. We move on foot, by night. If we are discovered, it will be when we are already among them."

Moone grunts. "And what are we after, Captain? Coin we can carry—or dreams of silver too heavy to move?"

Drake does not answer at once. He draws a line with his finger towards the clustered shapes that mark the town.

"We take the heart," he says. "The plaza. The noise. The confusion. Authority breaks first—always. When the bells ring and men run without orders, then we see what presents itself."

John Drake looks up. "You mean to divide us."

"Yes."

Drake straightens.

"John," he says to his brother, "you go with Oxenham. Back streets. Drums, trumpets, fire-pikes. Make them think more of us than there are. Do not linger. You are there to pull eyes and feet away from the center."

John Drake nods once. "Noise, then vanish."

"Exactly."

Drake turns to Moone. "You're with me. Straight in. Fast hands. We take what can be lifted and carried. Coin, jewels, plate—anything that moves quickly."

Moone frowns. "And if there's more?"

"Then we leave it," Drake says. "We are not here to sit under their guns."

The lantern swings with the ship's motion.

A soft knock sounds at the door.

Diego slips inside, rain-dark hair bound back, the smell of smoke and wet jungle clinging to him. He nods, brief and urgent.

"There has been movement," he says. "Men on the road. Mules came through not long past. The town is fuller than usual."

Drake's expression tightens—not with triumph, but calculation.

"Good," he says quietly. "Then they will be slow to understand what is happening."

John Drake studies him. "You think we can hold them?"

Drake meets his brother's gaze.

"No," he says. "I am certain we cannot."

He reaches for the mug, drinks, then sets it down.

"That is why we will not try. One strike. One moment. When the town wakes fully, we are already gone. No valor. No lingering. Living men return. Dead men do not."

Moone nods.

"Aye, Captain. That is the truth."

Oxenham rolls his shoulders, already preparing himself. John Drake allows a thin, sharp smile.

Outside, the *Pascha* presses on through the dark, carrying them towards a town that sleeps—armed, guarded, and utterly unprepared for what is about to step out of the trees. The vessel carries the crew on, the sea keeping their counsel as the jungle ahead waits to learn their names.

29 July 1572

The heat suffocates, a wet, living weight that clings to Francis Drake and his men as they slip ashore under cover of darkness. Their pinnaces kiss the sand without a sound. Oars are lifted clear. Breath is held.

Behind them the Caribbean lies flat and black; ahead, the jungle presses close, breathing insects and rot and unseen movement.

Drake crouches at the water's edge, hand raised.

"Steady," he murmurs. "No sound. Not yet."

They move inland, boots sinking into damp earth. Blades are wrapped. Match cords shielded. Sweat runs down spines and into eyes. The town of Nombre de Dios lies ahead—drowsing, but not unguarded. Music drifts faintly on the air. Pipes. Clapping. Laughter. A night of ease. A town that believes itself safe.

Smells follow the sound: roast meat, spilled wine, hot fat, the bite of aguardiente.

Drake tastes it and knows what it means. Goods have come in. Coin is near. Not in hand—but near enough to smell.

At the edge of the town he divides them without ceremony.

John Oxenham and John Drake take their men wide, slipping into the darker streets.

"Noise," Drake tells them. "Confusion. Make them think we are more than we are."

Oxenham's smile is thin. "They'll swear the devil's landed."

Drake turns inland with the rest.

The night breaks open.

Drums hammer. Trumpets scream. Firebrands flare—sudden suns lifted high. Shouts explode from doorways. Bells begin to ring, fast and wild. Arquebuses crack into darkness, shots fired more in terror than aim.

Drake drives forward through it all, straight towards the heart of the town. Spanish militia forms and breaks almost at once—men retreating, tripping over one another, dragged backward by fear. When Oxenham's noise erupts behind them, panic completes the work. The streets dissolve into shouting and flight.

The plaza opens before them.

For one suspended moment, Drake stands in it—at the center of the town that feeds the fleets of Spain. Stone. Shadow. Bells screaming overhead. Rain beginning to fall.

Then the shot comes.

No warning. No flash he sees. Just a brutal punch low in the left leg, hard enough to stagger him. He grits his teeth and keeps moving. There is no time for pain. Blood runs warm inside his boot, unnoticed, uncounted.

They surge past the plaza and into the governor's lower rooms, men scattering guards who flee rather than stand. A door is forced. A lantern is thrust forward.

And then—silver.

Not chests. Not coin. Bars.

Stacked against the wall in a long, gleaming mass—dull white in the lantern light, sweat-beaded, heavy beyond sense. A fallen rampart of wealth, rising chest-high, stretching away into shadow. Men stop short as if struck.

"Marry..." someone breathes.

Hands reach out. Fingers touch metal and recoil, as if burned. The weight of it presses into the room, into the lungs. Wealth so vast it feels unreal until it is touched.

Drake steps forward, jaw clenched. He knows at once what it is—and what it will cost.

"No," he snaps. "Leave it."

They stare at him, stunned.

"That will drown us," he says. "We take what can be lifted. Nothing that binds us to this place."

Rain slams down in earnest now—tropical, violent. The streets flood. Powder hisses. Matchcords die. Thunder rolls overhead. The storm flattens sound and sight alike, turning the town into a churning dark.

Men shout that soldiers will be coming from inland. That the town is waking. That the moment is slipping.

Drake stands tight to the lee of a house-front at the plaza's edge, men pressed in behind him under the shallow shelter of the eaves. Rain hammers the stones. A match hisses out.

He steps out from the wall into the downpour, soaked through, voice raw and carrying.

The storm does not relent quickly enough. Powder fails. The bells do not stop. Spanish voices gather closer now—fewer panicked, more ordered.

Drake takes another step—

—and his leg gives way.

He goes down without a cry.

For a heartbeat no one understands. Then Moone is there, hands slick with blood, staring.

"So much," he whispers.

The truth hits them all at once. Drake was struck earlier—carried it through noise and rain and command. The blood he has been losing finally claims him. The world narrows. Sound thins. His face goes gray.

Drake stirs, trying to rise. "On," he breathes. "Press it—"

"No," Moone says, voice breaking. "That's done."

They lift him as the bells ring on and arquebuses crack closer, sharper now. The wound is bound—linen blackening instantly.

Moone hauls Drake across his shoulders and turns away—from the plaza, from the rooms of silver, from the greatest prize any Englishman has yet seen and cannot take.

They retreat through water and darkness, slipping, swearing, dragging their captain away while Spain's treasure remains stacked and shining.

At the shore, a longboat waits.

Drake is laid down, shaking, pale as bone.

"How bad...?" he forces.

Moone swallows. "You'll live, sir. God willing."

A ghost of a smile touches Drake's mouth.

"...Hard...to kill."

He slips under.

The oars bite. The town recedes, bells still ringing.

The silver remains.

That night nearly ends him.

Instead, it teaches him something sharper than victory: that treasure may be seen, even touched—and still be lost if command falters for a single breath.

The lesson burns hotter than the wound, carried with him into fever and dark water.

From that night on, Drake counts weight before glory, distance before daring.

He learns that restraint can be a weapon sharper than steel.

That survival is not retreat—but selection.

And that Spain's wealth will wait for a man who can walk away alive.

30 July 1572

The shutters of the governor's residence shudder in the night wind. Inside, heat and smoke cling to the walls. A single candle burns low on a crowded table strewn with papers—witness statements, guard rolls, casualty lists, and hurried inventories, marked and remarked in different hands.

Don Diego Lope de Vera stands over it all, one palm braced on the wood, his shadow stretched long and distorted behind him.

Across the table, Captain Sancho Paredes of the town guard stands rigid, helmet tucked beneath his arm, sweat darkening the collar of his doublet. He has not moved since he was summoned.

Vera does not raise his voice.

"Explain to me, Captain," he says quietly, tapping a report with two fingers, "how Francis Drake's English raiders land outside the harbor, march inland unseen, divide their force, take the plaza, enter the governor's house—and withdraw—before my garrison forms a proper line."

Paredes swallows. "Your Lordship...the attack began with noise. Drums. Trumpets. Firebrands raised like standards. The men believed a larger force had landed."

"How many did you actually see?"

"Fewer than expected. Perhaps fifty. No more."

Vera exhales slowly, as if fixing the number in his mind.

"Fifty," he repeats. "Against a fortified port. Against cannon. Against three hundred soldiers."

He lifts another paper. Blood smears the edge where someone's hand was not yet clean.

"The bells rang," Vera continues. "The militia assembled. Yet authority collapsed before it could be exercised. Why?"

"The storm," Paredes answers. "The rain extinguished matches. Powder was spoiled. Men scattered for shelter. Orders were lost in the noise."

Vera inclines his head once. A storm excuses nothing—but it explains much. A clerk steps forward, holding a fresh sheet. Vera takes it, wipes his eyes, and reads in silence.

"At least this may be said," he replies at last. "The bullion remains here. The silver bars were seen, some even handled—but no chests were broken, no plate removed, no stacks dismantled. Only small items taken in flight."

He sets the paper down with care.

"A humiliation," he adds. "Not a catastrophe."

Paredes' shoulders ease a fraction—then tighten again.

"Drake was shot," the captain says, seizing the opening. "A single shot, fired from cover near the plaza. He fell later, they say."

Vera looks up. "Did we take him?"

"No, Your Lordship."

"Then the wound is of no comfort," Vera replies. "A wounded enemy who escapes still learns."

He turns towards the open window. Beyond it, the jungle lies black and steaming, the direction of the Camino Real swallowed by night.

"This Drake," he says thoughtfully, "does not behave like a tavern corsair. He divides his men. He strikes the center first. He withdraws the instant fortune turns, instead of dying theatrically in the street."

He pauses, eyes returning to the papers—not to the losses, but to their order.

"He tests us," Vera continues. "He measures how quickly we answer bells, how long fear outruns command, how much disorder can be made with little force. Tonight was not theft. It was instruction."

He turns back.

"That makes him dangerous."

Vera gestures to the clerk. "Write."

The quill scratches.

"*One: double the guard at the silver store. No lounging. No rotation gaps.*"

"*Two: recall coastal patrols and concentrate them here and along the mule-road crossings.*"

"*Three: send riders to Panama City at first light. Request arquebusiers accustomed to jungle movement.*"

"*Four: dispatch warnings to Cartagena and Veracruz. An English captain is operating deliberately on the Isthmus.*"

The clerk does not pause.

"And add," Vera says, "standing orders to observe unusual native movement along the Camino Real. Especially among Cimarron bands."

Paredes clears his throat. "Your Lordship...several men reported a guide. A native or escaped slave. He knew the streets."

Vera nods once. "Then he is the hinge."

He returns to the table and places his hand flat on the papers, pressing them into alignment.

"Find where such men move. Where they trade. Where they vanish into the forest. We will close the road—not with fear, but with patience."

He looks at Paredes fully now.

"And you will ensure the men speak of this to no one. Not in taverns. Not in markets. Panic spreads faster than fire."

"Yes, Your Lordship."

Vera gathers the papers into a precise stack and pinches out the candle. The room dims at once.

"This Englishman believes speed will save him," he says into the dark. "He has announced himself—to us."

Outside, the jungle listens.

And the treasure road begins, quietly, to harden.

***

Aboard *the Pascha,* the Captain's cabin reeks of blood, wet linen, and sour beer.

Francis Drake sits braced against the bulkhead, stripped to his shirt, his left leg wrapped thick in bandages already darkening through. His skin has gone gray beneath the lantern light, jaw set hard against the pain. With every roll of the ship, a dull, climbing throb runs up his thigh. He does not react to it—he simply endures.

On the table lie the spoils of Nombre de Dios.

A few small sacks. Loose coin. Trinkets scooped up in confusion and flight. Nothing more.

Drake does not look at them.

Thomas Moone stands nearby with a tin cup held in both hands, watching the captain the way a man watches a fire he fears might gutter. John Drake sits opposite his brother, elbows on the table, eyes fixed not on the money but on Francis's face. Oxenham enters last, ducking beneath the beam, rain still clinging to his coat.

"The men are restless," Oxenham says. "Talking. They say the town rang bells all night. Fired cannon at shadows. Some are already naming you."

Drake exhales slowly. It might have been a laugh once. It isn't now.

"Naming is cheap," he says.

John Drake breaks the silence. "They nearly killed you, Francis."

Francis turns his head and meets his brother's gaze. There is no bravado in his eyes—only the cold clarity that comes after survival.

"They almost did," he says. "And if I'd gone down ten minutes earlier, we'd have been finished. Every one of us."

Moone raises the cup anyway, his voice rough. "To your life, sir. By God's mercy."

Drake shakes his head faintly. "No."

Moone lowers the cup.

Drake gestures with two fingers towards the sacks on the table. "That," he says, "is what Nombre de Dios bought us. A handful of coin. And a torn leg."

He pauses, then adds quietly, "And we're fortunate to have even that."

Oxenham shifts his weight. "Still—it mattered. We showed them—"

"We showed them exactly where to look," Drake cuts in.

They fall silent.

"They know now how we come ashore," Drake continues. "They know we split our force. They know we have eyes inland. That road will be watched like a wound that will not close."

John Drake nods once. "Then we don't strike it the same way again."

Francis looks at him. Fever glints faintly in his eyes—but beneath it, calculation sharpens.

"No," he agrees. "We don't strike the chest again."

He swallows, breath tight.

"We strike the artery."

Outside the cabin, the *Pascha* creaks and slides through the dark water, pulling away from the coast. Behind them lies Nombre de Dios—its treasure untouched, its defenses shaken, its fear newly awake.

None of them speak.

Whatever Drake has seen in his mind's eye, he does not name it.

The ship bears on into the night, carrying men who do not yet know what they have agreed to risk.

Chapter 22
The Massacre of St Bartholomew's Day

1 September 1572

In the Palace of Whitehall, the rushes are fresh-strewn. The air smells of lavender crushed underfoot. Elizabeth sits in unrelieved black, the pearls at her throat cold as winter stars. Slowly, purposefully, she slips off a glove, finger by finger.

Monsieur de La Mothe Fénelon, the French ambassador, bows with measured grace.

"Madam, "he begins, "my master the King sends his grief. His Majesty deplores—"

Elizabeth cuts straight through the courtliness.

"Spare me the embroidery, Monsieur. It was a massacre."

Her tone is flat—controlled, lethal.

"Tell me—does your king deplore what he ordered, or merely what he failed to stop?"

Fénelon's expression does not change, but his eyes flick—to gauge the wind.

"Majesty," he replies, silky, "the court claims it was aimed at conspirators—rebels who plotted His Majesty's harm. After the villainous attempt on Monsieur l'Amiral Coligny, order had to be restored."

"Order?" Elizabeth leans forward. "I hear of knives in doorways. Children hurled from windows. Huguenot blood sluicing through Paris like rainwater."

She pauses. "And I hear my ally, Admiral Coligny, was butchered under the eyes of the court."

A brief silence. Cecil, seated nearby, keeps his eyes fixed on a sheet of parchment, though his quill has stilled.

Fénelon lifts a chastened hand. "In every tempest there are excesses, but the King's intent—"

"A tempest?" Elizabeth's brows rise, sharp enough to cut. "Your 'tempest' ran for three days, and somehow found only Protestants in its path. Very extraordinary weather you have in Paris."

Before Fénelon can respond, boots slap the gallery stones. A courier enters—cloak salt-stained, throat dust-choked.

He kneels and offers a packet sealed in green silk.

"From Paris, Your Majesty—at last—from Ambassador Francis Walsingham."

Cecil takes it, passes it to the Queen without a word.

Elizabeth slits the seal with her nail and reads. Her breath hitches once.

"Walsingham lives," she murmurs. Then again, louder: "He lives! Thanks be to God."

The chamber exhales as one.

She reads on. "He writes that his house stands ringed with armed men. He shelters Englishmen '*by the score.*' He says the streets are—red."

She pushes the plate of comfits away with two fingers; even sugared almonds taste of iron suddenly.

Dudley closes his eyes briefly. Cecil resumes his quill, but his jaw tightens.

Fénelon keeps his composure so absolutely that it becomes suspicious.

Elizabeth folds the letter precisely.

"You assured me not long ago that English subjects in Paris were safe—as safe as they would be in my orchard at Greenwich."

"And so they are, madam," Fénelon answers, gentle as oil. "Those under the King's protection—"

"My ambassador's house is under your king's protection," she snaps softly. "Yet it stands ringed by men with pikes. Must Walsingham raise a banner before French officers recall the law of nations?"

Fénelon bows his head a fraction.

"If there has been over-zeal, it shall be corrected. The Queen-Mother desires peace."

Cecil murmurs just loud enough: "The Queen-Mother desires survival."

Fénelon pretends not to hear. Elizabeth rises.

"You will write tonight—to King Charles and to madame, his mother. You will demand safe transit for every Englishman in Paris, named or unnamed.

You will demand safe conduct for Walsingham's couriers. And you will demand compensation for any English subject murdered in the streets."

Fénelon bows. "Madam, His Majesty will rejoice in your continued amity."

"Amity," she echoes, tasting the word like bitter wine. "I will have deeds, Monsieur. Not music."

Dudley steps forward, heat in his voice.

"Majesty, give leave to arm ten pinnaces for the Narrow Seas. Alba will smell weakness if we do nothing."

Cecil finally looks up.

"Ten will be noticed. Twelve will be unmistakable."

He turns to the Queen. "We should open our ports quietly to the refugees—Southampton, Rye. No proclamations. Quiet mercy buys strong loyalty. Better French hands at English looms than empty bakehouses and idle brewers in our port towns."

Fénelon's eyes flick. Once.

"Majesty," he warns, "to harbour rebels—"

"To harbour Christians who fled murder!" she corrects. "They will spin their lace, work their looms, and pray in peace. If that offends Paris, send them bread from your own kitchens."

A long silence. A clock somewhere strikes the quarter.

Elizabeth smooths Walsingham's letter, then issues orders like hammer blows.

"Burghley—draft my letter to the French King. Begin with courtesy. End with terms."

Cecil dips his quill.

"To the Admiralty: twelve pinnaces ready, Dover to the Foreland. No prizes taken without warrant. They show steel—not teeth. Lord Keeper Bacon: warrants to the justices for victual at Rye and Southampton. Silence the pulpits. No talk of sanctuary. Only hospitality."

Finally she turns back to Fénelon, voice soft—too soft.

"You will dine here tonight. And you will write your dispatch under my roof. Tell your king: I do not break treaties because Paris lost its reason. But let no man mistake my quiet for sleep."

Fénelon bows deeply.

"Madam is—magnanimous."

"Madam is watchful," she corrects.

He withdraws.

Elizabeth stands unmoving for a long heartbeat.

Dudley murmurs, "Majesty—if they march on La Rochelle—"

"They will," she replies. "But we will not be the ones to strike the first spark."

Cecil's quill scratches again.

"Yet we will be ready with water, if flames come across the Channel."

Elizabeth nods once.

"Ready," she echoes.

9 September 1572

Rain hammers the arrow slits and turns the inner ward to shining mire at Sheffield Castle in Yorkshire. In the solar, a brazier ticks and hisses. George Talbot, Earl of Shrewsbury, stands by the table with a damp dispatch beneath his palm. The seal of Cecil's hand has bled into the paper. Across from him, his wife—Elizabeth, Countess of Shrewsbury, "Bess" to the world that fears her accounts—stands straight as a pike, the heavy ring of household keys riding her girdle. She does not sit.

The door opens on a rush of cooler air and scented wool. Mary Stuart, Queen of Scots, enters with two women. One carries a dark mantle, the other a small coffer. Mary's veil is white. Her rosary clicks softly as it slips through her fingers. She takes in their faces, the spread papers, and stops.

"My lord," she says, voice low and courteous. "You sent for me?"

Talbot bows—deep enough to mark her rank, shallow enough to remind her of chains.

"Madam, news from France."

Bess's mouth tightens. "From Paris."

Mary's eyes flicker. "What news?"

Talbot lifts the sheet and reads, not trusting himself to paraphrase.

"*The bell of Saint-Germain-l'Auxerrois gives signal at midnight, the four-and-twentieth of August. Admiral Coligny slain, the King's guard in the streets, Huguenot houses marked, great numbers fall. The French court calls it preventing a plot. Our Ambassador Walsingham reports he barely escaped with his life.*"

Somewhere below, a dog barks twice, then falls dumb.

Mary crosses herself in one swift motion. "Jesu have mercy."

Bess's fingers find the ring of keys and still them. "Mercy? It is murder, madam."

She snatches up the trencher knife, meaning only to shift the cheese, and carves a sharper slice than the food requires.

Mary looks up, and the grief in her face is real, but complicated, lit from within by something like grim relief. "War breeds harvests of blood on both sides, my lady. You have seen the north of your own realm when rebels rise. I am told heads blacken on London Bridge."

"We do not call that mercy," Bess says. "Nor God's work."

"My lady," Talbot murmurs, warning in the word.

Mary steps towards the table. "What says the King of France?" Her French slips ready into her English, quick, taut. "What says the Queen-Mother? This—this frenzy—comes from the King's mind? Or Guise's blade?"

"Paris says what suits Paris," Bess replies. She does not yield the table. "England hears the sound that reaches us: Huguenots hunted through houses and hauled from beds, the Admiral's body cast to the stones. We hear it here, under your roof."

Mary's rosary slows. "Under my roof? My lady, I do not govern France from Sheffield."

"But you cheer it," Bess says, and the keys chime once at her waist. "We all know what prayers they say in your chambers when Mass is sung."

Talbot's hand lifts—calm, heavy. "Enough, Bess."

Mary's head tips, the smallest angle, as if tasting the insult. "If I rejoice," she says, very softly, "it is that the men who seek France's ruin are checked. But I do not rejoice in butcheries. I have buried too much of my own blood to clap at slaughter."

Bess's eyes rake her. "Your words will travel before breakfast, madam. Choose them."

Mary holds that hard look and does not blink. "I am a queen, not a cutpurse, to be lectured on trespass."

"And I am your keeper," Bess says, "not your maid."

Talbot moves—two deliberate steps that place him between them. "We will not have this. Madam, my duty requires I write this day to the Council with your answer, for all the realm runs high with this news. I advise you—as one who would see your condition no worse—speak with care. Master Walsingham writes from Paris with blood in the streets and terror in his mouth.

Her Majesty's shaken and angry. The City prays for the survivors. Rome claps. London curses. It is ugly."

Mary's hand closes on the rosary. The beads press half-moons into her palm. When she speaks, it is to Talbot, not Bess. "My lord, I pity those souls torn from this world without shrift. I pity France, where the crown must lean on daggers. And I pity England, if she thinks to use this grief to nail me tighter to my cross."

Bess's breath cuts sharp. "Call it a cross if you like. I call it a lock. And I will see it turned if you send one line that smells of praise."

Mary turns to her—sudden, bright. "And I call it malice to put words in my mouth before I utter them. Will you be a gaoler and judge both, my lady? Or is that office already filled at Whitehall?"

Talbot's fingers tighten on the dispatch. "Madam—"

"No," Mary says, the silk gone from her voice. "Let me say my piece, for once not wrapped in civility. I am not the butcher of Paris, nor the bell that calls the knives. I am a woman who sleeps in fear more nights than you can count, my lady, a mother torn from her child, a queen kept like a hawk hooded, lest she fly. I will not be made into your monster to ease England's conscience."

For the first time, Bess looks away—just a fraction, at the fire, at the steam lifting from a sodden log. When she looks back, her tone is colder, steadier. "You may not be the butcher, madam, but your friends sharpen the knives. Guise drinks Spanish wine. The Pope looses bulls against our queen. Do not tell me this blood will not stain your skirts if you step in it."

Mary draws breath to answer—and Talbot raises his hand, palm out.

"You will not," he tells them both. The authority in him—habit, office, bone-deep—fills the room. "Enough. Bess, stop tearing at raw flesh. And you, madam, no baiting when you know the hook is set. Listen: for a time I must halt even the small letters you are permitted. Anything to France will be opened and read. Anything to Scotland weighed before it goes. The Council requires it, and I will not gainsay them."

Behind Mary, one of her women stands with a small covered cup of spiced wine; it cools in her hands while queen and keeper fence.

Mary's chin lifts, queen to the last inch. "And my Mass?"

Talbot's jaw works once. "Your household may hear it—quietly. No triumph. No talk that can be taken for thanksgiving. I will not give Master Cecil cause to clap irons tighter."

Bess gives the keys the lightest flick, a muted chime. "And the French servants—watch them. The Guise favour creeps in with gifts and pearls."

Mary's laugh is a breath, almost a sob. "Pearls? Madam, I have traded all but pride for bread."

Bess's eyes soften a hair, then shutter. "Keep the pride to your beads, then."

Mary's gaze slides back to Talbot. "You will send my words as I speak them?"

"I will," he says. "And I will add my own—that you show sorrow for the dead and no joy for their killers."

Mary inclines her head: not thanks, not quite. "Then God judge us all, my lord. For Paris judges, and London judges, and neither is just."

A gust shoulders the rain against the stone. The brazier hisses. Talbot folds the dispatch and presses it with his signet. "We are done for now. Madam, if you would return to your rooms."

Mary gathers her mantle. At the threshold she turns. "When you write," she says, "do not forget to tell your queen that I pray for the souls of the Huguenots. And for hers."

Bess's mouth opens—closes. The keys are very still.

Mary goes out with her women, the rosary's soft click fading into the corridor. Talbot lets out the breath he has been banking.

Bess speaks without looking at him. "You will guard her tongue, George. If she writes to Flanders with so much as a tear of joy in the ink, Cecil sends us a chain for every window."

"I know," he says, tired to the nail. He touches the seal as if testing its cool. "God help us all, Bess. The world is on fire."

"And we keep the tinder," she says, and at last she sits, the keys settling in her lap like a verdict.

20 October 1572

The heavy oak door closes behind the courier with a dull thud, leaving King Philip alone in his private study in Madrid. A single candle burns low, casting thin light across a stack of dispatches newly arrived from Tierra Firme after weeks of transit. One bears Panamá's seal impressed in wax—blurred by handling.

Philip reads it once. Then again—twice as slowly. He sets the parchment down with deliberate care.

A knock. Juan de Idiáquez enters, bowing deeply before he rises. Philip gestures him closer.

"Sit," he says. His tone is flat, unreadable.

Idiáquez obeys, waiting.

Philip speaks without looking up.

"Nombre de Dios was struck. A night assault. English."

He taps the report with two fingers. "A Captain Francis Drake."

Idiáquez's brows draw faintly together. "We feared increased English incursions, Sire. But Nombre de Dios..." He exhales. "That is no minor port."

"No," Philip agrees. He finally lifts his eyes. They are calm—too calm. "It is the principal gate through which Peru's treasure enters Europe. Its loss, even for an hour, emboldens all our enemies."

He rises and walks to the window. The plaza outside is quiet, dusk falling over Madrid.

"Tell me what you observe," Philip says.

Idiáquez chooses his words with care. "First, that the defences were inadequate. The governor's estimates of readiness were...optimistic. Second, that English captains now strike with better intelligence than before. Someone guided them." He hesitates. "A Cimarron ally is mentioned—one called Diego."

Philip nods once, absorbing it.

"And the treasure?" he asks.

"Unmoved, Sire. The intruders took little. Their commander was wounded and withdrew. The loss is symbolic more than financial."

Philip's gaze sharpens. "Symbolic wounds fester faster than real ones."

He returns to his desk. He takes up a quill—not to write, but to hold between his fingers.

"We must avoid repetition," he says. "And we must avoid the appearance of disorder."

He hands the quill to Idiáquez, who inclines his head and sits at a desk to write.

Philip continues in the clipped cadence he used for ordinances:

"Draft for my signature:

To the Governor of Panamá—an inquiry into the state of defences at Nombre de Dios; an audit of garrison strength; a timetable for repairs; and proposals for a fixed battery at the harbour mouth.

To the Casa de la Contratación—review convoy schedules; ensure the treasure fleets sail only with full escort; and produce a report on losses to English and French corsairs in the past five years.

To the Viceroy of New Spain—recommendations for cooperation with Panamá regarding Cimarron activity; provisions for mounted patrols; and intelligence on this man Diego."

Idiáquez writes swiftly.

The quill rasps, the candle gutters, and the wine in Philip's cup has gone stale; he sets it aside rather than sip again. He adds, without a change in tone:

"And inform my ambassador in England that while Her Majesty denies sanction of these attacks, Spain holds her accountable for offering harbour to those who commit such attacks. No accusations—yet. Only the statement that such matters do not go unnoticed."

Idiáquez pauses. "Sire...shall I include instruction concerning pursuit of this Drake?"

Philip reflects for a moment.

"No proclamations," he says at last. "No grand gestures. But inform the admirals in Cartagena and Nombre de Dios that English vessels sighted off the Isthmus coast are to be shadowed, recorded, and—if engaged in piracy—seized. Quietly. Efficiently."

He goes to Idiáquez and takes back the quill.

"This is not a matter for anger, Don Juan. It is a matter for correction. England will learn our empire is not porous, and our memory is long."

Idiáquez bows deeply. "It shall be done, Your Majesty."

Philip dismisses him with a faint motion of the hand.

Only when Idiáquez has departed does the King pick up the report once more. His face remains impassive as he rereads the final line: *'The English commander is believed wounded—but escaped.'*

Philip folds the parchment neatly.

"We will see," he murmurs.

Then he extinguishes the candle.

25 December 1572

The great Yule log roars in the Great Hall at Whitehall, throwing sparks up into rafters dressed with holly, ivy, and bay. The Chapel Royal choristers have just completed their morning service. The air still holds a ghost of frankincense and wet wool. Trenchers are cleared from the high table—boar's head borne in triumph earlier to a muttered carol, marchpane castles dented at their parapets, wassail steaming in a broad-bellied bowl. Somewhere a scullion hurries past with a platter of spiced beef and another of mince pies cooling under linen cloths, the rich scent of cloves and nutmeg clinging to the air. The Office of the Revels prepares a masque for the evening. For now the Presence Chamber hums with murmurs and the soft clink of chains and rings.

Sir William Cecil, now Lord Treasurer, confers low with Sir Nicholas Bacon near the door, lists of New Year's gifts already being tallied, red-ink notes marching like soldiers down the page. A page tiptoes past with a dish of comfits. Outside, waites scrape at their shawms, trying for cheer in a winter light that refuses to thaw.

A bell tinkles.

Jane Foole blows in with the draught—cap a little faded, bells bright enough, a wooden spoon with a painted scowl peering from her sleeve. Jane snags one sugared aniseed from the passing dish, pops it between her teeth, and lets the sweetness sharpen her tongue.

Some whisper she is Will Sommers' daughter, others that she simply took the name of Jane to keep the mantle of Queen Anne Boleyn's fool alive. Only she knows the truth, and she never tells it straight.

She bears a shallow basket lined with straw and five eggs, each chalked with a word: SPAIN, FRANCE, NETHER-LANDS, MONEY, MARY.

She dips a curtsey to the room in general. "Make way for folly. Your wisdom looks overfed."

Bacon glances up, dry as the rushes. "Here is misrule without a warrant."

Jane sets the basket on a coffer and plucks up SPAIN. "Hot," she says, tossing it hand to hand. Up comes FRANCE—"Hotter." Then NETHER-LANDS, hyphenated and crowding the shell. "So low they drown if you spit."

Cecil's mouth almost smiles.

The Queen enters—black velvet taking the light, a small lace ruff, pearls at her throat like frost. She has heard the boys of the Chapel sing the Nativity, taken her wine at dinner, and now walks where temper and policy meet. The court parts without being told. Jane sinks a curtsey but does not stop juggling.

"Majesty," she says, "your fool's brought Christmas eggs. All of them laid by other people's hens."

Elizabeth pauses. "You have brought trouble."

"Breakfast," Jane says brightly. She risks a fourth egg into the pattern—MONEY—and the rhythm wobbles. "The one that breaks and glues us all."

A murmur snips through the Presence Chamber as Robert Dudley drifts closer to hear. A boy of the Chapel Royal cranes in the doorway until an usher gently presses him back.

Jane keeps the eggs in the air. "Three kingdoms in my hands," she sings under her breath, "two hands not enough." She quirks the fifth egg from her sleeve—MARY—and throws it a beat too high. Gasps nibble the air. She snatches it back with a sly little bow and tucks it safely into straw. "That one rolls," she says. "Best kept low."

Elizabeth's gaze rests on the basket, then on Jane. "And what do you advise on Christmas Day, when men are merry and princes are not?"

Jane flips MONEY in a shallow arc towards the Queen. Elizabeth catches it clean, unruffled. The court exhales.

"Keep that one upon your person, Majesty," Jane says, tapping her own bodice. "Else the others crack of themselves." She turns the wooden spoon so its painted frown faces the Queen and, in a gruff falsetto, intones: "Also, beware of French weddings." A beat. "They end in tears."

The room remembers Paris, the Massacre, without speaking it. The Queen's face tightens, then smooths. She weighs the egg once and settles it in the crook of her arm.

Cecil folds his gift-roll closed. "If she can juggle subsidies as neatly, we will have a miracle to match Bethlehem."

Jane nods briskly at him. "Set SPAIN nearer the fire—too cold, and it sulks." To Bacon: "Keep FRANCE in salt or it turns." A beat, pointed: "And NETHER-LANDS in a basket with the holes mended—else all your eggs run out in the night."

A ripple of laughter that is not laughter. The Master of the Revels peeps in, sees Her Majesty's hand out for silence, and retreats, clutching a painted visor.

Elizabeth looks at the straw, then Jane. "And Mary?"

Jane's bells barely stir. "Don't throw that one, Cousin Elizabeth. The floor is made of stone."

For a heartbeat no one breathes. Then the Queen inclines her head a fraction—acknowledgment without assent. The Gentlemen Pensioners shift their halberds an inch. The rushes whisper.

"Enough," Elizabeth says at last, but her voice is warmer than the word. "It is the day of Christ's birth, and we will take our lessons sugared." She gestures, and a page brings a small marchpane star. The Queen breaks it, shares a shard with Jane, another with Cecil, a third with Bacon. The almond paste is sweet and stiff with rosewater; for a moment their fingers are sticky with something simpler than policy.

"We shall eat peace if we cannot yet make it."

Jane pockets the wooden spoon, bells giving one small hopeful jingle. She returns the eggs to straw with fussy care—SPAIN, FRANCE, NETHER-LANDS, MARY—leaving MONEY cradled in the Queen's arm.

"Your licence saves your neck, Jane," Elizabeth says.

"Your patience saves my breakfast, Majesty." Jane scoops up her basket, throws the capering ghost of a bow to the door, and backs out into the corridor where the waites tune their shawms and a troupe of mummers in ivy are ready to caper. As she goes, she calls over her shoulder, "Mind your letters, my Lord Treasurer—thieves read faster than clerks."

Cecil's thumb settles on his seals, caught. "Duly minded."

The Queen turns slightly, so the fire warms the egg in the crook of her arm while the court hums back to life—twelve days ahead, a masque to see, a Christmastide to steer, and five eggs to keep from breaking.

10 January 1573

At Sheffield Castle, the cold comes up through the stone before dawn, a slow ache that settles into the bones. Mary sits wrapped in a mantle that smells faintly of damp wool and rosemary, her hands cupped around a cup long gone cold. Outside the narrow window, frost whitens the yard; a crow scrapes its beak along the sill and hops away.

They have brought her news again.

It comes, as it always does, sideways—through servants, through kitchen mouths—in whispers that dodge the listener.

Not a proclamation. Not a letter sealed with arms. A story—passed mouth to mouth, softened by fear, sharpened by wit. A fool at court. Christmas eggs. Laughter that was not laughter.

The woman who tells it—an old gentlewoman with kind eyes and a mouth trained to caution—keeps her voice low, as if the walls have ears. She does not embellish. She does not need to.

Mary listens without interrupting. Her face does not change. Only her fingers tighten, once, on the cup.

Five eggs.

Spain. France. The Netherlands. Money.

And then—Mary.

She sees it as if she were there: the basket lined with straw, the shells chalked white, the hands that toss and catch. She hears the gasp when her name rises too high, the careful snatch before it breaks. *Best kept low.*

When the woman finishes, silence thickens the room.

Mary sets the cup aside with care. It makes no sound.

"So," she says at last, her voice steady, almost gentle. "I am not to be thrown."

The woman swallows. "It was meant kindly, Your Grace."

Mary smiles at that. It is a small thing, precise. "Kindness is the blade that cuts deepest when it is sheathed."

She rises and crosses to the window. The frost has begun to melt where the sun touches it, leaving dark veins in the yard below. Stone, she thinks. Always stone.

"They juggle kingdoms," Mary says, more to herself than to the room. "They pass money hand to hand. They joke of weddings that end in blood. And when they come to me—" She lifts her palm, empty. "—they lay me back in straw."

Her reflection in the glass looks older than she feels. Or younger. It is hard to tell, these days.

"They are afraid," she says softly. "Not of me. Of what follows."

The woman nods, relieved to have something solid to agree with. "They fear scandal. War. God's judgment."

Mary's laugh breaks free then, sharp and sudden, and dies just as quickly. "They fear consequence," she corrects. "There is a difference."

She turns from the window. The mantle slips from one shoulder; she does not pull it back. Her eyes are bright now, wet with something she refuses to name.

"If I am kept," she says, "it is because I am heavy. If I am spared, it is because the floor will not forgive them. I live not because they are good, but because my death would cost them more than my captivity." She closes her eyes for a moment, seeing it—the drop, the shatter, the sound that cannot be taken back. "They call that mercy."

The woman shifts, uncertain. "Your Grace—"

"Do not," Mary says, and the word is not unkind. "I know what I am in their hands. I have known it since the first key turned."

She draws a breath and lets it out slowly, mastering herself as she has learned to do. When she opens her eyes again, the fire is banked, not gone.

"Tell whoever told you this," Mary says, "that I heard the fool clearly." A pause. "Tell them also that eggs hatch."

The woman's eyes widen.

Mary smiles again—this time with sorrow threaded through it, a queen's sorrow, practiced and terrible. "Stone floors crack," she says. "Given time. Given frost."

Outside, the bell tolls the hour. Mary gathers her mantle, straightens it upon her shoulders, and stands as if a court still waited for her to speak.

"They think me still," she says quietly. "They think me straw-bound."

She lifts her chin.

"Let them keep me low. I am patient."

And in the cold room, with winter pressing at the walls, patience feels less like resignation than like a vow.

Chapter 23
Drake Strikes Again

27 April 1573

In a jungle bivouac, four miles from the Camino Real in Panama, the air presses hot and swollen with the breath of coming rain. High in the treetops, howler monkeys call out, their cries echoing. Beneath the thick canopy, the small English-French-Cimarron encampment is a dark hush of movement and whispers.

A blackened iron pot hangs over the low fire, its thin broth of dried fish and plantain skins long since boiled to tastelessness. A gourd of stale water is passed from hand to hand.

Francis Drake sits crouched on a felled log beside the dying fire, his boots caked with mud and his shirt clinging to his back. A soaked scrap of parchment—a crude rendering of the jungle route—lies on his lap, weighted with a stone. Across from him sits the French privateer, cartographer, and explorer Guillaume Le Testu, sharpening his cutlass with the same care a priest might give a relic. Beside him, a strip of jerked beef lies untouched on a leaf; even hunger struggles against the heat and the stench of the jungle. The Frenchman's long face glistens with sweat, but his eyes dance with something close to joy.

"Two more days, Billy," Drake mutters, glancing at the dark tangle of trees. "The bells on their mules'll sing before dawn."

Le Testu chuckles low in his throat.

"Silver always sings before it kills, my friend."

Drake cracks a wry smile. "And we'll be there to catch the note."

A few paces away, Lázaro, a Cimarron leader, whispers to his scouts in a tongue Drake only half understands, his scarred arms pointing towards the northwest trail. Diego, sitting cross-legged with a musket across his knees, watches with sharp, wary eyes.

Le Testu breaks the silence by tossing a peeled mango pit into the undergrowth. "Do you remember San Juan? That night we stole two galleons and sailed through their harbour with Spanish cannons firing at our sterns?"

Drake laughs softly. "You were drunk off your boots."

"And you were singing Genevan psalms while loading shot."

They both grin. For a moment, the weight of jungle and death and silver lifts. Then the wind shifts, carrying the distant metallic jingle of bells.

Drake stands instantly, the firelight flickering across his face. "They're early. But we're ready."

Lázaro straightens, his hand falling to his machete. Scouts melt into the dark.

Le Testu rises, stretching his limbs with the ease of a man used to walking into danger. He looks at Drake, then towards the night-black path. "Well then. We've sharpened the knives. Shall we carve history?"

Drake nods. "We strike at my signal."

They clasp forearms, old warriors in a new world, bound by greed, vengeance, and something far stranger—trust. Soon, the jungle would either bleed treasure or men.

Perhaps both.

29 April 1573

In the black hours before dawn, when the jungle still holds the night fast, the bells begin to sound. Humidity clings like oil to every inch of skin. The dense foliage muffles all sound—except the pulse-quickening buzz of insects and the distant clink of bells. Beneath a tangled canopy of ceiba and mahogany, Francis Drake crouches beside Lázaro, whose scarred hand signals silently to his scattered warriors. The men of the Cimarrons melt into the underbrush like wraiths. Nearby, Drake's crew—soaked in sweat and silent as tombstones—clutch steel and musket. The men of Le Testu, lean and sunburnt, wait in a tense crouch, eyes glinting with equal parts anticipation and dread.

Drake turns to Moone and Oxenham, his voice barely above breath. "North and south. Flank them."

The bells grow louder—mules. A full train. The foliage parts, and there it is: near one hundred and sixty mules in a slow line, chests strapped to their backs like treasure coffins, escorted by wary, sun-drenched Spanish soldiers. The scent of Spanish gunpowder mixes with the rot of jungle earth.

Drake gives a sharp, birdlike whistle on his boatswain's pipe, and hell is unleashed.

Arquebuses crack and sputter. Cimarron bows hum death through the trees. Arrows and bullets rip through armour and flesh. Screams rise above the din as Spanish soldiers fall or flail, blood mixing with the soil. Half the matchcord sputters; some pans flash and fail. The Cimarrons surge from the shadows. One soldier manages a ragged shot—wet powder, more spark than aim—but too late. A crewman appears from the trees, a long dagger flashing in the moonlight. The soldier falls with a cry.

The Cimarrons, armed with clubs, overwhelm the remaining soldiers in melee. Near the rear of the mule train, Le Testu, bellowing in French and broken Spanish, charges with reckless gallantry into the fray, his cutlass gleaming red before it strikes. He moves like a dancer in a dream—until a Spanish arquebus cracks and his body jerks backward. He collapses to the ground. Two of his men rush to his side.

"Captain!" his men cry.

Drake arrives moments later, cutlass in hand. He kneels beside his friend. "Billy, you've done enough. Hold on. We'll get you to the surgeon."

But Le Testu's doublet is soaked red, and his breath comes in gasps.

Le Testu shakes his head weakly. "Leave me," he whispers. "The silver—your men. Don't waste them for me. I'll slow you down."

Drake hesitates, his face grim, but Le Testu waves him off. "Go!"

"You bloody fool," Drake mutters, choking on the words. "You should've stayed behind the line."

A tired grin tugs at Le Testu's mouth. "You would've done the same."

"I'm English," Drake says.

"Worse," Le Testu breathes, chuckling softly. Then, with fading strength and eyes wide open, he says, "Go."

Drake grips his hand one last time, then rises, face carved in fury.

"We get the silver!" Diego shouts, waving to Drake.

"Oxenham! Moone! Load the chests—fast! Move!" Drake commands.

The mule train's rear buckles. The guards give ground. Drake's men surge in—not to glittering coffers, but to the raw labor of empire: pack-lashings cut, hide-wrapped bundles rolled free, silver bars thudding into the mud with a dead, bright weight. Here and there a sack bursts—*reales* spilling like hail—while a smaller parcel, jealously wrapped, flashes pearls and stones before hands close over it.

Moone shouts orders. "Two men to each chest! Haul what you can carry—we don't hold this ground!"

Sweat-slicked mariners scramble in the undergrowth, stuffing coin into sacks, strapping ingots into netted bundles, moving with the desperation of men who know Spanish reinforcements are hours, perhaps minutes, away. One chest splits open and spills silver across the jungle floor like moonlight, drawing gasps and curses.

"Captain!" someone yells from the treeline. "More mules bolting down the path!"

Oxenham chases after one, cutlass drawn, while others pull bridles and lash broken chests shut. The Cimarrons move efficiently, wordlessly, securing the perimeter like men who had done this before.

Drake, eyes sharp, counts the mules, the men, the weight. Not enough time. Not enough backs.

"Take what we can carry!" he bellows. "Leave the rest for the Spaniards to weep over!"

And still, Le Testu bleeds into the ground.

By dawn, the ambush is done.

***

By late afternoon, Spanish boots entered the ruin of the ambush. They found blood pressed black into the leaf-litter, a discarded hat, and drag-marks scoring the mud—a sign that a wounded man, unknown whether dead or alive, had been dragged off—a Frenchman, by the look of the torn doublet.

Nothing else remained but churned earth, broken tack, and the slow, inevitable gathering of flies.

30 April 1573

Aboard the *Pascha*, anchored close to the coast, the mood is jubilant as Drake's men arrange the treasure in the hold. They had a brutal march back through swamp and ridge the day before driving straight for their hidden boats, and the sea had never looked so kind. On the quarterdeck, Francis Drake leans against the rail. He holds a goblet of wine while the crew celebrates below.

Diego stands on the deck, sweat-sheened, silver dust on his hands. He watches the men go to and from the hold. Drake approaches him.

"Diego," Drake says, clapping him on the shoulder. "You've been a free man in my eyes ever since we met. You'll be free in England as well."

Diego smiles, his eyes glistening with tears. "Thank you, Captain."

Below, the men cheer and sing shanties off-key. Someone has broached a small cask of Canary, and cups of the sweet wine go hand to hand with lumps of salt beef and hard biscuit, the men toasting their luck between mouthfuls. Drake raises his voice to his men. "Drink deep, lads! The Spaniard bleeds, and we're richer for it." The crew roars their approval, their voices carrying over the water.

On the quarterdeck, the captain broods, his face cast in shadow, his usual vigour subdued. "Captain," comes Thomas Moone's voice from behind. Drake turns, his expression expectant yet wary.

Moone's face is grim, and he holds a folded parchment written by a rough English hand from a shore camp, carried in by a Cimarron runner who rowed in from shore. Drake takes the message, unrolls it in silence, and grimaces as his gaze runs over the words.

"*Le Testu—dead.*"

For a long moment, Drake says nothing. He folds the parchment back and exhales. Then he crumples the note and hurls it into the sea.

He growls.

"We left him there, bleeding into the earth."

Moone's voice is low, steady. "He begged you to go—so the men say. You saved our men and a king's ransom. He knew the price."

"I knew we left him to his fate," he says softly. "But I held out hope."

Moone stands silent, watching as Drake turns back towards the horizon. "He was a good man, Captain," Moone says finally, his voice low but firm. "And he died fighting."

Drake turns away, fists clenched on the rail.

"He was a friend. He deserved better than a Spanish sword in the dark."

The shanty falters and dies.

Moone edges forward, speaking evenly, careful not to provoke. "Captain, you made the only choice you could. He knew the risks. He sent you away to save the silver and your men. He would not have wanted you to linger there, waiting to be slaughtered."

Oxenham approaches and places a hand on Drake's shoulder. "You honour him by pressing on, Captain."

Moone steps back, giving Drake space. "I'll leave you, Captain." Oxenham follows suit. As Moone descends to the lower deck, the faint sound of the crew singing a shanty resumes, though quieter than before.

Drake remains silent, staring into the vast expanse of the sea. He pulls a small medallion from his pocket, one that Le Testu had given him months ago as a token of their partnership. He holds it in his palm, staring at it, his thumb brushing over the etching.

He lifts it as if to throw it into the sea—then stops, wipes a tear from his face, and pockets it again. Then, with a deep breath, he squares his shoulders and turns to face the work ahead, his grief etched into the lines of his face. The celebration below deck quiets, the men sensing their captain's mood.

28 July 1573

The Audience Chamber at the Royal Alcázar has heavy velvet drapes drawn against the night. Candelabras illuminate the richly appointed room. A silver tray on a side-table holds a cooled cup of watered wine and a small plate of quince paste and almonds. Philip sits at the head of the room, his fingers steepled, his expression a mask of controlled intensity. Beside him stands one of his secretaries, holding a letter in his hands.

Across the table sits Father Ruy López, his golden rook pendant glinting faintly in the candlelight. A chessboard lies between them, its pieces mid-game, an echo of the strategies playing out in Philip's mind.

The secretary clears his throat, breaking the heavy silence. "Your Majesty, a letter from Panama." He unfolds the parchment, his voice calm but grave as he reads aloud. "'*This league between the English and the Cimarrons is very detrimental to this kingdom, because, being so thoroughly acquainted with the region and so expert in the bush, the Cimarrons will show them methods and means to accomplish any evil design they may wish to carry out.*'"

Philip's hands tighten into fists on the armrests of his chair. He exhales sharply, his voice cold and deliberate. "When the time is right, we will stop the English from robbing us of our wealth, stop them from helping Dutch rebels, and stop their Protestant heresy once and for all!"

His gaze shifts to Father López. "Father, what advice do you have for me? What are my next moves?"

The priest, his expression serene but calculating, lifts his gold rook pendant, holding it for a moment as if drawing strength from its symbolism. "Your Majesty, it is strategy that must guide us now," he begins, each word carefully chosen. "Strategy is key. You mentioned the time being right. When that moment comes, quickly overwhelm them with your army and fleet. Ensure your forces have maximum mobility—they must strike like lightning, leaving no room for retaliation."

Philip fixes López with a look that stops just short of a command—silent, heavy, expectant. López continues.

"You must anticipate how and where the enemy will counter you and prepare accordingly. Be willing to make sacrifices to gain a permanent advantage, and, most importantly, shield yourself from their powerful queen."

At the mention of the queen, Philip's jaw tightens. "Elizabeth," he whispers.

López reaches across the table, his hand hovering over the chessboard. With deliberate care, he picks up the white queen piece and holds it out to Philip.

"Do your very best to take her."

Philip hesitates for a moment, then takes the piece from López's hand. His fingers tighten around it, the sharp edges of the carved ivory pressing into his palm.

"Her time will come," Philip murmurs, his voice low but heavy with resolve.

The secretary, observing the exchange, steps forward. "Your Majesty, shall I send word to our admirals to accelerate their preparations?"

Philip nods, his grip on the queen piece unrelenting. "We do it prudently. We will slowly set the pieces. Then we wait for the right moment to strike."

The room falls silent. Philip sets the chess piece back on the board, his gaze lingering on it as if already envisioning victory.

9 August 1573

The stained glass windows of St Andrew's Church in Plymouth cast colourful patterns on the congregation that sits stiffly on the wooden pews. It is Sunday, and solemnity thickens the air. From the pulpit, Vicar William Moore, wearing a plain black gown and a surplice, thunders his sermon, gesturing passionately with his hands.

"*Dearly beloved,*" he begins, his voice echoing through the nave, *"believe not every spirit, but try the spirits whether they are of God. For many false prophets are gone out into this world.*" He pauses dramatically. "1 John 4:1."

Near the back of the church, a bored youth, his chin propped on his hand, sighs loudly. His gaze wanders to the open window where the faint sound of pipes and drums drift in on the sea breeze. His ears perk up. Curiosity gets the better of him, and he stretches his neck to look outside.

His eyes go wide. A ship glides into port, its crew playing a lively rendition of "Jouyssance Vous Donneray," a French tune Le Testu had taught them. The boy grins and slips out of the pew as quietly as he can.

Outside, the boy sprints to the harbour, watching in awe as Francis Drake's *Pascha* glides into Sutton Pool. The mariners, dressed in colourful garb, play their instruments with gusto as townsfolk begin to gather near the pier. The boy's heart races. He bolts back to the church.

Inside, Moore is in full flow. "Right honourable and beloved in the Lord, we have a prohibition and a commandment..."

The boy, breathless and red-faced, bursts in and whispers urgently to his father. The father's face lights up, and he whispers to the mother. Both stand abruptly, causing the pew to creak.

The vicar's eyes narrow as he notices their departure. "The Scriptures name plainly Simon Magus, Elymas, the Nicolaitans—Hymenaeus, Philetus—Diotrephes—"

The father leans towards a nearby parishioner and whispers. The parishioner gasps, nods, and rises to follow. The whispering spreads like wildfire, each whisper bringing more parishioners to their feet.

Moore pauses mid-sentence, his gaze darting over the steadily emptying pews. A child approaches the pulpit, tugging on the pastor's robe. She whispers something in his ear. The vicar's face transforms from confusion to joy. His hand freezes on the pulpit edge, knuckles whitening.

"Drake!" He snatches his robe and bolts from the pulpit.

At the pier, the *Pascha* is now docked. The crowd buzzes with anticipation as Diego, Drake, and his brother John stand proudly at the ship's bow. Drake's limp from the injury sustained during the Nombre de Dios raid only seemed to enhance his aura of indomitability. He pauses, scanning the throng with piercing eyes, before raising his hand for silence.

The crowd quiets, the air crackling with anticipation. Drake, with his familiar stride, addresses the crowd.

"Good people of Plymouth, I return not from some simple voyage but from the heart of the lion's den. Across the seas, in lands rich with gold and silver, I stood against the might of Spain—against their greed, their cruelty, and their arrogance. They believe their treasure untouchable and their dominion unchallenged. It is not. No empire is so vast it cannot tremble before free men."

The crowd cheers.

"The treasure we bring back today is not just wealth—it is a message! A message to those who would claim the world for themselves, to those who would harry the lands and chain their people. England will not bow to their tyranny! We are not cowards cowering beneath their shadow. We are sailors, we are merchants, and we are warriors, unyielding as the sea itself! So cheer not for me, but for England—for the winds that favour us, the courage that drives us, and the freedom that defines us! God save the Queen, and may England's glory never dim!"

The crowd erupts into jubilant applause, their cheers echoing across the harbour.

"Huzzah! Huzzah!"

"Welcome to England!" he declares, gesturing to Diego, who stands beside him. "Welcome to freedom, my friend!"

Drake bows with a flourish, and his crew waves enthusiastically, some doffing their hats. Diego, overwhelmed, grins broadly as the townsfolk call out welcomes and throw their caps into the air.

Amid the jubilation, the good vicar pushes his way to the front. "Captain Drake!" he bellows. "God's grace shines upon you this day!"

Drake smirks, tipping his hat. "Yes, good vicar. And may it shine upon us all. Now, who's ready for a tale of silver, storms, and Spanish fury?"

The crowd roars its approval, the sound carrying across the harbour, as Drake and his crew prepare to share their triumphs.

By dusk, the first wagons were already being loaded in the warehouses.

John leans in, his voice pitched low, meant for Drake alone.

"You've lit half the town, Francis. It'll warm you—or burn us."

Drake's smile thins. "Let them cheer. By nightfall they'll be counting their own hearths again."

John's eyes flick to the warehouses. "By nightfall," he says, "all the wagons will have been loaded."

***

Drake does not take the *Pascha* east into the Solent, nor under the formal gaze of Southampton's quays. That port looks east—towards merchants, ambassadors, and ledgers already half-written for foreign eyes. Plymouth looks west. It is a sailor's harbour, not a courtier's one: a place where cargo moves before questions do, and where a man may land first and explain himself later. What is carried ashore here can be divided, disguised, and quieted long before London begins to listen.

The harbour at Plymouth bustles with activity as the *Pascha* lies moored, sails furled, her hull heavy with treasure. Longshoremen and mariners swarm her flanks while chests of silver, jewels, and strange goods from the Indies are brought ashore under Francis Drake's watchful eye.

Soon the noise thins and the crowd drifts away, but the work does not stop. The chests do not linger.

Instead, they are taken—quietly—into plain, battered wagons already standing in the lee of a warehouse. Their boards are scarred, their axles creak, their appearance stubbornly unremarkable. Over the chests are laid sacks of salt, pitch, iron tools, and bundles of tattered clothing, as if the wagons carry nothing more valuable than refuse or seized goods.

At the quay's edge, John Drake keeps tally, brisk and exact.

"Careful," he calls. "If that splits, you'll hear it rattle all the way to London."

Francis Drake watches with his hands clasped behind his back, eyes already on the road east.

"The roads are thick with thieves," he says quietly to Diego. "They know we've returned. They know what we carry."

"And the escort?" Diego asks.

Drake's mouth tightens. "Not coming."

John steps closer. "Then we scatter the loads. Night travel. Different routes."

Drake shakes his head once. "No. We make them afraid."

John frowns. "Of what?"

Drake glances towards the wagons—and then towards the town, the courthouse, the gallows beyond.

"Of the Queen."

It is not the Crown's mercy Drake is counting on, but its weight. A thief may risk a blade against sailors, even soldiers; he will not wager his neck against writ and rope. Let the wagons look condemned, already touched by authority, already spoken for. Let rumor run faster than horses—that the loads are seized, watched, cursed with paperwork and consequence. Men who live by quick theft understand one thing well: there is profit in danger, but none in certainty. The Queen's name, once fixed to wood and seal, is heavier than any guard he could post.

***

In a warehouse near the quay, the crew assemble in disguise—not as old crones, not as corpses, but as something worse to a thief's mind.

They don dark cloaks, plain caps, leather jerkins stamped with crude marks, and carry staves tipped with iron hooks. Around their necks hang sealed leather pouches, heavy and official-looking.

Across the wagon sides, fresh boards are nailed bearing rough but unmistakable words burned into the wood:

QUEEN'S FORFEIT
SEIZED GOODS
UNDER COMMISSION

Drake supervises as a clerk's roll—real parchment, heavily sealed—is lashed to the lead wagon in a tin tube.

"No man in England wants to be caught robbing the Crown," Drake says. "And no thief wants to touch property already condemned."

John snorts. "And if they test it?"

Drake gestures to Diego, who has wrapped his hair in a dark cloth and marked his hands with ash and oil.

"Then they meet the Queen's watchers—and men whispered to have dealings with things best left alone."

Diego smiles thinly. "In the hills, they call men like this cursed."

"Good," Drake replies. "Cursed things are rarely robbed."

Only the Crown's portion goes east at once—the rest is buried in silence along the west-country lanes.

10 August 1573

The convoy leaves Plymouth at first light: three wagons, slow and deliberate, flanked by cloaked figures walking with staves, faces kept down, movements measured.

No laughter. No chatter.

Only the creak of wheels and the occasional muttered word that might be prayer—or something else.

As the road narrows beneath trees, riders appear ahead—three men, pistols loose in hand, horses restless.

"Halt," the leader calls. "What's this cargo?"

One of the cloaked guards steps forward and plants his stave in the mud.

"Queen's forfeit," he says flatly. "Seized under warrant."

The robber squints. "Looks like rubbish."

"Aye," the guard replies. "That's what remains after judgment."

Drake, bent beneath a hood, lifts the tin tube and gives it a light shake so the seals clink.

"Names inside," he adds softly. "And room for more."

One of the robbers swears. Another edges his horse back.

"What kind of men guard forfeit?" the leader asks.

Diego meets his gaze and answers without raising his voice.

"The kind who don't keep what they take."

Silence stretches.

Then the leader spits into the road. "Leave it," he snaps. "I don't like Crown business. Not worth it."

The riders wheel and vanish into the trees.

Only when the sound of hooves is gone does the convoy breathe again.

John lets out a low laugh. "Francis—you've made silver look like a hanging."

Drake allows himself a thin smile beneath the hood.

"Best disguise in England," he says. "Nothing frightens thieves like property already claimed."

The wagons roll on—plain, cursed, untouchable—carrying a fortune hidden in fear, bound for London under the Queen's shadow.

As the riders turn away, one does not.

He is younger than the rest, lean and sharp-eyed, curiosity gnawing harder than fear. He lets his horse drift closer, boots creaking as he leans from the saddle.

"Hold," he says. "Forfeit or no—I'll see what rubbish the Queen troubles herself with."

Before anyone can stop him, he draws a short knife and flicks it open with his thumb.

Drake feels the world narrow.

The blade bites into the nearest sack. Cloth parts with a dry rip. The robber hooks the tear wider—

—and the knife *rings*.

A thin, unmistakable sound. Metal. Not iron. Too clean. Too true.

The robber freezes.

For a heartbeat, the sack gapes just enough for a dull gleam to show through the pitch-dark lining beneath. One more pull and the lie would be naked.

Diego steps forward at once—not rushing, not reaching—his voice calm as if this were already decided.

"Enough."

The robber looks up, startled. "What's that sound?"

Diego lowers his stave until the iron hook rests against the wagon's rim. He does not touch the sack.

"That," he says quietly, "is the sound of your name being written."

The older leader swears and wheels his horse back. "You idiot—"

Diego lifts the tin tube and taps it once against the wood. The seals clack. Inside, parchment shifts.

"You cut a sealed load. That is defiance. You heard the metal—now you know it's worth counting." He meets the young man's eyes. "The Queen does not hang men for stealing refuse. She hangs them for proving it wasn't."

The robber's face drains. His knife wavers.

Drake steps forward then, just enough for the light to catch the edge of his hood.

"Close it," he says softly. "Or finish opening it and be remembered."

Silence stretches. Somewhere a bird lifts from the hedge.

The knife scrapes once more—*not* cutting, but clumsy now—as the robber shoves the torn sack closed with shaking fingers. He ties it in a knot so tight it puckers the cloth.

"Devil take you," he mutters, hauling hard on the reins.

The older man cuffs him as they turn. "Ride, you fool!"

Hooves thunder away, too fast, too loud.

For a long moment no one speaks.

Then Drake steps to the wagon and presses his palm against the hidden weight beneath the sacks—solid, unmoved, real.

"That," he says quietly, "is as close as silver ever comes to daylight."

John Drake exhales, half a laugh, half a prayer. "Next time, Francis—"

"There will be no next time," Drake answers. "Not like that."

The convoy moves on, slower now, every man keenly aware of how little cloth and nerve stand between treasure and the rope.

14 August 1573

A rain-soaked dusk presses against the mullioned windows of Elizabeth's privy gallery at Whitehall. The Queen stands by the hearth, warming her hands, a letter half-read on the table beside her. She turns as William Cecil enters, boots wet, hood cast back, jaw set like carved stone.

He bows, but not fully—he is too angry for courtesy to flow.

"Madam," he says, voice clipped. "We have a problem in Plymouth."

Elizabeth arches a single eyebrow. "A storm? A Spanish wreck? What now?"

Cecil holds out a parchment, ink barely dry. "Captain Drake. He has returned."

Elizabeth's expression softens. "Alive? Thanks be to God. And his men?"

"Alive," Cecil replies. "And loud."

He places the parchment on the table with a controlled slap.

"He marched straight into Sutton Pool playing shawms like a triumphal conqueror of old Rome. Half the town fled church to greet him. He proclaimed—publicly, and at length—that he struck at Nombre de Dios, that he wounded Spain's pride, that England's sailors defy the might of Philip."

Elizabeth closes her eyes a moment. "Oh, Spirit...must every raid end with a sermon?"

Cecil presses on, voice low and dangerous.

"He named you, madam. Loudly. 'God save the Queen,' he cried, as though the voyage were done under royal warrant. He boasted of Spanish treasure in broad daylight. Plymouth now believes he shattered Spain's empire with three guns and a drum."

Elizabeth turns back to the fire, lips tightening. "And Spain?"

"Spain, madam," Cecil answers, "will hear every word soon enough. Their spies sit in English taverns with better ears than our beadles."

Elizabeth's shoulders tense beneath her black velvet gown.

Cecil continues, sharper:

"This was supposed to be quiet. Your Majesty must be kept blameless. A discreet humbling of Spain's purse. Instead, Drake has staged a pageant. The Crown must now disavow, or own, what happened in Nombre de Dios—and neither choice is clean."

Elizabeth picks up the parchment, scanning the Plymouth report.

"What do you advise, Spirit?" she says, using that nickname when Cecil is in her good graces.

Cecil steps closer, lowering his voice even further.

"I advise that you call him to court. Not to punish him—the people would riot—but to bind him. To remind him that his tongue is more dangerous than any Spanish culverin. If he boasts again, Spain will claim we wage war by pirates. And then we will have war indeed."

Elizabeth exhales through her nose: not anger, but irritation sharpened to a knife-edge.

"Drake is a fire, Burghley. He burns what he touches."

"He burns *what we are standing on,* madam, if you do not rein him in."

Elizabeth's face hardens into the famous Tudor mask—cold, diamond-bright, unreadable.

"Summon him," she says. "I will deal with him myself."

Cecil bows—this time fully—relief and exasperation mingling.

"And Burghley," she adds, almost lazily, "see that no balladeer prints even a whisper of this in London. Plymouth may feast on his stories. The rest of England shall dine on silence."

Cecil's lips twitch—half a smile, half resignation.

"As Your Majesty commands."

He gathers his cloak, bows once more, and strides out.

Elizabeth lingers at the hearth, eyes on the flames.

"Francis Drake," she murmurs, almost fondly, almost furious. "You will drown me yet."

23 August 1573

London. The yard off Thames Street smells of damp stone, horse sweat, and ink.

The wagons stand in a neat line beneath a gray morning sky, their boards washed, their sacks re-tied, their seals intact. What passed as refuse on the western road now looks merely *ordinary*—which is precisely the danger.

Francis Drake waits with his hat in his hands.

No hood now. No disguise. A plain doublet, travel-worn but clean. He stands beside John Drake and Thomas Moone, both silent, both alert. Diego remains back with the drivers, eyes lowered, posture deferential in a way that draws no attention. To become the Queen's, the goods must pass once beneath the Crown's own ink. This was not all the silver—only what England meant to remember.

A clerk from the Exchequer approaches, flanked by a Customs officer and two warders. The clerk is young, precise, his fingers already stained with ink. He carries a sheaf of warrants bound with ribbon.

"Captain Drake," he says, not looking up yet. "By order of the Queen's officers, seized goods entering the City are to be inspected for levy and record."

Drake inclines his head. "As is proper."

The clerk glances at the wagons. "This one," he says, tapping the nearest sack with his quill. "Open it."

The word lands like a knife on cloth.

For an instant, the yard seems to tilt—not with threat of steel, but with the colder hazard of ink. Drake knows this danger well. A cut here would not spill blood; it would spill responsibility. Once the sack is opened, every ounce becomes a question, every discrepancy an accusation, every answer a chain of names climbing upward towards men who do not forgive being made visible. Thieves risk the rope. Clerks risk careers, patrons, and silence. That is why the quill, poised now above the ledger, is the sharper blade.

John Drake shifts his weight. Moone's jaw tightens. Somewhere behind them, a horse stamps.

Drake does not move.

"Before we do," he says calmly, "may I see the warrant that authorizes breaking a sealed forfeit?"

The clerk blinks, faintly irritated, and consults his papers. "Inspection is routine."

"So is record," Drake replies. He gestures to the tin tube fixed to the wagon—its seal unbroken, its ribbon stiff with wax. "That load was condemned under commission and marked for delivery entire. If it is opened here, it ceases to be forfeit and becomes—by law—diverted goods."

The clerk hesitates. He looks to the Customs officer.

"Is that so?" the officer asks.

Drake does not answer. He waits.

The clerk flips pages, lips moving as he reads. The yard seems to grow very quiet. The warders shift their halberds an inch.

"...if sealed under warrant," the clerk murmurs, then more clearly, "and delivered for audit without alteration..."

He stops.

The quill lowers.

"If opened," he finishes, "...the officer present bears responsibility for loss or discrepancy."

A bead of sweat appears at his temple.

Drake speaks gently now. "I do not object to inspection. Only to *alteration*. You may count wagons. You may count seals. You may record weights already declared."

The clerk swallows. "And the contents?"

"Are the Queen's," Drake says simply. "Not ours to expose."

Silence stretches.

The clerk looks at the sack—the one that once rang beneath a robber's blade. The cloth is thick. The knot tight. One cut would tell the truth.

He imagines the ledger entry that would follow. The summons. The questions.

He clears his throat. "Very well," he says. "We will note seals intact."

The quill scratches.

Drake does not exhale.

One by one, the wagons are marked. Seals counted. Papers stamped. No knife is drawn. No sack is cut.

At last, the clerk ties his ribbon and steps back. "Very well. The goods may proceed under seal to audit."

Drake bows his head. "You have my thanks."

As the officers move away, John Drake lets out the breath he has been holding. "Francis," he murmurs, "that was—"

"Closer than the road?" Drake says quietly.

He glances once at the wagon, at the place where metal almost saw daylight twice now—once to greed, once to order.

"Silver and gold tests every hand that comes near it," he adds. "The trick is knowing which ones to trust."

The wagons roll on, swallowed by the city.

And this time, the treasure passes not under fear, but under law—still hidden, still intact, having survived both knife and quill.

Drake wipes his brow, grinning at his crew. "Well done, lads. We've fooled thieves, nobles, and Crown officials alike. England's wealth is secured, and not a coin lost."

***

The hangings in the Presence Chamber at Whitehall stir with a faint draught from the river. Torches gutter. Court gentlemen stand in two discreet rows, the murmur of silk and whispered prayers mixing with the clack of a page's shoes on the rushes.

At the far end of the chamber, Elizabeth sits beneath the cloth of estate, the ropes of great pearls at her throat shimmering like frost on iron. Her face holds one of those courtly masks that can make a man sweat without raising her voice.

A herald strikes his staff.

"Francis Drake, of Plymouth."

Drake limps in—washed, combed, and buttoned. Behind him, Diego follows two paces back, hat crushed between both hands, eyes lowered but keen.

Elizabeth's nose twitches.

She does not rise. Instead, she tilts forward a fraction—enough for every courtier to feel the shift in air.

"Captain Drake," she says. "Either you have brought half the Indies home with you, or you have worn them home upon your clothes."

A thin ripple of laughter moves across the chamber—measured, careful, watching her.

Drake bows, stiff with the ache in his leg. "Your Majesty, the scent may be Panama itself. It clings to a man like burrs."

Elizabeth's eyes slide past Drake to the figure behind him.

"And this is the man who swam through Spanish shot to reach you?"

Drake turns slightly. "Diego, Your Majesty. Without him, I doubt I'd be standing before you."

Diego steps forward one pace, head bowed deep. "Your Majesty," he says, his English halting but clear. "I owe Spain nothing. England gave me...shelter."

Elizabeth studies him—not unkindly, but with the cool scrutiny she reserves for matters that may one day become questions in Council.

"A brave thing you did," she says. "And a dangerous one. You stand in England now, and England keeps faith with those who keep faith with her."

Diego's breath hitches, relieved despite himself.

Elizabeth's gaze returns to Drake. "Captain, I have heard whispers from Plymouth loud enough to reach my privy stairs. Trumpets on the quay, sermons interrupted, half the town racing to greet you as though you returned from the moon. Lord Burghley is pacing holes in my floorboards."

A murmur—half amusement, half apprehension—passes among the councillors.

She lets Drake feel a moment's weight before her tone softens a hair.

"You have done England notable service, Francis. Spain will gnash its teeth for months. But noise is tinder. We must not light a fire we cannot quench."

She rises—only slightly, but the shift commands the room.

"Your wounds aside, you are to go to Lord Burghley's closet. He awaits your accounting—and will speak to you of discretion. You will listen."

Drake bows deeper. "Your Majesty."

Elizabeth's eyes return once more to Diego.

"And you—Diego. England keeps those who come to her in loyalty. Lord Burghley will see to the writing that grants you freedom in this realm. Serve well, and you'll find honour here."

Diego presses a hand to his chest. "Thank you, Majesty."

Elizabeth gives a single, decisive nod.

"Go then. Let us hope the scent of Panama fades quicker than Spain's memory of your deeds."

She lifts her hand in dismissal—gracious, sharp, final.

"Now go. Burghley is in one of his tempers. Best to face him before he boils."

Drake stops at the threshold, bowing.

A genuine ripple of laughter moves through the chamber before the doors open.

Diego follows Drake out. Two ushers lead them down the passage towards the Treasurer's rooms. As they pass beyond the doors, the laughter ebbs and the chamber exhales. Elizabeth settles back beneath the cloth of estate, her smile already fading into calculation. Jests may dress a victory, but accounts must still be kept. Somewhere down the passage, Burghley's shutters are drawn, his papers laid out, and the true weight of Panama waits to be measured—not in silver, but in silence.

***

Before Drake is admitted into Lord Burghley's closet, Cecil already paces the narrow chamber, shutters drawn, a thin draught disturbing the candle flame. His voice is low but tight. Robert Dudley watches him.

"Dudley—does the man think himself King of Plymouth? Trumpets, pipes, half the town running from sermon to quay...bragging of striking the King of Spain in his own Indies." His hand fists at his side. "Spain will have every ambassador in Europe baying at our door by week's end."

Dudley, leaning one shoulder to the fire, allows himself a small smile. "A triumph makes noise, Lord Burghley. And Plymouth has long ears."

Cecil wheels on him. "Noise is the one thing we cannot afford. Not now. Not with Madrid already scenting English meddling in the Low Countries. Drake's shouts on the quay may yet cost us a year of peace."

A knock.

Cecil inhales once—long enough to swallow the fury—and exhales a man restored to statecraft.

"Bring him in."

For a heartbeat longer, Cecil does not move. He reaches out and stills the candle with two fingers, pinching the wick until the flame gutters and dies. Smoke coils upward, thin and acrid. "Remember this," he says quietly, not looking at Dudley. "War with Spain will come not from fear, but from exposure. What we do quietly can be forgiven. What is done in public cannot." He steps back, face settling into its practiced calm. "Now—let us receive our inconvenience."

The door opens. Drake enters—sea-worn, limping, Diego behind him—unaware of what he has narrowly escaped.

Cecil's face is unreadable now, the anger folded away like a letter sealed for later.

Drake sets a sealed inventory on the green cloth on the table. Cecil weighs it with his eyes. Dudley stands by the fire. No pageant, no chest—just numbers, names, and the Queen's quiet share. Their sea-worn clothes and rugged faces contrast with the courtiers' elegant finery.

Cecil breaks the seal with a thumbnail and reads in silence, lips moving once as he totals a column. He does not sit.

"Two score and seven bars of silver, assayed rough. Eight chests of coin, chiefly *reales* and *escudos*. Pearls—unstrung." His gaze lifts. "Provenance?"

Drake's jaw ticks. "Nombre de Dios. Mule train off the Camino Real. Spanish soldiers to either side and God in the middle."

Dudley lets out a breath that is nearly a laugh. "Always the short road through the long hedge."

Cecil turns a page. "Shares?"

"A tenth for the wounded, double for the widows. The men made good on powder from their own advance. My portion—" Drake taps the bottom line, "—set apart as agreed."

Cecil's finger rests on a small, neat notation: *For Her Majesty's privy purse*. He does not read it aloud. He folds the leaf over it like a lid.

"And witnesses?" he asks, mild as dust.

"Frenchmen saw the first light of it," Drake says. "Le Testu among them. He is dead now. The rest are Cimarrons—free men of the hills. No love for Spain. No letters."

Dudley's eyes warm. "See they are remembered."

Cecil makes no comment on remembrance. He closes the inventory, palm firm on the seal. "You will deliver everything to the Tower by dusk. Not to the Mint. To the Lieutenant." A pause. "No tally called in the yard."

"Sir Owen Hopton will have the keys," Dudley adds from the hearth. "I will see a guard on the wharf that does not look like a guard."

Cecil nods, already dividing the world into packets. "You and your men will keep shore quarters by the river—the back stairs, not the front gate. No tavern boasts. No pulpit tales. When Spain howls, we will deplore piracy in general terms and omit particulars."

Drake bristles. "We did not steal. We took back what Spain stole a thousand leagues deep."

Cecil's expression does not change. "You may carve that on your soul, Captain. I cannot carve it into a treaty." He taps the folded inventory once. "The Queen's share goes to the Privy Purse—quietly. Some will find its way to the Narrow Seas. Some to hungry English garrisons who never ask who baked all the loaves."

He slides a second sheet across—two short lines in Cecil's hand. "Receipts. One for the Tower. One for you. Keep yours dry."

Diego shifts in the shadow of the door, hat in his hands, unsure if he is meant to be seen. Cecil's gaze flicks, takes him in, returns to Drake.

"This man?"

"Diego. He swam to us under Spanish shot. Without him, we'd be counting wounds instead of silver."

Cecil considers, then reaches for a small wafer of wax. "Have him wait with the clerk. We will write manumission in English to begin with, and Spanish to follow. If he is to set foot on our soil as a free man, I prefer to use ink rather than hope."

Diego looks at Drake. Drake gives a short nod. Diego bows—awkward, sincere—and steps back into the passage.

Dudley moves from the fire, warmth in his voice. "You have put marrow in English bone, Francis. There will be a day for trumpets."

Cecil answers for him. "Not this day." He lifts the shutters a finger's width. A shard of grey light cuts the table, then he closes it again. "We do not mount a pageant while Madrid counts. Let them call you rogue and wind. Let the wind pay our bills."

He sets his signet to the inventory and passes it back, not as a gift but as a burden. "At dusk to the Tower. Your men go by twos, sacks wrapped in sacking, not velvet. If anyone asks, it is biscuit."

"And if no one asks?" Drake says.

"Then you were never here," Cecil replies.

Dudley claps Drake's shoulder once, quick, a soldier's benediction. "Eat before you go," he says. "The Queen likes her dragons fed."

Drake tucks the sealed packet under his arm. "And her dragons like to be useful."

"Good," Cecil says, already reaching for another stack of papers. "Then be useful by being invisible until I tell you otherwise."

Drake bows—a shallow curve, pride refusing to bend further—and turns for the door. In the passage, Diego waits with a clerk and a clean sheet of parchment. Behind them, the closet returns to its small orbit: fire, shutters, green cloth, and the quiet arithmetic by which England lives.

1 November 1573

The rain has only just stopped long enough to leave the world sodden and grey. A thin mist coils like smoke along the cobblestones, clinging to the cloisters of St Olave's by the Tower in London where crows watch from the eaves with mute judgement. From a nearby alehouse comes the faint smell of sour beer and frying eels, a reminder that London's belly is never far from its prayers. Somewhere beyond the Thames, the bells of All Hallows Church toll the hour, muffled as if the city itself feared to raise its voice.

Francis Drake steps down from his carriage with the swagger of a man newly gilded by glory. His boots splash into a shallow puddle, but he does not flinch. His doublet, dark with salt and wear, still bears the bloodstains of battle at the seam. A golden chain hangs proudly on his chest—the Queen's own gift she had set on him at Whitehall. Around him, London murmurs with reverence and envy. But here in the courtyard, there is only silence—and one man waiting.

Master Ezekiel Crowsley, gaunt as winter and clad in the unrelenting black of his office, stands like a monument beside the church door. His eyes are deep-set, his hands pale and veined, clutching a well-worn Bible. He is the same minister who had thundered against privateering since Drake was a boy.

He does not bow. He does not smile.

"Master Crowsley," Drake says, removing his gloves with a snap. "If you summoned me for prayers, you've wasted your morning."

Crowsley's voice comes like frost through fog. "I summoned you for an accounting."

Drake raises a brow. "Of what nature?"

The clergyman's jaw stiffens. "Of the soul. Or what remains of it."

Drake laughs—short, humourless. "So I am to be judged now by the likes of you? I have just returned from striking Spanish tyranny. You should be lighting candles in my name."

"I speak as a minister, not a magistrate," Crowsley says. "God needs no candles burnt for pirates. Nor does England need her sons to become the thing they claim to fight."

Drake takes a step forward, eyes hardening. "I've seen what Spain does in the Indies. I've seen men broken on wheels, priests ordering butcheries in the name of Christ. And you fault me for burning a garrison and seizing Spanish silver?"

"I fault you," Crowsley says, his voice sharpening, "for finding satisfaction in it."

Drake stops, struck silent.

Crowsley continues, "You have turned slaughter into spectacle. You return not in mourning, but in triumph. You say it was for England—but England is not your god. Silver is."

A muscle jumps in Drake's cheek. He lowers his voice.

"I fought to protect this realm. To weaken a tyrant king who would see your Bible burned and your tongue torn from your head for speaking it. I did what needed doing."

"And did you do it with shame?" Crowsley presses. "Did you ask forgiveness when your blade fell on men defending their own land? Or did you raise your cup and toast your own cunning?"

Drake grimaces. "You were not there."

"No," Crowsley says quietly. "But God was."

Words hang between them like smoke, bitter and heavy.

After a long pause, Drake speaks again—slower, wearier.

"You think I have not counted the cost?" he says. "You think I sleep easy? I do not. But I will not repent for keeping Spanish boots off English soil."

Crowsley nods once. "Then we are at odds, you and I. For I believe a man's greatness is not in what he takes—but in what he spares."

Drake meets his gaze. "And I believe a kingdom survives because some are willing to get their hands bloody while others wring theirs in prayer."

Crowsley's voice softens. "Then may your prayers come later, Francis. And may they not be too late."

Without waiting for reply, Crowsley turns and steps into the church, its heavy door closing behind him with the sound of finality.

Drake remains in the yard, alone now. The mist curls tighter around him. Somewhere, a seagull cries on the rooftops. He pulls his gloves back on slowly.

And walks away.

Across the yard, beyond the cloister wall, a clerk waits beneath a dripping eave, ledger tucked beneath his arm. He watches Drake go, then turns toward the river.

By dusk, the chain will be weighed and entered. By morning, the cargo lists will be copied—silver tallied, shares marked, names set down in ink that does not forget.

At the wharf, a lighter creaks as it is loaded, one chest after another, each stamped with the Queen's mark.

The tide will carry them east on the next turn, whether any man prays over it or not.

Chapter 24
The Birth of the Cooper's Son

16 July 1575

The bells of St Martin-in-the-Fields toll slowly, their notes muffled, a sound more fit for mourning than celebration. Smoke curls from pitch-fed fires lit in the streets—meant to cleanse the foul air—while the stench of sickness clings to Westminster's lanes. In a cramped timber house near Charing Cross, the midwife whispers prayers as she swaddles the newborn boy.

The cooper paces outside the birthing room, boots heavy on the boards, each cry from within pulling at his chest. The muffled toll of the church's bells creeps through the shuttered window. At last the door creaks open, and the midwife peers out, weary-eyed but nodding.

"You may come in now."

He hesitates at the threshold, whispering hoarsely, "God preserve us, Mistress Midwife. Born in a cursed year—but may He grant the boy strength enough to outlast it."

Inside, the room is close with heat and the sour-sweet scent of birth. A small pipkin of ale-posset cools on the hearthstone, warm ale frothed with milk and nutmeg—ignored now that the worst of the travail is past. His wife lies spent, her face pale, her hair clinging damply to her temples. But her eyes lift to him—alive, searching. The midwife places the swaddled child into his arms. On the stool beside her lies the heel of a coarse rye loaf and a clove of onion she had gnawed between pains, the sharp smell of it cutting through sweat and steam. The cooper stares down, undone by the fragile weight against his calloused hands. He looks at his wife, voice breaking.

"Wife—how can such a tiny soul breathe in a world so dark? If God has spared him thus far, perhaps He means the boy to see brighter days."

Her lips part in a faint, weary smile, and she reaches to touch the crook of his arm where the child lies.

"Then let him cling, husband—not only to us, but to God. It is His will that the boy lives this night, and in His hands rests all the rest."

The cooper bends closer, his rough hands gentled, and he is torn between dread and hope. "Will," he says, as if naming him could secure a future. "We name him William—Will. May the Lord make me worthy to keep him, wife—and give him strength where mine may falter."

At that, the midwife folds her hands, her voice soft but steady, rising above the crackle of the fire. "God shield this house and child, and keep death from the door."

The child's thin cries lift, and for a moment faith holds back the plague-darkness that presses at their door.

The cooper's wife, pale with exhaustion, looks at her child.

"Will he grow to manhood, with the pestilence and Spain forever in men's mouths?"

Her husband crosses himself. "If God wills it. He is the realm's child as much as ours. Born into a time when queens quarrel and kings covet, when our island waits for storm or deliverance."

The baby fusses; tiny fists clench as though resisting the weight of all these unseen enemies. And in that sweltering summer of 1575, Will's first cry joins the restless breath of a nation bracing for trials to come—plague in its streets, a captive queen in its midst, and the looming shadow of Spain on the horizon.

10 December 1577

Rain has wrung the colour from Plymouth at Sutton Pool and left the quay smelling of tar, wet oak, and salt. Men sweat in the drizzle, rolling barrels of biscuit and beef towards the *Pelican* while the boatswain's whistle cuts through gull-cry and hammer blows. Casks of beer and vinegar stand ready by the quay, and a boy staggers past with a sack of dried peas over one shoulder, the sour yeasty tang of the victual beer fighting the brine stink of the harbour.

Francis Drake stands with his cloak thrown back, a ledger tucked under one arm, his eyes skimming every coil of line and every face. This is his kingdom—the edge of land where order meets uncertainty and he bends both to his will.

A lone black-clad figure steps out of the mist, a lantern glowing through the fog in his hand, a small sea-trunk bumping his shin and a satchel of books on his shoulder. A Bible is pressed to his ribs as if it were a shield—narrow shoulders, scholar's hands.

Drake's jaw sets. "And who are you to bring a library to sea?"

The cleric bows, not too low.

"Francis Fletcher, sir. Ordained minister of the Church of England. I am appointed chaplain to your voyage."

"Appointed," Drake repeats, as if it leaves grit on his tongue. His glance flicks to the leather satchel. "By whom?"

Fletcher unfastens the flap and produces folded parchments, the seals still intact. He holds them out with steady hands.

"By order of Her Majesty's Privy Council and under the seal of the Church of England. Here is my licence and charge."

The words hang between them, heavy as any chain. Drake turns the seals under a forefinger, once, twice—then stops. His mouth tightens at the corners.

"Appointed, is it?"

A chaplain not of his choosing, but sent by crown and church alike—and bound to watch as well as pray.

Fletcher draws out a sealed letter. The wax bears the sober cross-hatched sigil of a London parish. "I come with commendation—and counsel—from Master Ezekiel Crowsley."

The name lands like a stone. For a heartbeat the quay noise falls away: Drake sees London's wet cloisters and Crowsley, a gaunt parson whose words had cut colder than November rain: "a man's greatness is not in what he takes, but in what he spares"—and the way he had stood immovable while Drake bristled before him. He sees again the yard of St Olave's, that cold November day in 1573.

Drake breaks the seal with his thumb. Crowsley's handwriting was tight and spare, the lines a web of watchfulness: "*the souls under your charge, the temptation of gold, the scandal of excess. Let the voyage be godly, not gaudy. Let zeal be tempered with mercy.*" Beneath the homily lies the barb—Crowsley had "discussed certain concerns" about Drake with Fletcher at length.

"You've been talking of me," Drake says flatly.

"Master Crowsley sought my conscience," Fletcher replies, steady. "He fears triumph can corrupt purpose. He bade me speak frankly where I must, and minister always."

Drake lifts his eyes from the page to the parson's pale face. "On land, Master Fletcher, you may speak as frankly as pleases you. At sea, frankness becomes sedition faster than you think."

"I do not intend sedition," Fletcher says. He is no firebrand in manner. His voice is mild, almost weary. "Men will be hungry, sick, and afraid. I shall pray with them, preach to them, and call all of us—captain not least—to remember that Providence is not licence."

A few nearby hands slow their work to listen. Drake steps closer until the light in the chaplain's lantern reflects in his eyes.

"Providence," Drake says, "is a word for men who've never reefed a sail in a black squall. Hear me. I'll have prayers at the change of watch, psalms on the Lord's Day, and thanksgiving after deliverance from peril. You'll visit the sick, bury our dead, and keep the boys from bawdy songs when the wind falls."

Fletcher rubs his forehead.

"You'll bless their mess of beef and biscuit as well, if they think it helps," Drake adds dryly. "Though I've yet to see a grace turn weevils out of bread. But you will not preach me a second helm. You will not take London's pulpit onto my quarterdeck."

Fletcher holds the gaze. "No second helm, sir. Only a compass. I understand."

"Good," Drake says, voice turning iron. He folds Crowsley's letter once, then twice, and pockets it. "And your compass, Parson, points where I say. You will write no letters ashore that pass my seal, and you'll keep your counsel with me—not with Master Crowsley, not with any man who thinks a ship is steered by sermons."

Drake's mouth twitches—not with humour, but with certainty. Words, like men, could be kept in order if the hand on them was firm enough.

Something in Fletcher's mouth tightens, but he bends his head. "I will minister within your order."

"Within my order," Drake repeats. He looks past the chaplain at the watching sailors. "Boatswain! Stow the parson's trunk. Put his hammock in the space outside my cabin where I can hear him snore."

A ripple of laughter, muted but real, erupts from the crew. The boatswain shoulders the trunk away. Fletcher puts a hand on his Bible as if to steady himself against the roll of an unseen sea.

"One more word," Drake says, softer now, almost companionable, though the edge remains. "I know the sort of talk that thrives in lamplight when rain keeps men below. If you must ease their fears, do it with prayers, not with doubts. There is only room aboard for one master of souls and one master of ships. Keep to yours."

Fletcher inclines his head. "I shall remind them that courage and conscience can share a deck."

"And I shall remind them," Drake replies, turning back to his ledger, "that courage without obedience drowns faster than any sermon can save."

The boatswain's whistle shrills again. Blocks creak. A cask thumps down the gangplank. Fletcher steps after his trunk towards the *Pelican*, the hem of his black coat catching spray. Drake watches him go—the bookish back, the careful gait—and feels, like the first prickle of a coming squall, how a quiet man with a Bible could make more weather on a voyage than any storm. He pulls his cloak close and shouts for the longboat crew, beating the quay back into motion.

Behind them the rain begins anew, soft and persistent, as if the sky itself meant to baptize the voyage—whether into blessing or judgement, no man yet could say.

24 September 1578

The candles in the King's private oratory burn themselves thin in the Royal Alcázar of Madrid, flames bowed as if already tired of pleading. Wax runs in pale veins down the silver stands and pools at their bases, cooling into misshapen white scars. Compline has ended, but the words linger—*custodi nos, Domine*—as though the stones themselves are reluctant to let God go.

Philip kneels before the altar, unmoving. His hands are folded with care, fingers aligned, spine straight as a blade laid flat. His shadow stretches across the saints carved into the wall, darkening their hollow eyes. His lips move once more—no sound—finishing what the prayer book cannot.

The door opens.

Anna of Austria enters without announcement. She does not curtsy. Not here. Not after prayer.

She pauses just inside the threshold. The smell of hot wax and cold stone settles on her like a second mantle. One hand finds the back of a chair—not for balance, but for steadiness—while she waits. She knows Philip will finish when *he* finishes, not when the world intrudes.

At last he exhales, controlled, as if releasing something reluctant to leave him. He rises stiffly and turns.

"You should be resting, Anna."

"So should you."

Her voice is calm. Too calm. A calm learned through discipline, not comfort.

Philip studies her. Candlelight hollows her cheeks, traces the faint blue at her temples, catches the gold threaded through her hair. She looks younger than her years—and older, too. Like someone who does not trust the night to carry its own weight.

"You were long at prayer," she says.

"I pray as long as God requires."

She inclines her head a fraction. Almost a smile. Almost.

"God asks much of you," she says. "He always has."

Philip does not answer. He gestures toward the chair again, more firmly. She ignores it and steps closer to the altar instead, careful not to touch it. She never does. Her gaze rests on the crucifix—on the bowed head, the ribcage drawn tight as if emptied by obedience.

"Did you pray for England?" she asks.

The question is soft. Exact.

Philip's shoulders tighten. "Why England?"

"You always pray in order," Anna says, as if reciting something learned by watching. "Castile first. Then Aragon. Naples. The Low Countries." She turns to him. "England always comes last."

"It is no longer mine."

"But it was."

"Briefly."

She does not press that. She shifts instead, just enough to change the weight of the room.

"Was she kind to you?" Anna asks.

Philip does not pretend not to understand.

"Mary Tudor was a queen," he says carefully. "She was earnest. She was kind."

His eyes return to the altar, as if the answer might be written there. "She was devout. She believed obedience would be rewarded."

"And was it?"

A candle pops. Another flame gutters, then steadies.

"She believed," Philip says, "that if she fulfilled every duty laid upon her, God would grant what she most desired."

Anna's fingers tighten on the chair-back. The wood creaks softly.

"And when He did not?"

Philip closes his eyes. Only for a breath. "She was not spared."

Anna nods once, precise, as if a calculation has reached its end.

"And Elizabeth?" she asks.

Philip opens his eyes. "What of her?"

"She does not obey," Anna says. "She does not submit. She does not marry." A pause, measured. "She lives."

"She lives," Philip snaps, "despite rejecting God's order."

"Or because she understands its cost."

The words fall between them and lie there.

Philip steps closer, his shadow crossing hers. "You should not measure yourself against her."

"I do not," Anna says quietly. "I measure myself against Mary."

That makes him look at her—fully, at last.

"You married me," Anna continues, steady and deliberate, "because the line required it. Because blood must remain intact. Because Spain cannot afford uncertainty. Because a king must not leave God unanswered."

"I married you because it was right."

"You married me," she says gently, "because duty is safer than desire."

Silence tightens.

Then Philip speaks, very softly. "Anna, you are wrong."

Her breath catches—just once.

"I loved her," he says. "I loved Mary. And she died believing she had failed me."

Anna turns away. Candlelight flashes along her lashes.

"And I will not fail you," she says.

"In God's plan, is that yours to decide?"

She turns back. Something sharper now moves beneath the composure.

"Everything I am is decided here," she says, gesturing—not touching—the altar, the candles, the enclosing night. "Every prayer you speak. Every flame you allow to burn down. You ask God to keep you. You ask Him to keep Spain." Her voice falters, then firms. "And I—"

She stops. Swallows.

"I fear I stand between the prayer and the answer."

Philip reaches for her hand. She allows it.

His grip is reverent. Controlled. Afraid.

"You do not stand alone," he says.

Anna meets his eyes.

"No," she says. "I stand watched."

A candle dies with a soft, final hiss.

Philip draws her closer and presses her hand to his chest, over the slow, deliberate beat of his heart.

"When you ask me about England," he says, "you ask whether obedience is enough."

"Yes."

"It is not," Philip says. "But rebellion is worse."

Anna studies him—this king who has buried wives, buried children, buried hope beneath crowns.

"Then pray harder," she says.

"I do," Philip answers. "Every night."

They remain before the darkening altar, unmoving, while the palace settles into uneasy silence—Spain holding its breath, and heaven listening, unmoved.

11 October 1578

London has grown harder, tighter, as though the whole city were under watch. As so often in the city, the sickness returns in waves rather than once. Plague is whispered in parishes from Southwark to Shoreditch. Plays are silenced, alehouses shutter early, and constables walk the lanes with orders from the Queen's Council in hand. Tavern men grumble as they pour unsold ale back into barrels and sweep untouched trenchers of pottage from their boards, cursing a plague that spoils both appetite and trade.

The cooper's household lives under these rules. A painted cross on a neighbour's door means confinement for six weeks, guarded day and night by parish watchmen. No one enters, no one leaves. Mothers wail from windows for bread and clean water. Now and then a parish officer thrusts up a rough brown loaf on the end of a pole, or a pail of thin broth, the smell of boiled bones and cabbage drifting out over the sour reek of shut-up houses.

Will runs sure-footed now. He learns early, without knowing why, that a marked door means fear and hunger, that the sound of weeping might mean another child like him will not live till winter.

His father curses the Council's ink-stained "Orders thought meet," calling them the work of men who have never smelled the rot of plague-stricken alleys. Yet his mother clutches Will tighter each time she hears of another house being "shut up," whispering that the Queen must keep her people alive, lest Spain find England already weakened before ever drawing sword or setting sail.

Talk of Spain drifts through the markets: King Philip's wrath still smoulders because Elizabeth's ministers keep Mary Stuart in captivity and deny Catholic hopes of her release. Every rumour is a threat—Spanish gold arriving to stir rebellion, or papal curses falling on England's Protestant crown. Fishwives at the stocks wrap eels and sprats in damp cloth while they gossip of Spanish gold and papist plots, and bakers mutter over their rising dough that if war comes, wheat and barley will grow dearer than ever.

For Will's family, foreign quarrels feel as close as the next cough in the street. One morning his father takes him to the wharf. Ships lie at anchor, crews idle while plague fears cut trade.

The cooper presses the boy's small hand against the timber of a half-finished barrel. "Remember this, lad," he murmurs. "England's strength lies in her wood and her water. If the Spaniard comes, it'll be ships like these that stand between him and us. You may yet see that day."

Will cannot understand the words, but he feels the weight of his father's voice—the mingling of pride and dread. In these years, the boy grows in a city where plague stalks each season, where a captive queen's shadow and a foreign king's ambition haunt every prayer, and where a cooper's son cannot help but breathe in the fears of an island bracing for upheaval.

16 February 1579

In the Queen's private chamber in Whitehall Palace, the light of late afternoon spills dimly through the velvet drapes, dust motes drifting in golden shafts across the floor. Beyond the closed doors, the muffled hum of court carries faintly—but here, inside Elizabeth's private chamber, silence holds like tension drawn taut.

Elizabeth sits rigid at her writing desk, the quill in her hand hovering above the parchment. Her grip on it is tight, too tight—white-knuckled with the weight of what lies before her.

Opposite her, Robert Dudley, Earl of Leicester, stands with his hands clasped behind his back. His voice is low when he finally speaks.

"Your Majesty..." he begins. "We have played this game with France long enough. If we are to keep Philip at bay, if we are to hold the Netherlands, we need this match—at least the appearance of it."

Elizabeth does not look at him. She stares at the letter in front of her—Hercule-François de France, called François, Monsieur, Duke of Anjou and Alençon—the lines penned in an eager, youthful hand, full of promises and poetry.

"Robin..." Her voice is quiet. "Do you, of all men, ask this of me?"

Dudley flinches almost imperceptibly. He takes a breath.

"I ask nothing for myself," he replies. "Not anymore."

She turns her head slowly, eyes locking onto his. A tension gathers there—not anger, but betrayal, heartbreak, restraint.

"You once swore you would never see me married to another man," she says, her voice barely audible. "Now you press me towards a boy scarred by the pox and a French army behind him."

Dudley does not flinch this time. He steps forward, lowering his voice.

"Because I would rather see you reign with a husband than be ruled by your enemies. This match is not love—it is armour. France at your side means Spain hesitates. The Pope hesitates. England breathes a little easier."

Elizabeth stands abruptly, her chair scraping back. The movement is sharp, wounded. *Enough of this.* Her hand comes down on the desk. The quill snaps beneath her fingers.

"You would have me haggled off like a girl with a dowry? Wrap me in French lace, bow to his ring, while Parliament gags?"

"No," Dudley says, firmly. "You must do what you have always done—command. Let them all think you will marry him. Let them twist in the wind. Use him. Use me, if you must."

He pauses, softer now.

"But do not let pride cost you your throne."

Elizabeth turns away from him, her eyes drawn to the window, to the pale February light casting long shadows across the chamber.

"They all want something from me, Robin. Spain wants obedience. Rome wants my soul. France wants my crown."

She looks over her shoulder at him, and the veil lifts for just a moment.

"What do you want?"

Dudley's face tightens. He crosses to her slowly.

"To keep you alive," he says quietly. "To keep you queen."

A silence settles between them. It is not cold. It is not even political. It is heavy with the truth neither of them will say aloud.

Finally, Elizabeth looks down at the letter again. She picks it up with trembling fingers and holds it for a long moment.

"Anjou will not have my heart," she says.

"No," Dudley replies. "But he may stay the weather for you a little."

She nods once. Not in agreement—but in acknowledgement.

"I will consider it," she whispers.

Dudley bows, and turns to leave. At the threshold, he hesitates and looks back. She stands alone at the window, her figure caught in shadow and fading light.

18 February 1579

Whitehall Palace—Shrovetide Masque. Lutes chatter, shawms bite, and painted clouds roll across the makeshift heavens of the old Banqueting House. Below the dais the sideboards groan under trenchers of venison pasties, marchpane castles pricked with gilded flags, and tall standing cups of hippocras and canary that pages refill as fast as courtiers drain them. Courtiers whirl with masks on sticks, ribbons flicking like minnows in torchlight.

Elizabeth stands just off the dais, pearls a cool weight at her throat, a velvet fan closed like a weapon in her hand. Cecil is a steady shape at her shoulder. Francis Walsingham waits a pace behind, all quiet edges. On the floor below, French envoy Monsieur Jean de Simier—black-silk doublet, eyes bright with mischief—plays the room like an instrument, trading quips with ladies and gentlemen who pretend not to orbit him. He plucks a sugar-plum from a silver dish as he moves, popping it between his teeth mid-compliment, as if England's sweetmeats and its favours were all one delicacy to be tasted and judged.

"Your Majesty," Walsingham says, low. "We have letters from the Low Countries. The Duke of Parma presses his advantage. The States beg for money and men that we cannot declare."

"So we must disguise our aid," Elizabeth says, watching the dancers. "Tonight's full of disguises."

Cecil's voice is softer still. "France offers a mask of its own, madam. And a suitor behind it."

"Ah," she says, "the French game." She flicks the fan open, then shut. "Fetch me the man who deals the cards."

Simier appears as if conjured, bowing just deeply enough. "How is Your Majesty's health?" he purrs, French smooth as glass. "The masquers pale beside your light."

"Flattery should come salted," she says. "You know my palate."

"Then I come with meat," Simier replies, his smile tightening. "France desires amity, and Monsieur"—he does not say the name everyone knows—"desires proof of it. England desires Spain contained. We could make all three true."

Walsingham steps in without stepping forward. "By massing French on our doorstep? Or by pushing a Catholic into the hearts of my lordships' nightmares?"

Simier lifts a mask from a passing courtier and turns it over in his hands. "Not massing. Moving. Quiet feet. Private doors. A visit where no heralds cry and no pulpits thunder. Two days. He sees the Queen's mind, and the Queen sees the man, not the pageant."

Elizabeth regards the mask. Its painted smile looks back, blank and perfect. "You propose that your master creep in like a cat."

"Cats catch Spain's mice," Simier says. "And men talk less when they are guessing."

From the far end of the chamber Dudley arrives, heat under his polish. He bows, but not before his gaze takes in Simier, Queen Elizabeth, and the angle between them.

"Majesty," Dudley says, voice careful, "there is value in show, too. A court can be steered by rumour, but a crowd is steadied by sight. If you mean to keep Philip wary, let London think you might marry France."

Elizabeth tilts her head. "And do you advise me to wed, Robin, or to threaten to wed?"

"To arm yourself," he says. He does not blink. "Let them sweat in Antwerp and Madrid and the Lords' chamber. We need not marry to make them fear that you could."

"And if fear turns to riot?" Walsingham asks. "If pulpits bellow 'Jezebel' and apprentices sharpen knives?"

Dudley's jaw works. "Then we remind them where the gallows stand. But we do not let Spain read our hesitations as weakness."

Simier's smile warms, false as a stage sun. "Or we do not let Spain read at all. No noise for Madrid to parse, no pulpits to rage. A private audience. A river after dark. No pageant, no sermon, no riot."

Elizabeth looks from one man to the other. The viols climb. The dancers part. A comic Mercury in silver tights declares a verse about peace while two papier-mâché dragons pretend to sleep. The court laughs in the right places.

"Spirit?" she asks Cecil, not taking her eyes off the masque.

"Truth?" Cecil says. "We cannot afford Spain's rage, nor can we afford to fear it. The appearance of marriage buys time. The promise of secrecy buys options. Choose both, and keep neither longer than they serve."

Elizabeth breathes once, slow, fan still closed in her hand. She turns to Simier. "If I agreed—if—what door would your cat use?"

"The river—at the stairs below the privy lodgings at Greenwich," Simier says. "He comes as 'Monsieur de Foys.' Two nights. He leaves before London wakes."

Dudley's voice is a shade rougher. "And while he whispers at Greenwich, what do I tell Parliament?"

"Tell them what they wish to hear," Simier says sweetly. "That your Queen's adored by princes and hunted by none."

Dudley almost smiles, then does not. "I prefer my hunting done in daylight."

"Gentlemen," Elizabeth says, and the word is a leash. Both men still. She lifts the mask Simier is holding and sets it back on the passing courtier's stick without looking. "I wear one crown. I do not borrow another to balance it. If monsieur comes, he comes invisible. If London must be fed, it will be fed appearances, not promises."

The comic Mercury finishes his verse with a flourish. Enthusiastic applause breaks like surf.

Walsingham bows his head a fraction. "Then we prepare Greenwich—and prepare the alleyways, too."

Dudley's hand flattens against his hip, grounding himself. "And I will keep the lords in a hopeful fever. Hopeful men are too busy to plot."

Simier bows deeper than before. "Madam, you will find me an obedient monkey."

"I find you useful," she says. "Do not confuse the two."

He laughs in a manner that is genuine enough to be disarming. "Then I shall endeavour to stay useful."

Elizabeth turns to the dais as the final dance forms. The torches spit. The dragons wake and chase Mercury to delighted shrieks. She lets the court see what it craves—poise, sparkle, the effortless centre—and lets the men at her shoulder feel what they fear—mind, edge, the quiet that precedes a decision.

"To work," she says, so low only the three of them hear. "Robin, salt the rumour. Sir Francis, salt the river. Monsieur Simier...salt your tongue."

She steps forward, and the crowd opens as if it always meant to. The masque swallows her with its painted heavens and tame dragons. Behind her, the plot she has chosen begins to move on quiet feet.

Chapter 25
Drake Off the Coast of the Audience of Quito

1 March 1579

The Pacific midday off the coast of the Royal Audience of Quito, on the Spanish mainland south of Panama, breaks pale and cold, a thin line of fire edging the world. The *Golden Hind,* once the *Pelican*, heels gently to the wind, sails full, rigging humming like a well-tuned instrument. Nearly sixteen months at sea have pared her down to something lean, purposeful—a hunting ship.

At the taffrail stands Francis Drake, legs braced, hands clasped behind him. Below, a pot of morning pottage—peas and slivers of salt beef—swings from its hook over a chafing fire, the steam whipped thin by the wind as men snatch mouthfuls between orders. His eyes sweep the horizon with a hawk's patience.

From the foretop comes the cry, "A sail to larboard!"

Every man aboard stiffens.

Drake steps forward without haste. "What trim?"

"She sits deep, Captain—deeper than any merchantman should."

A murmur ripples across the deck. Deep trim means only one thing.

Treasure.

Thomas Chappell—a gaunt crewman and one of the older hands, still sharp—moves to Drake's side.

"A Spaniard?"

"Or else the world itself's playing tricks," Drake says quietly, eyes narrowed on the horizon. "And I've no patience for a false compass."

The Sea Dogs gather at their stations: lean, wind-carved faces, calloused hands resting on tackle, pikes, and match cord. One or two still chew on hard biscuit, softening it with gulps of sour beer from leather costrels, swallowing fast as the cry of "Stand by!" runs along the deck. They are not the roaring caricatures of tavern tales. They are craftsmen of violence—measured, calm, deliberate.

Drake nods once to the master. "Ease sheets. Let our lady stroll like she's weary of the day. No sign of chase."

"Aye," Thomas Hood, the ship's master, answers, a ghost of a smile touching his mouth.

The *Golden Hind* slackens, her sails luffing just enough to look harmless. The strange ship ahead—the *Nuestra Señora de la Concepción*, a large *nao* with high quarter and swollen hull—plods northward on a languid breeze, unsuspecting.

Drake lowers his voice. "She's heavy—near to sinking on her silver."

A beat.

"And she's got no notion that we're wolves."

The men grin, silent and tight. Closer now. The *Concepción*'s decks are quiet. No guncrews mustered. Only a few idle sailors leaning on the bulwark, blinking into the sun.

Perfect.

Drake lifts a hand. "Topmen—stand by. When I give the word, shake every sail we have."

"Aye, Captain!"

Hood looks to him. "We show our teeth now, Captain?"

"Teeth," Drake says softly, "and manners."

Drake lifts the speaking trumpet.

"Spanish ship—ho! What vessel are you?" he calls, his voice rolling across the water.

The Spaniards look up. One waves lazily. Another shades his eyes with a hand, trying to see who hails them from the English bow.

And then the trap is sprung.

"Loose everything!" Drake cries.

Canvas booms out. Rigging snaps into new life. The *Golden Hind* surges forward like a suddenly awakened beast, cutting through the water with a speed few ships in the Pacific could match.

The *Concepción* erupts in confused shouting. A bell clangs. Someone runs towards a gun that has no powder laid.

Too late.

Drake's voice remains level. "Run up St George. Look sharp! Let them know who takes her."

The English flag whips out—red cross on white.

The *Concepción* tries a feeble turn, but she is sluggish, panicked, unprepared. Within minutes the *Golden Hind* is abeam of her, close enough for Drake to see the whites of the Spanish helmsman's terrified eyes.

A single warning shot barks from the *Hind's* bow, the ball skipping the water and thudding into the *Concepción's* rigging.

Drake raises both hands, palms open.

"Strike your sails," he calls in Spanish. "Yield. No blood spilled."

The Spaniards hesitate—but only for a breath. Their ship's no warship. Their guns half-mounted, their powder buried beneath cargo. They are a floating vault, not a fighter.

They shorten sail. Their colours dip.

A shout goes up on the *Golden Hind*—not a roar, but a release of long-held breath.

Chappell mutters, "She's ours."

Drake lowers his speaking trumpet. "Grapple her. Prepare a prize crew to board. The rest—stand easy."

No slaughter. Just skill and cold nerve.

***

The prize-master returns to the *Golden Hind* minutes after boarding, face pale.

"Captain...you must see this."

Drake boards the captured ship, boots ringing on planks sticky with pitch. Below decks the air is cool, heavy, unreal. Bales of cacao and baskets of dried figs and raisins lie wedged among the silver, rich cargo whose mingled scents fight with the close reek of tar, damp wood, and men.

And then—Silver. Gemstones. Bars of Peruvian silver ingots stacked in rows like cathedral pillars. Chests of coined plate. Silks, spices, porcelains, and lacquerware. A crucifix studded with emeralds the size of a thumb joint.

The air itself seems to glitter.

A single breath escapes Drake—not awe, but recognition.

"This," he says quietly, "will rattle Spain." He rests his hand on a bar of silver. "And this," he adds, "will buy England time."

Hood leans over a chest spilling with minted reales. "Captain...this could float a fleet."

Drake closes the lid with deliberate calm. "Aye. And one day, she will need one."

A faint smile touches his mouth.

"Mark this moment, lads. There's more coming after this."

The men look at him, not fully understanding—not yet.

The *Golden Hind* wheels northward, the treasure ship in tow, the prize's sails trimmed under English hands. Their sails blaze against the bleeding sky—two silhouettes on the edge of a world about to change.

17 June 1579

Months after Drake vanished into the Pacific—lost to rumour and calculation alike—rain troubles the window panes without ceasing. Inside the Privy Council Chamber at Whitehall, candles gutter. Maps of the Low Countries lie open like wounds across the table.

Elizabeth takes the head of the table. Cecil sits to her right, ledger-quiet. Walsingham stands lean and exact, a folded paper in his hand. Dudley comes late, bow already loaded with an apology that he refuses to fire.

"We have two roads," Elizabeth says without prologue. "One with torches. One in the dark. Choose."

Walsingham places the folded paper before her. "The dark road, Majesty. A passport—alias Monsieur de Foys—entry limited to two days at Greenwich, no heralds, no sermons, no parade. Landing by the privy stairs. Four attendants, no more. We hold London asleep."

If it succeeded, it would be written down nowhere—except as rumour, and even rumour would blur the truth.

Cecil taps a column of figures with one finger. "The Low Countries bleed silver. A whispering visit buys us breath without buying a wedding."

Dudley's jaw sets. "Or we step into a trap. We cannot show the realm. If you want Philip wary, let London see you might marry France. Nothing steadies a mob like a banner. Nothing."

Walsingham does not look at him. "Banners also steady mobs into riots."

The usher at the door clears his throat. "Monsieur de Simier awaits, madam."

"Let him in," Elizabeth says.

Simier glides in, silk behaving itself, smile already dangerous. He bows just deep enough.

"Madam, forgive the hour."

"We forgive nothing in June," Elizabeth replies. "Speak."

"Paris breathes truce since Nérac. My master waits on your word," Simier says. "Give me August, and I will give you silence. He comes, he sees you, he goes. Cats, mice." The smile twitches. "As we agreed."

Elizabeth's eyes never leave Simier. "And while your cat plays at silence, I am to keep the lords docile with talk of a marriage you swear is not a promise."

"Talk keeps Spain guessing," Simier says. "Promises end the game too soon."

Walsingham's voice is mild. "Promises also fill graves. We keep to the dark road."

Simier turns his head a fraction, the way a falcon notes a hare. "Majesty, if I may—one matter to clear before we walk anywhere." He does not look at Dudley when he says it. "Your Robin is, in fact, another woman's husband—married in secret these many months."

Silence sucks the heat out of the room. Cecil's quill stops. Walsingham's gloved hand stills mid-stroke.

Dudley does not blink. "I do not answer to French gossips."

"Nor do I," Elizabeth says, level, bristling inside. She does not move. She does not need to. "But I do answer for England. Robin?"

He takes the blow with a soldier's stillness. "Majesty, my loyalty is not divided."

"See that it is not," she says. The words are flat stone. Then to Simier: "And see that you never mistake my private life for your leverage."

Simier bows, not quite chastened. "I mistake nothing where your safety's concerned."

"Master Walsingham, write a safe-conduct pass for Monsieur."

He takes quill and parchment and writes.

"Read," she orders.

Walsingham recites as he writes. "*Safe-conduct for Monsieur de Foys, styled a gentleman of France. Entry by water to Greenwich, for two nights only, within August, on such nights as we name. No trumpets. No train above four. To be lodged within the privy lodgings. To depart before dawn on the third day.*" Walsingham signs.

"Copy it. Seal it. Burn the blotters," Elizabeth orders.

As Walsingham complies, Dudley breaks his stillness. "And if London wakes anyway? Mendoza keeps sharper ears than our watchmen keep pikes."

"Then London will wake to see nothing," Elizabeth says. "A rumour of a shadow. Let apprentices chase smoke. Walsingham, give him the pass."

Simier's hands open and he receives the pass. "I will carry this to Paris with speed."

"You will carry it clean, sir," Elizabeth says. "No letters in your sleeve that say more than I have said."

"On my life."

"Keep your life. I may need it."

Cecil shuts his ledger with a soft finality. "Majesty, one point of tide: if weather fouls the crossing—"

"Then he waits," Elizabeth says. "And we do not."

She rises. The men rise with her. For a moment there is only the sound of the river, patient beyond the open windows.

"Go," she says, and the room empties like a wound draining. Simier goes to the door. At the threshold he risks a glance back, rehearsing a charm that has worked on kings and housemaids.

Elizabeth is already looking past him, thumb on the coronation ring, calculating tides, sermons, streets, and August nights.

"Tell your master," she says without turning, "that England keeps cats—but feeds them on need, not flattery."

The door shuts. Elizabeth says, "Robin. Stay."

The word stops him before the lobby. She does not raise her voice. It does not need raising. He turns back, bows a fraction. That means habit, not peace.

She walks past him into the little closet, the one with the low window over the privy garden, the table scarred by old penknives. Rain needles the panes. He follows and closes the door.

On the table sits the sand-shaker for writing documents. She takes it up, feels its weight in her palm. For a heartbeat her arm cocks—an old hunting motion, the throw a girl learns in a yard—and the pewter lifts half an inch from her fingers.

She does not throw it. She sets it down too hard. A hiss of sand scars the map of Flanders like frost.

"You married," she says. No title. No veil. "You married and did not tell me."

Dudley stands very straight. "Majesty."

"Do not 'Majesty' me as if the word were ointment." She keeps her gaze on the ruined coastline. "I am not something for you to skirt, Robin. I am the very walls about you—and you do not pass them without my leave. Who is your wife?"

"Lettice Knollys. But my first duty's to you," he says, quietly. "That has not altered."

"It has." She lifts her eyes. "It altered the day you put a ring on a hand sustained by my favour."

He takes that without flinching. "I chose privacy because the world twists what you and I are. Because every whisper in Europe calls me your husband in all but name. I meant to spare you a cudgel."

"You handed them a mace." She taps the map where the sand lies white. "France will say you kept me as a jest while I bargained for her prince. Spain will call me a wanton. My own lords will write bills with your name in the margins. You have made me their sport."

"I have made myself their sport," he says. "Not you."

"Do not be noble at me, Robin." Her hand closes on the sand-shaker again and then loosens. "You know what I forbid. She will not cross my threshold. Not for christenings, not for deaths. Not for a play. Not for a day."

A breath. "I understand."

"You do not. You will absent yourself. Kenilworth will have you for a season. You will write when I ask. You will answer when I call. You will not answer to Paris. You will not breathe in Mendoza's hearing."

He nods once. "As you command."

"Do not make me command what should have been offered." The anger drains and leaves a colder thing. "You had only to tell me. I would have been cruel and I would have forgiven you. That is how we live."

His mouth twitches—pain, not smile. "Forgive me now."

She studies him: the soldier's stillness, the pride that serves and wounds in the same hour. Rain runs in threads down the glass.

"As Robin, you have my pardon. As Leicester, you will bear the weight of my displeasure."

She turns the sand-shaker on its side and draws a clean line through the spill with one finger, a channel cut in winter. "There. There lies a gulf between us, and we may call across it—but neither of us will set foot upon the other's side again."

He bows, deeper now. "Majesty."

"Go," she says.

He bows and then he hesitates at the door. "It was not meant to hurt you."

"It is the hurt that proves I am not stone," she says, not looking at him. "Now go, before I forget that I am queen and remember that I am a woman with a very good aim."

A ghost of a breath—half laugh, half ache—escapes him. He is gone.

Elizabeth wipes the sand from her finger onto the table's scarred edge, composes her mouth, and opens the door.

Walsingham's runners scatter towards the water stairs. Dudley pivots to the Lords' lobby with a smile that means hope and threatens nothing. Cecil sends for coin and quiet men. And downriver, the wherries sway and knock, already learning the path a small, dangerous secret will take in the dark.

17 August 1579

Late afternoon. The Thames smells of tar and tide. Inside Greenwich Palace the air tastes of beeswax. No masque, no trumpets—only a palace holding its breath. Only three doors in Greenwich knew he had come, and each was sworn to secrecy.

Elizabeth stands in the Privy Gallery, pearls cool at her throat, eyes on the Thames. William Cecil waits a step behind. Walsingham, lean and sleepless, hovers like a closed knife.

"He lands at dusk," Walsingham says.

Elizabeth's mouth tilts. "So the French whelp prefers doors to gates."

"Better a door we control than a gate they do," Cecil murmurs.

She glances from one counsellor to the other. "And London?"

"London hears nothing," Walsingham responds. "If London hears, it will not be from us."

From the court below, distant lutes begin to tune for the ordinary diversion—music meant to mask the unusual quiet above. Elizabeth moves, one deliberate pace, as if testing the ground for cracks.

"Ambition?" she asks.

"Abundant," Cecil says. "But aimed at Spain as much as England."

"And height?" she adds, deadpan.

"Insufficient to trouble a coronation ring," Walsingham replies.

Her laugh is quick and edged. "Bring me the man behind the alias. If he proves entertaining, I will decide whether to keep the actor."

She turns to the window once more, and the river throws back a hard flicker of light, as if winking at a secret it is about to keep badly.

Above them, the painted clouds turn on their ropes, obedient to unseen hands. Elizabeth watches their slow revolution and thinks—not for the first time—that power moves best when it appears to drift. Somewhere between river and court, between promise and refusal, a French duke is already being imagined into danger. And England, for one more night, dances while the board is set.

***

Late evening. The wherry kisses the privy stairs and goes still. No trumpet, no torch-line—only the Thames breathing damp against stone. A lantern lifts. Its circle finds a compact man, the Duke of Anjou, in a travel-stained cloak, hat brim low. He smells of wet wool and the sour dregs of wine from a river inn where he had gulped a rough red to steady himself before stepping into English hands.

"Your name?" the usher asks, already knowing.

"Monsieur de Foys," he says—French clean as glass. Then, careful English: "At Her Majesty's sufferance."

Two corridors on, Sir Francis Walsingham waits: awake, exact, dangerous because he never raises his voice. His glance takes in height, gait, the old pox pits. The eyes he lingers on. Young, yes. Soft? No.

"Your retinue?" Walsingham asks.

"None that will trouble you," Anjou says, a half-smile quick as a flicked knife.

"Good. Her Majesty receives you privately. No titles. If London hears of this, the blame's yours."

"Then London will not hear," Anjou replies.

"We will see," Walsingham says, and turns.

They move without hurry, footsteps swallowed by rushes and stone. Somewhere ahead, a door opens and closes again, softly, like a held breath.

Anjou straightens his shoulders, knowing that from this moment on, every word will cost him something.

***

The Privy Chamber is stripped to purpose: rush scent, wax smoke, a green-baize table with papers pinned by a knife-hilt. Blanche Parry keeps her station by the hearth, the kingdom's quiet metronome. At the table stands Elizabeth—light and hard edge together—the ruff a pale sunrise around a face that gives nothing until it chooses to.

Anjou bows, the deep French theatre of it, but he measures the floor first. When he rises, he lets his gaze meet hers, dip, then hold. Not insolence. Refusal to be invisible.

"So, Monsieur de Foys," Elizabeth says, silk drawn tight over iron. "You run a long way for a whisper by a river."

"Truly, madame," he answers in French, music without grease, "I would swim." Then in English, neat and spare: "I wish to see you before we speak of enemies."

"Wise," she says. "Enemies multiply when named."

He stands a fraction straighter. That is confidence—the kind that can steady a country or burn it. She clocks the pox scars and moves on. She notes the ungloved hands, the one small drift of the fingers before he quiets them.

Walsingham slides to the panelling and becomes oak. Blanche Parry becomes tapestry. The room shrinks to two minds and a table and the river scratching at the glass.

"You know the terms," Elizabeth says. "No eyes but ours, no ears but these."

"And you," he answers softly, "free to forget me when I am gone."

Her thumb brushes the coronation ring, England's ring, the promise she wears to herself. Candlelight flares on it. "Do you think I could?"

"I would rather you find you cannot."

She lets the corner of her mouth move. "Bold."

"True," he says, without blinking.

Silence—alive, not empty. She thinks of French envoy Monsieur Jean de Simier's letters, all lacquer and laughter. This is a different metal: less polished, more sturdy. She wants to test it.

"If you cleave to Rome, then you cleave away from England."

He looks at the ring before he looks at her. "If I cleave to Rome, then it is by birth, not by zeal. My faith is no friend to the Inquisition. And—if Your Majesty can endure it—there is one here who loves you still."

The word touches a live place. She looks to the window's black pane.

"Loved," she says, tasting the weight.

"You told me to answer every argument," he says more gently. "That one is the root."

A soft knock. Robert Dudley enters and stops dead, reading the air—and the distance between them: two bodies a shade too close, heat where there should be frost. His right hand presses flat to his thigh, an anchor. He bows lower than he means. He mutters, "Hmmph!"

Then he takes a deep breath. "Majesty," Dudley says. "The tide turns—if you intend—" He sees the guest. "Monsieur...de Foys."

Anjou tips his head—acknowledgment, not apology.

"You will wait," Elizabeth tells Dudley, eyes never leaving Anjou.

Dudley waits. His face learns stillness.

"Two days," Walsingham's voice wrung thin. "No more." They will spend those days like coin.

Elizabeth moves—only a pace—but it forces the Frenchman to pivot. He yields the angle, not the ground. Lesson taken.

"When Simier promised wit, I expected noise," she says. "Wit without teeth is a toy. Tonight you cut. Do not blissfully think you did not nick me."

"I would sooner cut my hand," he says. No show in it. Dangerous for that.

"You are very sure," she says. "Comfort. And hazard."

He steadies his breath. Risks one step nearer. The room changes shape—the scents of horse and damp wool, a quick memory of spiced pastry swallowed on the river. The scars lose their map. They are only his face. Neither of them reaches. It is nearer than touching.

"In my own tongue," he says, "allow me to be seen as I am. If you refuse me, let it be a man you refuse, not a cipher."

She cannot help herself. The full smile comes, bright and lethal. "A man? A small one."

It cracks his composure into a grin that makes him handsome. "A small frog, perhaps."

The word jumps before she chooses it. "My frog."

Dudley's jaw hardens by a hair's breadth. Walsingham's eyes go briefly to the rushes and back. Blanche Parry begins an invented task, the court's practiced veil.

Elizabeth cages the smile and sets it down. "My frog," she repeats, cool now, as if naming a hawk. "That will serve—for a season."

"For now is a kingdom," he says, and bows again—theatre scrubbed clean, the neck bared like an oath.

They work the hours to stubs: Holland, Parma, the States' letters, marriage as a wall against Spain—or a fire in London's streets. He uses swagger where it helps, sense where it matters.

Somewhere in the long drift of talk, duty frays into something warmer, something that makes him linger a heartbeat longer than he should.

At the threshold he pauses. "May I return tomorrow?"

"You will return tomorrow," she says—command, not plea.

"And after that?"

"After that," Elizabeth says, thumb on the ring that outlasts every suitor, "we return to war by other means."

He bows once more and vanishes into the river's keeping, a secret the Thames will fail to keep with any grace.

Walsingham lets go the breath he banks all night. Dudley does not move. Movement would concede ground. Blanche Parry brings a shawl her mistress does not need.

Elizabeth still smiles, and hates it. "Well?" she asks the room—and herself. "What say you of de Foys?"

"It is simple only for small hearts," Walsingham says. "Yours is not. We must be quick and precise."

Dudley watches the door the Frenchman uses. "He will not hold you," he says, almost level.

"No," Elizabeth answers, laying her palm flat on the green baize as if it is England's skin. "He will not. That is why he is dangerous."

She lets her gaze slip once to the dark window and the whispering river.

"My frog," she says again, tasting salt in the word. Then the smile goes away with the other jewels. The room turns back into a map. On it, Queen Elizabeth stands alone.

7 September 1579

Heat clings to stone. Philip stands by the high window, a crucifix catching noon light at his throat. Juan de Idiáquez waits with a leather portfolio and the look of a man who brings tides, not messages.

"From the Low Countries," Idiáquez begins, "and from England."

Philip extends a hand. A cipher from Ambassador Mendoza in London, unravelled and recopied. Another from Brussels, Parma's neat, iron script.

"Utrecht holds," Idiáquez says. "The northern provinces keep their union. The States court the Duke of Anjou—titles are floated, protections debated. And"—he chooses the next words like stepping-stones—"reports say that in mid-August Anjou met Elizabeth in secret at Greenwich, under the name Monsieur de Foys—two days of private audience, if the report is true."

Philip's fingers tighten. The paper creaks. "Secret," he repeats softly, as if tasting rust. "France at her ear while my towns bleed."

"He plays at sovereignty in the Netherlands to wound us," Idiáquez says. "He plays at marriage in England to hem us."

Philip sets the letter down very carefully, as if it were a sparrow he might crush by accident. "They think to draw a circle—France, the rebel States, that woman—in one chalk line." He looks past the window to a city that cannot answer him. "Circles are for children. We make sieges."

"What orders, Majesty?"

"Parma presses," Philip says. "Quietly increase powder and pay where it matters most. No parades, only results. In England—watch the ports. Let the friends of Rome know we will remember who stands firm when the world begins to shift."

"And if Elizabeth weds him?"

"She will not share her crown," Philip says, and the certainty sounds like a prayer he is forcing to be true. "But if their game becomes iron, we answer with iron." He looks down at Mendoza's hand, at the tidy report of a thing already done. "Until then, we move only when there is blood in the water."

Idiáquez bows. The door closes. The room returns to its slow heat.

Philip rests a palm on the dispatches, not quite a blessing, not quite a threat. "So," he says to the empty air, "let the frog leap. We will salt the pond."

Idiáquez pauses at the outer table. He opens the portfolio and removes three slips, already prepared.

One assigns powder from Namur to Antwerp — quantities noted, wagons counted.

One reroutes pay from Milan through Genoa — dates aligned, couriers named.

One lists English ports, ordered by tide and turn, margins marked for watchers already in place.

He sands the ink, closes the leather, and rings once for a clerk.

The orders go down the corridor, light as paper, heavy as iron.

Chapter 26
Elizabeth Betrayed

15 January 1580

Hundreds of candles flicker against gilded altars, lighting the Royal Chapel of the Alcázar in Madrid. The mournful tones of "*Circumdederunt me*" by Cristóbal de Morales echo through the grand space, sung by a choir hidden in the shadows of the high loft. Their voices swell, filling the chapel with solemn reverence.

At the centre of the chapel, Father Ruy López lies in state, his body draped in resplendent vestments. The golden rook pendant he had worn in life rests on his chest. A faint scent of incense lingers in the air. No wine or sweetmeats are set out tonight; Philip has refused even the light collation—a small morsel and wine—customarily offered in the palace before such long offices. He holds his vigil on an empty stomach.

Seated close to the bier are Philip and Don Bernardino de Mendoza, the Spanish ambassador to England, newly arrived from London on the King's summons. They sit in silence, their expressions solemn, their minds already at work.

Philip breaks the silence, his voice low but firm. "Don Bernardino," he begins, his eyes fixed on the body of the late priest. "The English court is a nest of vipers. I will need you to be both my eyes and ears."

Mendoza nods and places his right hand over his heart.

"At your command. I live to serve Your Majesty."

Philip turns to him, his face a mask of intensity. "The codes we devised—only you and I know them. Use them wisely. Send word of every whisper, every look, every suspicion. The stability of England is brittle, and we shall exploit every crack."

Mendoza kisses the King's hand, his head bowed and his other hand on his chest. "Your Majesty, I will not fail."

Philip smiles, a rare display of satisfaction. "There is a certain Edward Stafford with access to the English court who may yet prove useful. His mother serves among the women of the Privy Chamber, and so she stands close to the Queen's person. His loyalty, however, is flexible. It can be purchased, for his purse runs empty more often than not. Make contact with him. Offer him what he desires, and in return, he may deliver to us court secrets. England's court is a knot. You will untie it piece by piece."

Mendoza raises an eyebrow but remains silent, his face betraying no emotion. He understands the gravity of the task—betrayal within the English court could shift the balance of power in Spain's favour.

Philip rises from his chair, his long robes sweeping the marble floor as he approaches the bier. He stands over the late priest's body, his expression contemplative.

"Dear Father," he says softly, "in life, you guided me with your wisdom. In death, your example shall guide my resolve. The game we began together is not over. We will control the board...and eventually, we will take the Queen."

Philip reaches down and extinguishes one of the candles near the bier.

Philip turns back to Mendoza, his voice cutting through the silence. "Go, Don Bernardino. Leave for England at once. The winds are in our favour."

Mendoza bows. "As Your Majesty commands."

As Mendoza departs, the choir rises in a final crescendo, the mournful tones of the hymn blending with the heavy sound of Philip's boots as he walks down the aisle. Behind him, the golden rook pendant on the priest's chest gleams faintly in the candlelight, a silent witness to the King's growing ambitions.

4 February 1580

Winter presses against the leaded windows of the Royal Alcázar, a thin, needling cold that seeps through velvet drapes and whispers along the marble floor. A brazier glows low, its heat swallowed by the high chamber. Incense lingers in the rafters like a held breath.

A tapestry stirs as a servant enters, boots clicking softly. He bears a silver tray with a single letter, its red seal marked with the arms of the Portuguese royal envoy. He bows.

"A letter for Your Majesty."

Philip extends his hand, each movement precise, economical. He breaks the seal with a Toledo-steel opener. The parchment crackles. His eyes move down the page once—then again. His face remains still, but the air in the room tightens.

"Dead," he says.

A voice comes from behind him. "News from Lisbon?"

The Duke of Alba steps forward, cloak heavy with black wool, a steel gorget glinting like old ice. His face is carved with decades of war and court intrigues.

Philip does not turn. "Cardinal-King Henry is gone—word from Lisbon says the court is in uproar. No heir, no settlement."

Alba nods once. "Then the hour has come."

Philip clasps his hands behind his back, the gesture controlled, almost ceremonial.

"Portugal stands unmoored. The nobles will quarrel, the clerics will delay, and the empire's veins—India, Brazil, the Azores—run without a sovereign's hand upon them."

Alba's gaze sharpens. "And you mean to place yours?"

"I must." Philip turns now, fully, his eyes hard as forged iron. "My mother was Isabella of Portugal. The bloodline is mine. I will not see France or the pretender Dom António turn inheritance into farce."

A shiver of cold works through the chamber as he crosses to the map table. Lamps gleam upon the outlines of coastlines, sea routes, and fortresses. A small dish of sugared almonds and anise seeds rattles faintly as he leans over the charts, the little comforts of court life forgotten while he measures oceans and crowns.

"Portugal's fleet," Philip says quietly, "is the key to the Atlantic. With it, Spain commands the whole western Iberian coast, from Galicia to the Algarve. Every route to the Indies lies open. England cannot flank what she cannot approach. France cannot threaten what it cannot reach."

He sets one finger upon Lisbon, then presses it down.

"This crown is my right by birth. If parchment and envoys suffice, let them suffice. If not—" he lifts his hand, "—we march."

Alba bows deeply. "At once, Majesty. The Council will be assembled."

"See also that the fleet commanders are summoned," Philip continues. "I want the orders drafted tonight. Claims stated plainly. Troops made ready. We shall move before our rivals take breath."

Alba straightens. "Lisbon may resist."

Philip steps closer, voice softening into something far more dangerous.

"Then we will speak in a voice they cannot mistake."

A long, cold silence settles between them.

At last Philip adds, almost as an afterthought—but it lands like steel on stone:

"Send word to the governors of Castile and Andalusia. When Portugal stirs, I want no hesitation in our ranks."

Alba bows once more, the weight of the empire on his shoulders. "At your command, Your Majesty."

Philip turns back to the map, eyes fixed on the coastline that is about to become his.

"We begin at dawn," he murmurs.

And the brazier's fire gutters, as though the room itself recognises that a kingdom is about to change hands.

15 May 1580

The Thames fog folds over the London ward of Queenhithe like uncarded wool, muffling the clatter of chains and the groan of the tide against the pilings. An old spice warehouse—half-abandoned, half-forgotten—stands at the water's edge, its shutters trembling each time a gust off the river blows through the cracks. A single lantern glows within, a frail ember set against the dark.

Two of Bernardino de Mendoza's men keep watch at the door—still as carved saints, cloaks drawn tight, their sword-hands idle but ready. A rat skitters between their boots. Neither moves.

Inside, Mendoza waits. He had been Spain's ambassador to England since 1578—long enough to learn its damp habits, not long enough to stop despising them.

The air is sour with mouldy cloves and peppercorns—a ghost of spices long since carted away—mixing with the tarry tang of the river and the stale reek of spilled wine on the floorboards.

Tall, ink-dark, and wrapped in a heavy Spanish capa, he stands beside a crate marked with fading Lisbon lettering. His gloved finger taps once, twice, against his cane—an old habit when patience grows thin. He dislikes England's damp. He dislikes its smells. But he dislikes most of all the errand before him.

He heard Philip's voice as keenly as if the King stood beside him: "*You will untie it piece by piece.*"

The door rasps open. A blade of cold night slides into the room.

Master Edward Stafford steps inside.

He removes his hat with an elegant bow, every inch the court gentleman: lean, finely dressed, a man accustomed to good wine, good horses, and good secrets. Mendoza had been told that Stafford—between postings, and drowning in debt—had returned to court with more pedigree than purse.

"Your Excellency," Stafford murmurs. "You choose strange parlours for conversation. Most gentlemen prefer a hearth."

Mendoza regards him without warmth. "Hearths have ears. Cold rooms keep men honest." He gestures lightly towards the crates. "We will speak standing."

Stafford smiles at that—a small, knowing curve of the mouth. "Then let us speak plainly. You sent for me. Why?"

Mendoza studies him the way a falcon weighs a hare: measuring distance, risk, spoils.

"Because Her Majesty believes you loyal," he says. "And because loyalty in England is a thing that may be steered—not an agent yet, only a man being sounded for softness."

Stafford's eyes sharpen, though his tone stays soft. "If you mean to purchase treason, Ambassador, you will find the price steep—and perilous."

Without flourish, Mendoza reaches into his cloak and places a velvet pouch upon the crate. It makes a quiet, unmistakable sound as it lands.

"Spain asks for no oaths," Mendoza says. "Only observation. A letter, now and then. A whisper of what stirs behind your Queen's curtains. Nothing more."

Stafford regards the pouch without touching it. "You think my silence so easily rented?"

"I think," Mendoza replies evenly, "that a man of your standing deserves to live as comfortably as he appears. And Madrid has long arms. Long purses."

The river knocks against the pilings. A dog barks far off. The lantern gutters once.

Stafford's thumb works the seam of his glove—a gesture Mendoza does not miss.

"And if Walsingham gets wind of this?" Stafford asks quietly. "You should know his nets are wide."

"Then neither of us is here tonight," Mendoza answers. "And neither of us ever spoke. You know how shadows keep their counsel, Master Stafford."

A long silence settles between them—thick, heavy, testing.

At last, Stafford reaches out. He lifts the pouch. Weighs it. Not greedily—judiciously, as if assessing the worth of his own future. His eyes flick once to the door, as if he expects Walsingham himself to step through it.

"I will hear you. One letter. Nothing that hangs me."

Mendoza inclines his head, a single precise movement. "Then let this be the beginning—enough to test the seams. Tell me—what course does your Queen steer with France?"

Stafford pockets the gold, careful and composed.

"In England," he says, "nothing is given without its price." His smile thins into something colder. "Not even the truth."

1 September 1580

The scent of ink and beeswax clings to the panelled chamber like a second skin. At her writing desk, Elizabeth sits rigid as a carved figure, the quill poised above a half-finished letter. Only the faint tremor in her fingers betrays the strain of the morning.

Walsingham stands before her, hands clasped behind his back—but carrying the weight of bad tidings.

"Your Majesty," he says, "news hardens into certainty. Philip has moved. Portugal is lost."

Elizabeth's head snaps up. The quill tips, scattering a bead of ink across the parchment.

"Lost?" Her voice is low, steady, sharp. "Tell me what is meant by that."

Walsingham steps forward and lays a sealed dispatch in her hand. "Following the death of King Henry and the confusion over the succession, Philip marched his *tercios* into Portugal. The Duke of Alba led them straight upon Lisbon. Dom António's forces broke. Philip now styles himself King of Portugal."

Elizabeth breaks the seal and reads swiftly, her eyes racing across the page. Her knuckles whiten around the parchment. She presses it flat upon the desk, then looks to Cecil, who stands at the door as if rooted to the stones.

"Spirit—do you hear it? Philip holds Portugal as he holds Castile and Aragon. He commands the whole spine of Iberia."

Cecil moves closer, voice grave. "I hear it, Majesty. And it alters the balance of Christendom entirely. With Lisbon in his grasp, he controls the Atlantic approaches and the road to the Indies. He gains harbours enough to shadow our every voyage."

Elizabeth rises and goes to the great map hung on the wall. Her eyes travel the coastline with the precision of a cartographer.

"How long, Cecil? Before he uses Lisbon as a springboard against us?"

"In truth, Majesty," Cecil says, "he has the ports, the ships, and the will. That is the whole measure. Time is all that remains."

Walsingham adds, "Our watchers report preparations in Lisbon already—a great stirring in the yards. If he chooses to build at pace, he could have ships fitting out sooner than we like."

Elizabeth turns back. "He will not wait. He never has. Portugal was never his end, only a hinge."

She returns to her desk, but she does not sit.

"Walsingham—widen our net. I want eyes in every Lisbon tavern, on every quay, in every counting-house that carries his coin. If Philip breathes a thought towards invasion, I will know it—before his own ministers do."

Walsingham bows his head. "At once, Majesty."

"Cecil—our navy. Strengthen the Western Squadron. See the victuallers paid. No idle keels at Deptford or Woolwich. If Philip reaches for us, we will meet him upon the sea, not wait for him upon the shore."

Cecil's mind flicks, even as he bows, to casks of beef, biscuit, beer, and fish to be laid in along the Medway and at Plymouth—victuals as much a weapon as any culverin if the Queen is to have her will.

He inclines his head. "Your Majesty commands readiness. You shall have it."

Elizabeth stands before the map again—England a small shape in the upper corner of an encroaching empire. For a moment she is silent, assessing, calculating, the tremor in her hands gone.

When she speaks, her words carry through the chamber like flint striking steel.

"We have watched Philip gather his crowns—Naples, Milan, Burgundy, the Indies. Now Portugal. His reach grows long. England must not sleep while he builds his ladder."

Her palm rests flat upon the map, covering the narrow seas.

"If Portugal was his prize, England will not be his conquest."

4 April 1581

The *Golden Hind* glides into Deptford beneath a pall of overcast sky, its tattered sails and salt-stained hull bearing the scars of a voyage that had circled the globe and struck fear into Spain's empire. Crowds throng the quayside—nobles in their finery pressed against tradesmen and apprentices, foreign envoys elbowed aside by fishwives and sailors' wives—drawn by the rumour of treasure beyond reckoning.

Will, the cooper's son, is five, perched on his father's broad shoulders to see above the press. He is old enough to know the smell of tar and pitch, old enough to feel the boards of the quay shudder beneath the weight of the multitude, yet still young enough for the sight before him to seem like a dream.

The *Hind's* weary crew disembarks, their leather jerkins stiff with salt and powder-stains, their faces burnt brown by alien suns. Behind them, carts creak under plunder: gold ingots, silver bars, emerald rosaries, jewelled goblets, strange trinkets from lands the boy has never imagined. A gasp ripples through the crowd as a king's ransom spills onto English soil. Peddlers thread the press with trays of hot pies and hazelnuts, the greasy savour of mutton and onion fighting with tar, river-reek, and the sharp tang of spilled ale from an overturned jack.

At the river's edge, beneath a canopy guarded by halberdiers, stands Queen Elizabeth in regal splendour—white gown and jewels flashing even in the dim light, her presence brighter than the overcast sky. Will stares, wide-eyed, at the sight of majesty personified.

Then Francis Drake himself strides forward, sun-bronzed and battle-worn, his eyes still restless as if scanning horizons no one else could see. He kneels before his queen, laying open a chest whose contents glitter like fire.

"Your Majesty," he says, voice firm, "a token from your loyal Sea Dogs, who sailed in your name and for your glory."

Elizabeth smiles, her words pitched for all to hear.

"Captain Drake, you have made your queen and country rich not only in treasure, but in pride. Let Spain tremble, for England's Sea Dogs rule the seas!"

A roar bursts from the crowd, answered by the thunder of cannon from the river. Will's father spits in the mud and mutters, "A commoner honoured for harrying the Spaniard round the world. Mark this, Will. It tells you what

England honours now—not princes, not papal bulls, but men who dare strike Spain at sea."

But Will hardly hears. His gaze is fixed on the ship itself, its patched sails like battle scars, its timbers creaking with a tale too vast for him to grasp. Something stirs deep within him—not a longing for coopering or trade, but for sails, for rigging, for salt spray and the thunder of guns.

Around them, the gossip swirls: Spanish treasure plundered, Philip's rage across the water, Elizabeth possibly making a pirate into a Knight of the Realm. His mother, clutching Will's younger sister, murmurs that England will pay dearly for mocking Spain. She presses a heel of yesterday's manchet into the girl's hand, more to keep her quiet than to fill her, while Will's father swigs once from a leather costrel of small beer and wipes his mouth with the back of his hand. His father only answers, "Better we strike first than wait for Philip's galleons to come here."

Will looks at the *Hind's* battered hull. He cannot yet know the trumpet-blast of war that lay ahead, only that the roar around him made Spain feel nearer than the plague-cross on a neighbour's door. But already the world of plague-crossed doors and whispered plots gives way to something larger: an England that would live—or die—upon the sea.

In the evening, torches line the deck of the *Golden Hind*. The moon hangs low above the Thames, and a hush settles as Queen Elizabeth ascends the gangplank. Nobles, diplomats, and sailors line the rails as she steps onto the quarterdeck, clad in white and gold, her crown catching the torchlight.

At her gesture, Drake kneels again.

Elizabeth's voice carries clean over the water. "Francis Drake—your voyages have served England and stung her enemies. For these deeds, I grant you honour."

She does not take the sword.

"Monsieur de Marchaumont," she says—a French envoy steps forward at her bidding. A gentleman-usher presents the ceremonial blade to him. At the Queen's slight nod, Marchaumont touches the flat to Drake's right shoulder, then left—light, exact, nothing showy.

Everyone beneath the canopy understands the arithmetic: his hand, her will.

Elizabeth gives the words that make it law. "Rise, Sir Francis Drake."

Drake rises. The sailors roar. Courtiers trade measured smiles. And somewhere downriver, Spain will be told what it wants to hear—that the

Queen kept her hand from the steel—while everyone who matters knows exactly whose knighthood this is.

He places a hand to his chest.

"Your Majesty, this honour is greater than any I dared dream of. I accept it as your servant, and as your sword upon the sea."

Elizabeth's eyes glint with mischief and resolve. "Sir Francis, I suspect you will not rest until every Spanish treasure ship fears your sails."

Another cheer thunders across the deck. Wine is poured. Goblets clink. Casks of claret and Canary are broached for the great folk, while the mariners below make do with black jackfuls of ale and a greasy feast of salt beef, hard biscuit, and a rare treat—spiced pasties sent aboard from the royal kitchens. The Sea Dogs laugh and sing as musicians play a lively tune. And yet, amid the jubilation, the Queen's gaze is fixed not on the celebration—but on the horizon beyond the river.

Beyond Deptford's lights, the river bends towards the open sea, dark and unappeased. Elizabeth follows that line with her eyes, already measuring distance and risk. Tonight crowns a man; tomorrow commits a realm. The tide turns, and England turns with it.

***

Later, in the quiet of Drake's cabin, both he and the Queen sit at a table. She removes her crown. The room, lit by a single lamp, flickers with shadow.

"There is more," she says, voice soft and urgent. "You have missed much while abroad."

She produces a letter and sets it before him.

Drake frowns as he reads. His expression darkens.

"Philip has taken Portugal," Elizabeth says plainly. "Its ports, its navy, its riches. Lisbon belongs to Spain now. He controls the entire Atlantic coast."

Drake's expression turns to stone. "Then he can strike from there—move faster, send his fleets north unchecked."

"Exactly," the Queen replies. "Spain's power has expanded across Europe at a relentless pace. We must act before it reaches our shores."

His hands grip the edge, trembling with the effort not to shout. "Let him try. Let him send his Armada. We'll meet him in the Channel—or before."

"That is why you were knighted—not just for what you have done, but for what comes next."

Drake nods, his voice quiet. "The sea is his pride, Your Majesty. But it is our shield—and my battleground."

She meets his gaze. "Then let it be so, Sir Francis. Let Spain come. Let England be ready."

Outside, the revels carry on. But in that cabin, strategy replaces celebration. Elizabeth knew it with the kind of clarity that turns sleep to ash, and she would need this man again—and soon.

10 April 1581

London had not seen such fever in years. Since the Queen had ordered a sword to be laid on Francis Drake's shoulder aboard the *Golden Hind* at Deptford, the city seethed with ballads, bonfires, and fresh-pulled broadsides proclaiming him England's lion. Children played at "Drake and Spaniards" in muddy alleys, one boy always doomed to fall with theatrical groans. Taverns rang with his name, tankards raised until the ale ran thin and the boasting thickened. Hucksters sold crude woodcuts of the *Hind* with a red cross snapped like a whip above her mast, and apprentices pinned them to alehouse doors as if they were saints' images. Even the river seemed infected—wherries jostling for a glimpse of the ship's berth, oars dipping like conspirators' hands.

But where the people roared in delight, Spain fumed in silence. Bernardino de Mendoza felt each cheer in the streets like a stone flung at his dignity. For five days his quill had not rested, scratching dispatch after dispatch to King Philip—each sharper than the last—denouncing Elizabeth's audacity in honouring a pirate and daring Spain to answer it. He demanded audience, restitution, rebuke. At last, Whitehall opened its doors.

Not all the way.

The antechamber outside the Presence Chamber smells of beeswax and damp wool. Courtiers drift in loose knots, voices low, careful. Business moves here by glance and whisper rather than proclamation. Somewhere beyond the arras, a door opens and closes again. The room adjusts.

Francis Drake stands near a tall window, one hand resting on the pommel of his sword—not in threat, but habit. The knighthood has not yet worn smooth. Men look, then look away. This new honour still draws heat.

Across the chamber, Bernardino de Mendoza enters in black silk, chain of office heavy on his breast. He pauses at the threshold, takes in the room, and then—deliberately—his gaze fixes on Drake.

They have been placed to see one another. Not accident, exactly. No herald cries their names.

Mendoza inclines his head a fraction. Courtesy, stretched thin as wire.

"Sir Francis," he says, in careful English. "England honours her thieves quickly."

Drake does not move from the window. "Spain names men thieves when it cannot catch them," he replies mildly. "We call that envy at sea."

A couple of courtiers shift, pretending sudden interest in the tapestries.

Mendoza steps closer. "You wear honour stolen from Spanish blood."

Drake turns then, slow. "And you wear chains paid for by it."

The air tightens. Words like these, left standing, would grow teeth.

"Gentlemen."

Sir Francis Walsingham is suddenly between them—not hurried, not raised. He does not look at Drake. He does not look at Mendoza. He looks past them, as if the space itself has offended him.

"This passage is not licensed for debate," he says quietly. "Nor for misunderstanding."

"I speak for my king," Mendoza says, mouth thin.

"And I speak for the Queen," Walsingham replies. "Which is why this ends here."

William Cecil has appeared at Walsingham's shoulder, solid as stonework. His eyes meet Drake's—not warning, exactly, but inventory.

"Sir Francis," Cecil says, "you are expected elsewhere."

Drake inclines his head once—to Cecil. Not to Mendoza.

"As am I," Mendoza says stiffly.

"Indeed," Cecil answers. "In a different room."

The paths diverge. The moment dissolves. Conversation resumes as if it had never stopped—but the chamber remembers.

As Drake turns away, Walsingham murmurs, just for him, "Do not mistake applause for immunity."

Drake does not answer.

***

That evening, Elizabeth stands at a window in her privy gallery, the Thames dark below, the city's lights smeared by mist. Cecil waits with folded papers. Walsingham stands a pace back, hands loose.

"So," Elizabeth says without turning, "my lion showed his teeth."

"Barely," Walsingham replies. "Enough to be seen. Not enough to bite."

"And Mendoza?"

"Angered," Cecil says. "Which is his natural state."

Elizabeth hums, thoughtful. "Good. Anger makes men careless."

Walsingham shifts. "There is another matter, madam. The godly sort are muttering."

She turns. "Already?"

"They always mutter," he says. "Now they quote."

Elizabeth's brow lifts. "From whom?"

"Fletcher," Walsingham answers. "The chaplain from the *Golden Hind*. He says God preserved the ship to warn, not to bless."

Cecil exhales. "If pulpits take it up—"

"They will," Walsingham says. "Unless given something else to chew."

For a moment, Elizabeth is silent. Below, an oar creaks in its rowlock and a lantern winks out on the river, swallowed by fog. "Warnings," she says at last, softly. "Men are always fond of them—provided someone else heeds them. Let the godly weigh their souls. I will weigh my ships." She glances to Cecil. "There are sermons enough in timber and sailcloth, if one knows how to read them."

Elizabeth considers this, fingers tapping stone. "Spain howls abroad. Godliness frets at home. And in between stands Sir Francis—polished, dangerous."

She smiles—not kindly, not cruelly.

"Very well," she says. "Let Spain call us pirates. Let preachers scold. I will answer neither—yet."

She turns back to the river. "Drake will be useful again. And when he is not, silence will be."

Cecil bows. Walsingham inclines his head.

Outside, London sings his name. Inside, the Queen decides how much of that song England can afford to keep singing.

***

Whitehall's Chapel Royal vestry lies half in shadow, its door left ajar to air the smell of damp wool and snuffed candles. Beyond the thin wall, Whitehall goes on—pages calling, courtiers dispersing, the soft tide of a court resuming after the Queen's withdrawal.

Francis Fletcher stands at the narrow table, both hands braced against it. The psalter before him lies open where he left it in haste, still marked by the ribbon he pressed between the leaves when the Presence Chamber empties.

He can still hear his own words there—quiet, meant for no one in particular, offered as a clerical aside once Her Majesty rises and the formal air thins:

God does not crown every taking with His favour, even when it fills a treasury.

He speaks them in English, then repeats them in Latin without thinking—*non omne lucrum benedictum est*—as Mendoza passes within earshot. Not an accusation. Not a sermon. But enough.

The door shifts.

Fletcher does not turn at once. He knows the tread—measured, unhurried, the step of a man used to being obeyed at sea and indulged on land.

"Parson," Drake says.

Fletcher closes the psalter carefully before facing him. "Captain."

They regard one another across the small room. No crowd now. No diplomatic ears. Only stone and candle smoke.

"You choose your moment in the Presence Chamber," Drake says mildly. "After the Queen is gone. While men are still listening."

Fletcher draws a breath. "I speak as a minister of God."

"You speak," Drake replies, "where Spanish ears might mistake piety for policy."

Drake steps closer—not crowding, merely narrowing the space. The rushlight catches the scars along his jaw and lines set deep by sun and storm.

"You think I do not know what is taken?" Drake goes on. "What it costs? Do you think I sail half the world ignorant of judgement? If God wishes me stopped, Parson, He has oceans enough to do it."

"Not all reckonings come with thunder," Fletcher says, steadying himself. "Some come slow. Quiet. They wait until the cheering dies."

For a moment Drake studies him as one might examine a flaw in a spar—annoying, not yet dangerous.

"You are useful," Drake says at last. "You keep order when fear creeps in. You give the men a language when there is nothing else to hold. But usefulness is not command. And conscience—mine or yours—is not a rope you get to pull in public."

"If I am silent," Fletcher says, "I am false."

"If you are loud," Drake answers, "you are reckless."

Their eyes hold. Memory passes between them: hymns sung into wind, men clinging to faith because it is lighter than despair.

Drake breaks it first. "Pray as you must," he says, turning away. "But do it as a priest, not a judge. England has no patience for prophets who snarl at her victories."

At the door he pauses, just long enough to add, "And I have even less."

He is gone.

Fletcher sinks onto the bench once the echoes fade, the vestry suddenly too large, too empty. He bows his head, not in fear of Drake's anger—that he can bear—but in dread of what words do once loosed among courtiers.

He prays not for himself.

He prays for the soul of the man England has decided to call her lion—and for the country that has learned to mistake gain for grace.

14 April 1581

In the Presence Chamber at Whitehall, the Queen shines like a jewel in her high-backed chair of estate, pearls coiled in her hair, cloth of gold spilling over the dais. Courtiers, a small circle only—trusted faces and bought discretion—press close as Monsieur Jean de Simier, envoy of the Duke of Anjou, bows before her, hand pressed fervently to his breast.

"Your Majesty," he begins, his eyes bright with ardour. "Your frog, my master, burns with a flame no tempest nor eternity itself may quench. His love is immortal—lasting in the next world as in this."

Elizabeth leans back, dimples threatening. "My frog is a passionate creature. What of my monkey?"

"Ah!" Simier throws his arms open wide. "Your humble monkey kisses the very shadow of your footsteps. A fool, yes—but a fool blessed beyond measure to bow to magnificence."

A rustle stirs the council bench. Walsingham's lips thin.

"Flatterer," he whispers.

Cecil scratches so hard at his notebook that the parchment shudders. Dudley's glare is a sword drawn from the scabbard.

Then, shrill as a trumpet:

"Kisses the shadow! Kisses the shadow!"

The green parrot bobs furiously in its gilded cage. "Monkey! Monkey! Kisses the shadow!"

Half the court stifles laughter. Elizabeth claps her hands. "Monsieur Monkey, my bird steals your lines!"

Before the mirth can fade, another figure prances forward—a woman in motley, bells jingling, cap askew. Jane Foole somersaults across the rush-strewn floor, rolls to her feet, and wags a crooked finger at Simier. A sugared almond flies from her pocket, skittering across the boards as she rolls; she snatches it back up and pops it into her mouth mid-bow, bells chiming as she chews.

"Beware, Monkey!" she cries in a singsong. "The Frog'll swallow you whole, and the Queen'll roast him with garlic!" She flops dramatically on the floor, legs twitching like a gutted fish.

Laughter breaks again, though Cecil groans and covers his face. Elizabeth laughs so hard her fan slips from her hand.

"Jane, you wear that cap as if old Will Sommers himself handed it to you."

Jane bows, bells chiming, and picks up the fan and hands it back to the Queen.

"He left to me little else, Your Majesty."

Simier, undaunted, draws forth a folded parchment. Dropping to one knee, he cries, "Majesty, allow your monkey to be the mouth of your frog."

He reads aloud in rich, rolling tones:

"*Most divine Majesty, most peerless lady of Albion, each hour apart from your radiance is a wound without balm. My soul is captive to your eyes, my heart bound in your chains. If you deny me, I am undone; if you grant me, I live anew.*"

The parrot screeches, "Captive! Captive! Heart bound! Heart bound!"

Jane Foole topples over onto her back, legs bicycling in the air. "Undone! Undone! The frog is undone—boiled in butter!"

The Queen roars with laughter. Dudley mutters a curse under his breath.

Simier reads on, his voice swelling:

"Lose no more time, most sovereign of queens. Let me soon approach your charms. I live only for you. Your dearest François."

The green parrot still bobs: "Lose no time! Lose no time!"

"Lose no time!" echoes Jane Foole, plucking Cecil's cap off his head and plopping it onto Walsingham's head. The chamber dissolves into helpless laughter. Cecil even snickers a little seeing his hat on Walsingham, who, not amused, returns it to him.

Elizabeth, tears of mirth sparkling, extends her hand. Simier presses his lips to it.

"Monkey! Monkey! Kisses the shadow!" shrieks the parrot. Jane Foole flops to her knees, imitating Simier's posture, planting a loud smacking kiss on Elizabeth's shoe.

The Queen laughs so hard the Presence Chamber shakes with it—but beneath the laughter, tension coils tight as wire.

***

Later that evening in the Privy Council chamber, the mirth is gone. The firelight flickers over Cecil, Walsingham, and Dudley, who face their Queen in silence. The parrot dozes, feathers ruffled. Jane Foole crouches in a corner, whispering to her dolls.

Cecil begins. "Majesty, the Duke's suit is a trap. France offers chains disguised as garlands."

Walsingham's voice is iron. "And Simier—he flatters like a mountebank. I fear his tongue is sorcery."

Elizabeth turns, eyes blazing. "Think you me a child? That I cannot tell a chain from a garland? That a monkey's grimace sways my crown?"

Dudley, bolder: "Then why endure him, Your Majesty? Why let him strut and prattle while your court laughs at your parrot and fool? He steals your court, and mocks your council."

Elizabeth's face sharpens. "Because, my lord, while the monkey capers, Spain frets. While the frog croaks, Philip wonders if I will clasp France to my bed. And so he holds his sword. That is why."

Her words fall like iron on the floor. Silence follows.

Then Jane Foole springs up, bells jangling, waving her doll. "A frog in the bed, a monkey at the foot, a parrot on the pillow! What husband dares snore in that bed?"

The Queen laughs, sudden and bright, but her councillors do not.

Jane leans close, her voice lowering to an uncanny sing-song:

"Marry not the frog, nor wed the monkey,
Or England'll croak, and the crown look wonky.
Wed your realm, my Queen, wed your realm alone.
A husband may fail you—but the kingdom is your own."

The room chills. Walsingham crosses himself. Cecil's pen stills. Even Dudley's anger dims.

Elizabeth's smile softens, strange and distant. She looks at her fool as if hearing profound wisdom under the motley.

The parrot stirs in its sleep. "Lose no time...shadows...shadows..."

Elizabeth turns back to her men, her voice low, dangerous. "Lose no time, indeed. But it is I who choose the hour. Not the frog. Not the monkey. Not even you, my wise men."

Jane Foole, hugging her doll, rocks and whispers: "The Queen's hour, the Queen's hour...till the sun goes down."

Elizabeth takes Anjou's letter, holds it to her heart, and gazes into the fire. She laughs last—but with a shadow behind her smile.

Chapter 27
England Will Answer to Philip

18 May 1581

The air in Philip's council chamber swims with incense and foreboding, each breath steeped in unease. At the head of the long table, the King sits in a high-backed chair carved with the arms of Castile. His hands tremble—not from age, but from fury—as he scans the latest English dispatch laid before him. He reads the dispatch once. Then again.

Without raising his voice, Philip folds the parchment with exacting care and tears it cleanly in half. He drops the pieces to the table. The sound is small—yet it cuts the room to the bone.

"She knighted him—that pirate, Drake. I expected the gallows. Instead, Elizabeth places a sword on his shoulder and calls him 'Sir'?"

Courtiers flinch. A few lower their eyes. None dare speak.

Juan de Idiáquez approaches with the calm of a seasoned courtier, though tension coils in his shoulders like a spring wound too tight.

He had seen the King perform in anger before; this was not loss of control, but selection.

"It is a calculated insult, Majesty," he says. "Not just to your crown, but to all of Spain."

Philip turns abruptly, the heavy robes of state rustling as he moves once along the table's edge.

"Drake is a thief. A heretic of hell. A butcher of God's men. He burned my settlements in the Indies, struck at Nombre de Dios—then tore silver from the Camino Real, defiled my flag—and she dares honour him before the world?"

He turns on Idiáquez, eyes cold and glittering.

"Do you know what message this sends, Don Juan? The message that England may despoil us, and their pirates go unpunished. They are rewarded for it! Are we Spain, or are we nothing?"

Idiáquez bows his head slightly. "We must respond, Majesty, but with care. If we act rashly—"

The King interrupts, voice rising. "I have shown enough patience to saints and devils alike. Elizabeth cloaks herself in diplomacy, but it is the cloak of a temptress playing at power. Behind it, she sends wolves to tear at the flesh of my empire."

He stops, chest heaving. "And now she mocks us. The whole of Europe will see this and whisper: 'Philip of Spain was humbled by a common corsair, while a Tudor Virgin Queen hands out knighthoods like sweetmeats at court.'"

Father Diego de Chaves steps forward from the shadows, rosary beads clinking in his hand. "Perhaps this is a trial of faith, Sire. A crucible sent by God—"

Philip's gaze pins him in place. "Then God shall find me faithful. For I will not sit idle while heretics and pirates sail under banners of mockery. I will answer Drake's knighthood with fire."

He turns back to Idiáquez, voice dropping to a glacial calm.

"Find him. Wherever he hides—Africa, the Indies, the edge of the world—I want Drake hunted like a dog. Burn his ships. Hang his men. Let the oceans remember his name only as a curse."

He draws one measured breath, and the blaze in him banks into something colder—purpose.

Idiáquez bows. "We will see it done, Majesty. And...what of the English Queen?"

Philip snatches the torn halves back from the table, moves to the hearth, and holds them over the flame. The parchment curls, blackens, then vanishes in smoke.

"She toys with lions," he murmurs. "Let her keep her golden corset of power a little longer. We will wait—until her armour cracks, her fleet falters. Then we strike. We will strike with all the fury of Spain."

The courtiers are silent as Philip steps to the tall window. Beyond the glass, torches flicker against the night. His reflection, framed by firelight, is grim and unyielding.

"Let her bask in her hollow victories," he whispers, voice like flint on steel.

Then, slowly, he turns—eyes dark, resolute.

"But we shall pen the final chapter...and England will answer me at sea."

Somewhere beyond the walls, bells toll for Compline, slow and solemn. Philip listens, then crosses himself—not in doubt, but in vow.

10 August 1581

Heat clings to oak in Whitehall though the windows stand open to a Thames that smells of rope and low tide. Parchment lies on the green cloth—fresh copies of the States' instrument, already in circulation, renouncing Philip—translated into English, seals gritty with sand. The copies were sent ahead by fast packet; the formal seal follows.

Elizabeth sits at the head. Cecil is ledger-quiet at her right. Walsingham stands, lean and exact. Dudley paces near the hearth as if the floor has a current.

Two Dutch envoys wait with their hats in their hands—Heer Johan van Oldenbarnevelt, grave and watchful, and Heer Philips van Marnix, eyes alight with a tired zeal.

Walsingham reads the covering note aloud, spare as a docket. "From the States-General, confirming their renunciation of Philip and their appeal for succour. They add that Monsieur advances their cause"—he glances up—"and asks that Your Majesty countenance the same."

Elizabeth takes the vellum, skims, and lets it fall flat. "So. They throw off Spain in July and are here in August to borrow England."

Van Oldenbarnevelt steps forward. "Majesty, without a protector, our liberty dies. Parma presses. Towns waver. If England will not be sovereign"—he bows slightly—"let England at least be a shield."

Dudley turns from the hearth. "Shield, or purse?"

"Both," Marnix says, blunt. "Money for pay, powder for courage, and leave for English gentlemen to serve openly, not as shadows."

Cecil folds his hands. "You court France as well."

"We do," Oldenbarnevelt answers. "Monsieur keeps Philip from breathing easy. With your goodwill, he keeps him from breathing at all."

Dudley's mouth tightens. "Your French prince keeps himself."

Elizabeth lifts a palm. Dudley stills. She looks to Walsingham. "How loud can we be without being heard?"

"Loud enough in Middelburg, quiet enough in Spain," he says. "A loan through the merchants, powder through Flushing, and letters of marque that say nothing new while encouraging everything old. Volunteers—carefully—under captains who know how to salute and how to vanish."

Marnix leans in. "Names?"

"Men who do not need their names in pamphlets," Walsingham says. "You will know them by their discipline."

Elizabeth studies the Dutchmen. "You offer me France as a partner to your freedom and ask me to bless it. If I bless it too loudly, I buy a war I do not yet want. If I refuse, I let Philip grow fat on your bones."

Oldenbarnevelt does not blink. "Then bless it at the volume you choose. Only do not turn your face away."

Dudley cannot help himself. "Majesty, if the Netherlands fall, the Channel shortens."

"And if I march an army into Brabant," Elizabeth snaps back, "England empties."

Silence takes the table. Even the river outside seems to wait.

Cecil breaks it gently. "There is a middle: we acknowledge their act, we approve the French motion in principle, and we pay in coin, not in crowns."

Elizabeth's thumb finds the coronation ring. The gold is cool. "You ask for my name, Heer Marnix. Names are banners. Banners start trumpets. I prefer locks and tides."

Marnix meets her head-on. "Then give us the tide."

She lets out the smallest breath, the kind that moves kingdoms and not a feather. "You shall have the tide."

Oldenbarnevelt's shoulders ease a fraction; only then does he remember the beaker of Rhenish wine at his place, and take a single, careful sip as though to seal the promise on his tongue.

She turns to Walsingham. "A loan—renewable, deniable, routed through merchants—through the Merchant Adventurers' Low Countries channels, not the Exchequer ledger. Powder and match to Walcheren next month. Licences that let our Sea Dogs forget which flags they chase when Spanish silver swims by."

Walsingham inclines his head. "Mendoza will hear wind and see fog."

"To Marchaumont," she adds, "a note that says: *England does not stand in the door, but does not close it.* He may read between the lines and tell Monsieur to mind his."

Dudley clears his throat. "And soldiers?"

"Gentlemen may travel, as they have always done, with curious minds and light purses that somehow grow heavy in Holland," she says. "If they return with fewer teeth and more scars, I will scold them in public and thank them in private."

Oldenbarnevelt bows from the waist, relief and worry sharing the same breath. "Majesty, it is enough to keep a light alive."

"Then keep it," she says. "And keep your towns. Do not ask me to bleed for a cause that will not bleed for itself."

Marnix's mouth almost smiles. "We bleed."

"I know," Elizabeth says, softer, and it lands like truth.

She rises, and the men rise with her. "Tell your States this: England stands—cautiously. We fight with silver, sea-wind, and silence. If Spain prefers noise, I can be taught."

Dudley watches her face and finds no weakness. Walsingham already makes lists in his head. Cecil, being the treasurer he is, counts the coins twice.

The Dutch envoys back towards the door, gratitude careful on their tongues. When they go, the room exhales.

Elizabeth turns to the window, to the slow, iron water. "Gentlemen," she says, low, "one misstep and the fire jumps the Channel."

Dudley answers first. "Then we do not misstep."

Walsingham closes the dispatch case. "We misdirect."

Cecil nods. "And we pay as if every angel has two faces."

Elizabeth touches the ring once more, as if reminding it and herself. "So be it. Let Philip hear a murmur where there is a drum. Let France hear a drum where there is a murmur. And let Holland hear only this: the Queen across the water is awake. For every courtship I suffer, I buy one more season before Philip dares to strike."

23 October 1581

A pale hush fills the Privy Closet at Whitehall. A gentle tap of heels echoes on the stone as trusted court gentlewoman Anne Denny enters, curtsying softly. Elizabeth does not face her. She stands at the window, her back straight, one hand pressed to the cold glass. Her shoulders are stiff, her gown plain, absent its usual embroidery—as if even majesty itself feels too heavy today.

She speaks without turning.

"Come in, Anne. I don't want reverence today. My crown is outside the door. I need a woman's friendly ear. Not a courtier's silence."

Anne hesitates, her hands folded before her. She knows even here a woman might stand behind a screen and hear only what the Queen allowed.

"Yes, Your Majesty?"

Elizabeth turns slowly. Her face is composed, but only just—beneath the surface lies something storming. Her eyes are rimmed with sleeplessness, but not from restlessness of body—rather, from the heart.

"I have spoken to all the men," she says softly. "Cecil, with his reason and endless parchment. Walsingham, whose answers come wrapped in riddles and shadows. And Ro...the Earl of Leicester." She trails off.

Anne steps closer. "My lady?"

Elizabeth exhales, sharp and quiet.

"He looks at me with eyes that still think I am his to save. Or his to keep. But I am not a promise he can keep alive."

She turns towards the hearth, watching the last cinders curl in the grate. Her voice drops to near confession.

"They all think they know what is best for me—what is best for England. They speak of strategy, of alliances, of duty...but not one of them has ever stood where I stand now. Not one."

Elizabeth paces a few steps, then stops, her voice softening.

"They forget I am still a woman. I have built my life like a fortress, brick by brick, oath by oath. I have worn my crown like armour, held my heart behind battlements so high even I could not reach it."

She turns, her voice catching just slightly.

"And now—this—whatever this is...it feels like standing on a cliff with the wind in my hair. For the first time, I feel the air on my skin, and I don't know whether to breathe it in or run for cover."

She looks away, almost ashamed.

"I don't even know if I can live outside the armour I forged for myself. But God help me—I want to try."

Anne says nothing. She waits.

Elizabeth looks back. "You have loved, have you not? Not out of duty. But truly."

A pause. Anne nods slowly. "Once, yes."

"Then help me name it," Elizabeth says. Her voice breaks just a little on the last word.

She walks to a small table, her thumb tracing its edge absently.

"I used to think love would be like my father's temper—loud, absolute, something you obey whether you want to or not. Something that just...takes over. I thought that is what love was supposed to be." She pauses, her voice softening. "But now? I feel like some foolish girl at a masque. Giddy one moment, terrified the next. I do not know what I am doing, Anne. I feel like I am losing my footing—and I do not know if I want to catch myself."

Anne dares a step closer. Her voice is low. "You mean the Duke of Anjou."

Elizabeth lowers her eyes. She does not speak at first. Then:

"I do not know what this is. This ache. This...pull. Is it love? Or is it simply the idea of love?" Her voice drops. "It makes me feel alive. And I hate that I want to keep it."

She paces slowly, hands clenched.

"My sister Mary—she mistook a crown for a heart. She loved Philip like a girl loves a fairytale. And he turned her into a shadow. She wasted away waiting for him to need her." She stops. "I cannot be another Mary, can I?"

Anne's voice is almost a whisper. "No, Majesty."

Elizabeth turns sharply.

"Then what am I, Anne? A queen? A woman? Can I be both? Do I dare?"

Silence thickens.

Then, with sudden resolution, Elizabeth raises her chin.

"I will see him. In secret. This evening."

A flicker of sympathy warms Anne's eyes. "Majesty—if it wounds you—"

Elizabeth's voice hardens.

"Then let it. Better the sting of truth than the rot of wondering 'what if.'"

She moves back to the window. Outside, a blackbird flits across the garden wall. Guards change posts in the shadows. Life continues.

"God reward you, Anne."

"Your Majesty, if you ever need a listening ear...I will be here."

Elizabeth nods, her gaze still fixed on the distant garden. "Thank you."

And in that silence, Anne leaves, the weight of unspoken words lingering between them like the echo of a bell.

***

The crescent moon hangs low over the Thames, cloaking Whitehall's garden in a hush of ghost-silver. Leaves whisper in the breeze like silk brush on velvet. Somewhere deep in the trees, a nightingale dares a song—a single, fragile note in a world too heavy with consequence.

Walsingham's men had already turned the corridor into a throat—doors watched, servants dismissed, footsteps counted.

A narrow side door opens by the Queen's privy garden—so plain it might pass for a servant's gate. A shadow slips through. No escort. No trumpets. Just the faint glint of a jet-black ring catching firelight.

The Duke of Anjou moves like a trespasser in a dream. His cloak is damp with mist, his breath fogging in the chill. Each step down the silent corridor is a heartbeat, a trespass, a prayer.

She is already there.

Elizabeth stands at the far end of the gallery, still as stone, the stained-glass candlelight scattering across her gown. Her posture is regal, but her hands betray her—they are clenched at her sides, fingers twitching as if struggling to hold something in.

She sees him—and breath leaves her like a wave breaking. *Dearest.*

"François..." she breathes. Not a summons. A confession.

He pulls back his hood. His eyes are rimmed in exhaustion, but soft with longing. He does not bow. Does not speak.

She steps forward, then stops. "You came."

"You called," he answers, voice low, rough-edged from the road or restraint.

"They do not like you, my Privy Council. I almost told them I would not see you again," she murmurs, her voice catching. "And yet here you are. I must be mad."

He steps closer, slowly, as if she might vanish. Then he reaches for her hand and presses a jet-black token-ring into her palm—gently, reverently.

"Then let us be mad together," he says. "Just for this hour."

Her fingers curl around the ring. Her eyes flicker to his face. "This...what is it? A charm? A warning?"

"A vow and a promise," he says. "One that does not beg tomorrow to understand tonight, my rose."

She laughs—soft and bitter. "You speak like a poet."

"Only when I am near you."

She tries to look away, but her gaze is drawn back. She drinks him in—his presence, his scent of leather and rain, the hint of defiance beneath his tenderness.

"My Privy Council is sharpening daggers," she says. "They have seen how I look at you. I can barely breathe in their presence."

"You breathe just fine with me."

"I do," she says, voice trembling. "And that is what terrifies me."

She advances, close enough to see the rise and fall of his chest. "My sister Mary...she loved Philip. Or what she thought he was. She gave him everything and died broken, clinging to a dream. I cannot be her."

"You are not," he whispers. "You never were."

Her hand, still clutching the ring, lifts to his chest. He covers it with his own.

"I am not a queen when I am with you," she says.

"You are," he replies. "But more than that. You are a woman. And you are alive."

Her lips tremble. "If I kiss you again..."

"Then kiss me," he says. "And let the rest of the world burn."

She surges forward—not like royalty, but like a woman drowning and reaching for the shore. Their lips meet—urgent and trembling, burdened with truths neither has ever spoken. Her hands tangle in the fabric of his cloak. His arms enfold her like a haven.

It is not a kiss of state. It is a cry from the soul.

When they part, it is breathless—painful. As if to separate is to tear sinew from bone.

"François," she whispers, forehead against his. "If I lose you..."

"You will not, my rose," he says, cradling her face. "But even if you do, you will still be whole."

She almost smiles.

Outside, time ticks onward. But inside these walls—within the hush of candlelight and the ghosts of roses—there is only now.

And that is everything.

24 October 1581

In a shadowed alcove just outside the vaulted Grand Hall of Westminster Palace, Cecil and Walsingham stand in low conversation, their voices hushed but edged with conviction.

"William, I have misgivings about this. You cannot seriously believe it wise," Walsingham murmurs. "This Duke of Anjou is a libertine, a papist, and a Valois besides. His brother ordered the slaughter on Saint Bartholomew's Day—our Huguenot brethren butchered without warning. The Protestant world has not forgotten. Nor should we."

Cecil folds his arms, eyes fixed on the mullioned windows.

"Even so, we must consider what isolation will cost us," he says. "Spain grows bolder by the hour. With Portugal now swallowed, Philip commands the whole Atlantic coast. We cannot afford to stand alone."

He turns slightly towards Walsingham.

"Anjou is not Philip. He leans towards the Dutch rebels. That alone alters the balance in Europe."

Walsingham's jaw tightens. "But he is not one of us either. France wields a smiling knife. This marriage—God save her—would bind Elizabeth to their whims."

Cecil's voice softens, thoughtful rather than yielding. "I trust not France, Francis. I trust necessity. And necessity dictates allies."

Walsingham exhales through his nose, gaze distant. "Or it dictates a snare."

Before he can say more, the great doors open, drawing them towards the hall beyond.

The Grand Hall of Westminster glows with sobered splendour. Shadows tremble along the stone vaults; whispers drift like ghosts above the scratch of quills. At the centre, a long oak table stretches like the spine of the realm. Upon it lie illuminated scrolls, quills, and seals.

Queen Elizabeth sits at the head, poised as if carved from gold itself. Her gold-threaded gown catches the candlelight; the jewelled ring on her finger glints whenever she shifts. She seems serene, but Cecil—who reads her like scripture—sees the tautness beneath.

To her right, Cecil stands rigid, the morning's argument lingering in his eyes. Behind him, Walsingham watches the French commissioners with the hollow stare of a man measuring threats.

Monsieur Michel de Castelnau stands opposite, dignified, hands clasped behind him. Beside him, two envoys from Anjou hold fresh quills, awaiting Elizabeth's mark on the parchment before them:

"*Articles for the Further Advancement of the Marriage Negotiation.*"

Not a treaty. Not a contract. A gesture—and a dangerous one.

Elizabeth's gaze drifts to the scroll. Her breathing slows. Inside her chest, something twists: the knowledge that even this small stroke of ink may send ripples of consequence across Europe.

She lifts the quill.

Her hand trembles once before hardening. She signs—gracefully, deliberately—the draft articles that promise continued negotiation, nothing more. A flourish seals it, though her wrist falters at the final curve.

Castelnau inclines his head, satisfaction carefully masked. The envoys exchange murmurs in French—measured, pleased, hopeful.

Elizabeth places the quill down as though relinquishing a blade. Then she rises.

"You may tell His Highness," she says, voice bright and cold, "that I have set my name to these articles. But let him know also—my loyalty is to England alone. This gesture is for the stability of my realm, not for any foreign desire."

A ripple passes through the chamber. Castelnau bows, but the flicker in his eyes reveals how well he understands the Queen's meaning: she has granted a door, not a promise.

Walsingham steps forward, his voice low. "Majesty, I urge caution. France smiles today, but their appetite is long. And our Protestant allies—"

Elizabeth lifts her hand. "Enough, Walsingham. The ink is drying."

Then, turning to the French commissioners, her voice cuts like flint: "Let none mistake this for surrender. England yields nothing."

Formalities resume. Wax is melted. Seals are pressed. Clerks gather parchment with solemn care.

When the French delegation departs, Elizabeth remains with her council. She stands before the empty table, the scroll lying open like an unanswered question.

Walsingham approaches.

"This is no victory, Majesty," he says quietly. "It is a postponement."

Elizabeth does not meet his eyes. "Perhaps. But postponement is sometimes all that stands between ruin and survival."

Her fingers brush the edge of the parchment—so slight a touch, yet heavy as fate.

"It is done," she whispers.

And though she stands tall, crowned and resolute, she feels the invisible pressure tighten around her temples—the knowledge that every signature, every gesture, draws her closer to a choice she may not be able to unmake.

Somewhere beyond the Hall, bells begin to toll the hour, indifferent to crowns and ink. Elizabeth straightens beneath their sound, knowing that Europe has just been given something to wait for—and waiting, too, is a weapon.

15 November 1581

The chambers of Ribeira Palace in Lisbon lie in silence, cool stone swallowing every footfall. In his study, King Philip bends over a map of the Low Countries, tiny lead soldiers standing in neat formations. His quill hovers above a dispatch when the chamberlain hurries in, bowing, with his hand on his chest.

"Majesty...news from London."

Philip does not look up. "Speak."

The chamberlain hesitates, then hands over the parchment. Philip slits the seal with a thin blade, eyes narrowing as he reads.

"*Elizabeth of England has signed marriage articles with Francis, Duke of Anjou.*"

For a long moment, nothing stirs but the candle flame. Then Philip sets the letter down with meticulous care. His hand, pale and veined, rests upon it, fingers tapping once, twice, before stilling.

"So," he says softly. "The heretic queen courts the Valois frog."

Father Chaves says with unease, "A union of France and England, Sire. A union to hem in Spain on every shore."

At last Philip raises his cold blue eyes. "An intolerable danger," he says.

He turns back to the map. The Netherlands lie spread beneath his gaze, scarred with pins and notes of rebellion. Anjou had already courted the rebels. Now, as Elizabeth's husband, he might claim them with English support.

Philip's hand closes slowly over one of the lead soldiers. He presses until the figure bends, snaps, and falls in two.

"France and England," he murmurs. "A Protestant queen with a Catholic prince—so they say. But the Valois are not friends of Spain. With her crown, he may set the Netherlands aflame."

He looks up sharply. "Mendoza."

At once a secretary hurries forward.

"Tell my ambassador in London he is to protest this match in the strongest terms. He must remind the Queen that a Valois consort on her throne is an affront to Spain, to Christendom, to the peace of Europe. And he must...watch." Philip's voice lowers. "There are those at her court who despise this match—Leicester, Walsingham, even Cecil. Mendoza is to fan their fears, sow discord, break her resolve."

He stands, straightening his dark robes, and walks to the crucifix on the wall. He kneels, bowing his head.

"If the Queen of England will not bend to reason," he whispers, "then God's justice must be done."

Behind him, the lead soldier lies broken on the map, its head pointing towards England.

22 November 1581

The morning light filters through the tall windows of the Privy Gallery at Whitehall, pale and sharp as a blade. The Queen of England walks slowly between the leaded panes, her gown a blaze of gold and crimson damask. Beside her, the Duke of Anjou moves with a cautious, almost reverent gait, his delicate French boots making no sound against the marble floor.

At a distance, Robert Dudley, the Earl of Leicester, watches them both, posture tense, his arms folded not in ease but restraint.

"Hmmph," he says very quietly to himself.

Next to him, Walsingham remains impassive—except for the slight, deliberate way he winds the gloves tighter around his fingers.

Elizabeth's hands are clasped before her, her back straight, her chin high—but anyone who knows her well could see the tension in her shoulders, the way her lips press together when Anjou glances at her with soft eyes. She had worn a sovereign's face for so long that it rarely cracked. But now it threatens to crack.

The doors open, and Jean de Simier enters with a low bow.

"Your Majesty," he says with ceremonial formality. "I come with instructions from His Most Christian Majesty, Henri. He bids me ask—once and for all—your intention regarding his brother. Shall I write to him that this marriage shall go forward? Or nay?"

The gallery stills. Dudley shifts slightly. The only sound is the soft rasp of fabric. Walsingham does not move at all.

Elizabeth turns slowly to face Simier. Her eyes flick to Anjou, who stands now with anxious expectation, his pale hands clasped before him. The young duke says nothing, but his gaze searches her face as though trying to read a verdict written in glass.

Then she speaks—loudly, clearly, and without trembling.

"You may write this to the King: I am minded to take the Duke of Anjou to husband—if it serves England's peace, and mine."

A stunned silence follows, broken only by the rustle of her skirts as she steps towards the Duke. Colour drains from Dudley's face. Hands clasped behind him, he rocks once on his heels and forces his shoulders to stillness. Walsingham blinks once.

Then Elizabeth does the unthinkable.

She turns to Anjou and, with deliberate grace, kisses him full upon the mouth—a bold and unmistakable seal.

Gasps echo through the vaulted hall. Dudley's heart drops like an anchor.

As the ambassador's eyes widen and Anjou stands frozen in shocked delight, Elizabeth removes a ring from her own finger—an old piece, set with a ruby—and presses it into Anjou's palm.

"A pledge," she says quietly. "From my hand to yours."

The Duke exhales, his hand trembling slightly as he reaches into his doublet and withdraws a gold ring of his own. "And from mine to yours," he whispers, slipping it onto her finger.

The moment hangs there—tremulous, impossible, real.

Why must duty always demand her loneliness as its tithe? I will not wait forever.

Then Elizabeth turns, eyes flashing with something fierce—joy, defiance, or perhaps fear. She strides to the doors of the Presence Chamber and throws them wide open.

"Come!" she calls, her voice ringing like a trumpet. "Come all of you, and hear it plainly. The Duke of Anjou shall be my husband. Let it be known throughout the court—and the realm."

Courtiers pour into the gallery, stunned, whispering, bowing. Sir Christopher Hatton is in tears. A distraught lady-in-waiting mutters, "No, Majesty, no." Anjou stands straight and proud, chest lifted, the ring gleaming on Elizabeth's finger.

But behind them, Dudley does not bow. His eyes meet Walsingham's.

"She has done it," he mutters. "God help us all—she has truly done it."

Walsingham says nothing. He takes a deep breath. But in his mind, wheels begin to turn.

The French emissaries are overjoyed, believing they had finally secured their coveted alliance. While messengers get ready for Paris, Elizabeth stands in the centre of it all—crowned, ringed, and triumphant. But inside, beneath the silks and triumph, her heart beats wild as a war drum.

Because she knows nothing in her life will ever be the same again.

Chapter 28
Between Crown and Heart

23 November 1581

Before the court can turn declaration into decree, the chamber at Whitehall is dim. The stale scent of dying embers clings in the air. Beyond the door, footsteps and laughter drift down the corridor—carefree fragments of a world not yet shattered.

Elizabeth stands at a table by the window, her fingers splayed against the glass. Each breath fogs the pane, vanishes, and fogs it again. She wears no crown, no gleaming jewels—only a black gown heavy as her silence, a silence ringing in her ears like a bell struck too long.

The door creaks.

"Majesty?" comes the Duke's voice, tentative, almost tender.

She does not turn.

"You sent for me?" he repeats, stepping into the stillness, uncertain.

A long beat. Then, still to the window:

"I did."

He moves closer, hope flickering through the cracks in his fatigue. "If this is about the arrangements, I have written to my brother. They prepare a triumph in Paris—"

"No."

She turns—slowly. The look in her eyes halts him mid-stride.

"Not the arrangements. Not anymore."

The words hang between them.

His frown deepens, the room tilting beneath him. "What are you saying?"

Her voice trembles despite her desperate effort to hold steady. *I am hurting! Such pain!*

"I must withdraw what I declared yesterday. Cecil and Walsingham have been at me since dawn—plain as a writ."

Silence swallows the chamber.

"Withdraw?" His voice is a rasp, disbelief cutting deeper than anger.

Elizabeth shuts her eyes, breathes once, twice, before speaking again. "I should never have said it. I wanted to believe I could choose for myself. That I might be, for once, only a woman and not a sovereign. But I cannot. I never could."

"You spoke before your court," he says, hurt rising into his voice like a tide. "You kissed me in God's sight."

"I did." Her voice is soft, breaking. "But not because I was free to love you. Because I wanted to be."

His tone sharpens, laced with raw betrayal. "And now you cast me aside because your council mutters and Parliament brays?"

Her throat closes. "I cast you aside"—she forces—"because I have no other choice."

He stares, his face hollowing, the armour of diplomacy sloughing away from him. The courtly mask falls away; he looks suddenly very young.

"Was any of it real?"

Her breath catches. Her hand shakes against the sill.

"François...I have never loved as I loved you. And that is why I must let you go."

His chest rises sharply, as though pierced. He looks at her—long, unblinking—then speaks, low, steady, and devastating:

"You are not afraid of them. You are afraid of yourself."

Her lips part, but no words come. Only a small nod, weighted with lifetimes.

"I was not raised to be a wife," she whispers at last. "I was raised in a world of daggers and whispers. They took my mother's head before I was old enough to remember. Called me bastard, heretic, traitor. I am a queen because I survived—not because I was free."

His hand rises, then falters, dropping uselessly to his side. After a long pause, he slides her ruby pledge-ring from his finger. He had worn it since the gallery—hidden beneath lace and ceremony.

He does not hurl it in anger. Instead, he crosses to her with deliberate steps and sets it on the table, inches from her hand. His voice trembles.

"For when you remember what might have been," he says quietly.

He swallows, his throat tight, and adds, in a voice ragged with love and despair:

"I have loved you. You will never know how much."

He turns, each step dragging a piece of him away. At the door he stops, shoulders stiffening as though holding himself upright by sheer will.

"You will have your crown, Élisabeth. But you will lie alone without a husband."

The door shuts.

Elizabeth does not move. The mask fractures; her face collapses under the weight of what she has done. One hand seizes the table, clutching so hard her knuckles whiten. The other hovers—falters—unable to touch the ring.

She stares at it through a blur of tears until it seems a red wound against the dark wood. Her lips part, trembling.

"Forgive me."

The words fall into the silence. Then the sobs come—raw, helpless, uncontrollable—filling the chamber that once echoed with hope.

24 December 1581

Outside Whitehall Palace, the chill air hums with the sound of bells and of Christmas carollers singing a sombre nativity song. Within, three men linger over wine and spiced cakes, though none seem to relish the warmth of the fire or the feast of the season. The tapers burn in the council chamber.

Francis Walsingham stands near the hearth, his lean frame rigid, a goblet in his hand. William Cecil sits at the table, spectacles perched low on his nose as he fingers a scroll of Dutch correspondence. Robert Dudley, Earl of Leicester, stands apart, his arms crossed, eyes unfocused, staring towards the darkened window.

It is Dudley who speaks first.

"She did not attend chapel this morning."

Cecil does not look up. "She has not attended for several days."

"She has not spoken more than a whisper to me since the Frenchman arrived in October." His voice comes low, rough with something he will not name. "I know when she is unwell. And this time, it is not fever. It is...grief."

Walsingham turns from the hearth. "She is still the sovereign. Whatever hurt she carries does not change the game. Anjou lingers, the courtiers coo, the papists whisper—and Spain watches. Believe me, Philip watches carefully. He watches everything."

Cecil draws a breath and releases it through his nose, eyes fixed on nothing. "There was a moment—brief, but real—where I feared she might truly take him. She wanted to believe it was possible. That she could have both love and crown." He sets the scroll down. "But England has always demanded one or the other. Not both."

Dudley looks away grimly. "She loved him."

"She believed she could," Walsingham corrects. "But belief and rule make a hard marriage."

Dudley interjects, "Master Walsingham, you have a way with words."

A silence falls, broken only by the pop of the fire.

"Philip tightens his grip on the Netherlands," Cecil murmurs, "and our Dutch allies plead for support. With Elizabeth's refusal of Anjou, he can no longer play the role of suitor-diplomat."

Walsingham nods. "His usefulness lies not in marriage, but in war. If we send men and arms to the Low Countries under his banner, we may keep Spain at bay without directly declaring war."

He takes a measured sip of the mulled claret, now lukewarm, the cloves and nutmeg catching in his throat.

"It is necessary. But that buffer will cost us," Dudley says. "In blood, in coin. The Queen may yet balk at such a price."

"She must not," Walsingham snaps, more sharply than intended. He regains himself quickly. "If we do not act, the Netherlands will fall. And if they fall, England stands exposed. Philip will command the Atlantic from Lisbon. The Inquisition grows bolder. English Catholics—driven underground—will rise if given cause."

"Then Anjou must go to the Netherlands," Cecil says.

Dudley's expression darkens. "But he cannot remain here."

"No," Walsingham says. "He cannot. Their parting will come soon. And the farewell will not—fare well." He pauses, more sombre now. "But it is necessary."

Cecil speaks gently. "We must keep the Queen from retreating too far inward. The scars of her past are fresh again. And this—this wound with Anjou—reopens all of them."

"She will hide it," Dudley says. "As she always does. She will wrap herself in duty like armour. But I know the sound of her laughter when it is real—and I have not heard it since he kissed her."

He picks up a goblet of wine, then sets it down again.

"We ask her to be the Virgin Queen. But she is still a woman. And tonight, she mourns."

Walsingham's fingers fidget with the hem of his sleeve—not nervous, merely rehearsing control. "Then let her mourn. But let her rule also. And let us ensure she does not mourn in vain."

The bells toll at midnight.

Cecil says, "Merry Christmas, gentlemen."

He breaks a piece from one of the spiced cakes and crumbles it between his fingers instead of eating it, crumbs falling like grey snow onto the green baize.

Walsingham says, "Merry Christmas."

Dudley picks up his goblet of wine, takes a sip, and says, "A merry and sober Christmas to you, gentlemen."

2 February 1582

The wind outside sighs through the bare trees, rattling the leaded windows of Elizabeth's Privy Chamber at Whitehall. A fire crackles low in the hearth, the scent of beeswax candles mingling with the chill of approaching night. The court below still buzzes faintly, but here, all is quiet.

Elizabeth stands at the far window, one hand pressed to the pane, her other clutching the folds of her gown as if they could still her thoughts. Behind her, the door creaks open.

"Madam?"

She does not turn. She knows the voice too well.

"You have come to say goodbye then," she says softly.

Anjou enters, his steps slow, heavy with something unspoken. His velvet doublet, rich and embroidered, looks more ceremonial than celebratory. He carries no rose this time—only silence.

"I leave for the Netherlands in a few days," he says. "Preparations are... underway."

She chuckles. "How familiar that sounds."

Anjou says, "Élisabeth?"

Elizabeth nods once, her gaze still fixed outward. "So soon?"

"I lingered long enough. Some might say it is too long." He tries to sound light, but bitterness clings to the edges of his words.

She turns at last. Her face bears the careful mask of monarchy, but her eyes—those watchful eyes—betray more.

"I meant it, François. What I said last November in the gallery...in front of the court..."

"But not behind closed doors." His voice is sharp, though quickly softened. "First you call me husband before all of Christendom, then take it back like a vow spoken in sport."

"I could not wed you," she says, almost pleading. "Not because I did not care, but because I did—because I do."

He looks away. "You gave me no ring in private, Élisabeth—only in public splendour, and then silence—and a token returned in sorrow."

A beat passes between them, heavy with memory. Then, more gently:

"But you did give something else. Support. Funds. Arms and volunteers. You backed my campaign in the Netherlands, even after refusing my hand. You helped me fight Spain."

"I did what I could," she says, folding her arms as if to protect herself from her own sentiment. "Philip watches our every move. If I had married you outright, I would have bound England to a war it is not ready to fight. And I would have broken what little unity remains in this kingdom."

"You still sent your money," he says with a faint smile. "Your money and your blessings, if not your crown. Thank you."

"And you used your time here well," she adds, her voice tight with a mixture of pride and regret. "Secured your plans. Gained my Council's reluctant respect. My people may not love you, François—but they have come to see the man behind the mask."

He closes the last pace. "Then why does it still feel like failure?"

She is steady, voice low. "Because it is not a treaty we end—it is a promise I let you believe, a shield our friends counted on, and a story I told myself about what a queen is allowed to keep."

Their eyes lock. No more jest. No more pageantry. Only two princes caught in a web of history and longing.

Anjou sighs and steps back, collecting himself. "A royal prince cannot simply vanish. My departure will require ships, ceremony, farewells. No one slips away quietly from a queen's court."

"No," she says. "Nor from a queen's heart."

He bows his head, pain flickering in his eyes.

"I shall write to you, Élisabeth," he says.

"Do, please do," she whispers. "And send word of your triumphs. Let me hear how you throw back the Spaniards."

He turns towards the door, then stops.

She tries for their old joke—the one that had once made him laugh despite the court. Her voice is quiet, trembling but brave: "Farewell, my sweet frog."

He freezes. Slowly, he turns back, and for a moment—just a moment—his boyish smile returns.

"And farewell, my rose."

And then he leaves, the door closing behind him like the final note of a song never sung.

Elizabeth stands there long after he is gone, the fire burning low behind her. When she finally moves, it is to the window again—watching the winter sky darken over the Thames.

There were no tears.

But neither did she smile.

Only silence.

8 March 1582

In the Ribeira Palace of Lisbon, the echo of voices from the outer court fades behind the heavy oak door of King Philip's private study. A chill hangs in the air, sharpened by the draught slipping through the stone walls. Tall windows overlook the winter-bare gardens—orderly, silent, indifferent. Philip pays them no mind.

A small brazier smoulders beside his chair, warming a narrow table laid with olives, almonds, quince paste, and a cup of spiced cacao now cooling at the rim. On a larger table nearby, a chessboard sits untouched from the morning—its pieces frozen mid-campaign, as though awaiting a general who never arrived.

Philip shifts his foot beneath the robe. A violent throb bursts through the joint at the base of his big toe—far worse than the first faint pang he once felt in Brussels years ago. That one had been a warning. This is a massive siege.

He sucks in a breath, holding still until the worst of it passes. Sweat beads at his temples despite the cold.

A soft knock.

"Enter," he says, steadying his voice.

Juan de Idiáquez steps inside, face composed, though the folded letter in his hand carries an unmistakable gravity.

"Sire," he says, bowing. "A dispatch from our contact in London. It is...confirmed."

Philip does not reach for the letter immediately. His fingers rest lightly on the gilded arm of the chair. He studies Idiáquez's expression with a long, unreadable look.

"She has refused him, then?" His tone is calm, but curiosity threads through it. "The wedding is off?"

"It is," Idiáquez replies. "Queen Elizabeth has declined the Duke of Anjou's final proposal. He has left England. The French are...displeased."

A silence stretches. The fire snaps sharply, as if in answer.

Philip smirks faintly. "They would be."

He slowly extends his hand for the letter. The motion shifts his foot and another bolt of agony shoots upward—hot, merciless, blinding. His fingers falter for an instant before Idiáquez places the dispatch into them. The King closes his hand around it as though nothing is amiss.

He opens it carefully, reading the diplomat's neat French script. When he finishes, he shuts his eyes—briefly, just long enough to feel the weight of the information settle into place.

A thin, controlled smile creeps across his face. Not joy. Relief.

"So," Philip murmurs, placing the letter aside, "the mask has fallen. She remains England's Virgin Queen. No Valois consort. No French alliance."

He rises—but too quickly. His gout-ravaged foot rebels with a savage twist of pain. A gasp escapes before he can stop it, masked by the scrape of his chair legs across the mosaic floor. He steadies himself against the back of the chair.

Idiáquez pretends not to notice.

Philip walks—carefully—to the window. His robe trails behind him, his movements measured. Sunlight glints on the crucifix beneath his cloak.

"I will admit it," he says softly. "I feared she would accept him. For a moment—when she hesitated—I believed she might." He reaches for the chocolate. It has cooled and thickened, bitter as medicine, but he drinks it anyway.

The ache in his foot pulses violently, a drumbeat beneath his words.

"If she had married him," he continues, "England would not only be proud. It would be protected. France and England, united? That would have changed everything."

He glances back, eyes sharp despite the strain.

"But she did not. Could not, perhaps. Pride or fear...maybe both."

"Or the weight of her crown," Idiáquez offers gently.

Philip nods. "Yes. She knows what it means to rule alone. And perhaps she could not bear to kneel, even for a crown."

He turns towards the chessboard. Each step is a negotiation with agony, but he hides it behind an expression of iron discipline. He lowers himself into the chair with a barely stifled wince, pressing his fingertips together.

"Anjou will go to the Netherlands, alone and unloved. Without England he is a sword without a sheath—flashy, dangerous, but easily broken."

"Yet the Queen may still intervene," Idiáquez warns.

Philip's gaze hardens. "Then let her. Every move she makes binds her more firmly to rebellion. The world watches—and sees not a peacemaker, but a meddler in sacred order."

He leans forward. "But for now, we have been granted time. No Valois foothold in England. No Catholic prince beside her throne."

A fresh wave of pain knifes through him, sharp enough to steal his breath. He grips the table's edge until the spasm passes, sweat rising across his brow. Idiáquez's eyes flicker, but he remains silent.

Philip manages a long exhale, mastering himself once more.

"I do not rejoice in her refusal," he says quietly. "But I am...satisfied."

"Your Majesty," Idiáquez bows, "shall I send instructions to our envoys in Brussels?"

"Yes. And to Paris. Let them know Spain remains watchful. And gracious." A hint of irony touches his lips. "The Queen of England may yet regret what she has cast aside."

Idiáquez withdraws.

When the door shuts, Philip closes his eyes. The room swims. His foot feels as though it burns from within—his father Charles's old torment, inherited at last in full. The ember that once pricked him in Brussels has grown into a consuming fire.

He opens his eyes and looks at the chessboard.

Slowly, with trembling fingers, he picks up the queen piece—carved smooth as old bone. Even that small motion sends a tremor through him. He lifts the piece and studies it.

"Elizabeth plays for mate six moves hence..." he murmurs. "...so do I."

But beneath the table, the throbbing in his foot pulses harder—a merciless, intimate reminder that time itself has turned against him.

Philip places the queen beside his king, close as consorts, and sets his jaw.

He does not look at the board again.

Instead, he reaches for the bell cord and pulls once.

A clerk enters, young, precise, ink already staining his fingers.

"Prepare a memorandum," Philip says, his voice even. "For the Council of War. I want a full accounting—not of ships at sea, but of ships that *could* be made ready. Hulls laid up in ordinary. Timber under contract in Biscay and Galicia. Powder stores unassigned. Iron shot cast and uncast. Guns mounted, unmounted, and wanted.

"Count the men," he continues, without lifting his eyes. "Crews paid, unpaid, and owed. Pilots, gunners, carpenters. Victuals laid in and victuals still to be found—biscuit, cheese, beef, pork, oil, wine, water. How long each port can feed a fleet before it is felt?"

The clerk hesitates, then nods, grasping the breadth of it. "For when, Majesty?"

Philip's hand tightens on the table as another pulse of pain climbs his leg, hot as a brand. His face does not change.

"Not now," he says. "And not yet."

"And the ports?" the clerk asks, careful. "Lisbon, Coruña, Santander—"

"All," Philip replies. "List them by tide and season. Mark where stores can be drawn without noise. Mark where they cannot."

The clerk bows and withdraws, already murmuring figures to himself as if they were prayers. The door shuts. The room returns to its slow heat and the rasp of the brazier.

Philip closes his eyes for a moment, breathing through the flare in his foot until it dulls to a steady, intimate drum. When he opens them again, his gaze goes not to the gardens, nor the crucifix, nor even the chessboard—but to the dispatch on the table, the neat hand from London that has taken France off the board and left England alone.

Outside the palace windows, the winter-bare branches stand rigid in the wind, as if braced. Somewhere beyond the Tagus, ships creak against their moorings and settle with the tide, patient as beasts in a pen.

Spain has been granted time.

Philip does not waste it.

And far to the north, in waters no memorandum can tame, the sea turns on its own schedule—counting, always counting—toward the year it will demand its due.

Philip remains still, listening to the palace breathe—the distant scrape of shoes on stone, the muffled call of a clerk, the faint clink of metal carried from the yards below. He thinks of weight: of guns that must be hauled, of bread that hardens as it travels, of men pressed into service who will not return as they departed. All of it will move, not by impulse or passion, but by order—slow, deliberate, inexorable. When it begins, it will not ask whether it is just. It will only ask whether it is enough.

The time just may come when I must take the Queen.

To be continued...

Author's Note

This novel is a work of historical fiction. While major events, dates, and public actions are grounded in the historical record, private conversations, personal motivations, and certain sequences of events have been imagined for dramatic purposes. In some cases, timelines have been compressed, and minor characters combined, in order to serve narrative clarity.

Attributing motives to historical figures—particularly in moments where the record is silent—reflects narrative interpretation rather than definitive historical judgment. No character in this story is intended as a caricature; each is presented through a lens of plausible human motivation grounded in the political, cultural, and religious pressures of the age.

This work benefited from the responsible use of advanced AI tools as a collaborative aid during research, drafting, and revision. AI assistance was used to cross-check dates, terminology, geography, maritime practice, and linguistic consistency across a large and complex historical canvas, helping reduce factual drift and mechanical error while preserving narrative momentum. It also enabled faster comparison of conflicting sources, sharper continuity across scenes and volumes, and a more rigorous final polish than would otherwise be possible within a single author's working lifetime. All creative decisions, interpretations, and narrative judgments remain the author's own; the result for the reader is a novel that is clearer, tighter, more internally consistent, and more historically grounded—without sacrificing voice, drama, or human perspective.

Note on Dates

England and most of Europe observed the Julian calendar during the period covered in this novel. For clarity and narrative flow, dates are presented without adjustment for the later Gregorian reform. Where necessary, events are aligned for dramatic continuity rather than strict calendrical precision.

Acknowledgements

Many thanks to Professor Geoffrey Parker, co-author of *Armada: The Spanish Enterprise and England's Deliverance in 1588*, who was available to answer questions while doing my research.

To Bill Everatt of Celtica Radio (www.celticaradio.com) who was the first to play the theme song "Fallen by the Tide," a cinematic maritime ballad about the Duke of Medina Sidonia, the commander of the Spanish Armada of 1588.

To Allan Tee of Talk Radio Europe (www.talkradioeurope.com), Malaga, Spain.

To Nicola Kench for her encouragement.

Selected Bibliography

Hanson, Neil. *The Confident Hope of a Miracle: The True History of the Spanish Armada*. New York: Alfred A. Knopf, 2005.

Hutchinson, Robert. *The Spanish Armada.* New York: Thomas Dunne Books, 2013.

Martin, Colin & Parker, Geoffrey. *Armada: The Spanish Enterprise and England's Deliverance in 1588.* New Haven and London: Yale University Press, 2022.

Martin, Colin & Parker, Geoffrey. *The Spanish Armada*. New York: W.W. Norton & Company, 1988.

Mattingly, Garrett. *The Armada.* New York: Houghton Mifflin Company, 1959.

Pierson, Peter. *Commander of the Armada: The Seventh Duke of Medina Sidonia*. New Haven: Yale University Press, 1989.

Whiting, Roger. *The Enterprise of England: The Spanish Armada*. New York: St. Martin's Press, 1988.

Tilton, W.F. "The Defeat of the Spanish Armada." *The Atlantic.* (December 1895): 773-787.

Calendar of State Papers, Spanish, 1587–1603. Vol. 4. Edited by Martin A. S. Hume. London: HMSO, 1899.

"The Elizabethan Court Day by Day" by Marion E. Colthorpe, M.A. 2017 https://folgerpedia.folger.edu/The_Elizabethan_Court_Day_by_Day https://creativecommons.org/licenses/by-sa/4.0/

About the Author

Robert Oliver is a US-based historical novelist whose work explores power, loyalty, and consequence during periods of political fracture. Using rigorous research and restrained, character-driven storytelling, his fiction blends documented history with intimate human stakes. His work focuses on the collision between private conviction and public duty, where decisions echo far beyond the moment they are made.

He approaches historical fiction as an act of reconstruction rather than embellishment, grounding narrative drama in primary sources and lived realities of the past.

Learn more at www.prospectpacific.com.

The Story Continues
Coming Soon

Armada: The Fury—Book Two of *The Armada Saga*

The war did not end with survival.

It sharpened.

As England braces for retaliation and Europe tilts towards open conflict, alliances fracture, loyalties are tested, and the storm that was delayed now gathers force. The choices made in silence will soon be paid for in blood and fire.

Preview: Armada: The Fury — Chapter One (Excerpt)

Winter sunlight slips like pale gold through the frosted windows of the Royal Alcázar, scattering across polished floors and tapestries that hang still as tomb-cloths. In the great Audience Hall, musicians tune shawms and vihuelas for the modest festivities of the day: not a revel of France, nor an English masque, but the sober Spanish observance Philip permits even in a season of grief.

Pages carry trays of marzipan, quince paste cut in jeweled squares, and strips of candied orange peel, with small cups of warm spiced wine from Jerez to chase the chill from stone. Courtiers murmur polite wishes for the New Year, their voices hushed out of instinct more than decorum. Everyone knows it has been only weeks since the Duke of Alba—Spain's iron fist, Philip's blunt instrument—went to his grave in Lisbon.

At the far end of the hall, on a dais beneath cloth-of-gold, Philip II stands motionless, hands folded at his belt, eyes on nothing that any other man in the hall can see. His cap is trimmed in sable. His mourning is technically concluded, but the stiffness in his posture is not courtly—it is the residue of loss.

A herald calls out the names of grandees presenting their formal New Year's homage. One name cuts through the chamber.

"Don Álvaro de Bazán, Marquis of Santa Cruz."

He steps forward with a measured grace born of discipline rather than show. Fifty-six years old, beard salt-stained, eyes clear and steady, he wears the dark velvet of a Castilian grandee yet carries himself with the unmistakable bearing of a seaman: a man formed by wind, tide, and the smell of gunpowder.

Santa Cruz bows deeply.

"Your Majesty."

Philip's gaze sharpens. "Don Álvaro."

If Philip feels affection for any man living, it is hidden beneath this single, clipped greeting. But the shift in his stance betrays it—his spine easing by a fraction, the weight behind his eyes lightening.

Santa Cruz has served him since youth: scion of an ancient naval family, victor at Lepanto, scourge of corsairs in the Atlantic, guardian of the Indies treasure fleets, and commander whose squadrons never once lost a ship in battle. His record is a ledger of triumphs, unmarred by hesitation.

The court watches the exchange with careful eyes. It is rare to see Philip's features soften, even by a shadow.

"You have my condolences, Majesty," Santa Cruz says, voice low but firm. "Spain has lost a sword."

Philip inhales once. "A sword that served God and crown without wavering. Alba was...iron."

"And iron breaks when it has done its work," Santa Cruz replies gently.

A long silence settles, respectful rather than uncomfortable.

Philip's gaze drifts toward the musicians striking a soft chord for the Queen's entering procession—harps, vihuelas, recorders intertwining in an austere New Year's pavane. Even the sweetmeats went mostly untouched; sugar and spice could not soften the taste of mourning."

Then Philip looks back at Santa Cruz.

"Alba was my hand," he says quietly. "A hard hand. But he left me one truth: that storms come whether kings will them or no. And the sea...is a storm of its own."

Santa Cruz inclines his head. "The sea, Majesty, is where your enemies think you sleep."

Philip studies him with the still, exact assessment he gives to men he intends to test—and rely upon.

"I do not sleep, Don Álvaro. Nor will Spain."

A subtle exchange—brief, but weighty—passes between them. Some courtiers notice; most do not. But those who understand Philip's language of implication know this moment is deliberate.

Santa Cruz waits, silent, steady as the prows he commands.

"Tell me of Lisbon," Philip says. "Of the yards. The fleet."

Santa Cruz steps closer, speaking low enough that only the dais can hear.

"The Portuguese ports bend quickly to Your Majesty's rule. Their harbours are deep, their shipwrights skilled. With proper charge...they could birth a fleet to match any in Christendom."

"To match England?" Philip asks, with no change of tone.

"England grows bold," Santa Cruz replies. "And boldness is best answered before it learns certainty."

Philip's eyes narrow a fraction—not in anger, but in thought sharpened to a point.

The musicians shift to a livelier *villancico,* a nod to the Feast of the Circumcision. Courtiers pair for a stately dance. Yet around the dais, the air thickens with purpose.

"Santa Cruz," Philip murmurs, "Spain may soon need a hand that is iron...and another that commands the sea."

The Marquis bows—not dramatically, but with the surety of a man who knows exactly what is being offered, and what it will cost.

"Majesty," he says simply, "my life has ever been yours. My service remains so."

Philip's reply is quiet enough that only Santa Cruz hears it:

"When the time comes, I will give you charge of all. The fleet. The ocean. The judgment of God on England."

Santa Cruz rises.

"Then I will be ready."

A Fool's Request

Before you close this book and return to your own century, a small impertinence.

If you have read these pages—of queens who hesitate, kings who calculate, and a Europe inching towards fire—you now possess something of value: an opinion.

Fools trade in such things.

Should this chronicle have held your attention, stirred your temper, or taught you something you did not know, reviews may be left on Amazon (go to the next page for convenience), Goodreads, or wherever readers gather to argue with history. Praise it if it deserves praise. Criticize it if it does not. A fool respects truth more than courtesy, and silence helps no one but dust.

I have watched men lose kingdoms for want of plain speech. Books perish the same way.

Write what you think. History will manage the rest.

— **Jane Foole,**

Who has seen worse mistakes committed with greater confidence

Scan Me to Leave an Amazon Review

www.ingramcontent.com/pod-product-compliance
Lightning Source LLC
Chambersburg PA
CBHW020302030826
48979CB00027B/1995/J

* 9 7 9 8 9 9 4 4 4 3 4 0 8 *